Stolen
Santa
Monica

GINGER PENNINGTON

Fireroot Press
Los Angeles, California

ISBN: 978-0-9977570-9-5

www.gingerpens.com

For you
who saw me
through that year.

2013

WINTER

JANUARY

Stella Robertson wasn't entirely sure who she was at 28, but she didn't think she was the type to leave her husband. On New Year's Day, however, that's exactly what she did. She watched hands she recognized as her own, darkly possessed like the pointer on a Ouija board, as they took her belongings and placed them in black trash bags, leaving Andrew's things behind. They shut the door on her home for the last time, and her legs mechanically moved her outside and down the stairs. The salty breeze on her face tried to tell her what she was leaving, but she ignored it and kept walking through the cushioned grass, under the warm sun, past the Santa Monica palm trees lining the wide street. She may as well have been reading it all in a book then: one that a braver author would have made a memoir, but had become instead a novel; a story that began when she walked toward the smoky car where a bad boy waited to drive her away from her home on the coast.

But when night fell on that first day of the year, there was no novel. There was only Stella, lying on a hard motel mattress somewhere in Los Angeles with half her heart torn out. She had shattered Andrew's spirit. The truth scraped against her throat as she swallowed a mouthful of dry crackers. Wil, the boy she had left him for, was in the motel bathroom taking too long.

She looked down at her shoes and corked a sob before it escaped. She had reached a laughable low, eating Flavor-Blasted Goldfish under a motel art print of seashells, crying about leather Chuck Taylors.

Just six days ago she'd opened Andrew's Christmas gift, after a day she'd scheduled full of movies, ice skating, and Chinese dinner just to avoid dealing with her feelings. Andrew had known she'd wanted these shoes: the leather lowtops, size 10. He was always a great gifter; he had bought her shoes for seven years. This time he had fashioned the wrapping paper into origami-like triangles. Stella had felt sick ripping his artful creation under their tiny tree, knowing she'd be gone when the new year came. She removed the lid and there were the shoes: size 9 hightops. Wrong size, wrong height. Andrew, meanwhile, was opening the thoughtless wallet she'd purchased the day before, receipt in the box. She had exchanged his gift for the right shoes the next day. He had done the same with the wallet, which he'd hated.

Now he was probably at some bar, pulling out the wallet he had picked out himself and paying for his eighth whiskey, in quest of a lonely girl to occupy the vacancy in their bed. Or maybe he was working; he could never get away from the store on holidays, and though he didn't love his job, he rarely complained. He wasn't the type to voice discontent with anything except world politics. Even when Stella pressed, he always maintained he was happy in their open marriage, despite the film of malaise dulling his crystal blue eyes. She wondered if he had finally allowed himself to cry, or if he was still stuffing the torment down into the pit of his stomach where he kept the rest of his feelings. Stella had spent most of November and December in tears as the truth of what she had to do came into focus.

A deep voice was speaking behind the bathroom door. Was Wil talking to himself or God? Stella needed to talk to God herself, but she didn't feel worthy. The closest she came to feeling God lately was when she was with Wil, embarking on a fearless life where there were no guarantees, where she was true to herself in the moment and all seemed to be beauty and magic and love.

When Wil finally emerged from the bathroom, he did something Stella had never seen another man do in person. He got a blow dryer and a brush and began styling his hair. "You're my baby now," he said over the noise, beside himself with glee now that he had finally gotten what he had been working for since September.

I am not afraid, Stella told herself silently, walking toward him. *I am not, in this moment, scared about our love, the money, the jobs, the fallout, the sadness, the change.*

Wil put down the blow dryer, his dark Morrissey hair flipped to one side, and he looked down at Stella from his six-foot-four vantage point, placing his huge hands on her shoulders, a little too close to her neck. "You had the guts to follow your heart," he said. "No one does that. No one does that for love. Your life is fucking changed," he said, big lips twisting into a smile. "Are you happy?"

She looked at him: articulate anarchy in human form, youth and exuberance bursting forth from him like the creation of a universe, and she saw the love like madness in his eyes, all of it aimed at her.

"Yes," she said.

***

She woke up choking on cigarette smoke in the non-smoking hotel room.

"Good morning, baby," Wil said, exhaling.

"Good morning." She walked over to the sink and splashed water on her face. She had blue almond eyes and white teeth people commented on since she usually smiled, even when she didn't feel it in her gut. She had recently gotten her hair cut pixie-short and dyed it dark, so she and Wil looked like members of the same rock band. But Wil wasn't in a band, and Stella's band, the Ladidahs, was comprised of all women: twelve of them, in fact, who sang cult-like choruses over guitars and drums. She would be rehearsing with them this evening after babysitting. She looked forward to feeling normal for three hours, surrounded by her friends like all Wednesdays.

"Is something wrong?" Wil asked, seeing Stella study herself in the mirror. "That hair suits you perfectly. The long auburn was the old you, the yoga you. This is the badass you."

"Yeah, I feel more like myself."

"Listen, tonight I'll buy you some nice dinner, then we'll get in the hot tub and talk about all the incredible things we are going to do starting tomorrow. Our first apartment together! We're going to rule the fucking world! I can't wait to start my life with you, Stella. Our life."

"Thanks, baby. But sorry; I have Ladidahs practice after babysitting so I'll have to just see you later tonight."

"Are you serious? You're already going to leave me alone?"

"Uh, I rehearse every Wednesday, you know."

"Can't you just skip it tonight? I've been waiting for months to have you to myself and this is only our second night together—" He would have gone on.

"I don't want to start this relationship off on the wrong foot. I'm sorry, but we're learning some new music tonight, so I need to be there."

He began pacing. "What am I supposed to do while you're gone? Just rot in this room by myself?" He took a nervous drag off his cigarette, lips agleam with drool. The shadow that blackened him with desperation was the same shadow that sometimes played as seductively dangerous and edgy.

"Wow," Stella said, trying to find air amid the secondhand smoke. Tears came again. "I'm starting to wonder if I made the right decision."

His pale eyes flashed and he seethed, "Well, if you feel like you lost something so good, then you're welcome to go back to it!"

But Stella had made her choice. Anyway, she liked the passion of a good fiery argument.

She and Andrew had never argued. There was the one time

years ago, after months of his repressing his feelings on Stella hanging out with a wrestler named Trev, when she had pleaded for it: "Just fucking tell me what you're thinking, Andrew! If you don't like the situation, let me know! Give me something!" Andrew had yelled out every truth he'd been containing, and it had ended well, with understanding and a good lay. But then he'd reverted to his usual manner of snuffing out any thought that contradicted Stella's wishes.

"I'm sorry," she lamented. "I don't want you to constantly feel like I'm regretting this. But I want you to know that I'm not going to give up the things that are important to me."

"I understand," he said, pulling her tight enough that she could feel his hard-on pressing into her hip, which turned her on a little. "I don't want you to give up anything you love. Go to your rehearsal. I'll see you when you get back." They kissed. Four months in, she barely minded the taste of tar and ash.

***

Wil had been building up this red-letter-day since they'd first met in September. It was their official beginning, even if it was only in a one-month sublet. After babysitting, Stella was on the L.A. city bus heading down Santa Monica Boulevard past the Mexican bodegas and check cashing stores of grimy East Hollywood to meet Wil at their new temporary apartment. He had taken her Corolla, which he drove more than she did, to get there early so he could pay the owner couple before they left for their month-long vacation. Stella had barely scraped together the $400 to pay her half. She had fifty-three cents in her checking account and no real job, but she thought if she kept the faith, she would eventually be financially solvent, and then she'd repay Andrew $650 for her half of the rent money she had stuck him with when she left with no warning.

She felt she owed Andrew so much more than the rent money. The previous summer, when she had complained to him of feeling purposeless, he had supported her. "Why don't you just quit all these jobs," he had said. "Catering, babysitting, bartending, background acting: You hate it. I make enough to get us through. You should focus on your writing and acting, and your music." Eventually she had agreed. She started a blog that garnered a small following, she told her agent she was available for auditions, and she joined the Ladidahs. She slept in, glammed up and scolded herself often for procrastination and lack of productivity. And for all his generosity, all Andrew had expected in return was for Stella to be his lady. She had failed.

Wil was still spending thoughtlessly and convincing himself that he needed things like root beer floats and foot scrub from Target. When she met him, he had worked at a PR firm with a made-up title— "Director of Social Initiatives" or something—given to him by a CEO he met in rehab. He would fling his money everywhere, buying $500 sunglasses from the Tom Ford store in Beverly Hills, taking Stella to lavish dinners, memorializing even non-occasions with gifts. But a month ago, after one-too-many hospital stays thanks to his bad heart, his CEO friend fired him. Wil's real goal was to be a director, and with his charisma, creativity, and film school credentials, that seemed like a possibility. His bad heart rendered his odds steeper than most, but his zest for life enthralled Stella, who still thought frequently about the night they'd first met, just four months before.

***

Andrew was in Cupertino for two weeks of work training and Stella was dog-sitting at her friend Deb's house. She wasn't used to spending nights without Andrew, and she was missing their nightly routine of *Midsomer Murders* and cheap wine. She went online to find the perfect songs to make Andrew a mix CD like she used to. She found one song that might fit, but she didn't feel passionate about it so she took a break and checked her email. There was a message from a guy whose name she didn't recognize, from a dating website she and Andrew had played around on in the past. Stella clicked on the message.

Wil Mallory:
Want to come celebrate with some wine and jazz?

Stella:
What are we celebrating?

Wil Mallory:
It's September 11th. That's a holiday, right?

Stella didn't know whether to be appalled or interested. He looked cute in his photo. She assumed he was joking and figured hearing his voice would clear up the confusion.

Stella:
Call me so I can decide if you're worth getting dressed for. And to make sure you're not planning to chop me up into bite-sized pieces.

His voice on the phone was deep and leathery, and he had an invigorating way with words. Soon Stella was leaving Deb's in a cotton dress. The lighting at the hotel was dim, but she recognized Wil's big lips and Mick Jagger hipbones jutting from under his jeans through a crisp white button down. He was a tall, black denim oil-slick of a boy, hair obscuring one eye, who smelled like vanilla and tobacco. He

5

bought Stella a glass of red, got a tonic for himself, then coaxed her outside so he could smoke. Within minutes, he told her, "I'm a recovering addict. Heroin."

Stella replied, "I'm married. Open relationship. Not looking for anything serious."

"Perfect," he said. "How does that work, anyway?"

"We did it for a year before we got married. I instigated it out of boredom and he went with it. That first night, we actually made a Word document of mutually agreed-upon rules to keep our relationship sacred."

"How romantic. Rules like what?"

"Like, 'you may only spend time with other partners when your primary partner is already busy,' and 'no banging friends,' and 'no bringing outsiders into our home.'"

"Weird."

"Oh, and, the number one rule is, you have to be honest with everyone at all times."

"So if you develop feelings for someone else, you have to tell your husband?"

"Hopefully that won't happen. But theoretically, yes."

Wil's candor was magnetizing; he wore his scars on his sleeves, which were rolled up to reveal scrappy tattoos that looked like they were drawn by an eight-year-old. One covering his forearm read, "Die Yuppie Scum." He took Stella's hand and placed it on his chest under his heart. She felt her own heartbeat accelerate. "Do you know what that is?"

It felt like an Altoids box. "Um. Your rib?" she asked.

"No; it's a defibrillator. I'm one of the seven people in the world who have this kind: It's an experimental one. They gave it to me after I died the last time." His heart had stopped after a seizure, he said, and he had ended up in a nine-day coma. The doctors told him he'd probably have a short life.

Stella hadn't felt this invigorated since she was 19 with pink-and-platinum hair, wearing fishnet shirts and driving to Cincinnati in her neon green Beetle to sweat with strangers in the pit while NOFX played. Two hours passed without a lapse. Stella didn't really want to kiss Wil because of the cigarettes, but when he propositioned her in such a charming way—"Do you think that when we're old someday, sitting on the front porch, you'll remember how I asked you if I could kiss you at this moment?"—she couldn't say no.

One of Stella and Andrew's rules prohibited bringing flings into their home, but Stella was house sitting. She would not remember inviting Wil back to Deb's, but she would remember being devoured like she was Wil's last meal, and her soft flesh would be left with the bruises from his sharp pelvis for at least another week.

***

At 2:00, the bus finally dropped her off in the no-man's-land past Hollywood Forever Cemetery. She knocked on the door, excited to plop down with Wil on the couch in their new temporary home, finally at rest.

But it wasn't Wil who answered the door.

"Oh my gosh! He hasn't gotten here yet?" Stella asked.

"No. He called and said he was on his way," said the girl, annoyed.

"We were supposed to be on the road over an hour ago," said the guy, pissed.

"Let me call him," she said.

Stella paced back and forth on the stoop. "Where are you?"

"I left my wallet at the hotel," Wil said. "By the time I got back there, I had to convince the front desk lady to let me in the room, and when I finally found it, two-hundred dollars was missing from our rent money."

"No!"

"Yeah, it was probably that cholo maid."

"Well these people really want to leave. What are we going to do?"

"I'll be there soon. I'm on my way. We'll figure it out," he said.

She sighed, sat down on the steps, and waited.

***

"I'm really not supposed to lift anything over twenty pounds, but forget it; I'm going to help you," Wil said once they had procured a U-Haul to pick up the stacks of boxes at his sober living house.

"No way," Stella said, lifting one of the boxes, which was huge but very light. "Your surgery hasn't even totally healed. Back off, bucko."

Wil spent the rest of the evening holding doors and smoking while Stella unpacked everything at the new sublet: all her possessions, which fit into her Corolla, and all Wil's boxes, which filled the entire U-Haul truck.

***

It felt good to wake up in an actual apartment instead of the gritty motel. The bedroom wall was hung with vintage women's hats. The living room had high ceilings, wood floors, a guitar and some lute-like instrument, though Wil's stacked boxes obscured it all. The kitchen had shiny pots and pans dangling from the ceiling, and every kind of tea in the cupboard. Stella wanted to stay and enjoy it, but she had to drive back to the Westside to babysit again.

"I promise I'll unpack all of this as soon as possible," Wil said before she left.

Evan and Kara were watching *Animal Planet* and drawing anime characters at their house on the Westside. Stella was all too aware that Andrew and her old apartment were only a bike ride away. His nearness constricted her breath: She felt as if she was homeless and Andrew was as good as dead. She stared at her computer as her mind cranked, desperate to understand why this ill-feeling decision had forced itself upon her, how it had appeared so quickly and capsized the boat on the placid lake of her life. Having been adopted at birth with no biological clues, she had spent her life trying on identities to see which one fit, but she had always tried to be kind and thoughtful in the process.

"What are you writing, Stella?" Kara asked cheerfully.

Stella clicked on a Facebook message from Rob, a friend who had gone to college with her and Andrew.

"Just working on my blog," she lied. She hadn't written in months.

Stella,

Jen and I are embarrassed for you. We've seen too much on Facebook recently from this guy Wil. While ultimately you must do what you think is best for you, we would rather not read about it. I can only imagine the pain Andrew must be feeling. If you really care for Andrew, put him first here. Don't allow Wil to share these inappropriate "joys" publicly, no matter how poetic his words may sound or how protected you may feel. You've made these decisions and, not surprisingly, the repercussions are great. I write you this message to let you know why I am removing you from my friends list.

Rob

Stella ducked into the bathroom so the kids wouldn't see her crumble. Rob's friendship was no detrimental loss: He was more Andrew's friend than hers. But he was right. While Stella had been discreet when she realized her feelings for Wil, only telling her sister, her best friend Claudia, and Andrew himself, Wil announced his feelings in social media posts:

Had an incredible night bowling with the infinitely-talented, beautiful, (in every sense of the word), always-surprising love of my life, Stella Robertson!

Stella hadn't wanted to stifle his excitement—it felt good to be the object of such praise—but it was causing alarm from loved ones who thought she was happily married. Stella and her mother had always been close, but lately, Stella had been dodging Linda's calls.

She dried up and came out of the bathroom. A grizzly bear on TV killed and ate a deer.

Kara moaned. "Oh."

Her brother Evan rolled his eyes. "It's just the way it has to happen, Kara."

Stella wished she could be that grizzly bear. The bear didn't have to justify himself for eating the deer. He didn't have to write an apologetic Facebook message to an uninvolved outsider, he didn't lose the love of his tribe, and he didn't have to carry the weight of the dead deer on his back.

On the way back to east Hollywood that night, Ray Lamontagne's voice rasped through the speakers. Stella turned it off immediately, sobbing as she remembered lying in the extra-long twin bed back in Kentucky, listening to that song with Andrew during her last week of college.

Andrew was the son of her British drama professor Dr. Foss. Senior year, when Stella finally broke up with her boyfriend Matt, an iconoclastic swimmer with loud, strange philosophies who became addicted to snorting crushed-up Vicodin, Andrew was there. He was a pale, easygoing blonde who hated making plans as much as Stella did, and he was always up for a good time. When Stella graduated, they traveled around the south together eating buffalo wings and drinking beer, working for theater companies and being broke. Stella got a Master's degree in writing while she waited for Andrew to finish undergrad, and four years into their relationship, they moved to Los Angeles, because Stella wanted the ocean and she wanted to write, act, and sing. They settled into a studio in Santa Monica, Andrew got a job at the Apple store, and Stella worked at a clothing store she hated. She wore bleached pincurls and polka-dot dresses from the 1950's, and rapped "Big Pimpin'" at karaoke like an irreverent-gangster Marilyn Monroe.

Another year passed. Every day Stella met interesting guys of all shapes and colors who asked for her phone number and told her they'd never met anyone like her. She loved Andrew, but he was just the same as when they'd met, and she wanted more. She had read about non-monogamy and asked Andrew if he'd be willing to try it. He said yes, and the experiment began.

Stella quickly realized she was getting the bulk of the benefits. While Andrew enjoyed a couple flings per year, she was meeting up with a Brad or a Jesse or a Chris monthly for no-strings-attached sex. Though the flings usually made her more interested in coming back home to Andrew, she felt the imbalance and worried that he wasn't truly happy. She offered many times to return to monogamy, but Andrew said, "Even if you and I split up, I would never go back to being in a monogamous relationship."

Stella looked around at her life one afternoon when Andrew was at work: blue curtains, sunshine and sea air, a potted violet on the glass-topped table, a date with a wrestler later this evening, and the promise of Andrew snuggling with her in the night. She and Andrew had spent five years together—one of them non-monogamous. This arrangement, she thought, afforded her everything: freedom, love, and commitment. She felt an impulse and texted Andrew

Will you marry me?

They had an Indian-inspired rebel wedding on a Kentucky farm. They wrote their own vows, eschewing the bit about being faithful. Family and friends flew in from all over the world, clueless about the couple's arrangement, wishing them babies and many happy years together. Stella and Andrew had bucked the antiquated marriage system by inventing their own rules for commitment, they thought. This was it: sustainable freedom and love.

Back in California, Stella tried to write a novel and gave up. She taught writing at the community college until the semester ended. When people saw her wedding ring, they gushed at her like she was a blushing newlywed, asking how Andrew proposed, and if she was going to have kids anytime soon. Stella hated it. She didn't know who she was, but she wasn't an old married lady; she was a vital, sexy rebel who did what she wanted. She moved her wedding ring to her middle finger and started wearing a leather jacket and black sunglasses. That was around the time she met Wil.

***

It was Stella's first AA meeting, and it felt a bit like the Appalachian church she grew up in. They intoned mantras in unison and referred to "The Big Book." They held hands and asked for serenity to accept the things they could not change. They told their ugly stories at the podium, describing their backslides and the people they had hurt along the way, but here they were: living proof that the human spirit could triumph, that lives could change completely. Stella needed to know that.

Soon two of Wil's friends were dragging her up to the podium, holding a cake they got for his "sober birthday." Stella was the only "normie" among all the addicts.

"Wil is one year sober," said the announcer, giving Wil the microphone as everyone clapped.

Wil blew out his candle. "Wow. Thank you. I can't believe I'm standing here right now. And I wouldn't be if it wasn't for my friends here, and most of all, Stella, this kind beauty who came into my life and saved me when I was about to give up. She is an angel, and I am thrilled to say we just moved in together." Stella shrank a little behind him as the girls in the audience all gave an "aw."

Wil continued, "My life hasn't been easy. I have a heart disease called catecholaminergic polymorphic ventricular tachycardia, and I have been in and out of lots of very painful heart surgeries." He began to cry a little and Stella gave his hand a pulse. "There have been times when I've wondered if it's even worth all this—the struggle to stay clean and sober. It is a struggle. And when there are no highs, when there's nothing but lows, you don't have much to live for. There was a time just about a year ago when I had told myself that if I ever had to go back in the hospital for another surgery, I would just push the morphine drip button until I killed myself." The audience was a blanket of concerned looks.

"And then it happened. Back in September, one of the wires from my defibrillator popped through my chest and I got put into the hospital for surgery. It was the week of my birthday. That could have been the end for me. But as fate would have it, I had just met this wonderful woman a week before. I have never truly loved anyone, but it was the strangest thing. I just knew that this was God, sending her into my life to tell me I had a reason to live. And Stella stayed by my side. She slept beside me almost every night and made sure I was comfortable. I couldn't believe my luck. I knew I had to do anything in my power to stay alive and keep her around. And I'm glad I did, because I ended up having to have another surgery in November, and she stayed with me through that, too. So if you're out there wondering if it's all worth it, I am here to tell you that it is. Love is worth it."

Applause filled the room.

On their way home, Wil said from the driver's seat of Stella's Corolla, "I don't know why you're with me, but I'm glad."

When Stella looked back at September, remembering the force of Wil's tsunami wave—the second date, the third and fourth, all in a week—she felt that being with him was never a choice. He had impulsively bought a Vespa and had taken her on it to see a movie. He had bought her dinner at the Chateau Marmont and as they held hands, paparazzi had taken their photo, thinking they were *somebody*. He had told the people at Cold Stone Creamery her name was Juliet, and coaxed them into singing her "Happy Birthday." He had written countless flowery texts to tell her how perfect she was. He had fucked her in the car and in a skeezy hourly motel and in the dressing room at Bloomingdale's before buying her a sweater. And then, on the Friday she had planned to go to Cupertino to stay with Andrew, Wil had texted her at 5 in the morning:

I'm in the hospital. I have to have heart surgery.

She had only known him for five days, but she couldn't leave him all alone in the hospital when his family was thousands of miles away. She stayed by Wil's bed all day and went to Cupertino six hours later than she'd planned. She had hugged Andrew hello, but her heart was still in that hospital room back in Los Angeles, and that's where she returned two days later.

***

Stella awoke in the temporary Tempur-pedic bed, in a brief panic about where they would sleep in February. With all the worry and lack of self-care, her body felt like it had been put into a trash compactor. Wil looked beautiful, even if his snoring grated like the chainsaw scratched onto his arm in permanent ink.

She pulled a sweater and a robe from the pile of clothes on the floor and tiptoed into the kitchen, shivering. She couldn't believe how cold East Hollywood was. She tried not to miss Santa Monica and the mild mornings by the beach. She made coffee and opened her computer, searching through Craigslist's "Education Jobs" section to bookmark anything that looked promising.

An hour later, she heard some tinny, atmospheric indie rock, which meant Wil was awake and had taken up residence in the bathroom as usual. What did he do in there every morning for hours behind the locked door?

"Hey sweet thing," she yelled through the door. "If you could just let me grab my makeup bag out of there, I have to go to that audition in a little while."

"God, I love your voice," he said. "You have the projection of an actor and the huskiness of a phone sex operator, and then once in a while, you have that hillbilly twang that comes out."

"Thank you!" She waited. "Now, about that makeup bag."

"Just give me a minute," he said. Stella could hear his wet lips sucking on a cigarette, followed by his loud exhale, in an apartment owned by people who had asked him not to smoke.

She went back to the job search, and thirty minutes later he emerged with a huge kiss.

"I made coffee," she said.

He looked at her as if she had just cured his heart disease. "You are the best thing that has ever happened to me."

"You have to eat something for breakfast," Stella said.

"Yeah, I will. I'm not hungry now."

He always said that, but then he never ate. His skin was nearly translucent. "Do you want me to make you one of those peanut butter and jelly English muffins you said your mom used to make you?"

"You would do that for me?"

"Of course, my love." Stella went to the kitchen and made it just the way he had described, toasting the two halves of the muffin and then spreading natural peanut butter on one side and fruit spread—not jelly—on the other half. He was very particular.

"Wow," he said when she gave it to him on a little saucer. "Wow." Stella was mollified when he ate it, like a toddler's mom.

She felt raw driving through Santa Monica to get to the audition, realizing how much the city had meant to her for four years. The skaters clack-clacking down sunny sidewalks, the sage-smelling yoga studios, the people walking little dogs in front of 1960s stuccoed apartments, the ferris wheel turning slowly: None of these belonged to her anymore.

Auditions were brief blips that rarely amounted to anything, but Stella had to go, just in case. At best, she could win a fun, high profile job that could get her out of debt for good. At worst, they could be embarrassing, or inspire comparison and self-loathing. With the right attitude, they were a chance to work on some new material, get dressed up, exchange energy with someone new, and learn the value of non-attachment.

She walked into the brick waiting room, signed her name inside a box on the sheet, and grabbed a paper on which was a little comic strip: a storyboard for the commercial, in which a weather woman has an on-air meltdown. Stella looked around at the other beautiful late-twenties women sitting on benches. A couple were chatting, but most were moving their mouths silently as they stared intensely at the storyboard in their hands. They had shoulder-length hair and pencil skirts, and Stella immediately wondered if her dress was over-the-top or if it made her look fat, and if her short hair was too short. She'd never seen a weather woman with a pixie cut. She tried not to think of the generous pay rate as she mentally rehearsed. Casting directors could smell desperation.

"Stella." A woman poked her head out the door marked "3." Stella said hello and followed her into the tiny room where she obediently stood behind the tape mark on the floor and stared down the barrel of the camera.

She smiled and chatted with the woman and a man beside the camera, who explained that Stella was to say the line that was on the cue card, then improvise a meltdown in which she quits her job as a meteorologist. "Are you ready?"

Stella mustered her best acting skills to say, "I'm ready!" with a subtext that said *I am a capable, together actress who doesn't need anything, much less this paltry commercial!*

"And action."

The on-air meltdown was no trouble at all.

Afterward, Stella found herself at the edge of the water.

The last time she had been at this beach was the week of Christmas with Andrew before the tragic gift exchange. She remembered the scratch of his wool sweater. She remembered being desperate to be swayed by his hopeful smile but only being able to return his kisses halfheartedly.

She buried her feet in the sand and wondered again if it was too late to go back.

Then something came to her and she whispered as if reciting lines, "Everything is working out exactly as it's supposed to. There is really nothing to worry about in this present moment, which is an amazing thing. I am going to make my way back here, to my home on the Pacific, in a month, with the guy I love or with my precious self."

She wrapped her arms around herself and gave a squeeze, then got up and turned her back on the ocean.

***

A new week came and Wil was out looking for a job. Stella went into the bathroom to get ready, and a note was stuck to the mirror. Big red letters.

Don't even bother—you look marvelous.

She laughed. She was starting to feel like a human again.

It seemed that she could feel happy for spans of time without letting her head enter that sad museum where hung the portraits of Andrew's devastated face next to all the scowling people who had lost faith in her. It was hard to visit that place when she was busy smiling, and Wil did keep her smiling. If he wasn't engaging her in never-ending conversation, he was listening to her, leaving her notes, breaking a social norm and making her gasp, screwing her silly, or building her up with his endless supply of compliments. But it wasn't just the way he made her feel: It was who he was trying to become every day. Wil, unlike loves of her past, knew he could be better and he was always on a journey of self-improvement. Stella admired that.

***

If Wil was ever to get a job in L.A., he would need a car, so his dad had sent him $2,000 expressly for that purpose.

"I'm sure you can find something on Craigslist for two thousand dollars and just have it checked out," Stella told him. She thought guiltily of Andrew, driving that beat-up old Civic. "Andrew's car isn't worth more than five-hundred bucks, but it gets him everywhere he needs to go. Good gas mileage too."

"You know what I'd like to have?" Wil said. "One of those new little Fiats."

"Hmm—I think those cost a little more than two-thousand dollars."

"Well, I can work out some sort of financing plan, probably."

"You don't even have a job yet," she said as kindly as possible, her breath hollow.

"Don't you believe in me?" he said. "If I put it out into the universe that I am going to have a job, then I am going to get a job. Can we just go around to a few dealerships that have used cars and see what they have? I won't buy anything today."

She thought about it. She did want to believe in miracles.

"Sure, baby."

***

Wil's trash heap of boxes still hadn't budged, despite his pledge to clean them up. Stella gave in and decided to do it herself. She opened each box, finding only receipts from gas stations and Target, old to-do lists and notes, cigarette packs with one or two smokes in them, and a couple rolls of toilet paper. She was irate to think she'd allowed herself to be pinned in all this time by such insubstantial shit. She threw out all the rubbish, took the boxes to the dumpster, and stacked what was left—a few books, notebooks, videotapes, little toys, and greeting cards—in a few neat piles on the floor next to his twelve heaps of clothes. When the living room was clear, she was conscious of something missing. She didn't want to do it, but she had to email Andrew.

Stella <stellawrites84@gmail.com>
to Andrew

I'm sorry it's taken me so long to write you. My life has no structure right now, obviously, so I am kind of winging everything. I saw you're going to be having a birthday get-together. I hope you have a wonderful birthday.

I wondered if you would mind if I came to get the Santa Monica sign. I left it because it was bolted to the wall. I feel bad asking, but it is my favorite thing and if I could only have one thing it would be that. It just reminds me of good things, and I really could use good feelings now. I know you like it, too, but I found it and carried it back that day, so I hope you won't mind. If you want it, that's okay. Just let me know. Thank you.

I want to say more, but I know your disdain for what I've done to you makes any well-wishes null and void. But you know how I feel about you and what I want for you, which is all of the best and everything you deserve. I hope you will let me know when you might ever want to see me again and talk and be amicable, though I know it will be a while.

Wil came out of the bathroom in designer jeans and a crisp Paul Smith button-down covered by a trench coat, hair pomped with styling putty. "Wow! This place looks great! You are amazing!" he said.

"Thanks." Her mind said, *I can't believe you made me rent a U-Haul and spend all day carrying in boxes full of trash*. But the garbage that had been his property had changed her view of him. She saw him now as someone damaged and on the mend. He had been through a lot, and these things that seemed crazy to her now were things he would sort out in time. She only allowed herself to say, "I couldn't stand living in this heap anymore."

Stella let him drive her car to find a dealership. On the way he said, "I was doing some research, and it looks like I might not be able to actually get a car in my name in the state of California."

"What?" she said. "Why?"

"I will be able to soon. I just have to get medical clearance since I sometimes have seizures."

"How do you do that?"

"It's just a bunch of paperwork. I'll have to get my doctor to sign off on it before they'll let me get a California driver's license." Stella knew his was a Pennsylvania license because she had seen it the day his first lie to her was exposed. In September, the first time he'd stayed in the hospital, he had said he was turning 25, so she had made him a special mixtape with 25 carefully selected songs. When she brought it to his hospital room, there was a big birthday balloon there that said "24!" He had told her, "That's from my boss. He's an idiot and doesn't know how old I am." A few weeks later he had left his wallet lying around and Stella had seen his birth date. When she confronted him, he said he'd been worried that she might not go for someone four years younger. Stella had excused it when he'd promised never to lie to her again. As if a promise meant anything, ever.

"So when are you going to send in this paperwork?" she asked.

"I've submitted it to my doctor, so as soon as they approve it."

"Oh. Okay," she said.

"Baby?"

"Yeah?" They were passing the Chateau Marmont on the hill with its classic neon sign, and Stella briefly flashed back to that magical dinner four months ago.

"I'm going to ask you something, and you're welcome to say 'no'. But you know that it's me and you forever and you can trust me because I'll be right here beside you."

Her stomach lurched. "Okay..."

"If I found a car that was a little more than two thousand dollars that I could make payments on, would you consider signing the papers for me?"

"Um—"

"It would actually be good for you because I'd pay for it, so your credit score would go up, and you would get the payment history without even having to pay for it. It would be my car, but it would just be in your name."

"Um—"

Wil converted his face to upset. "I'm sorry. I should never have asked. You've done so much for me and here I am just asking for more. Don't worry, Stella. I'm going to figure this out on my own."

"Like I said before, we can get you a car with the money your dad gave you and there will be no payments necessary."

"Yeah."

They drove on in silence for a minute. He put his hand on Stella's knee. "You are the best thing that's ever happened to me," he said. "You know, a few days before Christmas, when I was so in love with you but I didn't think you'd ever leave Andrew, I actually looked for ways to kill myself." She recoiled a little from his touch. He continued. "You were the one person who has shown me that I am capable of giving and receiving love." He started to tear up as they stopped at the red light. "I didn't feel like I had anything left to live for if you weren't going to continue on this journey with me. But I knew you were mine the night I showed up at your door with the signs."

She started to cry a little, too. "You don't feel like doing something that extreme now, do you? I'm here."

"No, not since you decided to share your life with me."

"I love you." She put her hand on his shoulder.

"I love you too." He smiled. "Look. There's a Toyota dealership. Can we go take a look over there?"

"Sure," she said.

"My girlfriend here wants to find something affordable but reliable," Wil told a hungry salesman.

"I'm really not looking to buy anything today, though. Just looking."

The salesman asked Stella question after question about her preferences. She looked at Wil after each question and said, "What do you think?" and let him answer.

The salesman said, "Well, I have the sharpest little Prius right now. 2010. Red. Would you like to take a look?"

"I'm sure that's probably out of my price range right now," she said, adrenaline pumping.

Wil said, "Let's just take a look at it, baby."

"Yes, it won't hurt to look!" said the salesman. "And we have financing plans to fit almost everyone!"

Stella was sure they didn't have a financing plan to fit an unemployed girl with an overdrawn checking account and an unemployed boyfriend who was trying to buy a car in her name that he couldn't afford.

"Okay. Just a look."

The salesman brought the car around and told Stella to sit in the driver's seat. It was "sharp." She thought of how much gas money she would save if she ever had a car like this. "This is nice," she said. "Do you want to try it, Wil?"

Wil slithered behind the wheel. "This seems perfect!" he said, high-beaming that "Here's Johnny!" smile. "He looked at the salesman. "What would the pricing be like? We have two-thousand that we could use as a down payment today," he said.

"The full price is $26,000, but as far as financing goes, we would have to look at Stella's credit history and employment to find what's right for her. I'll be right back." He went inside.

Wil backed Stella up against the wall of the building and kissed her. "Mmm," he said, "that car would be perfect for me! I've always wanted a Prius!"

"I don't know if I would feel comfortable putting it in my name, sweetie," she said.

"Why? Don't you trust me to pay you? You know I would pay you every month. When have I ever let you down?"

"It's not that. It's just—"

"Baby, if we are going to make a life together, we have to go all the way. You know I'm good for it. I'm looking for jobs. Besides, you could drive it anytime you wanted."

"I already have a car," she said.

"I promise you, Stella. I will do everything in my power to get that medical clearance so I can get this car in my name. They told me that max, it would take three months. You're still going to be with me in three months, right?"

"Of course."

"Well, in three months, you just sign it over to me, and it'll be like nothing ever happened—except you get some good credit from it." Just then, the salesman returned.

"Stella! Great news! We can get you this car for as little as four-fifty a month."

"Wow," she said, knowing full well that even at the best of times in the past four years, she had probably never made much more than six-hundred a month. And they still had rent to worry about and a deposit coming up...that is, if they ever found an apartment.

"I think she wants it," said Wil. "But can you go any lower on the monthly payments? I think the most you could afford, Stella, would be four-hundred a month."

"Follow me," said the salesman. When he turned his back, Wil looked at Stella and whispered, "you don't know how happy this would make me. Stella, I promise you that I will give you the moon."

They reached the salesman's office while Stella's guts churned. He made some calls, and then turned to them. "Stella, good news. Because your credit is so good, we can give you the car today for the down payment of two-thousand, plus three-ninety-nine a month." Feeling woozy, she put her name on the dotted lines without reading anything. It wasn't her car, she reasoned. It would all be fine.

Surely the salesman knew the car wasn't for Stella because when he handed her the key, she gave it to Wil. She just wanted to get out of there.

Wil pulled her outside, running, then sat in the driver's seat of his new car, thrilled.

"I'll see you back at the apartment," Stella said, and went to her Corolla. On the way back, she stopped at a convenience store and got a six-pack of Arrogant Bastard.

"Are you okay?" Wil asked at the apartment when he saw her open the first beer. She glugged it down in response. "I'm not judging you. I know you're scared about this. But you have nothing to be scared of."

"You know," she said, "I'm not only scared, but also pretty jealous. I've never bought a car. Here I am, buying my first car, and it's the one I want, but it's not even mine!"

Sitting down at the kitchen table inside, she continued gulping down the beers until she had drunk three of them. She felt used.

"You're right, baby," he said. "I don't deserve it. I have been only taking and not giving lately. Tomorrow I am going to treat you like a queen. It'll be your day. You deserve better than this. I want to thank you from the bottom of my heart. You are an angel."

Instantly, Stella felt cruel. Her head swam with all the back-and-forth. How could she suck all the happiness out of this occasion for him? She was glad he had a car. She just needed to let go, take care of herself, and embrace the spontaneity of her new life.

***

Andrew had replied brusquely and said to come get the sign. When Stella got to Santa Monica, she parked on 9th Street and walked shakily up the stairs, guts fermented at the thought that this was now "Andrew's Apartment." They had been so proud of their first one-bedroom, which they'd moved into after their wedding. Stella had been training to be a yoga teacher. She'd had long auburn hair, wore mala beads on her wrist and burned incense. She and Andrew had picked out three calming periwinkles and painted a big *om* on the wall together.

Stella knocked. The knob turned and the door swung open. On the floor inside sat a pile of her belongings—a couple of pots, a salad spinner, and the giant Santa Monica Boulevard street sign she had pilfered one day on her way back from the gym. She had been on fire when she'd found it: one of those streaks of fortune that arises from a combination of perfect gratitude and trust in one's place in the universe. She had been in love with her city, enjoying its food and balmy weather and community of people who smiled back. She'd been getting every acting job, singing with her band, feeling at home in herself. She had, on the very morning she was to take the sign, said to Andrew, "I really want a Santa Monica Boulevard sign." And later that day, running home from the gym, it was lying at her feet on a corner, detached from the metal pole like a fallen palm frond. She stole it from the city, and saw it as an icon of the most vital version of herself, a version from which she now felt so far removed. It shattered her to think that after all she had done, Andrew had taken the trouble to unbolt it from the wall so she could steal yet another thing from him.

He watched her from the bedroom, as far away as he could get. He had gotten rid of their fluffy chair and brought the desk into the living room. He had taped his artwork over the *om* on the wall; mostly stencils of children with guns. He hadn't shaved; maybe he hadn't slept. He had a grisly beard and seemed shaky and ready to bite, the way a dog does when it has been beaten repeatedly. Stella's tears came again. She loved him. She always would. She apologized in five different ways, knowing the futility of her weak words. Then she waited for him to speak.

He stared from swollen eye sockets. Her own eyes continued to leak. Who was this person? He had been her sweet, mild partner, and she had made him feral.

"You don't have anything to say?" She asked tentatively.

He snapped. "What do you want me to do! Yell at you?"

Salty streams ran down her cheeks. "No," she said, "no." She stooped down to gather her things. The Santa Monica sign stretched from the ground to her armpit, the way it had when she'd found it. She turned and looked at him one last time, felt the pain in her heart make its way through her entire body, and said, "I love you. I'm so sorry." She walked out the door, hating herself.

***

She couldn't believe the year had only begun ten days before. It felt like a lifetime since she had given up her comfortable home life for Wil, who had since been strewing his promises at her feet like petals from a flower girl's basket.

"Don't you do those dishes this time," he said after she made him breakfast. "I'm going to do them.

"I'm doing the laundry. I just have to go get quarters," he said as she sat applying for jobs.

"Tomorrow is going to be your day. I am going to give you an amazing massage and cook you dinner. Oh, and I'm almost done with that mixtape for you. This one is going to be the best you've ever gotten," he said as she left to go running in the Hollywood Forever Cemetery.

"I promise I'll get my stuff off the floor so that we can actually walk in this place," he said after seeing her nearly collapse with exhaustion, attempting to pile some of his shit into a tiny closet.

She was trying to be laid-back; it was so unsexy to feel like her boyfriend's nagging mom instead of his lusty partner. But the dishes were overflowing and the pile of dirty clothes was taking over. Before she left the sublet to babysit Kara and Evan, Stella checked her credit card statement to total up Wil's tab of "I'll pay you back if you get this" purchases. They totaled more than a thousand dollars.

Then there was the sleeping. It seemed all Wil did was sleep, and he always had an excuse. If he wasn't sick, he said it was the medicine. The surgery in September to implant a new defibrillator hadn't worked, so he'd gone back for a second surgery in November. His pain management doctor had supposedly put Wil on a titration schedule to wean him off whatever cocktail of drugs was flowing through his veins at any given moment. Stella had seen different pills come and go. He was open about all of them: suboxone, klonopin, tramadol, bisoprolol. But yesterday, after sending her regular text messages detailing how he planned to defile her, the unthinkable happened: Wil fell asleep right in the middle of sex.

He was still clinging to his "One Year Sober" title, but she started to wonder if this really counted as being sober.

It was almost time to drive to the Westside to pick up Kara and

Evan from school. Stella caught herself in the mirror. Who was she now? She felt mixed up, idiotic, and ugly. The skin around her fingernails was ripped up and bleeding.

What started as a trickle—"Wil? I know you're going through a lot, but it seems to me that you've been making tons of promises you never keep"—soon became a waterfall that omitted nothing. She mentioned the dishes and laundry and trash, the constant promise that tomorrow would be her "special day," the sleeping, and at last: "Do you know how much money you owe me?"

"How much?" he asked.

"More than a thousand dollars."

"No I don't!"

"Do you really want to argue this? I can print out the statement and highlight every one of the things that you promised to pay me back for! Most recently, for example, when you insisted you'd 'take me out' to that nice dinner and pay me back if I put it on my card. You never did."

"What? I didn't say that. You wanted to go out to the restaurant."

"Wil! Are you insane? I would never have gone to a restaurant if you weren't paying for it. I have no money! I would have eaten pasta for dinner!"

He continued to deny his actions until Stella began to doubt her every decision and everything she thought she knew about love. Maybe she was the crazy one. "I have to go pick up the kids," she said, and left, defeated.

***

Stella found reasons to be grateful. She was alive, after all, and young and healthy, and she had gotten an email response to one of the jobs she'd applied for—a real estate office secretary job—so there was hope. She glanced at her stolen Santa Monica Boulevard sign, which she had propped against the wall on top of the bookshelf. The bright blue and yellow reflected into her eyes as it caught light from the small window.

Wil was different after the confrontation. He made Stella a bath and a cup of tea. He went out and bought her a stack of trashy gossip magazines to read in the tub while he cooked her dinner. He made delicious marinated chicken with quinoa and pancetta brussels sprouts. He did the dishes and the laundry. For the first time in weeks, Stella felt at peace. They watched a movie together and talked for hours, munching cereal and then accidentally super-gluing their fingers together while trying to fix a cassette-tape picture frame Stella had made him for Christmas.

***

"We only have two weeks before February, and we have no place to live. I really don't mind where we live at this point," Stella said. "As long as it's a little closer to the ocean." The sublet was nice, but it was freezing and cramped and in the ghetto and it wasn't hers. Stella was so tired of not having free cabinets for her toiletries or a closet for her clothes.

"Stella. You are going to live in Santa Monica. That's your home. You deserve it. I will not hear of anything different," Wil said, wrapping her up in the long sticks of his limbs like a mantis embracing its prey.

As he drove them west in the Prius, the blue of the ocean appeared on the little GPS screen. Maybe Santa Monica would be Stella's city again someday, but until now it had only been Stella-and-Andrew's city. Overlaid upon every sight, she saw a funerary filmstrip of once-happy memories, now grainy and out of focus.

They got out to look at a way-too-expensive apartment north of Wilshire. "Imagine us living here!" Wil said. There was a giant dining room and wood floors.

"Yeah," Stella said, looking at the application on the countertop. "Sixteen-hundred a month. Maybe someday." She briefly fantasized about returning home from a movie set, waiting for Wil to come home from his own set where he had been directing, the two of them showering and putting on designer clothes to go grab a bite without worrying about the price of food. She couldn't tell if this was her own fantasy or one Wil had imposed.

"It'll be someday before you know it." His eyes had a dreamy, faraway look in them as he said, "We're actually doing this. This is it. We are making a life together!" Stella reached up and rubbed his bony shoulders. His zeal made her feel old and cynical.

"Let's go see that other place that was fourteen-fifty just for fun," she said. "That's the cheapest we're probably going to get around here."

The cheaper apartment was only three blocks from Andrew. Stella tried to suppress the nausea, the impulse to jump out of the car and just run back to 9th Street, walk through the front door, get into her old bed, under the red duvet that used to belong to her little sister, and never leave again.

"Well, it's closer to the beach than I've ever lived," Stella said, looking around. It was cozy, with fluffy white carpet. "We could walk to the sand in less than ten minutes."

A smile grew across Wil's face. "Do you want to do this?" he said.

"Of course I'd love to live here," she said, but it wasn't that simple. They literally had no money for a deposit. She thought of the years it had taken her and Andrew to make it as close to the beach as they had.

"I know we could do it," Wil was saying. "As soon as I get a job, I am going to be bringing in some hefty paychecks, and it'll be no problem to pay my half. And you'll be able to do 725 a month easily."

"Yeah? Didn't you just buy a car that you have to pay four-hundred bucks a month on?"

"Listen. Stella. You have to believe that it is going to work out. My counselor told me that the ones who believe are the ones who are most likely to receive. And I've seen it. I'll tell you what. That thousand dollars I owe you for the credit card? How about I give it to you and you use it to pay the deposit. I'll pay the first month's rent. Then by March we will both have jobs and we can split it normally."

"Do you honestly think they are going to rent an apartment to two people who don't even have jobs?"

"How about I call," he said.

***

Wil had slinked into the landlady's office and somehow charmed her into skipping over the credit check. In lieu of three months of paystubs, she accepted Wil's word that they were both gainfully employed. Stella was a well of doubt and fear, but the fact that it had worked out must have meant something. Her impatience and uncertainty drove her from east Hollywood toward 7th Street, the deposit and February's rent in hand.

Wil was shivering in bed back in the dark sublet, trying to self-detox from the pain meds against the advice of his doctor. Stella had begged him to follow the titration schedule per his doctor's orders, but Wil wouldn't have it. "I have gotten sober from heroin three times and stayed for at least a year. Once I stayed sober for three years. This is the best way. Trust me. It's like ripping a band-aid off."

Stella couldn't wait to live where she could walk and bike again instead of being stuck in a hunk of metal all day. She pulled into the parking spot outside her potential new apartment, pausing to contemplate her immediate future. Was it wise to sign a year lease on a $1,450 apartment with a volatile person she'd only known since September, when neither of them had jobs? She felt rickety, light-minded, and queasy. It was the same feeling Wil induced. The high from his love had been so intense, she was afraid of who she'd become if it abated, leaving her to detox. She thought of all the times when she might have had the chance to turn it all around and go back to Andrew. But those were cowardly thoughts. Every great reward started with great risk. *Stella, be strong. It's too late to do anything but move forward,* she told herself. She walked inside and handed the check to the landlady, resolving not to regret it.

***

Stella wouldn't be babysitting Kara and Evan for a while, so she had to return their house keys to her friend Dani, their regular babysitter. Dani was at her job, where she managed the kid-watching services at the fanciest gym in town. She stopped by, taking in the shopping-mall scale and grandeur of Equinox West L.A.

"Wow. You have an office!" she said, handing Dani the keys. "Thanks again for thinking of me as the fill-in babysitter. I seriously don't know what I would have done without that gig."

"Why? Do you need a job? We're hiring."

"What? Yes! Definitely!" Stella hadn't gotten the real-estate office job, so she was back to looking for anything. She always tried to stick with part-time jobs or gigs, so that she wouldn't have to say no to auditions or meetings. But since any guarantee of real money usually meant wasting her life doing something she didn't care for and thus shortchanging her own art, she wondered if she'd ever know what it felt like to be financially solvent.

"Well, we're hiring for front desk and Kids Club. I think you'd be good at both. It doesn't really pay well—"

"That's okay—anything is welcome right now."

"—But you do get a free gym membership, which is worth a lot." Dani passed her an application, "Here. Why don't you fill this out and I'll make sure it gets to the right person."

***

5:17 AM (5 hours ago)

Everly <evrobertsonsmith@yahoo.com>
to me

Sis! Here's the thing—I understand that it's not my life. But sometimes I think that if I am going to be a part of this sister relationship, it is my responsibility to tell you what I think is true. I know you haven't been talking much to Mom, but she is really concerned about you. I was going to send you the gist of what Mom wants to say, and maybe fancy it up to make it sound better... but I'm not going to. I thought I would just try, though, to be the mediator / messenger between you two. I request— especially this time—that you communicate back to her through me. Here's Mom:

I have some questions in my mind that I want to address with you as a mother...the most important of which is: What do you plan to do if you need to go to the doctor when you're no longer on Andrew's health insurance? Also, what do you plan to do about your signed legal obligation on the apartment lease with

Andrew? In your job search, are you applying to larger corporations that would pay consistent with your education so that you can take care of your responsibilities and come home if we had an emergency, and pay your student loans? While you may think none of this is my business, these are things which are causing extreme stress for me. I know that you are stressed too, but I did not bring this on. The last time I heard, this other person does not have a job either and was picking up whatever he could. Doesn't sound very dependable. In an idealistic world, you can live on love, in a realistic world, you cannot.

While nothing you could ever do will change the fact that we love you, do not delude yourself, you must know that this will change your life forever and in a big way. I truly hope he will be worth it, because you are going to lose the respect of many, many people in your life. Whether you think so or not, you do owe us a certain obligation. You are our child. We raised you, provided all your needs and most of your wants, and gave you many, many opportunities and sacrificed to do so. Life is not just all about you, everything you do affects us too.

Everly here again! Ok. Now, I already know that some (or all?) of what she said is very bothersome to you. I agree that it is your life and that your mother no longer can tell you what to do. But some of what she says makes sense. I seriously think that at the first sign of "hey, this might come between Andrew and me" you should have split with Wil. You did make a commitment to Andrew. You know, Aaron and I have had insurmountable troubles. It is so tough and sometimes I think "what if I didn't have to deal with this anymore and what if I fell in love with some charming guy and felt like a teenager again" and all this. But I can't do that. I promised. What's right is not always easy.

I would also like to say that I have learned something from this. I have learned to be a little less judgmental. Say if a friend of mine came along and told me about some girl she knew who sleeps around and then leaves her husband for some dude who used to be a drug addict and she doesn't have a job and neither does he and... DO YOU KNOW HOW CRAZY THAT SOUNDS?!?! Now I know, though, that everyone has a story. It is not all black and white, no matter how much it seems to be.

The truth is that the damage is done. Like I said in the letter I sent you in the Christmas package, though, I think I can be honest and supportive at the same time. I love you and am so glad you are my sister. :)

Everly

***

Stella's sister's email spawned nightmares. She tossed, tormented by all the people she had let down. When she awoke, she wondered how she could justify her actions. Had the problem been blandness on Andrew's part or blindness on her own? She burrowed deeper under the covers next to Wil. All she could think of was Christmas.

The week of Christmas, the walls of the 9th Street apartment were closing in. Stella had tried to watch *Love Actually*, the way she did every year with Andrew, but this year she turned it off halfway through when the holiday cheer went rancid in her stomach. While Stella spent all her free time with Wil, Andrew would leave for the evening, come in late and drunk, and cry himself to sleep next to Stella in the bed they had bought together. One day he drank a whole bottle of wine until he was uncharacteristically angry and maniacal, then he overturned a chair, yelling, "You did this! You don't care about me! You don't even consider me!" She had, in fact, spent the day alone crying. She couldn't stop feeling like she needed Wil, even when it was destroying the life she knew.

She had a desperate idea. She suggested to Andrew that maybe the two of them could pick up and move to Europe together. "We could just leave, and live with your family in England for a while, travel, and get Wil out of the picture for good," she had said. But Andrew said that the glamour of Europe would wear off, and that Stella would again realize that he could not give her everything she needed, and she would probably just fall for some Pablo or Sven.

Christmas Eve, Stella lay beside him in a state of tortured unrest, until she received a text at three in the morning that said "Come outside." She got up and walked out the door onto the balcony.

Below, Wil was holding giant cue cards, á la Love Actually. He put a finger over his lips and held up the first sign, which said,

Shh! Say it's the Dreadlocked Hobo.

Stella couldn't believe it. Instantly, all the sickness in her stomach transformed into fireflies. He flipped to the next sign.

With any luck, by Christmas next year, you and I will be ___ (wherever the hell we want.)

The signs were in his big scrawling handwriting, same as his

27

"Die yuppie scum" tattoo. She laughed. He flipped to the next sign.

But under the same roof.

He wanted her so much. He wanted her to live with him. She imagined a cozy Christmas around a fireplace, with matching pajamas, the way he had described it. He flipped to the next sign.

But for now, let me say, with GREAT hope and an agenda...

His eyes were trained on Stella, whose tears welled.

To me (and to the rest of the entire fucking world) YOU ARE PERFECT.

No one had ever gone out of his way to be so romantic. Stella let the tears fall.

So, although we won't be in our own place with our own tree on Christmas morning this year...WE WILL NEXT YEAR.

Yes, she thought. Of course they would.

And...
my catecholaminergic-polymorphic-ventricular-tachycardia-riddled heart will love you until...well, forever.

She ran down to give him a hug and he whispered, "I'll see you soon. Now go have a nice Christmas with your husband."

She climbed back up the stairs and back into bed with Andrew, who didn't ask where she had gone. She curled away from him in the fetal position, and that was when she saw no other choice. It had been a good run, but she would have to leave the man she had loved since she was 21.

***

Sun was soaking the Westside as Stella interviewed with a youthful, smiling woman at Equinox. "I want you for both positions," the woman said within fifteen minutes. Stella's heart flooded with warmth. Finally, she could start feeling a little secure. "It would still be part-time to start out, but people will be asking you to cover their shifts so you could end up working almost full time if you want."

"Thank you. That sounds great."

Stella called Wil.

"That's amazing, my little *femme fatale!*" he said. "Are you coming

28

home now?"

"Yep."

"I'll cook you something. And I want you to go do something for yourself. How about getting your nails done?"

"Well—"

"You're getting your nails done. I'll see you back home, you working woman. Now I just have to get a job that's more impressive than yours."

"Thanks, baby."

"I fucking love you so goddamn much. We're meant for each other, baby. I feel like the most blessed person on the planet for a lot of reasons, but having your love truly makes it unbelievable. I'm going to treat you accordingly."

Stella felt pierced by a thousand darts of dopamine. She had a way to make a little money. Wil was starting to do things for her again, the way he used to. The sun sank, pink in her rearview mirror. The ecstasy was surely worth the pain.

***

Stella booked a small commercial for a makeup mirror, and to celebrate, she and Wil went to the Dresden, a bar frozen in time, all green and brown decor with huge Flintstones-style rocks set into the wall and gaudy tile on the floor. Marty and Elayne, a geriatric lounge act, sang "Stayin' Alive" around a grand piano that doubled as a table with bench-style seating around it.

"I love how they're still together," Stella said.

"That's going to be us," Wil said.

Stella had brought Andrew here once toward the end of their relationship. By then, it seemed they had exhausted every possible conversation, so when they went out, they just drank and looked around for interesting people to talk to. But with Wil it was different; the world orbited around them. Stella took a sip of a gin and tonic.

"This place is so rad," said Wil.

"I know!"

"You know what?" he said. "I've been talking to some of my sober friends—not the alcoholics, but the addicts. And a whole lot of them actually drink. Because drinking is not a problem for them."

Stella cringed. "Interesting," she said.

"I even talked it over with my counselor and my sponsor. And both of them agreed that I'm not an alcoholic. Opiates are what I am addicted to, so it's a totally different thing altogether. I've talked to them about maybe starting to incorporate alcohol back into my life, not to get drunk, but just to be moderate about it."

"I really don't think that's a good idea. You just celebrated your one-year sober birthday."

"Look, I know how I react to alcohol, and since I have you, you can help me monitor. I would only drink one or two and then be done for the rest of the night. You know, just so I can enjoy social situations. I hate always having to tell everyone I meet that I can't drink because I'm an addict and all that, you know? It's not even my problem. I'm pretty sure that I can drink like a gentleman. But, like my sponsor said, the only way I will know is by trying. And since I'm in a safe place with you, I feel like I can try now."

Stella's tipsy brain swirled around in her head. She didn't say anything.

"Baby, if you don't want me to, then I won't do it. But I feel really confident right now that I am a changed man. I know that if I take one drink, I don't have to drink anything more after that."

"This scares me. But I don't want you to do anything just for me. You need to do things for yourself."

He ordered a whiskey and with one sip, broke a year of sobriety. He didn't do anything strange and he only drank the one. When they got to the apartment, he ravished Stella until they both came three times.

She didn't know what to do other than trust him. He trusted her. *Love saves*, she told herself, drifting to sleep.

***

Stella sat in the Equinox parking garage, waiting anxiously so as not to be too early for her first shift. She realized that, with all the excitement of someone actually hiring her out of her rut, she had forgotten to ask about the pay. But something was better than nothing. She just wanted a place to go, to finally feel like she was contributing to society instead of being a leech.

An hour later, she was sitting on a foam-cushioned floor, building boats out of giant blocks with two kids under the age of five.

"I'm the captain and there's an alligator!" said the little girl.

"I don't think that's an alligator!" she said. "That looks like a gootledoo!"

"What's a gootledoo?" asked the little boy.

"It's a very colorful and rare creature. If you be very quiet and lay down like this, and cross your arms, sometimes you can get one to come up to the boat."

The kids lay down and crossed their arms. Stella was amazed at how quickly they were willing to go along with her absurd suggestion, trusting and unafraid.

On her way out the door, Stella saw Dani in her office. She thought about asking how much money she was making, but she felt weird about it, so she just passed by with a wave. Dani yelled, "How was your first day?"

"Great!" Stella said, heading to her car.

***

After a shift at the front desk, Stella took a gratitude-driven yoga class that had her counting her blessings all the way back to Hollywood.

I am grateful for this sunshine in January. I am grateful for my health. She opened the door to the apartment and Wil was watching TV on the couch.

"Have you seen this show?" he asked. *I am grateful for Wil.*

"Nope, I haven't really had time to watch anything lately." She sat beside him, put her arms around him. "Did you see those emails I sent you about the jobs? Maybe you should try to just P.A. on a couple things until they get to know you, then you could move up."

"Yeah. You're right. Thank you so much for finding those for me. It's so frustrating how hard it is to get a job just because I don't know that many people out here. I obviously have the talent. I just don't want to have to settle for doing things that are so beneath me."

"I know, but keep plugging away. You are so talented. You're going to find something."

"Thanks. I'm not feeling so good about myself right now. But I do have a friend who used to go to rehab where I went, and now he's driving a Maserati. I emailed him, but he hasn't responded yet. He might be able to get me in as an editor for his company."

"What? Keep emailing him! That could change everything!"

"I know. The only thing is, his company distributes porn."

"So you'd be editing porn all day?"

"Well, yeah. Would that bother you?"

"No," she said. "I like porn just as much as the next pervert. But wouldn't it, like, desensitize you to sex or something?"

"I don't know, but it's not like I'd be doing it forever."

"Well, hey. I say go for it." *I'm grateful for porn.* "That rent is going to be expensive. And you can obviously look for something else while you're working there." *I'm grateful for opportunities.*

His expression was overtaken by the familiar grin that said *I'm in disbelief at how amazing you are.* He squeezed her tightly. "Stella, thank you for believing in me. I have never known what real love feels like, but this is it. Even if you were an okay-looking dude, you would still be one of the most incredible people that I've ever known. The fact that you are an absolutely stunning, heart-skip-a-beat-when-I-see-ya, sexy sex master that happens to have a penchant for me, makes me feel like I'm the most amazing guy on the planet."

Later, Stella's friend and band mate Jo had a glitter-themed birthday party. Wil, in a sequin shirt he borrowed from Stella, drank a rum and Coke and made people laugh nervously with his political incorrectness.

Stella stood in a glittery pod with Tessa, Erin, and Jo—all members of the Ladidahs.

"Wait. Isn't Wil sober?" asked Tessa.

As she explained how he was reincorporating alcohol in moderation, she heard how insane it sounded.

She started talking to two guys who were Jo's friends. Out of thin air, Wil claimed her from behind with his long arms and whisked her away, saying he felt like he was coming down with something, and would she mind if they just slipped out and did the Irish goodbye? Stella said sure, of course, so he pulled her outside into the hallway and pressed her up against the wall, kissing her hard with wet cigarette lips. They'd only been there for twenty minutes, but Stella figured her friends would forgive her.

***

Stella knew there was a world beyond the one she saw, and one night she caught a glimpse of it.

She was chatting over a table of hors d'oeuvres with Neil Patrick Harris, who was laughing at a joke Stella made. Kerry Washington came through in a shimmering gown and said, "Well aren't you cute!" and took a photo of Stella with her phone.

Javier Bardem was chatting with Daniel Day Lewis a foot away, and realized he didn't have Daniel's phone number. "Do you have a pen I could borrow?" Javier asked Stella.

"Sure," she said, and handed him the pen she used to write in her journal.

Stella wasn't dreaming; she was working in the green room at the SAG awards.

When the show wound down and celebs started leaving, one of the bouncers turned to her and said, "What are you doing after?"

She thought about her real life, held together with rickety clothespins. She thought of Wil, sick in bed again, and considered leaving. But instead she said, "That depends. Can you get me into the after party?"

When he said he could, Stella changed from her all-black catering outfit into a minidress she'd brought just in case. She drank some Taittenger straight from the bottle and sat in on a banquette with celebrities, laughing in glamorous anonymity.

She was at the open bar when a young guy with a movie star face and white suit approached her. A few feet away, people were dancing to Billie Jean.

"I love this song!" said the guy.

"Who doesn't?" she said, taking her cocktail. "Are you even old

32

enough to drink?" she asked him. He had caramel skin and light green eyes, a jawbone that could crack nuts.

"How old do you think I am?" he asked.

"I'm going to go with...twenty," she said.

"Twenty-one!" he said.

"So you're legal!"

"I am. Now come dance with me before Michael goes off! I have this tattoo because of Michael Jackson. He's my hero!" he yelled above the speakers, pulling up his sleeve to reveal the ink on his wrist.

They grooved over to the dance floor where he pressed his crisp white suit up against Stella. His hips were wise beyond their years, and soon they were sweating, gyrating, laughing, and singing along, their noses nearly touching. Then, the boy put his 21-year-old lips right on Stella's. They tasted clean and ready to go places. She kissed him back until she was tingling in all the most sensitive locales.

"Are you an actor?" he asked.

"I am," Stella said, hoping he wouldn't ask what movies she was in. "What about you?"

"I'm nominated," he said.

He must have written music for some movie or something, Stella thought. "What for?" she asked.

"I'm an actor on a TV show you might have seen," he said.

"Oh," she laughed, and they kissed again.

After a few more songs had come and gone, he said, "Let's go somewhere."

It was then that Stella remembered the fact that her life was far from a celebrity-studded fairy tale. "Okay," she said. "But first I have to go to the bathroom."

"I'll wait right here," he said.

She slipped through the crowd, past the flashing lights to the bathroom, and sat down on the toilet thinking of Wil, and how vulgar and sweaty she felt, and that the liquor that was wearing off, fatigue setting in after the long work day. What had she been thinking? She and Wil were monogamous. She felt guilty. Back outside, she saw her makeout partner in a group, talking to his mom. Midnight struck, and something felt different. Stella didn't belong to this world yet. She wasn't ready. She walked off the red carpet and out the door of the after-party tent, back to her regular universe.

***

Wil had three times more clothes than Stella. He had trench coats and sweaters and tons of pants she'd never seen him wear. He had shoes for every occasion and at least four matching flannel pajama sets. It was the first day of moving to their real apartment, and Wil was ambling in and out, smoking and claiming that he felt feverish.

"Your head does feel hot," Stella said, putting a palm to his forehead. "You need to start sleeping regularly instead of staying up all night and passing out on the couch."

"When we get to our new place and get our bed, I'll start coming to bed with you, I promise. I'm just hungry right now."

"Want me to make you something?"

"No, I'm going to go get one of those burritos." If he ate anything lately, it was a pastor burrito from the stand down the street. "Want one?"

"That's okay," she said. "I'll get these clothes packed so we can go."

Stella made trip after trip to her white Corolla with all the clothes from the floor. Once she was done, Wil was back, eating the burrito, pacing back and forth outside the door, on the phone with his dad.

"Stella, my dad wants to talk to you," he said, and passed her his iPhone.

She pressed it to her ear. "Hello!"

"Stella, it's Pat."

"Hi, Pat."

"I just wanted to say how wonderful I think you are for what you did for Wil regarding the car. You have no idea how much that is going to help him. You are truly a selfless person, and Wil is so lucky to have found you."

"Oh, thank you. I just want what's best for him."

Pat said, "Well, it warms my heart to know he has found someone like you."

She said goodbye and handed Wil his phone, pantomiming her need for him to hang up so they could drive this load of stuff to the new apartment. He kept talking for another half-hour, then went into the bathroom and closed the door. Stella waited.

She went online and saw how much she had been neglecting her writing. She'd kept her blog for years and gotten thousands of page views every day, but her last post was from late September, right after she had met Wil. Once he had come into her life, productivity had shriveled.

She clicked the "New Post" button and watched the cursor blink for a while.

"Okay baby," Wil said, emerging from the bathroom to pull her off the futon with a dancer's flair, "I'm ready. Let's do this."

The light was pale yellow in Santa Monica, and a breeze was blowing sweet jasmine through the air. Stella walked into the empty white apartment with armloads of clothes, taking great pleasure in opening the closet and hanging them all up. That was a start.

Wil kissed her in the living room. Rivulets of daylight gushed through the blinds. "This is the beginning, baby," he said.

As Stella drove them back to east Hollywood, she put in the mix Wil had made her when they first met. It still tugged at her heart with kitten claws, every song dripping with romantic longing for a true love that would last a lifetime. That kind of Romeo-and-Juliet desperation was something she'd never experienced with easygoing Andrew, and she never knew she had wanted it until Wil convinced her. They both sang along until they were back at the sublet where the wood floor was entirely visible for the first time since they'd moved in. Stella touched the track pad on her laptop and saw the cursor still blinking on her attempted blog post. But what could she write? She was too emotionally bound up in her own story to think of anything else, and writing the truth would expose the worst of her. She already felt judged enough. Not writing hurt, but writing might hurt more. She closed the laptop and drank a Guinness with Wil.

***

An unexpected email awaited Stella when she woke up.

6:17 AM (1 hour ago)

Helen Foss <h_foss@aol.com>
to Me

Dear Stella,

When you and Andrew were in Kentucky less than two years ago for your wedding, we had no idea how things would unfold. I can only state how sad, angry, disappointed, and downright dumbfounded I feel to know what has passed between you and my son. I feel for you and the feelings you must have had to have made such decisions.

I have always been glad that you and Andrew made the move to the West Coast - I felt it would force you two to stand on your own more than you ever would in Kentucky. But that place does change people. Relationships suffer - there is such a sense of freedom, of excess, of possibility.

That said, you had been together for several years, and we were delighted to find out that you had decided to marry. You must have thought you were ready - as you popped the question. And I understand the impulse because a lot of your friends were making that decision.

Yes, I had been told that a pattern had been observed in your relationships prior to you and Andrew getting together. "Use them and lose them" was the basic mode of operation; a very intense, all encompassing, passionate relationship that then ended soon after. When you and Andrew started dating, I was warned by several people to be prepared. I basically told folks that Andrew could make his own decisions and that I wouldn't be prejudiced by their rumors, gossip, and attitudes.

However, this pattern seems to have happened again. It is a pattern that feeds your insatiable need for newness and change and excitement. At this point, after the commitment of marriage, the sphere of people who are then involved increases, and the hurt increases exponentially. But doesn't it hurt you too? Perhaps you should look for the reason you have repeated the behavior - if you do you may discover some truths and may then be able to find true happiness with someone.

In these past years I have enjoyed getting to know you - as shallowly as we have been able to because of personal reticence on both of our parts as well as by distance. I understood your appeal and saw - indeed see - your talents and abilities. You have a joy of being, of exploration, of freedom that must in some ways be intoxicating. Andrew once told me that he never felt he would be bored by you. However, there is usually another side to this. I know, because I share some of your characteristics.

I found a partner who has been willing and often encourages my itinerant interests and lopsidedness. You had also found such a partner in Andrew. It saddens me to know that you have willingly thrown it away. The old adage states that "the grass is always greener on the other side of the fence." So, you've broken the fence and gone to the other side. Go on, do good work, play and have fun and live your life. Please don't insist on Andrew telling you that "it's okay," that "you are a good person." He has given you the freedom to leave him - because he loves you and you have been unhappy being with him. THINK. How must that have been to live with each day for the past months? Mend the fence behind you and don't look back.

At some point you may recognize, truly recognize what you have given up. Maybe. You will have some real disasters in your life before that happens.

I've said more, and probably have sounded uglier, than I intended. I'm sorry for that. I hope that at some point in the future, you and Andrew can become friends. It can't be for a while because the hurt and broken trust you have caused are too fresh.

Stella, I hope that you grow and develop and use your talent in wonderful ways in the world. I truly believe in karma, I've had my share of good and not so good, and in large part I can tell you why the 'not so good' has happened. I am working on becoming a more understanding and open individual and wish the same for you.

Helen Foss

***

Kara was trying to make lip gloss in the microwave with coconut oil and crayons. Stella had to use every shred of energy left in her cold bones to summon interest and excitement. January was ending and she needed help. Her phone rang. It was Wil's mom.

"Hello?"

"Stella, hi, it's Judy."

"Hi Judy," Stella said, excusing herself to the bathroom.

"Wil tells me you're having a really hard time lately. I just wanted to call and check on you."

"Yeah," she said. "I just can't move past my guilt. I love Wil so much, but I was married, you know? And I have done irreparable damage to someone I love. I just want to feel better. I know my problems are nothing compared to people out there who are self-immolating and living as refugees and locked up in cells, but it's hard to put things into perspective when everything in my life is so up in the air."

"I know, dear. You know I left Wil's dad, don't you?"

"I think Wil mentioned that."

"Pat was such a sweet guy, but there was a time when I just couldn't do it anymore. I realized I was in love with my boss who I'd worked with for twenty years. That was years ago, and now I am so happy with my choice. I'm moving in with the real love of my life this week."

"That's great," Stella said.

"But I know how you feel," Judy said. "It took a long time for Pat and I to be friends again, but we are. But change is the hardest thing, and all the best things in life all come from the hardest decisions. I think you were very brave to make this decision."

"I guess so."

"Is there anything I can do for you, Stella?"

"I guess I just need someone to tell me that it gets better."

"It gets better. I promise you it does. And just think, you're moving into your new apartment with the love of your life—right?"

"Yeah."

"You've got my number, so feel free to call me anytime. And if there's any way Pat or I can help you guys, we will do it."

"Thanks so much. It really helps just to know that someone has been here before."

"You're welcome," she said.

Stella left the kids and got into her car, which was stuffed to the ceiling with the last load. She had packed it last night before crashing into a six-hour coma. She zoomed over to the new apartment and unloaded everything into neat piles in each corner of the living room. Then, she went back to east Hollywood one last time to clean and repair the sublet before she could join Wil to sleep in Santa Monica. The place was in shambles. Stella felt so irresponsible. Wil had broken two glasses and a ceramic dish. He had crusted up pans that wouldn't come clean, stopped up the bathroom drain, and imbued everything with the smell of cigarettes. Stella fixed what she could, still carrying the weight of Andrew's mother's email, which had been crushing her for 14 hours. Before she said goodbye to the place for good, she wrote Helen back.

She apologized, leaving nothing out. She assured Andrew's mother that she already recognized what she'd given up. She set Helen straight on the rumors: Stella's last three relationships had lasted years, not months. She explained why she had to leave—that she and Andrew had become strangers who lived in the same house and had agreed to date other people. Stella thanked Helen for her candor, and then closed the door on January and the destroyed apartment.

She arrived at their new place at almost midnight, where Wil sat in the living room, face pressed against a glass terrarium.

"Surprise!" he said.

"What's this?" she said.

"This is our new pet. A bearded dragon," he said. "I hope you like him. They're really easy to take care of. I got him in a fire sale. Look at this." He pointed to the side of the glass where the price was written with a Sharpie. "He was originally $559.99! I got him for fifty bucks!"

"Wow, that's a good deal, then. Even though we don't actually even have fifty dollars. Why was he on sale?"

"The lady told me her pet store was going out of business. I think she had to be out this week, so she was trying to get rid of everything. He eats meal worms, and we need to give him a little salad every day. Isn't he cool?"

"He's pretty cool," Stella said, taking a closer look at the price on the side of the glass. The first "5" in "$559.99" looked like an afterthought, lighter than the other digits. Stella thought for a second that maybe Wil had penciled it in to make me believe his story about the major discount, *but why would he do that?* She let the thought go. She was too tired to put up a fight anyway.

"Are you going to take care of him?"

"Of course I am!" he said. "I was thinking we should name him Hemingway. Because of the beard."

"*The Sun Also Rises* is one of my favorite books," Stella said, petting the soft belly of the scaly creature with a finger. "Hello, Hemingway," she said, and then she blew up the air mattress they'd bought and fell asleep.

FEBRUARY

On the carpet in their new apartment, surrounded by boxes, Stella removed the lizard from his terrarium and let him walk around the floor. She flopped onto her back like a starfish, wondering if she'd ever wake up again without the throb of a knife stuck in her heart. Her hand hit a box of books and she sat up and looked into it. A bunch of her old journals.

Wil was in the bedroom, sick again, coughing and then saying "ow." The doctors had said it was pneumonia, yet he still smoked a cigarette every fifteen minutes and wouldn't consume anything except the Vanilla Ensure she'd bought him at CVS.

She cracked open the blue journal from 2008. *Andrew surpasses my expectations always. He surprised me by coming to visit early this weekend. He had made me a fur stole, just like I'd tried on in the thrift store. He sewed it in the costume shop. We bought champagne and I was his forever.*

Stella closed it and flung it back into the box like a mousetrap that had snapped on her finger. She tried telling herself she didn't miss him. She put her head down onto the floor and closed her eyes. *What am I missing? His warm hugs and kind eyes.* She tried to remember him at his best, but his image was in a rearview mirror, getting smaller and smaller until she couldn't make out his features. All she could see was a sweet face pleading for something she couldn't provide. She put Hemingway and her feelings back into their boxes and sat up. There was work this afternoon, thank God. She'd go early and work out first.

In the box of books she spotted her copy of *The Sun Also Rises.* She propped it up beside the lizard's glass as if he was reading it. Wil would get a kick out of that if he ever got out of bed.

***

40

Stella sat at a miniature table at the Kid's Club, coloring with toddlers who were making cards for their moms. She thought of her mother and how long it had been since they'd talked. The last time Stella heard her mother's voice was when Linda had left her a voicemail to say that Janice's father had died. Janice was the only "family" Stella had out west. She was a spunky 60-something distant cousin who had let her and Andrew live with her for two months when they first moved to California. They'd called her their "mom away from mom." She had encouraged them until they found their first jobs and apartment. Stella wasn't sure whether Janice would want to hear from her now, but she had recently gotten divorced so maybe she'd understand. Stella made her a card with hearts on the outside and a note on the inside.

Dear Janice,

I'm thinking of you. My mom told me about your dad, and I'm so sorry. I can't believe it's been almost four years since we moved here and you took us in and helped us get started. I will always consider you family and I know Andrew feels the same. A lot has changed in the past few months and I understand if you don't want to get wrapped up in it. I am having a really hard time, but he probably needs you more than I do. I miss him, but I know this is for the best. I really miss you, too. I haven't gotten to see or talk to you since that Ladidahs concert back in October. I'd love to see you soon for lunch or something if you're ever free. I am sorry for everything, and I really hope you are finding the light at the end of your tunnel. I can see mine, though it is far away. Sometimes life takes you in directions you didn't expect to go, but I know that things will be better for everyone in the end.

I love you and hope to see you soon,
Stella

Back on 7th Street, Wil was outside the apartment, crouched in the corner of the stairwell, wearing a big winter coat, smoking as he talked on the phone.

Inside, she looked at the messy floor—boxes, clothes, one of Wil's sweaters pooled with festering green lizard shit—and her legs decided they didn't want to stand anymore. She slunk down onto the floor and let herself cry.

Wil came inside. "Baby! What's wrong?" he said, crouching over her and wrapping her in his arms.

"I don't know," she said. "I'm worried about everything. I just want to feel okay again."

"You talked to Judy the other day, didn't you?" He always called his mom "Judy" instead of "Mom."

"Yeah," she said.

"Something she told me is that you can't keep waking up and expecting the pain to be gone and then thinking something's wrong with you when it isn't gone." He looked pensively into her eyes and spoke with the innocence of a little boy. "You have to give it time. It will hang around for as long as it needs to, and then once you finally learn to live with it, that's when it will start to subside."

Wil grabbed Stella's hand and let her climb his lanky body until she was standing. Sometimes looking up at him made her feel like her neck was going to snap. She accepted a slurpy kiss. "You are going to be just fine," he said.

She escaped his grasp. She had to get to the Valley and bartend a 1960s-themed party. She pulled a mod houndstooth dress out of the closet, which she accessorized with the thick-framed Oliver Peoples glasses Wil had given her as a gift months ago.

"See you when I get back," she said.

***

Stella woke up stuck to the plastic of the air mattress. No work. She made coffee. Wil got up and announced that he would cook breakfast and that today was going to be a good day. He had bought some cinnamon sugar yesterday, and now he was making toast to put it on. "This guy might be buying my scooter this weekend," he said. "I definitely want to use that money for a camera. All these jobs I keep finding, they want someone with equipment, but a good camera is a couple thousand bucks. If I can get one, I'll be able to make a killing doing film jobs for people."

Stella felt like a refugee. They still had no hot water, no internet, no gas. She looked over at her beloved Santa Monica Boulevard street sign, half buried under boxes. She'd put it up soon. "Awesome, baby," she said. "I think I need to get out of here and walk to the beach."

They walked the seven blocks and sat down on a bench near the pier. It was the perfect day: warm sand, waves crashing, kids on monkey bars, people blasting "California Love" from bicycle speakers. They held hands as they watched the ocean sparkle in the light. Stella wanted to jump in, but she knew Wil wouldn't.

"I will never get tired of this city," she said, though she felt like she was looking at it through a diving helmet.

"I am so pale right now, but now that we're here, wait 'til you see. Last summer I was so tan, and I looked so healthy." In the airy sunlight, she could remember what optimism felt like.

Since they had no utilities, Stella took Wil to the gym later for a shower and some internet. She breathed deeply, alone in the steam room, letting sweat pool in her belly button and run down the backs of her knees. When she was done showering with the expensive products, blow-drying and slathering on the rich lotion, she went to the computer and checked her messages. For some reason, she had a message from Jeff, Wil's rehab buddy who was the owner of the porn distributing company. Weird. Stella hadn't even met Jeff.

Mrs. Wil,

Tell Wil to call me ASAP. I need him to come in tomorrow for an interview.

Best Regards,
Jeff Barnard

Back on the air mattress in the bare apartment, Stella coaxed out a little more hope. Maybe Wil would get a job and things would start sailing gently forward. That night Stella felt like Wil was so deep inside her that the only way they could get closer would be to turn into ghosts and merge soul particles.

***

At 6 a.m. Stella would've been sleeping, but Wil's job interview was in an hour in the Valley. When he kept snoozing his alarm, she had to get out of bed herself and shake him. On eight occasions he said he was getting up and then fell asleep again. In between jostling him and saying, "Wil, baby, come on, you have to get ready," in the sweetest voice she could muster, she made coffee. She finally had to bring it to his bedside and use it as smelling salts. This got him to sit up, at least. Finally, he took the coffee into the bathroom and Stella had to knock on the door every few minutes to alert him of the time so he wouldn't be late for the interview. At last he emerged, looking like a young Keith Richards trying to disguise himself as a regular person. He wouldn't eat, of course, so she sent him off with an Ensure.

Stella was still stuffed with the leftover love from yesterday's sun and spa excursion and the rough sex that had been her lullaby. There was a bruise on her butt from where he had bitten her so hard.

"You're gonna kill it, mister," she said.

"Thanks sweetie," he said, and closed the door behind him.

She knew by now that he wasn't the easiest person to love, but she did, as evidenced by the fact that she was making a tiny salad for a lizard that she had not asked to care for. An image of her college boyfriend Matt came to her, his kind eyes turned volatile from the drugs, her stapler exploding as it hit her dorm room wall. Stella hoped she could by now distinguish the difference between commitment and addiction.

Going back to sleep wasn't an option so she walked to a yoga class. Yoga stopped the spinning wheels in her head and stripped her down to her essence. Two hours later she left the studio covered in sweat, holding tight to the intention of caring for herself as much as she cared for others.

Back at the apartment, her phone rang. Wil.

"Hello?"

"Guess who is employed," he said.

"You got the job?"

"Yeah. Jeff loved everything I had to offer. I'm starting tomorrow. So I'm gonna have to look at inflatable tits and hear fake moans all day."

"Well, get ready then!" Stella was sure that once he got into a routine, she wouldn't have to get him going every day.

"I love your small boobs," he said.

"Well I love your giant schlong."

"Oh, and guess what else. The guy is going to buy my scooter today, so I am on my way to not being completely broke."

"Awesome. Come on back and we'll celebrate. Should I get some champagne?"

"That would be perfect."

"Done! I'm so proud of you."

"I couldn't have done any of this without you, Stella."

***

Clouds marred the morning. Stella didn't have work until the afternoon and was angry to be awake at six again overseeing Wil's departure. It was the same as yesterday: six alarm snoozes, Stella shaking him awake six times while making coffee, Stella pushing him out the door. She poured herself coffee and then slid her back down the slick stove until she landed on the kitchen floor. She took a sip. Nothing tasted good anymore. She put her forehead on her knees and tried to cry, which sometimes helped. But she was numb. She wasted the rest of the morning pacing and futilely trying to organize things around the barren room.

Hemingway looked sad. Stella had been the only one to feed him since Wil had brought him home. She cut up some salad leaves and dug two mealworms out of the little plastic jar and added them in. *Get into your car,* Stella's mind implored, *and drive until the gas runs out. Or just walk over to Andrew's. You always loved how sweet he was when he slept. He's probably in bed only three blocks away.*

When nothing else would help, Stella called her mother. Linda didn't mention how long it had been since they'd talked, except to say she had missed her baby. Her sweet Appalachian accent soothed Stella and tore her up all at once. When Stella told her how hopeless she felt, Linda said, "Honey, they'll be cloudy days everywhere, no matter where you are. You have to pick yourself up. Start walking toward the light."

"I don't know where the light is, Mom. I just keep thinking"— *Don't say it*—"about Andrew."

She got quiet. Then, in her sweet southern accent: "Do you think he'd take you back?"

"Mom. I can't do that. I can't keep looking backwards: It's going to drive me crazy! I have to make the best of the situation I'm in, otherwise I am never going to heal!"

"Well, honey, stop worrying; Andrew is taking care of himself. Now lay off yourself. It's not easy. It'll take a long time to get over it."

"Okay, Mama," she said. "Thank you."

"You're going to be alright," she said. "No matter what happens, the world keeps on turning."

Stella dropped to her knees and asked the universe or God or whatever was out there to dissolve her stress and fear. She closed her eyes and pictured these walls warm and calming, covered with pictures and paintings and mirrors and signs. She pictured lying with Wil on an oversized couch, legs on top of each other, reading, watching movies, writing novels. She pictured them taking sex breaks, ordering takeout, walking to the beach. She pictured friends coming over. She pictured trips to visit family. She pictured a time when they wouldn't even have to talk about money. She pictured her credit cards paid off, a loud sun, and a rosemary-scented breeze blowing the curtains.

***

At the front desk, Dani was wearing a new engagement ring. Stella feigned polite interest and Dani launched into a romantic beach surprise story she had earned after years with the perfect guy. "Do you think you'll ever get married again?" Dani asked.

"I hope so," Stella said. "I never felt this way before, but now I just want to believe in long term love with one person. I don't know if I'm capable of it, but I want romance, you know? I want someone who wouldn't dream of sharing me, who would fight for me."

"I know just what you mean. Do you feel like you have that with Wil?"

"That's why I left. He convinced me. He's just so confident in what he wants. Sometimes when I'm around him I forget I even exist."

"That sounds kinda scary."

"Yeah, I know."

***

Stella needed her bike. Her rusty old cruiser was still locked to the street sign outside Andrew's apartment on 9th Street. She braced herself and walked the three blocks. She unlocked her bike and looked up toward the balcony. The door was cracked and Stella heard his voice, deeper than she remembered. She saw his shadow move past the gap in the door and felt so distant from this person she had effectively grown up with. She quickly rode away, stopping at Starbucks to use their internet.

On Craigslist she found an entire house full of furniture for $330. She called her mom to regretfully ask to borrow some money, which she assured her she'd pay back. She biked to the ATM and used her emergency credit card for a $400 cash advance. She biked to Budget Rent-a-Car and got a big truck for $60, then drove to the West LA apartment where an Armenian couple was moving out in a hurry. She had promised over the phone to load up all the furniture herself, and she did: She carried out a dresser, a bed, some mirrors and lamps, and a little table. She was perspiring as she drove the truck back to 7th Street where she began unloading it.

Wil arrived as Stella was carrying heavy bed boards up the stairs. He tried to take the wood from her and she said, "No, I'll get this. You're not supposed to lift more than 30 pounds."

"Well, here, let me at least—" he made a move to help her carry it, but he was only in the way.

"No, seriously. I got them on the truck by myself. I can get them in the house. Don't worry about it, baby," she said.

As Stella went in and out, Wil relocated outside to smoke, and hollered at two guys who were skateboarding by. "Hey you two!" When they came over, he said, "Would you two be so kind as to help this lovely lady unload this truck? If you can help, I'll give you each ten bucks."

"No, Wil," she whispered. "Seriously, I'm fine."

The guys looked at each other with a "what the hell" resignation and said, "Okay."

They were done soon. "Thanks so much, guys," Stella said, and Wil sent them off with his money.

"Now let me just put this stuff where it belongs and then our place will be perfect. Except that we have no couch. Or mattress."

"You just made me feel like such an idiot," Wil said.

"Huh?"

"You know what? All I wanted to do was help you. You make me feel like I'm not even a man!" He coughed.

"Baby, you have fucking pneumonia and you just had another heart surgery a couple months ago. I'm just trying to look out for you since you don't do much of that yourself."

"I just realized something," he said. "I just realized that you might not be the person I thought you were."

"What?"

"We have different priorities. I am the type who will allow things to slide 95 percent of the time, like the fact that you still haven't bought a mattress for us and you are making my back hurt every day."

"Are you kidding me?" she said.

"While *you* are the direct type who confronts aggressively."

"Okay, I can't believe you are bringing up the mattress when you know I have negative fifty dollars in my bank account and a million bills to pay." Her mind went back to that shadow through the crack of the door—the ghost of Andrew, his lonely body wandering around their old apartment.

"Well you promised that you would buy the mattress, and you still haven't," said Wil.

"Are you completely inept? I don't have any money! You just sold your scooter. Why don't you use that for the mattress if you want it so badly?"

"That is my money. I have to use it for my camera. And I am never going to get better if I have this aching back every day."

"Well, you're fucking out of luck, I guess. I won't have the money for a while. I just borrowed money to get us an entire house full of furniture and now I am four-hundred more dollars in the hole."

"You are nothing like what I thought you were!" he said. "You are so abusive!"

"Abusive? What the fuck? All I do is take care of you! You're like an invalid! I don't know what happened to the guy I fell for a few months ago. You're acting like a psycho!"

"See!? You are verbally abusing me!"

"I'm verbally abusing you? I am at the end of my rope here! I am doing everything for this situation and you can barely get yourself to work in the morning. How is this going to work out?" Stella started crying. Not for Wil: She was crying for the destructive, careless person she had recently come to know as herself.

Wil got calm just to contrast her outburst. He quietly said, "Stella, I don't know what your problem is. I have done everything I can for you and I can't believe you'd expect more when I've gone through all that I have. You just have to have faith, and be patient and try not to hurt people. You hurt people, Stella."

Stella went and stacked the air mattress on top of the platform bed, got into it and covered up her head, sobbing. Here was more evidence that she shouldn't be allowed to love anyone because all she ever did was hurt people.

***

Stella's friend India smelled of lavender and sandalwood, even after the sweaty yoga class. India was a Venice hippie who had left her southern family and her Christian roots to change her name and become a life coach.

"I only worked four hours today at the gym," Stella told her, sipping wine at an outdoor Venice café, "and they pay minimum wage, so every time I'm doing anything other than looking for jobs, I feel guilty. I'm trying to stay positive; I just can't find anything."

"You know what, Stella?" India said. "I have this girlfriend from Sweden who worked as a very high class 'escort' for wealthy businessmen. She absolutely loved it. I know it sounds weird, but wouldn't that be perfect? Showing people how to love and getting paid extravagantly for it? Too bad we don't really have anything like that here."

"Yeah," Stella said. "I've had unenjoyable sex with a quite a few people, and now that I look back on it, I wish I had gotten a thousand bucks an hour for it."

"If there was a classy, regulated way, I'd do it," said India.

"If there was ever a time when I would be considering it, that time would be now," Stella said. She couldn't imagine making that much money in an hour, being able to get anything she needed. "It seems like a terrible idea on paper, but I guess you couldn't know if you never looked into it."

"Exactly. We have to be open to unlimited possibilities. This world holds so many opportunities as long as we are open to them. So tell me more about Wil."

"That's another idea that sounds horrible on paper. But I'm here because I felt led here."

"You have to do what lights you up!"

"I just want a way not to worry about money. And I want to keep doing the things I love."

"Tell me what those things are."

"Writing, acting. Singing."

"You can do those things, Stella. Just do them. The money will follow."

"Yeah. I know that's true but—"

"Are you going to do the things you love?"

"Yeah."

"Just do them. You're going to be just fine."

***

Stella was working a Bar Mitzvah somewhere near Beverly Hills. Flashing DJ lights swirled around boozy adults and hyper teens grinding on a dance floor. Stella's friend Vince, an adorable gay Filipino and today's bartender, had been secretly plying her with drinks.

"Thank God I'm here making twenty bucks an hour instead of

eight," she said. "Can you believe that's all I get paid at the gym?" She had found out when she received her first check.

"I feel ya, girl. I haven't had any massage clients lately," Vince said. "So you were saying, about moving in with the new boy?"

"Yeah. Oh, but I have to tell you how it happened." At least she always had a good story.

Stella embellished the familiar tale of falling in love with Wil against her better judgment, and as she told it, she was hit with a boozy realization: Repetition had created her very identity. She wondered if she could choose any story and repeat it until it became truth.

The fact that she was from Kentucky, for example, had never been a defining characteristic growing up; it was just background noise. But since living in Los Angeles, the hills of Appalachia had become etched into the stone of her self, simply because she was forced every day to answer the question "Where are you from?" With every detail she reiterated about her hometown and its mountains, its coal and vegetable gardens, four-wheelers and churches, she dug the groove deeper. Now, whether it was true or not, she credited the Bluegrass State with everything from her bluntness to her big smile.

Standing beside the dance floor at the bar mitzvah, rounding out the Wil story with the *Love Actually* scene, she saw that the monologue had become a performance. She was reciting passages from the novel of her life. By now she'd perfected the phrasing and pace. The story had become bigger than Wil himself. But Vince took the bait. He widened his eyes, handed her another vodka tonic, and said, "How could you possibly have said no to *that?*"

"I know," she said, taking a drink.

By party's end, Stella's eyes were glassy. She found herself texting Andrew.

Andrew. Regardless of the things I have done, I just want you to know that there will never be a day when I don't love you. Until the day that we can have some kind of relationship again, please know that I am always here for you, no matter what.

In Santa Monica before she got out of her car, she saw his reply:

Say whatever you want. You don't get to be my friend. You don't get to do whatever you want anymore.

Somehow at the moment, that was all she needed to hear.

***

Wil and Stella had argued again and she felt the need to make up for it. She spent the day doing laundry and putting the heavy mirrors and photos up on the walls. First she hung her stolen sign front and center over the kitchen. It took some might and some drywall screws, but once it was up, the white Helvetica letters looked so friendly, declaring "Santa Monica," accurately at last. She was back, though she didn't feel it yet. On one living room wall she hung their paintings. Stella's was a black-and-white nude with an old-fashioned camera for a head. The background was neon and covered in all her favorite quotes from Emerson's "Self-Reliance" essay. Wil's was a spray-painted quote in hot pink, dripping with the words of his favorite fictional sociopathic killer, Patrick Bateman. "I just want to have a meaningful relationship with someone special."

The apartment looked nearly homey now; they just needed the couch and mattress. Stella had made chicken for dinner, and Wil came in after work, smiling. "Look at this! You are so thoughtful. I did some thoughtful things today, too. Valentine's Day is coming up, you know."

"Yep, but you know how I feel about Valentine's Day," Stella frowned.

"Well, you're going to feel differently this year. I've been working so hard to do this special thing." Then he coughed. "Ow." The pneumonia was still here, and he was still smoking, still not eating much.

"I don't want any more grand gestures at this point. I just want to live a drama-free, casual, fun, easygoing life. Don't stress yourself out over it." She made herself a plate, hoping he'd get himself one eventually."

"I have this Buñuel movie I've been wanting to watch for three days," he said. "Will you watch it with me? We can drink some wine!"

"Okay." She sat with him, gulping wine through *The Exterminating Angel.* Halfway through, Wil lost interest and began nagging at her about finding a job that would pay the rent. "I'm looking for one," she said. "What do you want me to do, become a hooker?"

"I can't believe you'd consider that, but it might be your only option now," he said.

"Are you serious? I'm *not* considering that," she said, though his tone made her wonder what she might do in dire enough circumstances.

"Good," he said, "because I might get jealous. I wonder sometimes how much I can trust you."

Stella shook her head in disbelief, took her wine glass into the bathroom, got into the shower and let out an angry scream. Wil went outside and smoked.

Back in the living room, the movie was paused and grainy. Stella's brain was seeing everything in black-and-white, too. She said quietly, "I feel like I'm dating my college boyfriend Matt all over again."

"How could you say that about me?" he said.

"What am I supposed to say? I'm miserable every day. I was with Andrew for almost seven years and we *never* argued."

"Maybe you never argued because you didn't actually care enough to," he said.

Wil saw Stella considering this and retracted his claws. "I'll tell you what," he said, "I'm going to quit smoking tomorrow. That's going to be your Valentine's present."

"What about that stuff you said about the pneumonia and how it will hurt to cough and everything?"

"Fuck that. I'm gonna have to do it sometime," he said.

"I'm definitely okay with that, as long as you are doing it for you."

"I am. I've wanted to quit for a long time. So I have this one pack left. I have to get rid of it." He walked into the bathroom. Stella waited for him to dump the cigarettes into the toilet and flush. Instead he sat down on the toilet lid, opened the window, took out a cigarette, and began to smoke.

"Having a last one?" she asked.

"I'm just going to smoke all the rest of this pack right now," he said, "because then I will be so disgusted that I won't want to smoke ever again."

"Not to be pushy or tell you what to do, but that sounds like the worst idea ever. You have pneumonia. That means your lungs are full of infection. You don't need to smoke twenty cigarettes one right after the other."

But he puffed away, determined to chain smoke the whole pack. Stella shut the door in disgust.

***

A blaring question woke Stella with a start. *Have I made the worst mistake of my life?* She breathed deeply to try and slow her heart. Her mind flashed back to one of the last times she had sex with Andrew. She had choked down a lump in her throat, wishing she could feel something.

Wil had called in sick to work and was asleep on the air mattress. Stella ran errands, looked for jobs, and went to yoga until it was time for Ladidahs rehearsal.

The girls were planning a trip to Vegas.

"I can't go," Stella said. "I've never been so broke."

"But Stel, you *have* to go," said Tessa.

"Yeah," said Erin. "Who else is going to entertain us in the car?"

Stella thought about how much she could use a weekend away. "You know what?" she said. "Fuck it. I think I will go."

"Yes!" said Jo. "I can't wait to pick up guys with Stella."

It was nearly eleven when she got back from rehearsal. Wil hadn't responded to her "Coming home!" text. She opened the door and called out his name. No response.

When she walked into the bedroom, she found him hunched over the dresser looking vacant.

"Wil! What's wrong?"

"I have last night the bathtub rib crack," he said, his eyes empty and looking around.

"What? What are you saying?" She hoped to God he wasn't on drugs again. "Are you okay?"

"I have—I brain work and then hit the side and fell in. A seizure." His black leather voice was raspier than usual.

"You had a seizure!?"

"Yes, but please don't tell my family. Don't tell my mom when you talk to her, please. I'm sorry."

"Just sit down. Come in here and sit down on the floor until you can talk to me."

He sat down and eventually said, "When this happens, my brain gets all mixed up. I was taking a shower and I had a seizure. I hit my rib on the side of the bathtub and now it hurts to breathe."

"Why did you have a seizure? Probably because you smoked that entire pack of cigarettes last night."

"No, it's lack of sleep. I haven't been sleeping more than three hours the last few nights because I have to wake up early for the job so my schedule's all fucked up. Now I have the worst headache. But don't worry, I'm used to these. I just have to sleep it off." Stella searched his face. He said, "But I had these huge plans for you for Valentine's Day tomorrow. I am still going to do them."

"No! I do not want anything for Valentine's Day. It doesn't mean shit to me! All I want is for you to take care of yourself! Go to bed right now."

"I will after I sit here for a minute and watch some TV."

"Seriously, go to bed." Stella knew she'd have to stay up and keep an eye on him, and it was already 11:30. She was tired.

"I will soon. Don't worry sweetie. I'm going to be just fine and we are going to have the best Valentine's Day ever. Listen, can you do me a favor and call Jeff for me and tell him I won't be able to come in to work tomorrow?"

"Sure. I'll call him."

"And then tomorrow morning I want you to do something for me, okay?"

"What?"

"I want you to set your alarm for 8:30 and wake me up, and I am going to make you breakfast in bed." `

She knew it would be *her* waking up early on the day she wanted to sleep in. He was already keeping her up late. She knew it would be *her* spending an hour dragging him out of bed so that he could "do something nice" for her.

She said, "I really just want to sleep in tomorrow. If you're not going to work, you should sleep, too."

"No, please. You deserve a good Valentine's Day. Tomorrow's going to be your day. We are going to do something awesome."

"Fine," she said, exasperated. "I'll set the alarm for 8:30 but you better get up immediately. I'm not going to spend an hour making you get up like I have to every morning."

After an hour watching TV, Stella went to bed alone. Wil said, "I'll be there in ten minutes, I promise." Thirty sleepless minutes passed as Stella worried about him. She peeked into the living room.

"You need to come to bed, Wil."

"Just ten more minutes."

***

Valentine's Day began how Stella expected. She woke to the sound of Wil's alarm; Wil did not. She didn't bother trying to wake him. He couldn't care for a lizard, or even himself, so it didn't follow that he would take care of her. She was furious by now from all the repetition: "Eat something, baby," "come to bed, baby," "you don't need to do that, you need to do this." She felt used up, stressed out, under-slept, wrung dry.

She went to the gym, and when she returned, Wil was gone. He arrived an hour later with a giant heart balloon that said "I love you."

"Thank you, sweetie, but really, you didn't need to do that." Pity coursed through her.

"Well, I had to do something," he said. "Plans A and B can't happen now, and I just feel terrible. I'm the worst boyfriend ever. So I got this fucking balloon. Do you know how much this cost? Twenty-seven dollars!"

"What? We could have eaten dinner or gotten groceries at the 99 Cent Store for that much. I do not need a balloon!"

"You're right. What an idiot." He picked up one of the gifts he had gotten her a month ago: an Airsoft handgun. He turned it toward the balloon aimed at it. "Maybe you should do the honors." He put the gun in Stella's hand.

She did feel like shooting it, but she didn't have the heart. He couldn't understand that he was enough.

He held Stella's shoulders and looked down at her. "I want to tell you what I had originally planned, though," he said. "First, I tried to book the Griffith Observatory for just the two of us. Because, remember how I said I had done something so nice for us the other day?"

"Yeah." Stella hoped he hadn't had a star named after her or something.

"I had a star named after us. Stella and Wil's Lovestar. They're supposed to send me a certificate and stuff, but the fucking thing hasn't come in yet. We were going to get a private tour of the Observatory, then I was going to show you the star through the telescope. But then the booking got cancelled. So there was plan B, which was to hike up to this place I found where the stars are so bright, but now I have this aching rib from the fall yesterday after the seizure, so I don't think I should hike—"

"Wil."

"What?"

"Calm down. I don't care about any of this stuff. Why don't I just go get some Indian food from Main Street and we'll just eat and watch a movie, and then we can go to bed early and forget this day ever happened."

"Are you sure?" he asked.

"I'm sure," she said.

She got in the car, glad to get a breath as she drove the few blocks down Main Street, looking through restaurant windows at the couples holding hands across the tables. At that moment she would have traded every grand gesture in the world for the predictable peace she'd had with Andrew.

***

At Starbucks Stella charged a coffee to the credit card that was almost maxed out. She used to come to the coffee shop for a change of scenery while writing, but writing seemed an impractical luxury now. This time she needed the free Wi-Fi to see if her Equinox check had gone through. *Shit.* A check that was payment from a recent catering gig had bounced. The gym check hadn't cleared, and once it did, it would barely cover the three-hundred-dollar overdraft.

She opened her email to see if there were any responses to the Craigslist jobs. An older guy sitting beside her tried to start a friendly conversation. Stella wondered if he could tell that beneath her politeness, her stomach was folding in on itself. The only new email was some lady named Anne, asking if she'd like to join a high class escort service. Stella deleted it. The man beside her asked her out. Stella told him she was taken. The sadness was palpable. She unplugged and left the coffee shop, calling her mom.

"How are you doing, honey?" Linda asked dimly.

Tears poured out as Stella walked to her car. "I'm not good, Mom. I can't blame Wil for coughing up blood and being nearly helpless after the seizure. I know it's not his fault, and I have to be there for him. Maybe this is my destiny, Mom," she sobbed. "Maybe I am just meant to be a—caretaker. I'm good at caring for other people. I thought I had a lot more to offer the world but I am not so sure anymore." She opened the driver's side door and collapsed into the seat.

"Honey, have you thought about just coming home? You're always welcome here."

"No, Mom. If I come back, I'll just be another one of those people who gave up when things got too hard. I have to figure it out on my own this time." Stella thought often with love of her tiny coal mining town with its dogwood tree canopies and muddy hollers, but moving back there sounded as appealing as moving into a cage.

"I'm just worried about you, honey."

"Please don't. I am going to be okay," she said, unsure if she could trust her own words. So many times when she called her mother desperate for encouragement, Stella ended up doing the comforting. But she kept calling anyway, because Mom was always there. Frustration mounted. "I need encouragement, not handouts."

"Don't get snappy with me, now, Stella. You made this decision and that is why you're in this boat. Have you talked to Andrew lately?"

"No! Mom! Why would I talk to him? He hates me! I ruined his life!"

"Well I don't think it's over in his mind. I get the impression that it's his family who is pressuring him not to talk to you."

"Please, Mom, please don't say things like that."

"Well, he's hurt. I think you should try again to talk to him. Just see if he would be willing to give you another chance."

"Really?"

"I don't think you have anything to lose."

"I don't." Her brain felt like a worn-out, smoking engine that she couldn't stop revving. "I'll call you back." She drove to her old apartment. She parked outside and patted her face dry, fixed her makeup, and then got out and walked up the stairs.

She knocked on the door. Andrew answered, looking wooden under his scraggly, wolf-child beard. All the blond in his hair had turned to dishwater. All the blue was gone from his eyes.

"Andrew, I'm sorry to bother you, but can I please come in?"

He stepped back, wordlessly allowing her in. On their old table Stella spotted a card from his mom with two wolves on the cover.

"Andrew. I know this is a shot in the dark," Stella began. He studied her like a specimen in a jar. "But I can't do this anymore. I have made the biggest mistake of my life, and I have hurt the person I loved the most. You. I am so sorry, Andrew." She cried more. "I am so sorry. I didn't know what I was doing." She fell to her knees on the floor. "I am asking for you to please forgive me. Even if you can't forgive me now, I am asking for you to consider it. Would you consider taking me back, Andrew? I have fucked everything up and it's my fault, but I love you and I always will, and I promise you that if you would have me, it can be on your terms. Anything you need. I'll be there for you. I will not take you for granted. And we don't ever have to do this open relationship thing again. I will be loyal to you for the rest of your life. I will, Andrew."

He still hadn't responded. Stella sank lower until her forehead was on the floor. She sobbed. When she looked up again, he had ducked into the bedroom. He had gotten in the bed, and he had covered up his head with Everly's old red comforter. He was crying.

Stella stood up and walked to the threshold of the bedroom. She didn't want to overstep her bounds. She whispered through the tears, "Do you want me to leave?"

"Yes," he said.

"Will you just think about it? I will be waiting. I'm not far. I just want to fix this. We can fix this."

"I don't know what I think right now," he said gruffly, his face turned away from her. "Just please go, Stella."

She turned and walked out the door, unable to hold back her sobs, which sounded idiotic and alien to her.

It was all she could do to get through work without breaking down in a customer's face. Halfway through her shift at the desk, she received a text from Wil.

I'm in the emergency room.

Wil was at the apartment when she got off work. The doctors had decided not to keep him overnight, as they could do nothing for aggravated pneumonia and a pulled muscle in his chest.

Stella wanted to feel sorry for him, but his family and internet friends had the saccharine sympathy and encouragement covered, so all she could do was lie inert, detesting herself, wondering for the first time which had come first: the heroin use or the heart condition. She'd never asked him—doing so was bound to ignite some "who do you think I am?" argument full of made-up stories—but she had done enough Googling to know what too much of the drug could do to a heart. And Wil had certainly abused it. Once he had showed her a photo from a few years back. "See that bruise below my eye?" he had said. "That's because I had used up all the veins in the rest of my body."

But Stella's real questions were internal. Her life, in the 12-step terms she'd learned at Wil's meetings, had become unmanageable. Did she regret what she'd done yesterday, intruding on Andrew and begging him to take her back? She didn't know. But now, somehow she hoped he'd never want her back. Surely she had taken this path for a reason. Miracles did happen, and they could happen to her.

***

At last, the cable people turned on the Wi-Fi. Stella could finally look for jobs without having to buy coffee. On a friend's Facebook she saw that Andrew was selling tickets to an art show he was having downtown. She was so proud that, unlike her, he was finally doing something creative. Maybe being without her had energized him. She didn't have the money, but she bought a ticket anyway and sent him a message.

Hey, I bought a ticket to your show on Thursday. Would you mind if I come?

He texted back quickly:

Please don't come.

Stella felt a stab of pain and responded:

Okay, congratulations.

***

Wil had asked Stella to accompany him to the pain management doctor. He drove them in the Prius down Santa Monica Boulevard, into the parking structure at St. John's hospital, and all the way up to the roof. They got out and walked toward the edge where they could see all the lights of Santa Monica, the traffic backed up on the boulevard. "The air feels so nice tonight," Stella said.

Wil gazed down over the edge at the street. "It is beautiful," he said.

"That's a long way down."

As they sat in the dismal grey waiting room, they held hands. "Will you come in the office with me when they call me?" he asked. "This doctor is such an asshole. I just want some backup. Ever since I tried to get off this medicine cold turkey he treats me like I'm a goddamned criminal."

"Okay."

"Wil Mallory," the nurse said. Stella got up and walked with him through the door. Wil made her sit up on the examining table with him, and the roll of paper crinkled beneath them. Wil tried to slip his fingers into her bra.

"Quit!" she laughed.

The doctor came in. "Wil, have you been following your

titration schedule?" he asked.

"Yeah. I've been using one Suboxone strip every night."

The doctor looked at Stella. He had a sober face, a red beard and glasses. "Is this your girlfriend?"

She stuck out her hand for a shake and introduced herself.

"Nice to meet you," he said, and shook his head.

"Wil, your eyes are really glassy. You're not doing drugs are you?"

"No," Wil said.

"Stella, is he telling the truth?" She felt the doctor's eyes pierce her own, so that she doubted herself briefly.

"Yes. I'm with him every day and I haven't seen him do anything except take the medicine he's supposed to take," she said. Wil patted her thigh.

"Okay," said the doctor. "Wil, I'm going to keep you on the same dose you've been on," he said, pulling out a prescription pad. "Come back same time next week and we'll see if we can lower it." Stella wondered why he couldn't lower it now. Wil told Stella that if she ever tried to take one dose of his medicine, it would knock her out completely. He said that his body was so used to opiates that they had to give him an extraordinary dose of non-narcotic painkillers to do anything at all.

They got back in the car and drove west. "I'm sorry that guy treats you so bad," Stella said.

"I know." Wil was unusually quiet today.

"What's wrong?"

"Stella, something is different. I know that you've been feeling one foot in the door and one foot out. Have you been thinking about Andrew?"

"I never really stopped thinking about Andrew. He was part of my life for almost seven years and I basically discarded him like garbage, so yeah."

"It's fine that you're thinking about him. I just get the impression that you might be regretting leaving him."

"I can't lie, Wil. I have been feeling so guilty. I cry every day about it." Stella started to cry again. "I'm trying to make this work, but there's something inside me that keeps wondering if I've made the right decision. And when I wonder that, I feel guilty about you. And then I'm so worried about money. How are we going to pay March's rent? It's coming up and I still only have this job that pays eight bucks an hour. What the hell are we going to do? We're one step away from being homeless!"

"I wish I could take away your pain. You've taken such good care of me through all this. I know it's weird, but I kind of just wish you'd get sick so I could do everything for you and show you how much I care."

"You wish I'd get sick?"

"Well, I'm sick so much, and all you do is take care of me. I want to show you how it feels."

"Why don't you just take care of me now?"

"I do! I do everything for you."

"You do?"

"But if you'd just get sick, you could lay in bed every day and I'd cook for you and clean the house and give you your medicine."

Stella stopped crying and let the sour feeling settle in her stomach.

***

She spent the entire day drinking French press and combing the internet for jobs. She composed thoughtful cover letters and sent off resumes to "LA Instructors Needed Immediately - Tutoring, Music, & Arts," "ESL Teachers Wanted," "Hiring Star Server," "Santa Monica Locals Needed for Bar," "Customer Service Experience Needed Westside," "Models Wanted - Live Hostess Gig," "Seeking Assistant to TV Producer," "Administrative Assistant, Full Time Only!" and "Staff Editor - Digital Content."

Wil was feeling better and had finally gone back to work. All week he'd been talking up a big date he had planned. "I'm going to make up for Valentine's Day. You be ready," he'd said.

"How are you going to pay for this?" Stella asked as he opened the car door for her in Beverly Hills.

"I got us a deal. Three course meal plus dessert and champagne. So you have nothing to worry about. Tonight, you are going to be treated like the queen that you are."

Wil chatted up the waitress, schmoozed with the manager, and shared dessert with Stella over candle light. The night was as light as champagne bubbles and just as temporary.

Back on the air mattress, he pinned her by the wrists and ravaged her the way she used to love. Just as she left fear and worry behind and became aware of her bliss, Wil froze, then let himself collapse on top of her. He covered her completely. Stella felt the heaviness of his bones and the darkness that lived within him.

"I just got really light headed," he said.

"It's okay," she said.

He rolled off her and smashed his face into the pillow, suddenly crying. "I'm a freak. Why would you want me?"

"What are you talking about, Wil? I love you!" The heady buzz gave way to a bad taste in her mouth.

"Stella. You could have any guy, and you're trapped here with me. I am damaged. My heart doesn't work! I can't even do something as simple as fuck you without feeling like I'm going to die."

The self-pity surprised Stella a little: She had never seen him fully discard his cocky outer shell. "That is not who you are, Wil. That is a *condition*. It doesn't define you. You have a lot to offer the world, and I love you now and for who you are going to become."

"But what about you? You don't deserve to have to take care of me all the time."

"I don't know what *deserve* even means. Sounds like bullshit to me," she said. "And I take care of you because I choose to."

***

Ladidahs rehearsal ended early. Tessa was too upset to sing. She had decided to break up with Jared, a guy she really loved, because he wasn't the one and she knew it. Her band mates told her she was brave.

"Nothing hurts worse than admitting that everything you hoped for has been cut short," said Victoria, "but you'll be happy you did it when you find the person you truly want to be with."

"I know," Tessa said. "I just can't stop wondering if I'm doing the right thing."

Emotions mounted as they sang in harmony. They hugged in a circle, then laughed at their own corniness.

"Just remember," said Jo. "None of this weepy shit is going to go down in Vegas. I will hold you down and force feed you alcohol while playing Beyoncé."

Stella didn't even like Vegas, but she was relieved that Friday's drive would distance her from her current situation, however temporarily.

***

"Jeff was super pissed that I came in two hours late this morning," Wil said when he got home, "But I explained that I've had this pneumonia and he said it was okay as long as it didn't happen again. I just can't believe I'm doing all this for a job that pays eleven dollars an hour. I'm worth so much more than that."

"Yeah, I know how you feel."

He enveloped her. "I know what, baby. Let's do something nice for you. I've been telling you that I'd get you a smartphone. We have to get you into the 21st century."

"Yeah, but I like not being available, you know? It took me, like, two years just to embrace texting. I don't like feeling like I'm attached to the internet wherever I go. I want to be free."

"But you're going to have to sometime. Why don't you just let me buy you the phone? I owe you something for all you've been doing for me."

Stella thought about it. "Okay."

"Let's go. This way you can send me pictures from Vegas this weekend!"

Wil paid fifty bucks for a phone whose contract Stella worriedly signed, knowing she wouldn't have the extra hundred dollars next month to pay the bill. She used it to get on Facebook and post a status that said

> Living in Santa Monica four years and FINALLY I am a 310 area code! Not to mention, I am the last person under 65 to FINALLY get a smart phone! THANK YOU, Wil Mallory!

Then she saw an update from Janice, who had posted a photo of her and Andrew at his art show. She still hadn't responded to the card Stella had sent her.

***

"This is the longest we will have been apart since we moved in together," Wil said as Stella kissed him goodbye.

"I know," she said, feeling a bit of guilty excitement at the prospect.

"But this is good!" he said. "I'm going to catch up with some friends I haven't seen in a while, and you get to hang out with the Ladidahs."

"I'm glad you feel that way," she said. "But I'll be back before you know it."

"Hey," he said, "Do whatever you want. You know that you are free with me. I'm not going to expect a call every hour on the hour. Just send me a pic on that new phone once in a while."

"I don't really know how this thing works yet, but I'll try. Love you," she said.

He held her for longer than usual. "Love you, my little tater tot."

"Wow, Stella, this is a nice Prius. It's technically yours, isn't it?" asked Victoria.

"Well, it's in my name for right now, but it's really Wil's." He had let Stella drive it since it was the most fuel efficient car of the group.

"He's actually been paying for it?" asked Rebecca from the backseat.

"Well, yeah, there's only been one payment so far, but he's going to."

"Girl, you need to get him to put it in his name as quickly as possible," said Victoria. "That is bad news."

"Yeah. He's waiting for medical clearance from the State of California. It should only take three months, they said."

"I am so ready to get out of here," said Tessa. "This has been a tough week."

Later, Stella's friends were sitting around a coffee table drinking something blue out of plastic hotel cups.

"You losers better take some shots!" Jo said, thrusting flavored vodka into their faces. Stella went to the bathroom and attempted to text Wil a photo of a TV built into the mirror.

"Stella! Get in here!" called Kerry from the next room. "We're gonna go to all-you-can-eat sushi, then we're gonna go to the club, so let's get ready."

"What do you think? Retro, or slutty?" Erin asked, holding up two dresses.

"I think retro-slut," said Stella. Then her phone buzzed. "Um. Oh my gosh. This is a new phone, and Wil just sent me a dick pic so I quote-unquote wouldn't forget about him."

"Stella! How do you deal with that thing?" said Kerry, looking at the photo.

The night was an eardrum-crushing blur of flashing lights and half-naked cirque performers hanging from club ceilings. Stella texted Wil at midnight.

I'm in the middle of a loud club. I really hope you're asleep and don't get this until the morning. Kerry says to tell you that your ding-dong is huge!

He wrote back,

Well, actually, I was asleep and you just woke me up to say some lewd thing to me about your friend. I'm going to try go back to sleep now. Maybe you shouldn't call me until you're on your way home.

She thought this was weird and assholesque, but she was too full of firewater to give a fuck. She would talk to him in the morning. She pounded a syrupy gasoline-tasting Jäger bomb Jo bought her, then walked around hotels in heels until there was no sensation in her feet.

***

All of Stella's friends had congregated in one room. She waited until after 10:30 to go into the hallway and call Wil. "Hey baby! Good morning! Hope it's not too early."

"Yeah, it *is* too early. I was *asleep* since I didn't get any sleep last night because you took it upon yourself to text me and wake me up after midnight for *no reason.*"

"Huh? Why are you mad?"

"You didn't even text me *one* picture!" he spat. "And why did Jo and Erin get there hours before you did? *They* posted pictures on Facebook. Where were you? You have completely fucked up."

"Wil. What the hell are you talking about? I thought I was allowed to have fun this weekend."

"You *are*. But if you're doing things that you're hiding from me, maybe this relationship isn't such a good idea."

"Are you kidding me right now?" The conversation spun in circles for as long as Stella could stand it, and finally she talked him down enough to let her get off the phone.

"Holy hell," she said, re-entering the room where her friends were getting dressed. "I do not know what just happened." She explained what she understood of the talk she'd had with Wil, then moved on quickly so as not to kill their buzz. "So what's the plan?"

"Buffet. Then pool," said Jo.

"He's mad at you for not posting photos? What, is he, like, eight years old?" said Kerry.

"I guess! That can't really be it, can it?" Stella dug a sundress out of her suitcase and pulled off her pajamas, which consisted of Wil's Joy Division T-shirt and some penguin pants.

"Sounds to me like he's trying to manipulate you," Victoria said. "This is not a healthy relationship. I think you should consider getting out of it when you get home."

"I've been thinking that for a while," Stella said. "But we just moved into the new apartment a week ago, and I'm still just working at the gym. I'm stuck with him for now."

"Girl, you can sleep on my couch if you want to get rid of that loser," Victoria said.

"Or mine. I'm sure any of us would be willing to help you out," said Tessa. "Because, Stel, this is serious. He sounds truly insane."

"I know. I'm going to leave my phone here so he can't call me."

"I think that's a good idea," said Tessa. "But are you going to make some plans to break up with him?"

"I don't think I can break up with him as soon as I get home, but I've been applying for a ton of jobs, so as soon as one pans out, I will get the fuck out of there."

"Yes. And we will be here for you no matter what," said Tessa.

"Thanks guys. That means a lot."

They crammed into a van-taxi, laughing and forgetting their attachments and jobs and diets and resolutions. After lunch, Jo and

Tessa both got a *bloop* on their phones.

"You have to be joking," said Jo.

"Stella, he's at it again," said Tessa.

"Wil?" Stella asked.

"He even tagged *me* and I've only met him, like, once," said Victoria, looking at her phone.

"Me too!" said Erin.

"What is it?"

Tessa said, "He put out a public alert on Facebook looking for you, and he tagged *all* of us."

"I'm going to untag myself from this shit," said Jo.

"Oh my god, can I see it?" Stella asked. Erin handed over her phone.

The post said,

Well, Ladidahs, it appears that Stella has left her phone at the hotel or it might be on silent, but I really need to talk to her ASAP. Erin, Tessa, Jo, Victoria, Kerry, Rebecca. Please let Stella know I need her to call me. The cable people need me to give them her social security number and I don't have it, so she needs to contact me as soon as possible. Can you beauties give her the memo for me? :0)

"I am so sorry," Stella said. "What the hell? I am just going to wait until tonight before we go out, and I'll call him for like two minutes and tell him to cut this shit out."

"This is first-class insanity," Rebecca said. "I've never seen anything like it."

Stella sweat shame beneath the hot judgment of her well-meaning friends. If she tried to redeem Wil by telling them how great he used to be, she'd sound like one of those conspiracy theorists who swears that the moon doesn't exist. She probably already seemed like one.

That evening, before they headed out, she gave Wil one last courtesy call.

"Hello," she said curtly. "I am going to talk to you for no longer than five minutes. I don't want to spend my entire getaway stuck on the phone in the hallway while my friends have fun. Now what is it that you need?"

"I just couldn't get a hold of you. Why did you leave your phone at the hotel? Never mind, I know why you left it at the hotel. You were trying to punish me. I'm totally stupid."

"All my friends are really creeped out that you put them on blast on Facebook. What could possibly be so important?"

"The cable. I just need your social security number for the…to hook it up, because—"

"We already took care of the cable over a week ago. I need you to get a grip."

"You're out having sex with people. I know you are."

"What the hell?"

"Why else would you be avoiding me like this?"

"Wil. I am having fun with my girlfriends like I said I was going to. What is wrong with you?"

"Yeah? Well maybe I just need to kill myself. I could just jump off a building and nobody would even care."

"Wil. Don't you dare talk like that while I'm five hours away and can do nothing about it."

"I could, though. Maybe I should. What's the point anymore, anyway? I'm just inconveniencing everyone with my existence."

"You know what? This is manipulation, and I refuse to have this conversation. I love you. I have done nothing wrong. I am having fun for a matter of about 24 more hours. Then I'll be home and everything will be fine, okay?"

"What about the photos?"

"I am not going to take photos on this trip because I want to enjoy it. If you want to see photos, look at Facebook. Erin loves to post stuff. That's not my thing."

***

The next morning, after a night moving as a herd in spangled dresses, skipping lines and getting free drinks from desperate bachelors, the Ladidahs left Vegas puffy and stringy-haired. Victoria drove the Prius back. "So, what's your plan?" she asked Stella.

"I'm going to go home and smooth this whole thing out for the time being. If anything, I can use sex to bridge the communication gap."

"Seems like you've got that covered," said Rebecca.

"Yeah, but I'm still looking for a full-time job, hardcore. So as soon as one comes through and I can afford to move, I am going to get out of this situation."

"But just don't get lost in him," Rebecca said. "He's manipulative. Remember what you're telling us now, because when you see him, you're probably going to feel differently."

"I know," Stella said.

"You can call us if you need a reminder," said Tessa.

"Thanks, ladies."

The sun was sinking when Stella walked into the apartment. She heard the splashing of the shower. The lizard was walking around on a mound of clothes. Two piles of lizard crap glistened on the carpet.

Stella stripped down as she walked into the bathroom.

"Hey you," she said, and stepped into the shower behind Wil, wrapping her arms around him. He bristled.

"Hey. Did you kiss anybody else?"

"I'm going to kiss *you*," she said, turning him around to face her, planting her lips on his. They were big, wet, and familiar, and they kissed back. "You missed me, didn't you," she whispered. "I still want to talk about some things. Let's work on this."

"I don't want to work on this if I can't trust you!" he said, breaking away.

Stella grabbed the soap and quickly lathered herself up, rinsed off, and got out. "Okay. I don't know why you think you can't trust me."

He turned off the water and grabbed a towel. "You didn't answer me when I asked if you kissed anybody else."

"Well, there was this Irish guy who sat down next to me on a banquette and tried to kiss me, but I nipped it in the bud and sent him to hang out with Erin."

"You kissed someone else! I knew it! I knew I couldn't trust you!"

"I didn't kiss anyone!"

"What did you just say? You kissed an Irish guy?"

"I *said* he tried to kiss me and I pushed him off of me, telling him that I was not interested, but I know that my single friend Erin likes Irish guys."

"I know you did more than kiss him."

"Huh?"

"Why else would I get a text from someone saying 'I just fucked your girlfriend'?"

"What? Who texted you? Obviously it was someone who doesn't like you. One of your so-called 'friends' trying to get a rise out of you."

"I don't know. It was an unknown number."

"Let me see the text."

"I don't have it anymore. I didn't want to look at that shit! Evidence that the woman I love is out fucking someone else!"

"I didn't fuck anyone or do anything! I was with my friends the whole time and you know it! You can ask them!"

"Like they would tell me the truth."

Stella racked her brain thinking who could have sent him such a text message. There were so many friends who'd come and gone: people who now hated Wil for various reasons, most of which involved him lying, borrowing something and not returning it, or suddenly turning on them when they needed him. She listed a few of them. "Wil,

I don't know who could have sent you this message. Could it be Ryan?"

"No, he wouldn't do that."

"He was mad enough at you to get you kicked out of your last job. I'll confront him."

"It wasn't Ryan! I know it wasn't."

"Who the hell would do such a thing, then?"

"I don't know—who did you sleep with?"

"I didn't fucking sleep with anyone!" she said, losing control. "Look at me! What is wrong with you?" She grabbed him by the shoulders when he avoided eye contact. "You're delusional! What happened to you wanting to spend your life with me?" She shook him a little. "I left my husband for you!"

"You're laying hands on me!" he said. Then he got very quiet and put on a reasonable-sounding, conversational voice. "Stella, this is enough. You are not only verbally abusing me, you are physically abusing me."

She would have loved to choke him until he turned purple, then punch him in the face so hard he fell to the ground bleeding, but instead she removed her hands from his shoulders and said, "Yes, this *is* enough."

She walked over and pulled her painting off the wall.

"What are you doing?" he asked frantically. She didn't answer.

She took two of the four pillows and some sheets off the air mattress. She left the stupid framed print of Stella and Wil's Lovestar.

"You owe rent for next month! You signed the lease!" he said. Stella didn't answer. She took the crock pot, some pans and cups. She took her books and clothes, and piled them neatly by the door. "Oh, so you're going to just leave me now, like you leave everybody?"

She took a screwdriver, stood on a box of books, and muscled the bright blue Santa Monica sign down from the kitchen wall. "Yes," she scathed. Wil hung around, stammering. "Don't talk to me," Stella said.

She opened her computer and drafted an email, adding every female friend she had in Los Angeles.

Hello ladies...

I wouldn't normally do this, but I feel that I need to reach out to any and everyone I know right now. I am going through a very tough time. My marriage recently fell apart. I had to move in with my boyfriend, which I knew was a bad idea, but there was nothing else I could do, I thought, because of money.

At the same time, I lost my only source of income, which was working at Santa Monica College (they only hire temporarily, per semester, and the semester ended). I ran up all my credit cards and now they're maxed out. I have been applying for jobs like crazy but all I have been able to find so far is a part-time job that pays less than $300 every two weeks.

Now, as I thought might happen, my boyfriend and I are breaking up. I need a place to stay tonight (and for a couple weeks, I guess.)

Basically, I am very in debt, without a place to live or a real job, and I am asking you all for any help you might be able to provide:

-Do you know of a full-time job ANYWHERE that is hiring? I have a Master's degree in English and I have worked a ton in production, writing, teaching, and customer service. I am attaching my resume. I will do anything as long as it will get me back on my feet.

-Do you know anyone who is renting a room or needs a roommate, or any other living situation that could help me?

I know everything will work out in the end, but this is the most difficult period I have ever been through in my life, and if anyone has any ideas, I would so appreciate it. I really don't want to have to move back to Kentucky.

Thanks so much,
Stella

She went outside and pulled her Corolla close to the house. It was dark. The old muchacho next door who usually cat-called Stella when she wore running shorts stood and gawked as she made trip after trip to the car. She wept a little as she carried the few items that still belonged to her. She knew she was on the right road, but the map had been stolen.

Once the car was full, she flopped down into the driver's seat and cried shamelessly. For the second time this year, she drove away from the ocean. Maybe she wasn't worthy of Santa Monica. She didn't bother turning around to take a last look at the God-forsaken apartment that was never going to be home.

She was going east, but she had no idea where. If this had happened a year ago, Janice would have been her refuge. But she had fallen so far, it seemed even Janice hated her.

She drove aimlessly past Century City on Santa Monica Boulevard, past Beverly Hills and West Hollywood. She drove past the old sublet, north toward the mountains. She looked at her phone for a response to her email, but nothing was there. Her brain was overloaded.

She thought of going to a bar, but she didn't have the money to waste on drinks or the energy to be near people, so instead, she drove up the winding roads at Griffith Park where the darkness covered everything. She pulled over onto the dusty shoulder, locked the doors, and tried to sleep. She passed into a few hours of blackness, followed by a nightmare of being buried alive in a desert.

A knocking startled her and she screamed. She sprung up and saw a figure looming by her car.

It was the park ranger. She cracked her window.

"I'm sorry ma'am, but you can't sleep here."

Stella nodded and started the car, then drove away, down the mountain. She found a Starbucks and parked. They would open in another hour. Then her phone buzzed and buzzed. She had seven texts and three voicemails. She must have had no service on the mountain. She picked one of the voicemails and listened.

"Hey Stella, it's Diana from Ladidahs. I got your email. I have a whole duplex to myself in Tarzana and I would love if you came to stay with me as long as you need. I know it's far, but you would have your own room and bathroom. Call me."

***

"Come here," Diana said when Stella climbed out of her jam-packed Corolla. Diana was thin, straight-haired and tall like Stella. As Stella fell into her arms, the motherly comfort she provided unleashed another cascade of tears. Diana was a little older than the rest of the band members, a real adult who didn't have time to go to bars with the others or stay after rehearsal and chat. Stella had only ever had about two real conversations with her, and yet here she was, to the rescue.

"Thank you so much for this," Stella said.

"It's my pleasure," said Diana. "I have all this extra space and it gets lonely here."

Diana showed Stella her room, and Stella made the two-story trip at least twelve times, bringing her belongings in before taking a hot bath, then sinking corpse-like into the downy comfort of Diana's guest bed where she stayed the rest of the day.

"Make yourself at home!" Diana said. "I'll be gone the rest of the day, but I'll see you tomorrow morning.

"Thank you so much," Stella said, wondering if she'd regret her choice by the morning.

***

Stella cracked her eyelids open. The room was still dark and

69

smelled of coconut bubble bath. The soft bed swaddled her; pillows surrounded her like a fortress. She rolled onto her side and looked at the clock. It was nine. She had slept a full day. She opened the blinds, letting in a stream of desert light from the San Fernando Valley.

She surveyed her surroundings: a mirrored closet and soft carpet, two lamps sitting on nightstands on either side of the bed. A sparse bookshelf. A clean bathroom with a tub; bare shelves inside the vanity mirror. A closed door. It was far from the ocean, but it was the nicest room she'd lived in since she had moved to California, all thanks to the kindness of Diana, a woman who barely knew her.

But here was the light, and it was warm and not stark, and Stella regretted nothing.

Stella's new phone was full of messages. One by one, Stella opened eleven responses to the email she'd sent.

Stella, honey. I am so sorry. You can stay with me, but I only have a couch.

Here are some jobs you might be interested in. Good luck!

Girl, I will give your resume to my boss. We're looking for someone and you might be perfect.

You know are always welcome at my place. I am so proud of you for this.

She took a couple steps toward a hill of cloth shopping bags by the wall, containing everything she owned, which wasn't much. She felt like she had just returned from a long trip. She peeked inside to find her clothes, books and papers, a couple frames and flower vases: the storied artifacts from dead relationships. She pulled out her massive metal sign: over four feet of bright cobalt stamped in white with two soothing words—Santa Monica—and she propped it against the wall opposite her bed.

She inhaled and all she could hear was her own breath. Here she was, Stella Robertson, age 28, truly alone for the first time ever.

***

Stella spent a full day in Diana's extra bedroom sending out resumes and cover letters, looking for a real job. In the meantime, she had babysitting and catering.

Today, one of the parents from the Kids Club at Equinox had hired her to babysit. She in a Beverly Hills condo, halfway through a sink of dishes. The baby was crying for attention from his little swing in the corner. "Just a minute, Ben," Stella said in a sing-song voice. "Just let me wash these last few, baby. Juuust a minute." He kept wailing.

Beneath the bottles and cereal bowls was a coffee cup that read, *Peace. It does not mean to be in a place where there is no noise, trouble, or hard work. It means to be in the midst of those things and still be calm in your heart.*

Stella finished the dishes and walked over to lift Ben up. He was heavy as she pulled him in close, one hand on his tiny back and the other on his diapered butt. She walked him back and forth from the kitchen to the living room, bouncing him gently as he continued to wail. She looked at the clock. Still two hours before his mom would return, and it would be time to go to work Kids Club at the gym. "Shh, baby boy. It's not so bad. Shh."

Stella began humming to him. The tune that came out was "That's Life" by Frank Sinatra. Little by little, he started to quiet. She rocked him back and forth and began to sing the lyrics. "That's life, and I can't deny it. I've thought of quittin' baby, but my heart ain't gonna buy it." By the time she got to the chorus, Ben was quiet and sucking his thumb, his little face calm and lying on Stella's tear-stained, burdened shoulder. She kept singing, and her voice began to quiver. The tune became barely a whisper: "Each time I find myself flat on my face, I pick myself up and get back in the race." Now it was baby Ben whose shoulder was catching Stella's tears.

***

She re-stocked coffee cups and carried trays of mini quiches, working at a bris in a Westwood penthouse, berating herself for all the undue pain she'd brought into her own life. She couldn't stop trying to make sense of how a person who had regarded her as a Heaven-sent angel could change his mind overnight.

She smiled for an old man who flagged her down. "My dear, would you mind bringing me a gin and tonic?" he asked.

"Absolutely," she said. "Be right back."

She returned with a rocks glass. "Here you go."

"Did you take a drink of it?" he asked.

"I thought about it, but I decided not to."

"It is early," he said.

"Eh, who's watching?" she said

"What is it that you do, honey, when you're not at an event like this?"

"I'm a writer," she stuttered. She didn't feel like a writer lately.

"No kiddin'," he said. "So am I. Do you do screenplays? Fiction?"

"Not yet. I hope someday to write a novel. Then maybe screenplays after that, so I can act in them."

"You act too? Well, let me tell you. I can tell that you're probably good at both, because you clearly value what's important."

71

"Gin and tonics?" she joked, then: "Have you written a lot of screenplays?"

"I've written forty-three that were made into movies. The first one I wrote was in the forties!"

"Wow. That is something. Do you have any advice for a young writer?"

The old man took a sip and said, "No matter what they say, stick to the truth."

"Huh. That was my impulse."

"Trust me. You'll be fine."

Just then, the baby's wail filled the space as his foreskin was cut.

"Ouch," Stella said.

"Time for another drink!" said the old man.

***

She walked into Ladidahs rehearsal carrying a stack of posterboards. "I need you guys to help me."

"Are those the ones Wil made you at Christmas?" asked Victoria.

She nodded. "I've had these in the trunk of my car forever, and I just hate knowing they're there, because—they're such a symbol of this lie I believed. So I want to destroy them. I just need backup."

"This is such a good thing," said Tessa. "Let's make a ceremony of it."

"Okay," Stella said. The first poster in the stack said,

To me (and to the rest of the entire fucking world) YOU ARE PERFECT.

She tore into Wil's scrawled words with a satisfying *schwoop*.

"Do it, girl," said Erin.

She ripped another, violently. It said,

But for now, let me say, with GREAT hope and an agenda...

"Fuck your agenda," Stella said. She continued ripping until the trash can was filled with useless white scraps, as insignificant as the Taco Bell wrappers beneath them. The sting of triumph came to her eyes.

"Come here," said Diana, holding out her arms. "That must have been hard. But don't you feel better?"

"Not yet," she said. "But I will."

***

Morning came and another day loomed ahead. Stella forced herself out of bed and into her Corolla to drive two hours to Santa Monica, where she had another catering gig. Commuting to her rightful city as a migrant worker felt like being disowned by a loved one. She would never see the money she was working for: It would go straight to all the debts she'd accrued.

The job was just around the corner from Wil's apartment. She parked in the spot that had been hers for a few weeks, plugging up her tears with force. A red-skinned homeless man in tattered cargo shorts loped by, looking for something on the ground, then looked up and made eye contact with Stella. Stella wondered if Wil was just inside the apartment, if he was doing drugs, and if he was planning on paying March's rent, which was due tomorrow. Then she unlocked her beach cruiser from its sign post and rode to the convention center in her black pants and button-down.

When she wasn't attending the buffet, she ducked into the wings to sit down and breathe through her headache. "You seem like a free spirit," said a kindly black man who caught her stretching behind the curtain.

"I am," she said, smiling through the ache. And that was just it. Stella was free; completely free and with nothing to lose for the first time ever. And she was scared to death.

Her phone buzzed. It was an email. One of the full-time jobs Stella had applied for! A man named Chet wanted to interview her today! Oh no. She couldn't do today. She wrote him back and asked if he had any time available tomorrow.

He replied, "You can come in at 10 tomorrow. You'll be the last interview."

It was an office manager job on the Westside. It would be a long drive from Diana's, but Stella would find a way to move back soon enough, she hoped.

Nine hours later, when she returned her bike to its signpost in front of her ex-apartment, her spine was compressed, her feet were throbbing, and her heart felt like a pincushion. She locked the bike, walked to her car and saw something flapping on the window. A seventy-five dollar parking ticket. The sign she had missed (was happiness contingent on what signs you saw and what signs you missed?) read "NO PARKING THURSDAY 3pm-5pm."

On the drive back to Tarzana, all her limbs were heavy, the way they were when someone died. She thought of her interview tomorrow, trying not to attach to its outcome. Resentment toward the whole city of Santa Monica enveloped her heart like a snowball. Its message to Stella was clear: It had not only disowned her; it had stolen every last cent from today's work.

MARCH

Stella dressed in her most capable clothes—a pencil skirt and wispy blouse—for her meeting with Chet Goldstien, CEO of TV Partners. Kerry from the Ladidahs had sent her the posting, and her resume had gotten her the interview. It was a small company in a quaint Victorian building nestled between Marina del Rey and Venice Beach, and Chet, a middle-aged Jewish man wearing embroidered jeans, was gregarious and receptive to Stella's charms.

"I've reached a point where I'd like something steady that will keep me engaged," she doubletalked confidently.

***

Back in Tarzana, Stella made coffee and sat on the sunny balcony.

"Hey stranger," Diana said, emerging from her recording studio.

"Hey buddy. What are you up to today?"

"You know how I've been composing that Star Wars tribute? We're going to be teaching it to an orchestra so I'll probably be MIA this weekend. How are you doing?"

"Hanging in there. I had that job interview today and I'm working the late shift at the gym tonight."

"Well, I was thinking," said Diana, "I'm allowed to give away one of my massages at the place down the street. Would you be interested?"

"Are you serious? Yes!"

"I think it might help. You've been through a lot."

"Oh man, you're the best. If there's anything I can do for you, please let me know. I did your dishes last night."

"That's the best thing you could do. I *hate* doing dishes." She popped into her office and emerged carrying a stack of CDs. "And I copied you a few audiobooks. I know that when you're in traffic for hours, you might get tempted to call Wil."

"Ugh. Yeah."

"So anytime you feel like you want to call him, just put in one of these and listen to it instead."

"Thank you."

"And if you're in a hurry and don't have time to eat, there's a box of nutrition bars in the cabinet. You're welcome to grab anything you want."

"Seriously. Thank you."

Her phone rang as she was watching HBO on Diana's giant projector.

"Stella!" came a booming male voice. "Chet Goldstein."

"Oh, hi Chet!"

"I'm calling because I'm making my decision here about an assistant."

"Yes..."

"And I have to tell ya, I was very impressed with your resume and your energy. I bet we could even use you for voiceovers and writing commercials."

"Oh!"

"So if you think you could do the boring spreadsheet part, I'd love to offer you the job. What do ya say?"

"I accept." Her heart was leaping. She was almost safe.

"Alright. Can you come in on Monday?"

"Yes!" she said without checking her schedule.

After she hung up—"Yes! Yes! Yes!"—she pulled the mini trampoline from behind Diana's couch, turned on a pop radio station, and jumped until she was sweating.

***

She was in a fetal position on a mat as three toddler boys built a fort around her at the Kids Club. She tried to remain fun-loving, though her exhausted mind was trapped in an eternal loop of confusion. Wil had emailed her last night saying he felt guilty. *What did he feel guilty for? Pretending to be her "soulmate" and then flipping out? Doing drugs?* She hated that she cared.

"AAAAGGGGGHHHHH!" The toddler boys violently kicked down the fort they'd been building, leaving Stella open to enemy fire. She fell suddenly into a desolate trench in her mind. She got up and walked over to Esme, an older coworker who was in a playhouse pretending to cook eggs with two little girls.

"Esme, do you mind if I take my break right now?"

"Sure, darling," Esme said through an Eastern European accent.

"These boys are getting picked up in five minutes, anyway."

"Okay, I'll just wait until then."

"Are you okay, Stella?"

"Yep. I'll be okay."

She returned after fifteen minutes of resting in her car, and all the kids were gone.

"The Saturday morning rush," Esme said. "I guess their parents are going to take them to the beach now. You are so good with kids, Stella. Do you have any?"

"Oh no," she said, shuddering. "I still feel like a kid myself. Ugh. Nope. There's still a lot I want to do before I tie myself down like that."

"Oh. How old are you, if you don't mind me to ask?"

"I'm twenty-eight."

"I had kids at twenty-two. Well, my daughter."

"Oh!"

"But it is so hard here in Los Angeles, you know? It is so expensive here, and you can't find a job that pays anything. My daughter is looking for something. We live so far away because it's cheaper up north."

"I know how you feel," Stella said. "But I'm probably not going to be working here for much longer. I just got a full-time job as an administrative assistant."

"Oh, that's wonderful! Congratulations! Where did you find your job?"

"I have a friend who sent me the info. But I applied for a lot of jobs on Craigslist. Maybe your daughter could try that."

"Oh yes. Maybe." They picked up toys and sanitized them with wipes. Then Esme said, "Are you married, then, Stella? Or have a boyfriend?"

Stella hadn't practiced answering this question. Yes, she was married. Yes, she had just stopped having a boyfriend. Yes, both of these people were now enemies. Yes, she was all alone. She must have looked like she was going to cry, because Esme put a hand on her back, like a mom.

"It's okay."

"I'm just going through some hard times right now," she said.

"Sweetie," Esme said, "you are going to do fine. Your heart is as big as the ocean. People like you always come out on top."

***

Stella stripped naked and dropped herself on the table.

"Go as deep as you can," she told the masseur, who worked her muscles like he was tenderizing meat. An hour later she left light-headed, her fragile spirit released from its crustacean shell.

She ignored fourteen texts and two emails from Wil, some of them saying "I miss you" or "let's work this out," others demanding her personal password for the car insurance website. Since Wil's Prius was in Stella's name, it was on her insurance policy, which was auto-paid via her bank account. Until Wil transferred the car to his name, Stella would have to collect his half of the insurance money from him each month.

She'd spent her last day of freedom before her full-time job happily alone, but by evening the quiet was heavy. Stella was used to having someone waiting for her, someone texting and asking when she was returning, someone missing her. But now the aloneness darkened her like the shadow of a cliff. She went cold with worry about having real responsibilities, about financially extricating herself from Wil—the car, the apartment, the cable bills—and about Wil's health now that she was gone.

She found distraction in finally cleaning her piled-up room in Diana's house, and in doing her taxes: joint taxes with Andrew, of course. She had to email him to ask him questions. She missed him and told him so. He wrote back to answer the questions, adding,

Stop saying nice things to me. You're making me angry.
***

"Chet really didn't give me any instruction on how I'm supposed to train you...so I guess I'll just come up with some stuff," Britt was a dirty blonde in a black hoodie. She and Stella were sitting in two office chairs side-by-side at the same desk.

"This is a cool building," Stella said.

"Yeah," said Britt. "When I first started, the whole operation was running out of Chet's house. Awkward."

Stella could see Chet through his office window. He was wearing a paisley button-down shirt, his capped teeth gleaming as he guffawed over the phone.

"So why are you leaving?" Stella asked Britt.

"Well, I have another job doing promotional stuff for a radio station, and I told Chet that I was going to be getting more hours over there, but really I don't have a plan. I also work at a restaurant."

"Oh. So how long were you here?"

"Just six months. He was going to give me a raise after six months, but I just felt like it was time for me to go." Britt selected an internet radio station and atmospheric rock tinkled out of the computer speakers.

"Oh good. I'm glad we can listen to music."

"Yeah. I try to keep it quiet, but I would go crazy if I didn't have something to listen to. I also keep Facebook open down here in the corner. He never gives me enough to do."

"So you're just over this job?"

"I mean...it's pretty boring. I needed it at the time, financially. It was the first time I could pay for stuff without worrying about money."

"I'm here for the same reason. Whoa, but I'm kind of nervous looking at that," Stella said, watching her pull up a spreadsheet full of figures and built-in formulas.

"Don't be. I just pretend I know what I'm doing. I don't think a day has gone by without me making a mistake."

Stella sighed. "Oh, good. I think. Should I feel hopeful since you still don't know what's going on, or should I be scared?"

"I promise you'll be great."

Britt went over the spreadsheet line by line and explained it, saying things from time to time like, "I don't honestly even know what this number stands for."

Stella took notes until her head spun. "Is it always this freezing in here?" she asked.

"Yeah. The vent is right above our desk, not in Chet's office, so he's always complaining about how hot he is and cranking the AC. I used to come to work looking cute like you are, but after a while I just started wearing hoodies every day. Nobody sees us anyway."

"Man. Well, I'm just glad I'm going to finally be able to stop worrying about money for a while," she said.

"It is nice, I can tell you."

"Sitting this long, though..."

"Yeah. I took a lot of walks, pretending to go to the bathroom."

"Good idea."

Stella had been in traffic for an hour after work when her phone pinged with another text from Wil, still demanding passwords and private information. At a stoplight she finally replied.

YOU ARE NOT GETTING THOSE PASSWORDS. GIVE UP.

He wrote back:

I'm in the hospital again at St. John's.

And for a second, as she slugged through two hours of traffic on the way to Tarzana, she couldn't help thinking, *if I were still living on 7th Street with Wil, or on 9th Street with Andrew, I could have ridden my bike to work today.*

***

Stella woke up at four a.m. and got in the car. She hadn't wanted to let down Dani or lose her gym membership when she got hired at

TV Partners, so instead of quitting Equinox, she had the bosses work around her new schedule. Now she was working 60 hours a week and driving at least 20, waking before daylight and spending her days talking to no one.

In the early morning, Dani was as silent as a black hole, which Stella wasn't used to. She considered the fact that she had more or less been on someone's arm since she was thirteen. With her new schedule and singlehood, silence had become a part of her life, and she would have to grow into it.

The morning shift ended at eight. She changed into business attire in the spa-like locker room and waved as she walked out the door with a no-nonsense click-click-click.

When she got in the Corolla she saw another text from Wil.

> I really need that password for the insurance website if I'm going to get the clearance to get a California license. If you ever want the Prius to be out of your name, you need to text me that right now.

Her internal temperature rose. She noticed she was passing St. John's hospital. She still had twenty minutes to get to work. She pulled over and parked, marched up to the desk and sweetly said, "Hello, I'm here to see Wil Mallory."

"Room 332, dear," said the receptionist.

Stella clacked up the stairs and down the hallway into Wil's room where he sat on an automated bed, puffing an e-cigarette like Louis XIV on his throne. Suddenly powerful and independent, she stopped a foot from his bed in a wide stance.

"You need to get the car transferred to your name, and then leave me the fuck alone," she said. "I printed out the insurance information you needed. There is nothing you need my password for. I don't trust you as far as I could throw you, so I am not giving you access to *anything* of mine *ever* again."

"I can't believe you would come into my room at the *hospital* and start yelling at me like this! Who would do such a thing?" he said, grabbing his phone.

"I was just passing by, and I really hate that it has to be this way, but you should know that I am not going to continue being manipulated by you. You have no right to ask me for anything. We are not together."

"Well, if you don't give me the information I need, you *do* realize that your name is still on the lease, don't you? I can stick you with all those debts that you owe for walking out on it."

"You gave me no choice but to walk out on it! I tried to make it work! But I am not your mom, your babysitter, your nurse, your cook, or your banker. *You* are the reason all this happened. I have to go to work now because I am actually a human being who is contributing to society. So straighten up and get out of my life."

She walked toward the door, but stopped when she heard his voice say, "Stella." She turned around. He held up his phone. "I've been recording all of this."

What a toddler. He was probably going to share this conversation with his mommy, and Judy would probably call Stella and tell her what a terrible person she was for barging into poor William's hospital room and making it impossible for him to get well.

Stella tramped away without turning around again, almost excited for the eight hours of work that followed and the fact that the only person she'd see afterward was herself.

What do you want to do tonight? She asked herself on the way to her second job of the day. *Whatever the fuck I want*, she answered.

***

Stella had no time to respond to Wil's texts, no time to drink or socialize. She was losing weight, since eating and sleeping were afterthoughts. Her crying came at strange intervals: in the car or in the women's bathroom at TV Partners. Sometimes she laughed at herself for the ridiculous incidents that caused her tears, like seeing an inflatable flailing-arm man at a car dealership. There was no time to masochistically stalk Wil or Andrew online, though her sister had taken care of that.

Everly called Stella at work to alert her that Wil had been tagged "in a relationship" with Tyler, a waifish ex-coke addict who had once tried to "steal" Wil from Stella. She remembered meeting Tyler in September when Tyler had brought soup to his hospital room. Tyler had told Wil she loved him and had given him concert tickets and expensive gifts she bought with her trust fund money. When he'd seen Stella was unhappy about it, Wil had ceremoniously blocked Tyler's number from his phone and said, "I would never date that batshit crazy, skinny rich girl. Her desperation is overwhelming. She's like, 32 and she's trying to get with a 24-year-old."

And now he was probably taking Tyler for joyrides in a Prius that was legally Stella's, then leaving it parked in illegal zones while the two of them made out in the backseat, their bony ribs bruising each other. Happily, Stella was too busy to contemplate this new information. She had a three-hour Ladidahs rehearsal tonight, after which she was going to stay on Rebecca's Westside couch so that she could sleep in until 4:30 a.m. tomorrow.

An hour before rehearsal, Stella ran to Venice Beach and sat looking off into the horizon with her little notebook. Writing, which had once been her ultimate purpose in life, had become relegated to a few words here and there in her journal. She wondered if getting it back could help save her. She listened to the waves, which assured her she didn't need to ask anyone for help or approval. She knew what she needed to hear. As a friend, she opened her notebook and wrote herself a letter.

Stella, sweetheart,

You feel like you've lost everything, but you haven't.

This is an opportunity for you, whether you see it all the time or not. You are free! Nothing's holding you back.

Who cares what Wil does now? That's his problem. Be thankful to Tyler for taking him off your hands. You escaped, and look at how drastically life has improved. No more dealing with someone whose insecurities eat you both alive, someone who doesn't take care of himself, who blames you, who sucks your time and energy, who lies. Face it, he is a helpless, juvenile, skeletal, crude addict with no empathy for others, no care for humanity. He is a spoiled, lazy know-it-all with NOTHING to offer YOU.

You thought your purpose on this earth was to take care of others. It is, but in a bigger way. Through writing, or through the way you live, someday you will be able to help others just as Diana is helping you.

Tonight you can go to sleep and not give a second thought to the past. You are okay in the present. You are okay being alone. Your heart is as big as the ocean. You are so much stronger than you know. I love you.

Stella

***

She ordered a gin cocktail at the Roosevelt. She was talking to Jesse, a handsome, suited-up black man at the bar who teased her when he found out she was waiting for a blind date. Her friends thought dating around might show her that good guys still existed. She admitted to her low expectations. "He's going to be some stiff guy with, like, Donald Trump hair, who wants to talk about his years rowing crew boats," she said.

"Then why are you meeting him?" asked Jesse.

"My friend Tessa went to college with him. She said he saw a picture of us and asked about me. According to her, he's a good-looking Canadian millionaire, and in college he was the founder of the best men's *a capella* group."

"Well then!"

"Yeah. I don't know how much I'll have in common with a man named Chip, but we'll see."

"I gotta say, I'm pretty excited to see what he's like at this point," said Jesse, who had by now told Stella all about his silence retreats in India, his favorite books, and his home in New York.

"Meanwhile, I'm getting more and more nervous," she said. "Or is it drunk?"

"Yeah, your drink is looking a little low. Let's get you one more," said Jesse.

An hour later, a blonde guy approached in a dark grey suit and tie. He had a dynamic smile, though it was the smile of a guy who probably said things like, "let's circle back."

Stella stood up to greet Chip with a light hug.

"I'm so sorry I'm late!" he said.

"No worries," she said. "I've just been hangin' with Jesse here."

"Hi," Chip said in a lily-white voice. Stella looked around at the empty candlelit tables for two nearby, assuming that Chip would suggest that they find a good place to talk, but instead, he sat down at the bar. She and Jesse exchanged judgmental glances at Chip's decision to make their date a group affair.

Then Jesse said, "Why don't I buy you two a drink?"

For the next half-hour, Chip leaned over Stella to talk to Jesse, answering questions about his real estate company and recent history. Stella was getting a little sloshy and, since nobody was talking to her, she tottered away to find the bathroom.

"Well," said Jesse when she returned, "I guess I'll allow you two to get to know each other." He ambled off to his room, leaving Stella in Chip's shaky, well-manicured hands.

Chip jumped right in, telling her he wanted kids and asking if she did, too. "I'm a long way off from even thinking about that."

"My, my. You are not what I expected. I bet you don't usually go out with guys like me, do you?"

"I'm an equal opportunity dater, but no."

"Who do you typically date?" he asked. "Let me guess: the drummers and the dreamers."

"I guess you could say that," she said. "I like artists. People with interesting stories and philosophies. Romantics." She hadn't planned on talking about the whole open marriage and the 24-year-old junkie with a heart condition, but the more Chip played into the stereotype of the straight-laced square, the more pleasure she found in shocking him. She brought out the heavy artillery and smiled inside when it produced the exact result she was going for.

"Wow. It strikes me as odd that Tessa would set us up," he said. "We don't really have much in common, do we?"

"Nope," she said, probably slurring, "but at least we had an experience."

***

Onstage at a charity show in West Hollywood, Stella sang with the Ladidahs, front and center because she was the tallest. She wondered if the audience could hear her life's recent events unspooling through her voice. Wil had texted today to tell her he had a potentially lethal blood infection.

I bet now you wish you had treated me better.

Her mother had called to update her on Andrew (*Why?*), who was visiting family in England.

She burrowed deep between the notes of the music, feeling the meaning of every word while the heat of the stage lights revealed her to the audience of strangers below.

After the show, sipping a gin and tonic with her bandmate Erin, she felt a hand on her shoulder and turned to see a dark-haired guy. "Hey, you really stood out up there," he said. "Are you the lead singer or something?"

She laughed. "No. We don't have a lead singer."

"I'm Paul."

"I'm Stella. What's brought you here?"

"I'm Tessa's friend."

"Who isn't?" she said. "You look like somebody."

"A lot of people say that when I wear my glasses I look like Rivers Cuomo."

"Oh, I grew up loving Weezer," she said, sucking down the last of her drink, "but it's actually my ex-boyfriend I was thinking of." He reminded Stella of Trev, the wrestler she had dated for half a year while she and Andrew were only open-dating.

She and Paul talked for a while about the rise and fall of nerd rock and his life as a lawyer, writer, professional foodie, and DJ. He was charming, so when Paul wanted to exchange numbers, she agreed. She exited into the West Hollywood evening, and rainbows shone all around from shop windows, coloring her boldly with their lights.

***

The stabbing menstrual cramps were preferable to the mental anguish Stella had been suffering, but they weakened her resistance to Wil's advances. She was working at the gym when he texted.

I'm out of the hospital. I'm still hooked up to a PICC line and I
have to give myself antibiotics.

She wrote back without thinking:

Need me to bring you anything?

Wil:
No. I'm okay. My mom's flying in from Philly tomorrow.

It was strange that Stella had never met Judy Mallory after all the
times she had consoled Stella over the phone, advising her on how to
deal with her son. A misplaced pang of jealousy hit Stella like a blow
dart.

I could just come say hello, if you want.

Wil:
No. I'd rather you not. I don't think I'd be able to stand to
see you leave.

Stella:
Then I'll stay.

Stella knew she'd gone too far, but she still felt a responsibility
toward him, and a longing to figure out what had changed in him.
Hours passed. Work ended. *Why was she checking her phone again for a
response? And why had he not written back?*
   Tyler's pretty, malnourished face appeared in Stella's mind,
attacking her brain like a swarm of gnats. Tyler in the apartment whose
lease bore her name, Tyler bringing Wil food, Tyler kissing him on the
forehead. She wanted not to care, but she was possessed. As a
distraction, she texted Nick, her most reliable friend-with-benefits.

Hey you. Are you still with that girlfriend, or are you back in
public domain?

Nick:
That's up in the air. Do you want to come over?

Stella:
Yes.

"I can't fuck you just yet," said Nick, descending the stairs from his apartment, "but I can buy you a coffee."

"Sounds like a good consolation prize," she said.

Nick worked in post-production on some reality show and lived in the fancy part of Santa Monica, north of Wilshire. Stella had met him at Father's Office last year while she was having a burger. He was direct and low-key, and once she got to know him, she found out he was a genuinely nice guy with no ulterior motives and also a highly skilled human vibrator. Stella hadn't seen him since September, when she'd agreed to be monogamous with Wil because he'd blocked Tyler from his phone.

They walked toward the little coffee shop. "So you're still on the leash?"

"For now. She's really possessive." Nick told a story about his girlfriend and some jealous stalking over a camping trip. "I told her if she acts like this again, I'm outta here, but I really love her, you know. So I'm going to give her another chance."

"I get that."

As they walked through the golden, palm-studded streets with their cappuccinos, Stella relayed the whole saga.

"I didn't want to tell you," said Nick, "but I could tell this Wil guy was a fuck-up from the beginning. You didn't even have to say he was an addict. His behavior is textbook addict behavior."

"Yeah," she said, "but nobody could have told me anything at that time. Oh well. It was my choice." She added sarcastically, "Who'd-a-thunk this was a bad idea?"

"Yeah." They sat down on the curb outside his apartment. "But don't get too down on yourself. From what it sounds like, your relationship with your husband was doomed."

"Really? Some of my girlfriends have told me that, too."

"Yeah. If you really wanted to make a life with him, why would you want to fuck other people?"

"I don't know," she said. "I just thought that monogamy was a total lie, that it was impossible. I thought that finding a companion who shared my lust for lust was the best option for someone like me. And along the way I sort of realized that it wasn't about lust anyway."

"Well, it sounds like you would've left him anyway. But it probably would have been way down the road."

"Hmm. Maybe. But now that he's gone, I keep picturing him as some kind of saint."

"He's not; trust me. Or else this wouldn't have happened."

"I think it did have to be something this extreme to wrench me away from him."

"Yeah. So just put both of them behind you and keep walking."

They hugged and Stella left to go to a yoga class. "Call me if you're ever single again," she said.

"You'll be the first to know," said Nick.

***

Monday was back in town, ruling with an iron fist. Chet wasn't cutting any breaks. Stella had screwed up a list of things that had made no sense last week, and here they were again, needing to be fixed. She asked Chet to explain the first item, and he went ballistic.

"What does it say there? Do you see those words on the page? Just do what it says!" he condescended. When Chet went to lunch she called Britt to ask advice.

"He used to do that to me all the time," Britt said. "That's why I stopped asking him questions. I'd rather just keep getting it wrong than get yelled at like that."

"I know—and the wack thing is, when he's in a good mood, he's always saying, 'Feel free to ask me anything. There are no stupid questions; only stupid people.'"

"He said that to me, too!" said Britt. "Did I tell you about the time he made his wife bring me some UTI medication so I wouldn't skip work?"

"No!"

"So embarrassing. First I had to tell him I had a pee infection because he kept pressing me as to why I was calling in sick. I wanted to stay home so I could go see a doctor. But he insisted that Karen come over and pick me up for work. She brought me medicine. And that was when the office was at his house, so I couldn't get out of it."

"Horrifying. Be glad you're gone, my friend."

"I am."

"So, do you know how to fix this?"

"I don't, but I'll tell you what I used to do."

"Thanks."

She went outside to take a call and get some sunshine.

"Can you walk Bosley for me this evening? I have a dinner." It was Deb, whose dog she'd been sitting when she met Wil.

"I wish I could," Stella said, "But I'm no longer your neighbor."

"You're not in Santa Monica anymore?" She sounded shocked.

"No. I'm in Tarzana right now." Stella explained her situation.

"Oh," Deb said. "You know I used to be married, right?"

"I didn't."

"My husband worshipped me, but five years ago I left him for another man and it didn't work out."

"Oh," Stella said.

"Not a day has passed that I haven't regretted it."

After she hung up, she saw her world as a prison. The prospect of returning to work to figure out the tasks on her list with no guidance sounded as promising as trying to break out of her cell with a toothpick. Her own ineptitude swallowed her. She had no plan to get her mind and heart under control, and she was too busy to make one. Being busy *was* her plan, she figured.

She ducked into the handicap stall in the bathroom and sat on the floor, draining what she hoped was the last reservoir of tears. "God. Universe. Higher Power. I know I don't deserve it. But please help me. I don't know what is supposed to happen in my life, but if you could please help it to happen soon? The guilt is so heavy. My brain hurts from all the back and forth. Am I supposed to be channeling my energy into getting Andrew back? Or figuring out why Wil rejected me? Or moving on? I am so, so lost. Please help me to keep my eyes open and make the right decisions. Please help me to be wise and kind and smart. Please make this pain go away."

She returned to the uncomfortable chair in the cold office, staring at the screen. Chet yelled from his office, "Hey! Stella! Where were you?"

"The bathroom," She said, trying to sound normal.

"Well, can you start letting me know when you're going to the bathroom?" he barked. "I don't even notice you're not there until I'm sitting here talking to myself!"

She wondered why he couldn't just look up to see if she was there or not, so she wouldn't have to report her every urination. But she just replied, "Yeah, sure."

***

Chet was out of the office the next day, thank God, and had left nothing concrete to accomplish, but the clouds had rolled away from Stella's mind. She knew what she needed to do. She stretched, cracked her knuckles, and got to work.

First, she needed to move by the end of March. She needed a place that belonged to her. She needed her city back, so when people asked where home was, she could simply say "Santa Monica," instead of, "Well, for now I'm living in the Valley, but it's only temporary," which only led to more questions with depressing explanations. She'd require roommates, of course. Even the smallest kitchenless studio on the Westside would be at least a thousand a month, and she could barely afford six-hundred. But she searched online and found a few that sounded promising. She emailed them. One, with the headline "Come Live With Us!" seemed especially inviting, with two male roommates and a female just outside of Santa Monica.

The second thing she needed was to quit the gym job. It wasn't contributing financially and she couldn't even use the free membership since she was always working, driving, or sleeping. She emailed Dani and her bosses to give them notice.

The third thing she needed was a drink and some intelligent conversation. She stayed until 5:30 in case Chet called to check on her (he did, at 5:28), and once work was over, she drove to Santa Monica to meet her friend Serena at Bodega. Serena was a Cuban photographer and yogini who still lived on 9th Street in Andrew's building.

"Happy hour wine special?"

"Yes please," Stella said. "I'm going to skip Ladidahs tonight because if I go, I'll never be able to wake up at four in the morning."

"Is that when you have to leave for Equinox?"

"Yep."

"I don't know how you're doing it."

"I'm not. Man, I am just scraping by. Last night I went out with this guy. We went to the Silent Movie Theater, and as I sat in the seat, I realized the movie was, like, two hours longer than I thought."

"What the hell kind of movies are you watching?"

"It had an hour of short films at the beginning, then it was a three-hour movie. Anyway, I realized that today I was going to have 12 hours of work—both jobs—and then rehearsal for three hours, and then have to drive back to the Valley, so do you know what I did?"

"Please tell me you said you had to go to the bathroom and didn't come back."

Stella laughed. "Almost. I did tell him I was leaving. But I just walked out in the middle of the date! And he was nice."

"Well, you're doing better than Andrew."

"Really? Do you see him a lot?"

"I see him, but I have to tell you, I try to avoid him. He looks awful. He comes in drunk almost every night, slurring his words and saying really disturbing things."

Stella felt a pang of responsibility for the guy she had fallen in love with because she thought he was idealistic enough to change the world. "I did that to him," she said. "And now I can't help but think that I gave up the only chance I had at a good relationship."

"Honey. I'm telling you. I always thought this, and I still think it: You can do better."

"Really? My mom doesn't seem to think so. Anytime I call her with sadness or confusion, I hang up feeling like there are only two options: get Andrew back, or be alone forever."

"Girl, please," said Serena.

Stella couldn't believe it hadn't occurred to her before that Andrew might not be a good match for her. But here was Serena, a happily married, grounded friend, telling her just that. Not fully convinced, Stella sent Tessa a Facebook message to see what she thought. Tessa responded:

Tessa
to Stella

Stel,

First of all, don't apologize for missing rehearsal. You need to rest. You HAVE to make sure you are taking care of yourself health-wise, or you won't have the strength to get through everything else that you're dealing with.

I think it's fair to say your life has exploded, Stel, and your heart is suffering from that combustion. And that's not necessarily a bad thing. A couple of months ago you had a husband, a boyfriend, a home, and financial security. At this point in your life you have none of those things. But for the first time in your life you have complete freedom and independence. You have a full time job. You have friends that are willing to support you as long as you need. And because you're not one to be defeated, you have the ability to do and be anything you want to.

I would feel defeated and frustrated with your current lifestyle as well— having no home, the long drives, the insane work hours, the loneliness— it's enough to drive a person into a black hole of sadness, and that's totally understandable. But the amazing thing is, you now have a plan. You'll quit Equinox, you'll find a place on the Westside with roomies, and you'll eliminate the commute. At that point I assure you that life will already feel easier. You'll have people to go home to, and you'll find so many hours in your day that previously didn't exist. At the very least, you won't feel like a wanderer.

As for Andrew, here's the thing: If you want him back, make sure it's for the right reasons. The first thing that happens when we feel alone, is we scramble to squash that loneliness by trying to get back with the one person who offered us security. It's instinctual. The second Jared and I broke up (even though it was my decision) I panicked and wanted him back. Because it hurt. But I didn't want him back because he was the perfect fit or because I wanted to be with him until I was 90. I wanted him back because he had a steady hand, and I knew that could stop my heart from aching. But that's not the right reason. You have to go through the pain to move forward. You can't be with someone just because breakups hurt and you want to avoid that pain. It seems like such a simple fix: Get Andrew back, the pain goes away, life stabilizes, money isn't as tight, and everything will be back to what it was. But is that what is best for you, Stel? It is definitely what will cause the least amount of sadness. But is that what you want for the rest of your life?

If you go back to Andrew, you should be prepared to be in it for the long haul. And not until the next Wil comes along, but for a long, long time. Because it isn't fair to you or to Andrew to go through another break up a couple of years from now. You've already wept. You've moved. You've come a long, long way. And if you go back to him, all the progress you've made, all that you've done to move forward, will be reset back to zero.

I'm not saying don't reach out to Andrew. But remember what it was like when you DID have him. You wanted something else. You wanted another man, and a different life. Don't try to get Andrew back just because your life feels like a fucking mess. You need to want Andrew back because he's the love of your life, you'll never love another man the way you love him, and because you want to be with him forever. And what happens when your life stabilizes by your own will, which it will, I promise? What happens when a few months from now, you're in your own place with your roomies, you've got your steady job, you have a normal schedule, summer is in full swing and you're getting asked out by other men? Will you still want Andrew as much as you want him now? If the answer is yes, then by all means, get him back. Fight for him.

Whatever you choose, I support you, Stella. But don't be mistaken, you DO have a purpose. Your purpose isn't about who you're with. It's about what you're going to do for YOURSELF. Where do you want your life to go? You're blessed with being remarkably intelligent, talented, drop-dead gorgeous, and young. Not everyone gets to start with those qualities—but you're lucky enough that that is the hand you were dealt. You can play it any way you want. If you want to use your cards to get Andrew back, then do. If you want to use your cards to just focus on yourself, then do. But know that even in this dark period, you're enough, alone. This is the sort of strife that comes right before you blossom. I swear it's at these darkest moments when we find out what we're really capable of. And I think you're capable of doing anything you want to, Stel. Anything.

I love you and will back any decision you make. Truly. Let me know if you want to talk more about this over email or on the phone. I'm here.

Tessa

***

Stella left Kids Club with a check in her pocket and drove to Venice to look at two apartments, which were decent but swamped with inexplicable bad vibes. Next she visited the "Come Live With Us!" apartment on the outskirts of Santa Monica proper. It had a gym, a pool, a sauna, and a Peet's coffee machine. The potential roommates, Jeff, Danny, and Angie, were warm and lively. There was only one iffy issue: She'd have to share a room, which she hadn't done since undergrad. But Danny said that Angie usually slept at her boyfriend's house anyway. And Stella would probably be a lot less depressed if there were people around laughing and watching TV on the couch.

As she was waving goodbye to Danny, her phone *blooped*. It was Nick.

It's officially over with Crazy. Want to come (over)?

The last sex she'd had was the week of Valentine's Day, after caviar, when Wil had crumpled halfway through, calling himself a freak. She hadn't even successfully masturbated since then. She was in the neighborhood so she figured it was fate.

Nick answered the door and they quickly hugged hello. There was no romance, no deviance or dirty talk; a little requisite kissing and then straight to the chase. Nick whipped off his clothes and Stella pulled off hers. Nick pushed her on the bed, her feet still touching the floor. He knelt down and went to work quickly: tongue, fingers, some fancy swirly vibrations, all the precise machinations to get her off exactly twice. Then he climbed up on the bed and let her suck him until he couldn't wait any longer. He put a condom on, not even bothering with missionary; it was doggy-style every time so he could stare at her ass and pull her hair. He kept at it until they were both dripping with sweat, then handed her a towel after he came, like a cornerman patting her on the back after a good fight.

"So what happened with your girl?" Stella asked when they were at coffee around the corner.

"More of the same. I just got tired of dealing with her paranoia. Are you still on the wagon?"

"Yep. I'm trying to talk to that idiot as little as possible. He sometimes tries to lure me back in but I ignore it for the most part. Being alone for a while is probably the best thing for me."

"I agree," said Nick.

***

Dressing up for work had become uncomfortable and pointless, as Britt had forewarned. Stella was wearing yoga pants and a sweater. Chet's patronizing became unbearable by midmorning so she excused herself and took a walk around the sunny block.

She called Wil to find out when she could collect his half of the insurance money.

"Hey. Good to hear from you," he said, annoyingly casual.

"What, are we buddies now? Just a couple weeks ago you were texting me every other day, saying you hoped we could get back together someday."

"I just want you to be happy, so if you want to move on, I support that."

"I just can't make sense of you. Not even a month ago, you were so jealous of delusions you had made up. You were accusing me of sleeping with people, and now I'm actually moving on for good, and you're this relaxed about it?" She knew she shouldn't let him have power over her, but some unchecked thought had left her feeling discarded and worthless.

"If you and I are ever going to get back together, you are going to have to change yourself," he said.

"*Change* myself? Can you see anything that's going on outside you?" Of course he couldn't. Apparently neither could she.

Wil flipped. "Are you saying I can't *empathize?* How can you say that about me?"

"Because I'm over here trying to understand—"

"I can't *believe* you would say I can't empathize with you! How could you say something like that?" he interrupted.

"Because you basically ruined my life! And you have no remorse! You are so cold. Have you looked at Hare's Psychopathy Checklist? I bet you would be off-the-charts if you answered the questions correctly."

He screamed, "You're calling me a psychopath?"

She hung up. She might never know what he was hiding from her, what had caused him to push her away, whether it was drugs or another girl, or maybe he just lost interest when the chase ended. But that all-encompassing feeling they had shared, she knew now it hadn't been love. Addiction, maybe. Whatever it was had changed Stella. But maybe that was a good thing. Maybe someday she could look in the mirror and say, "You are a good person," and believe it.

She cried a little more, climbed back up the stairs, and finished out her day of work. She checked her email every hour, hoping for news from the apartments she'd looked at, but nothing. She did have a message from a guy, Jake, whom she'd met a few months back when she'd been acting in a movie that was being shot on location at his house. She'd been playing the devil's girlfriend and it had been a fun fight scene, flipping backward off the wall. She remembered talking a lot with Jake that day while munching on pistachios from craft services between scenes, listening to him play his grand piano, beautifully. Now Jake was inviting her to come and "jam" with him this evening.

I'm dying to sing with you.

She decided she'd go.

***

Stella certainly hadn't intended to sleep with Jake. But when she arrived at his house, he was wearing a crisp oxford shirt and he smelled like sandalwood. She sat with him on the piano bench and they harmonized deliciously, drank Shiraz and talked philosophy.

After the wine was gone, it was late and she was too sloshed to drive. He kissed her. He talked a big game about his sexual skills and then, like most talkers, disappointed in the delivery. But she blamed the wine and happily accepted his caring touch as she drifted to sleep.

***

She arrived at work in yesterday's clothes, fatigued but high-spirited. Wil texted before she had put Chet's coffee on.

Stella, I have been doing some thinking. I love you. You are my true love. I want to make this work. I am seeing a therapist and a counselor. I am doing my part to become a better man, so if we are to make this happen, I need you to be willing to do ABSOLUTELY ANYTHING for this relationship.

She turned on the computer on and sat down at her desk. She replied to Wil hours later, when she had decided.

Stella:
Can I come over after work and talk to you about this?

Wil:
Yes. I'll be here.

That evening, at the door to the apartment they had briefly shared, Stella hugged Wil.

"Thank you for the text," she said. "But I think this is over."

Something had shifted inside her. She looked at his face—sad, with atmospheric eyes advertising an innocence he never possessed—and saw him completely in past-tense for the first time. She picked an eyelash off his cheek and waited for him to make a wish.

In response, he let a tear roll off his face and he kissed her with those lips and a finality that told her he was just as true as he'd ever been. She kissed back for the last time, knowing that she wouldn't have to try to memorize them, the lips and all they had been to her: They had long since singed themselves into her gray matter. Her anger for now was gone. Her confusion no longer mattered. Here they were at the end.

The little world they'd created with a big bang had burned bright and hot, and now had become a black hole.

"We are just two little kids trying to figure out how to live in this world. And a lot of people get to this point a lot earlier than we have. Everything is new to us. But that's the fun of it."

"This isn't much fun," he said.

"But it *was* fun, wasn't it?"

He nodded.

They said "I love you" and then turned each other loose, promising to take care.

***

TV Partners was sucking Stella dry. She did yoga on the floor because Chet was out.

As she put the finishing touches on the last slide of a Power Point presentation, her email dinged.

She braced herself for rejection when she saw it was from Danny, of the "Come Live With Us!" apartment.

<3efbf70@reply.craigslist.org>
to Stella

Hey-o Stella!

It was awesome to meet you! You seem really nice and like someone I'd totally love to hang out with. The other roommates and I just talked it over, and we decided that we are not going to require a talent show or swimsuit competition for the roommate selection process, though I *am* sort of curious to see each person's talents, haha. Drat, I should have thought of that before hand....

Anyway, we thought you were the coolest candidate by far, and we would love to invite you to our humble abode. If you have any other questions or pertinent information for us, feel free to email me or text me. The room will be available the first of April if you'd like it!

Danny

***

Instead of the freeways, Stella took the streets to work for a change of landscape. She twisted through the canyons to a soundtrack as rocky as the scenery. A bass guitar thrummed until the rhythm nearly burst through the skin on Stella's arms and all the hairs stood up in recognition: God's creation, humans' creation—it was all one. Violin strings swelled to a mighty crescendo as she came down off the mountain and onto the Pacific Coast Highway. The view of the ocean smacked her like an endless blue truth.

She had to write.

Not for anyone else. For her. She didn't need to wait for life to happen to her. She could be the author of her own existence. Writing was the one place she knew how to leave behind what that didn't move her story forward, entertain her, or show her some instance of synchronicity that reminded her of life's magic.

She tried calling Claudia, then Serena, then Everly, but she only got voicemails. So she called the one person she knew would be home.

"Hello?"

"Mom!"

"Hi honey! You sound good," Linda said.

"I am. I just realized something amazing."

"What is it? Are you in the car? I hope you're being careful."

"I am. I just decided: I'm going to write every day for the rest of the year."

"Good, baby. What are you going to write?"

"I'm just going to write my life. Just for...clarity. Do you have anything like that, that you *have* to do?"

"No, I don't. I'm just not creative like that."

"It doesn't have to be something creative. You know, like, basketball players have to play basketball."

"Do they?"

"It's like—music. That's something everybody can relate to, right? When you listen to the right music at the right time, it's supernatural. It's the perfect reflection of a feeling. It magnifies everything and you suddenly *understand* things you didn't before. Have you ever felt that?"

"Yeah, I guess I have. I don't know."

"So maybe everyone can't relate to my thing. But words are my thing. They're the building blocks of meaning. You know?"

"Hmm."

"It's like, no wonder I've spent so much time confused lately. I stopped writing my blog because it was about me and I didn't want the judgment. But I have to write to sort things out. It's my way of making life what I want it to be. Thoughts are just running rampant in your mind and they're not even yours until you claim them, but writing lets me take those thoughts and filter them through a sieve."

"A sieve?"

"Like a strainer. That gets all the nasty chunks out. And it's just a reflection of life, because in life we're all just playing characters. So once you get control of your thoughts and decide which ones to keep, you're writing your own life. Does this make any sense?"

"Not too much, but it sounds good."

"Okay, let me try one more time. If I'm telling my story through a character, I'm seeing my life through eyes once-removed, right? And the space I'm writing from is the space of the being that exists *beneath* me. Beneath Stella, this persona I wear. Get it? So I'm this *power* underneath Stella, this eternal force that isn't affected by the trivialities of life. Operating from there takes away my fears. Acting does it for me too, but in a different way. You know what? I'll just shut up. Sorry. I love you, Mom." Stella wondered who would get it. *Wil would.*

"My creative girl," said her mom. "Your brain and mine just work on different planes, I think. I'm proud of you. Now, are you planning on writing something that'll make money?"

At work she wrote her first story. She turned herself into a character, and the character's feelings didn't need to be her own. Her story was as made-up as she wanted it to be. She wrote about going to her ex-lover's house and saying goodbye to him in the kindest way she knew how. In choosing her words, she was in control of her own viewpoint, her own path. She was the author; she was free.

***

Stella's last Friday evening at Equinox came and went without fanfare. It was overshadowed by a short film Stella got to act in on Saturday: a comedy where she played a superhero. The producers had secured a small studio in Hollywood so they could use a green screen for special effects.

She loved her latex costume and the sultry makeup that allowed her to pretend she was someone funny, powerful, and one-dimensional for a day. She felt light and important, making people laugh on set and kissing her co-star, a boring, good-looking guy named Matthew who she could leave behind without offense when the day was done. And the best part about film was that in a couple of months, she'd have a shiny, tangible product to watch: proof of the work she'd put in.

***

Sunday, before a small Ladidahs show in the Valley, she was back to writing. The last few months she'd been paralyzed at the page, terrified for her ego's sake, but now that it was only a character whose life had blown apart, Stella's fingers moved quickly over the keys. She gladly played the part of herself, unglamorous as it was at times.

"Yoo-hoo!" came Diana's voice as she was finishing up.

"In here!" Stella yelled.

"Good for you, writing! Are you ready to sing?"

"Yep. Just got to throw on a dress."

"Legs or boobs ?" Diana held up two dresses.

"Both options are tantalizing, but for tonight, I think legs might be the best option on the menu."

"Legs it is, then," said Diana. "I know we didn't get to see each other a lot, but I'm going to miss you, girl."

"I hope my new roommates are half as incredible as you," she said.

***

Stella was knocking on Andrew's door. He answered with sad eyes.

"I'm sorry," she said. "Can we try it again? I'll make it up to you." He stood silently for a few minutes, then pulled her into a hug. His body felt familiar: stout but slightly soft, just her height.

"Go get your stuff and come home," he said. She cried with relief and lay her head on his shoulder. His embrace felt safe.

"I never stopped loving you," she said.

She went to pick up all her belongings from Diana's. On the way back, every street sign was a blue Santa Monica sign. She followed them west, but a rock slide on the mountain blocked her way. She turned and tried a different road, but the road was flooded. She got out of the car and tried to walk, but the trees all grew together and kept her from returning to Andrew. She tried to call him, but his number was disconnected.

Stella realized she was dreaming and sat up, head thrumming under a layer of fatigue. She remembered Diana leaving early last night with her boyfriend. She remembered driving herself back after the Ladidahs concert, after having way too many drinks with Tessa—*so stupid; must not do that again*—and then stalking Andrew on Facebook before bed. She couldn't tell if she was hungover or still drunk, but it was time to leave for work. She grabbed her makeup bag and slipped carelessly into a cotton dress, making sure to take two different jackets for the cold office.

Chet was always late. Each morning Stella jumped when she heard his keys rattling heavy in the lock, followed by his used-car voice resounding, "Good morning, Sunshine!" He made requisite small talk, asked for his coffee, and gave her a monkey-caliber task. Stella knew not to work on it right away, but to make it *look* like she was toiling. If she finished it early, Chet would find more busy-work for her, then examine it with a fine tooth comb, yelling, "You rushed this! Look at all these mistakes! This line is supposed to be a *thick* line! This box is supposed to be connected to *this* box!"

She opened Excel as a decoy, but turned her attention to a tiny window she hid in the bottom corner of the screen. She wrote a page about a Valentine's Day seizure—until Chet asked if she was finished with her task.

"Just finished it!" she chirped, before finishing it in five minutes. By then it was lunch time. Instead of wasting her precious hour waiting in lines and stuffing her face, she ran all the way to Venice beach and back in the blazing sun, just to remind herself that she had a strong, athletic body and there was a joyful, free world outside the frosty office.

***

The long week was over. Stella took a bath and crawled in bed early, excited to spend Friday evening reading and dozing.

Diana had left a photocopied page on her bedside table. "Let Love Go, If She Will" by Robert Louis Stevenson.

> Let love go, if she will.
> Seek not, O fool, her wanton flight to stay.
> Of all she gives and takes away
> The best remains behind her still.

It began to vibrate within her and she whispered it aloud, and by the time she was speaking the last stanza—"one thing is ours that nothing can remove"—she had tapped into the well of tears that she thought was nearly dry.

So much love had come and cleanly gone. Boxes of photographs sat under her bed back in Harlan—she and her first love Bret making faces on a school bus, she and Matt lost on a cobblestone street in Rome, she and Trev kissing on the rocky beach, she and Andrew eating cake at their Bollywood wedding—each memory as far away and also as close as the text on the pages of Stella's favorite books. *One thing is ours that nothing can remove.*

She realized this would be her last Friday at Diana's. She was moving in two days.

She couldn't deem these relationships "failed" because they didn't last forever. She wiped her eyes and pulled up the covers.

> Joy she may give and take again,
> Joy she may take and leave us pain.
> O Love, and what care we?

An hour later, when she was at peace, reading a copy of *Walden* she'd gotten from a "free" box at the library, Victoria from Ladidahs called. She was moving in with her boyfriend this weekend and said that if Stella would like her bed, she could have it for free. She'd just have to pick it up somehow tomorrow, when she was already slated to work catering at a wedding.

"I know that's short notice, but it would actually help me a lot," said Victoria.

"Oh, me too," Stella said. "I need a bed. I can do it. I'll see you tomorrow at, like—"

"Ten?" offered Victoria.

"Ten." She'd make it work.

***

Early Saturday morning, all was still. Stella cleared Diana's kitchen and drank coffee, then sat straddle-legged on the living room carpet, relishing the excruciating stretch in her hamstrings. Soon the outside world would sweep her into a rank, sweaty day stuffed with driving and serving stuffed mushrooms and navigating difficult logistics. But now, even the fog-filtered light through the windows was quiet. She let the hush envelop her as she closed her eyes and meditated on the distinctive lives she'd lived across these 28 years. When she opened her eyes, a question had arisen. *What is it that you want for now?*

She took her journal and wrote it down:

I want to feel stable again. I want to feel happy and excited about life. I want to be kind and inspiring to everyone and let people know how much they mean to me. I want to write a novel, pay off my debt, buy a condo, travel anytime I want. I want to be in love with someone worthy of my love, who is communicative and can take care of himself. And is an awesome lover. I want to start enjoying the beach and outdoors again. I want to leave the office job as soon as possible and find a way sustain myself with work I enjoy.

She stood up, signing a silent contract that said, *from now on, I am the arbiter of my own fate. Henceforth, I and only I am responsible for myself.* Then she called U-Haul.

"We're all out of trucks. It's Easter weekend," said the guy on the phone, mockingly.

"Oh." She called two more U-Hauls and a Budget and got the same answer.

"Everyone's moving this weekend," they said. "You should have reserved."

"Oh."

Finally, she found an Enterprise Rent-a-Car in Culver City. She drove there and spent the last of the week's pay to rent a giant Dodge pick-up truck. She played country music on the way to Victoria's, just to get into character, and they loaded up the bed.

As Stella drove away, Victoria said, "That mattress has seen a lot of action, so don't disappoint it!"

"I don't have anyone new to introduce it to now, but give me a little time and your bed will be back in action, I guarantee."

"I don't doubt it!" said Victoria with a wave.

Danny let her in at the new place, but Stella refused his offer to help move the mattress, as he seemed busy working in his room. In two hours she managed to unload the mattress and box springs on the fourth floor, drive to the site of the wedding she was working, change into her all-black outfit, freshen her makeup, parallel park the enormous pickup truck, and greet Vince, who was serving drinks as usual. Sweat pooled on her chest and ran down the backs of her knees, but at least she'd make a few bucks today.

"This wedding is so cute," Vince said, his hair and tie perfect as usual.

"Yeah." Stella looked around. A couple was dancing. A groomsman walked up behind his lady and massaged her shoulders. The newlyweds kissed. She remembered how she used to take simple gestures of affection for granted, just like these people. But now she had no one in her life who would willingly massage her shoulders, hold her hand, or place a palm on the small of her back. The only way she could feel a tender touch right now was to pay for a massage. Her muscles tensed with longing.

***

Early on Easter, the murky sky did not bode well for starting anew. The clouds were visual manifestations of Stella's usual worries: the fear of not having money for an apartment deposit or this expensive truck, the awareness that she had to move all by herself again, the knowledge that signing a new lease meant truly abandoning the possibility of returning to Andrew's safe haven. She felt the pain all over her body, every muscle balled up.

She thought with wonder of the whole wedge of the population out there, festooned in pastels, celebrating the Resurrection. The word *impossible* came to mind. But if Jesus had done it like they used to tell her in Sunday School—if he had pried his defeated body off the floor of the tomb and rolled the stone away—then surely Easter was a good day for Stella to do the same.

While eating her toast, she browsed a Feng Shui book from Diana's shelf that gave birthdate-specific decorating tips for maximum energy flow. She looked hers up—August 3rd—and found a warning against fire. "You are in danger of destroying your wood element when you bring candles into your space." She finished her food and returned the book to the shelf; it was time to get ready.

She put her body into a bath and lit some candles around the tub and sink. She sighed and buried herself underwater, officially recognizing her status as a stray. She'd left 9th Street in January, left East Hollywood in February, left 7th Street before March even arrived, and now she was leaving Tarzana. *Please*, she thought as the heat seeped in through her pores, *let this be the last time I move for a while.* She stepped out, baptized and ready. She brushed her teeth and bent over to take a sip from the sink faucet.

It was an acrid stench that hit her first. Burning. When she stood back up, swishing the toothpasty water around her mouth, she saw it. Flames rising from her forehead. A little piece of her hair, the sideswept part of her bangs, was on fire. She bent over and doused her hair with sink water.

Fuck you, Feng Shui, she thought.

Tessa texted:

> Are you coming over for Easter dinner? Everybody wants to see you.

She felt too daunted to answer. She sank onto the bed and closed her eyes. Thoughts skittered around like spiders, hairy and full of venom. *I don't want to pack this all up for the fourth time this year. What if the new roommates aren't home and I can't get in? What if they decide they don't like me? Andrew and Wil don't even know where I am. Wil's probably on drugs again. How am I going to take this truck back in the morning and get to work on time? I'll probably get fired. I am so broke. And so alone. I may never be loved again.*

The fire had opened up new channels inside Stella. She allowed the fear to engulf her for over an hour, excreting desperate, lonely sobs. Then she got up, washed her face in cold water, put on a flowery dress and Doc Martens, left a goodbye note for Diana, and packed up the truck.

She stopped halfway to her new place, pulled over and parked the full truck beside Tessa's apartment in West Hollywood.

> I'm here!

Tessa came out. "I'm so glad you were able to make it! We're just having some wine while the food gets done. Is this *your* truck?"

"Just for the rest of today. I'm in the middle of moving, but I can stay for a couple hours at least."

"Great. It's just a few of the ladies and some friends from work. I'm so proud of you, Stella! You're doing it! Are you hungry?"

"I could eat," she said.

She grew stronger, bolstered by the energy of friends, and left smiling again, ready for her new life.

SPRING

APRIL

Freedom, came a whispered word, a wake-up call at the end of a dream. Stella found herself in a strange bed, licked through the window by bird songs on a calm breeze. Though she was a few blocks shy of Santa Monica, she was finally west of the 405 again, boxes still stacked all around her. Angie had, as promised, never come home last night. Stella walked into the open living room-and-kitchen area where nobody was stirring. The sun shone through the French doors, inviting her outside. She stepped onto the balcony, taking in her new view, where the ocean-tinged air smelled cool and familiar.

It took just fifteen minutes to get to TV Partners. She sailed through the workday on the air of this new lifestyle, rich with all the time she had gained. Everything was new. Even Chet, with his explosive condescension, couldn't touch her; she churned out two assignments before lunch.

***

High on nostalgia, Stella sang along with a punk band at a private Hollywood rooftop show. The band was getting older and so was she. She talked to them—a feat the younger Stella would never have believed possible—and then descended to street level. The black no longer smudged her eyes, but somewhere buried in the fissures of her rib cage or her hip bones, she could feel exhilarated stirrings of that reckless young soul.

A missed call from Andrew stunned the smile off her face. She called back, strengthened by the confidence of her younger self.

"Hello?" His voice stung like lemon juice in a paper cut.

"I saw you called."

"Yeah. The lease is finally up so I can move out of this

apartment. But they need for you to go and sign the papers to release it," he said heavily.

"Okay," she said, longing to comfort him. "Anything you need."

Silence.

Then she said, "Andrew, I know I left you in a terrible place. I promise you that whenever I get enough money, I'll pay you back for those months you were alone in the apartment. I know it was expensive. I just felt like I had no choice. It was so sad there. I was only bringing you down."

"It doesn't matter," he said.

"How are you now?"

"How am I? I'm angry."

"I understand," she said. "So, you don't think you could ever love me again? Even someday in the future?" She didn't know what she was saying until the words escaped.

"I don't know, Stella," he said. "Even just talking to you makes me feel bad."

"What's the worst part?" she asked. "What can I do?"

"You can't do anything. Because the only reason you want to do anything is to help yourself feel better. Everything is about how *you* feel. At this point, my heart is the site of a forest fire. I don't know when, or if, I will ever be able to love again."

"I am so sorry, Andrew." A sob got caught in her throat.

"You know what I keep thinking of?" he said.

"What?" Stella became the tears; she had no other choice.

"One time, toward the end, you told me that you had been unhappy for a long time. You told me that for two whole years, you had been imagining other people while we had sex." Stella could tell that he had gone over and over this thing she had said, his hurt hardening like layers of rock.

She didn't even remember saying it. All she knew was that toward the end, she kept trying to be as honest as possible. When she felt he had refused to confront the situation, her truth became more and more harsh, in hopes of sparking a real conversation. But he had remained silent.

"I am so sorry I hurt you. You mean so much to me," was all she could say now.

"Stella, move on," he said.

"You don't want me to—"

"Move on," Andrew said, and hung up.

***

Angie was getting her things together to leave for the night while her little black dog, Mary Ann, followed her around. Stella put some new sheets on her bed—sea green, to invite the peace and vastness of the ocean into her dreams.

"Are you almost unpacked?" Angie asked.

"I've got everything here," Stella said, "but it's a matter of putting everything in a place. Sorry my stuff's everywhere. I'm gonna have to get a dresser. I don't even have a surface to sit things on."

"Please. I need to get my stuff off the floor. These boxes have been here forever," Angie said. Her bed, a modified IKEA futon crammed into the corner of the room, was barely visible, piled with clear plastic boxes and old shopping bags full of photo frames and folders. "But I'm going over to Jackson's. I'll be back in the morning to take out Mary Ann."

Once Angie left, Stella arranged her side of the room and hung her framed Lichtenstein prints on the wall by her bed, then lay down and took it all in. Here she was: alone in a situation of her own design. Stella Robertson, Single Woman Working 40 Hours a Week, Paying for Her Own Shit, Answering to No One. She was boundless: She was a newly-inflated balloon.

***

Claudia, Stella's best friend from Kentucky, called crying. "Stel, I'm getting divorced."

Luckily Chet wasn't in the office today. "What happened, my friend? Talk to me."

"You know all the problems we've been having, with Carter's drinking and the DUI. That's not even half of it. I think I told you about the sex. I don't know if it was my fault or what, but we hadn't done it in months. I just didn't want to, Stel. It felt like I wasn't even a part of it."

"Oh. That's not good."

"I know, and he just works all the time and stays gone. I don't know if he's been cheating on me, but it feels like it. I basically make all the money around here and he doesn't even try to contribute. He just expects me to bail him out. And you know? I wanted a family. And I just don't think we're on the same page at all anymore."

"I'm so sorry, Claude. I know it feels like severing a limb." She and Andrew had yet to even speak of legitimate divorce, but Stella knew it was coming.

"Stella?"

"Hmm?"

"Was it ever real?"

"Of course it was!"

"I keep looking back at myself and I keep thinking that maybe I knew even then that I was forcing it, that I was just dying to be in love. And Carter was convenient."

"I don't know, Claude, I think it was real. I was at your wedding and I got misty-eyed. I remember when you were telling me about how he asked you to marry him, that whole Beatles song by the fireplace thing. You were in love. We all loved Carter. And when love is at its peak, we want to believe it's going to last forever, but one of the things I've recently learned is that usually it doesn't."

Claudia let out another sob.

"But you are going to love again. So am I. We have to believe this. You're so strong. You'll make it through this dark time and I'll be right here with you."

"Thanks, Stel. I know you will be. I miss you."

"I miss you, too." Stella hadn't seen her in person since a friend's wedding last summer in Kentucky, but they'd been friends for years and through phone calls, they'd grown even closer in the seven years since college had ended.

"Love you. Call me if you need anything."

"Love you too."

She hung up wishing there was more she could do for Claudia, but she was grateful that all her pain had at least made it possible to console a friend with real understanding.

***

Now, it only took five minutes to get to her place from Ladidahs rehearsal. Jeff, Danny, and Danny's girlfriend Ariana were strewn about the kitchen when Stella came in. They poured her wine and asked for her fucked-up stories.

She regaled them with an anthology of this year's rock-bottom moments, and Jeff said, "Damn, girl. You could write a novel."

"I am writing every day now, even if nobody ever sees it."

"I'd love to read it," said Ariana.

"Thanks, girl. Hey Danny, I never found out—is there a deposit on this place that I need to pay in addition to rent?" Stella asked.

"Yeah, there is. It's, I think, nine-hundred fifty bucks. I'll check to make sure."

She stifled the panic.

"But you can pay it in installments if that's easier."

"Okay," she said. "It's stupid; I feel like I'm wasting my life away at this nine-to-five, and I'm not making much more money than I was when I was just hustling with all my gigs."

"Stella, I don't worry about you," said Danny. "If anybody's going to make it, it's you."

"Man, I hope so."

"You will," said Ariana. "Do you know Angie's story?"

"Nope, I haven't really gotten to sit down and talk to her yet."

"We joke about this place. We call it Passages West LA. Because everyone who moves in here starts out in kind of a bad place, but within a year, they're living their dreams. Like, the roommate before

Angie, Hope. She was a mess. She had dropped out of school and was broke, but after living here for a year, she got a scholarship and now she's doing a study abroad program in London!"

"Wow."

"And Angie. I'll let her tell you about it, but when she came, she was about to move back to Chicago because she'd almost given up on L.A., but now she has this great boyfriend, Jackson, and, like, they're probably going to get married. And she has her own production company and makes movies all the time."

"It's true," said Jeff.

"I can't wait to see what you guys can do with me," Stella said.

This segment of her life did feel like a rehab, come to think of it. Or summer camp. In middle school, her dad had sent her to the same camp where he'd gone: a Christian retreat deep in the mountains with a swinging bridge and bunk-bedded cabins, an Olympic-sized pool and a mess hall, campfire singing and athletic competitions. Stella remembered always returning slightly transformed—more adult, more rugged.

Likewise, at this apartment, she was dedicated to a list of temporary endeavors that weren't exactly her own. Someday she wouldn't have to work in cheesy advertising, she wouldn't be sharing a room, she wouldn't be tethered to anyone by marriage certificates or car titles. Someday she'd be able to dictate the terms of her own life, but until then, she had to play by the rules of this summer camp, and that was okay for now.

The door opened.

"You guys are partying without me?" Angie said.

Angie joined them and divulged her stories of fights, failures, and broken relationships. When the wee hours came, they got into their beds in the same room and turned out the light.

"Night," said Angie.

"Good night," Stella said, closing her eyes and feeling a bit dizzy.

Thank you, God, she said to herself, falling instantly to sleep.

***

"Hey," Everly said. "Just making sure you're still alive."

"You wouldn't believe it, but I'm super alive."

"Good. Are you moved in?"

"Yes, and I hope that'll be the last time for a while."

"What's it like?"

"It's really fancy. I'm actually going to be spending my evening reading in the Jacuzzi."

"Wow," said her sister.

"Yeah, and my roommates are awesome. Hey, did you hear

about Claudia?"

"Ugh...yeah. Everybody's getting divorced. Have you and Andrew started that yet?"

"We haven't even mentioned it. I don't want to cause Andrew any further pain, so I'm just waiting for him to say something." There was a long pause before Stella said, "I can't imagine loving anyone again for a long time."

"That's okay. Being single is probably what you need right now. I mean, you've pretty much been in a couple since—how old were you when you started dating Bret?"

"Thirteen."

"Man. Have you even been single since then?"

"Yeah. For maybe six months."

"By the time you're ready to date again, you'll know what to look for," said Everly.

"Oh, I already know what to look for. Do you know what I realized?"

"What?"

"I have never actually sought out specific qualities in a guy. I just kind of get involved with somebody and then fall in love with whatever they've got going on."

"Interesting. Yeah, you're pretty open."

"I have been. But I have learned a lot from this whole rock-bottom experience, and what I've figured out is that both of the guys I gave up were good in their own ways, but neither was for me. So next time I get into a relationship, I have some requirements. I want the guy to be kind and caring and laid-back like Andrew, but I want him to be more...*alpha*. You know?"

"I know," she said.

"I want him to have some *throw*-down, ya dig?"

"Oh my gosh. Don't say 'ya dig.'"

"Like, I need someone who can put me in my place once in a while. Challenge me, so I can evolve."

"That's gonna be hard to find, but you can do it."

"Yeah. I want someone who is completely confident and interested in everything. That was the one thing about Wil that really lured me in. He was full of all these ambitions and fantasies. He had all these lofty goals and he was always working on himself. Or so it seemed."

"But he was psycho," Everly said.

"But he was psycho. Exactly. So what I want in my new man is someone who is exciting and full of vim and vigor like Wil, but without all the baggage and addiction and mental illness. I want someone who is easy to hang out with, and smart and artistic like Andrew, but I want him to have more important things going on in his life than just me. I can't be someone's everything."

"You're right. I think Andrew was a little too devoted to you in a lot of ways."

"I think so too. I think this breakup will end up being the best thing to help him find himself."

"Are you finding yourself?"

"I'm doing my best."

***

Stella met her friend India for lunch in Venice. She was so proud of Stella for committing to a writing goal. India had just gotten a weed stash with her medical marijuana card. Stella gave her 40 bucks and bought weed for the first time in her life.

"Am I a real adult now?" she joked. She smoked a little in the car when she got home from work.

Upstairs, she floated over to the dining room table, opened her computer and stared at the screen. It was time to write. She typed five words when she desperately yearned for kettle corn. Jeff had some. Stella popped and ate the entire bag. But her calves hurt. She had gone to get a massage the day before, trying to reprise the one Diana had gifted her. But today, the masseur was blind. "Don't hold back," Stella had told him, figuring his blindness made him especially sensitive to touch. But she was wrong. She had spent the entire hour wincing and crying on the table, letting him dig his dagger-like fingers deep beneath the gristle of her muscles. He never let up.

Her computer screen went black from inactivity. She saw a smile on her face in the reflection. It looked so much better on her than the two vertical lines between her eyebrows that had etched themselves deeper over the winter.

She picked up her phone and sat looking through her contacts. "Who *are* you?" she said aloud to no one, and began deleting names she didn't remember. She deleted a Christophe, a Dan and a Darnell. Then she arrived at a name that gave her a rush of strange excitement: Dylan.

Dylan. She tried to picture his face, but all she could remember was that he was a handsome half-Japanese guy she'd met at a warehouse party. She didn't remember what his voice sounded like—it had been six months since they'd met—but seeing his name made her juicy with optimism. She had nothing to lose, so she clicked on his number and composed a message.

> Dylan, it's Stella! Remember me? Got a new phone and was going through my old contacts. If you happen to be free sometime, I would love to hang out...

She put her phone down and walked over to the balcony. He probably wouldn't remember her. But her phone *blooped* right away.

Dylan:
Course I remember you! And I seem to also remember you sing very well. I'm free this Friday. You?

Blood rushed to her head and all her extremities.

Stella:
:) I am! What shall we do?

Dylan:
Are you still in Santa Monica? If so I wouldn't mind trekking down to the beach. Know any good spots on the beach?

Stella:
Why yes and yes! We could take some wine in water bottles (a favorite pastime of mine...) and explore the pier, maybe even ride the ferris wheel! Then walk north where nobody bothers, or south where we could swing on the swing set! Depending on the mood...

Dylan:
That would be quite epic. The only thing more epic would be to duct tape flashlights to a couple surfboards and catch waves in the dark. Next time maybe? I'm down for wine and water bottles.

Stella:
Ooh...I like your idea better! We'd just need the equipment...

Dylan:
Do you surf? If so all you'd need is a wetsuit. I've got plenty of boards.

Stella:
I want to surf, but never have (yet)! So maybe I could procure a wetsuit before Friday...to start my surfing career.

Dylan:
Haha let's start you off in the sunlight. There is a swell coming in though...

Stella:
Tell me when and I'm there! (I have a 9-5 now, though...ick!)

Dylan:
You really want to try? Right now is probably not the best time because it's cold. You'd last about 5 minutes without a thick wetsuit. But if somehow you can find one, I'll take you out.

Stella:
Oh I can find one...:) I am all about it!

Dylan:
Well then I have a board for ya! Let me know when you get that neoprene.

Stella:
You shall be the first to know!

Stella felt renewed and triumphant, like she had recently pointed herself in a more positive direction and maybe she was getting somewhere. But writing wasn't going to happen until later.

***

With all the time Stella wasted stuck to this ergonomic chair, it seemed impossible that her bank account was at zero again. Jonas, the part-time accountant and only other employee, came in at ten. "Hey Jonas. Um, you do the payroll here, right?"

"I make the checks out, yes."

"Well, I'm dead broke. Should I *ask* Chet if he'll give me a check today or what?"

"It's time for you to get paid?"

"Yes. I haven't been paid in two weeks. I'm kind of scared to ask. He jumps all over me every time I talk to him."

"I'm meeting with him in a few minutes, so I can ask if it's okay to cut you a check."

"Really? *Thank you.*"

Maybe when these checks started adding up to something, making her life less stressful, she'd start to appreciate this job. After all, she *was* actually writing, even if she had to hide it in a two-inch window. And she wasn't having to drive all over Los Angeles finding gigs, not knowing where her next check was coming from. For this she could be grateful.

If she got paid, then tomorrow maybe she could buy the wetsuit. Slightly nervous that she was coming off too excited, she sent Dylan a message.

What thickness of wetsuit shall keep me warm in the frigid waters?

Dylan:
4/3 mm. That'll keep ya toasty.

Stella:
I'm on it :)

Dylan:
Damn, I hope surfing doesn't disappoint you! If you stick with it, it won't, but it'll probably be rough the first few times. Think you can hang?

Stella:
I know I can! I am a yogi. Plus, the ocean is my muse. I must know her better. *him, in my case

Dylan:
Well you'll definitely get to feel her power. Pretty sure it's a she. Although Dylan in Welsh means ocean, so could be a he.

Stella:
Let's see, then...

Dylan:
The ocean can't be described. Just respected, loved, and enjoyed.

Stella:
I totally plan on enacting all three of those verbs.

Dylan:
I just hope you like it.

Stella:
Don't you worry...I try things a million times before truly deciding if I like something. Like olives. Took me years to like olives.

Dylan:
Hopefully it'll only take a few times to realize the orgasmic quality of catching a wave, but we'll see.

Stella:
Can't wait :)

After lunch, Stella took the little glass bubbler out of her glove compartment and inhaled three deep hits of the sour-smelling weed to make the four remaining hours tolerable. It worked. Back in the office, she was encased in a cushy bubble, detached from the sound of Chet's demeaning gripe. By the end of the day, Jonas had procured her a check, and the mild high was gone.

***

Stella had only been in the new apartment for a week, but she was starting to feel some ownership. Home alone, she stood on a chair and installed her Santa Monica Blvd. sign over the doorway to the room she and Angie shared. She unsheathed bits of a particle board dresser from a box she'd bought at Kmart. She sat on the floor and started piecing it together, considering the phrase, "building something from the ground up." Wil used to say it all the time. "I want to build a life with you, from the ground up," he would say. It was one of those statements that was both naive and all-powerful. How romantic it sounded; how pure.

But, she thought as she put her might behind the screwdriver, *I am the only one to build something with from the ground up. At least for now.*

When they decided to open their relationship, it was because she and Andrew used to say there was no such person as The One. Then Wil came along and insisted that there was, and he was it. He had tapped into a desire Stella hadn't realized was there: she wanted The One to exist. And though Wil could not be that, her hunger still stirred. She still wanted a Love of My Life. She knew now that there was not one solitary individual to "complete" her. She was complete already. She'd have to make compromises and deal with some shit if she wanted to share her life with someone.

But she still believed in The One. It was just a different kind: one imperfect person she would *choose* to make it work with. Wil was not that person. Her person would not lie to her or steal from her or doze off while she read him a Raymond Carver story in bed. No, Wil was not, in the end, the love of her life. But for some reason, it had hurt to find out that she might not be his.

Her heart was still cracked. She still felt sick anytime she heard lo-fi indie rock. But she was making money, eating her vegetables, going to the gym, even finding time to meditate a little. And, in an effort to enjoy being single, she had not one, but three upcoming dates with interesting men: Tessa's friend Paul from the Ladidahs show on Tuesday, a blogger named Mike on Thursday, and Dylan the hot surfer on Friday.

She finished the dresser. It wasn't perfect. She had driven certain screws too far, leaving rough dings in the particle board. But it belonged to her and it would serve her needs.

***

She peeled herself off the bathroom floor at work where she had been sobbing again. Hours ago she'd woken up at peace, fished her folded clothes out of the dresser she'd built, ready for a day's work. Then…surprise! It was strange how grief came in surges, as if she were part of an experiment where some almighty scientist was pressing a button to electrocute her. Maybe it was her newfound stillness that made it possible to hear the faint, persistent clanging of her broken heart still trying to beat. In the quiet moments she wondered what was wrong with her. *Was she cruel? Was she unlovable? Was she destined to slave away in jobs she hated? Why did it seem so easy for others to just live? Were they happy, or did they just have lower standards than she did?* She scribbled in her notebook the first words that came to her mind.

WAKE UP, STELLA! You are not perfect, but you are worthy! You will experience romance again. You will go to Costa Rica and Hawaii and India. You will learn to surf. You will continue to have lots of friends and great L.A. experiences. You will write a novel. You will start acting more often. You will someday know how it feels not to worry about money. And there await a million other untold happenings too fantastic for you to predict.

When she stepped back and saw herself from the outside, she saw that she was just another well-meaning, flawed person doing her best, and she understood how to care for herself. On her lunch break, she bought a wetsuit at the Rider Shack. She texted Dylan a selfie from the dressing room, with the caption

I'm READY!

He wrote back.

Oh hell yes. We'll have to go at some point this weekend and get your stoke on!!

***

She had gone to a movie screening with Tessa and Erin the night before, and now they were sitting in a circle with the others at Ladidahs rehearsal.

"Stella," Erin said between songs, "Tessa told me Paul was going to be your date last night."

"Yeah. But then his uncle died and he ended up having to fly to

116

Texas," Stella said.

"Do you like him? He's such a great guy," said Tessa.

"I do like him," Stella said. "We've been texting a little, and he asked if we could reschedule for a real date when he gets back. But I'm not trying to get close to anybody right now. Just having fun."

"Who else have you been out with?" Erin asked.

"About a month ago I went out with this guy Chip—"

"Chip!" said Tessa. "He called and told me that you guys weren't a match. But for the record, it wasn't my idea, it was his. He was the one who saw your picture and asked me to set you two up."

Stella laughed. "It's okay. I still had a good time. And there was the guy Jimmy who I walked out on early, and Jake, the Lebanese Jake Gyllenhaal pianist."

"He sounded great," said Tessa.

"He was, but the chemistry was off. And then there's this dude named Josh who was really charming, even though he was clearly using cheesy pickup artistry. I went out with him and he tried to psychoanalyze me and tell me about my Return of Saturn. He kissed me and I was not feeling it, so I went home. And I have a date tomorrow, too."

"Who is it this time?" asked Victoria.

"It's this guy named Mike. He writes this actor blog that I've been following for years, and I didn't know he'd even heard of me. But recently he started messaging me. Turns out he had been reading *my* blog, which I haven't written in since last year, but—"

"That is so cute," said Kerry.

"I think so," Stella said. "He's really funny, though I can't tell how attractive he is from his photos. But there's something a little creepy about him that I can't put my finger on."

"Where are you guys going?" asked Tessa.

"The Galley in Santa Monica. I guess he lives close to me. He wants to pick me up, but I'm like, 'Nope! I'll ride my bike!'"

"Yeah; you don't want to get stranded," said Rebecca.

"Exactly."

"What's creepy about him?" Erin asked.

"Uh, well, he's already been calling me 'Babe' over text, and we haven't even met. He's like, 'We're definitely going to work well together,' and stuff. Not complete red flags, but..."

"Yeah," said Victoria. "That's a little forward."

"But what I'm really looking forward to is Friday. Remember how I slipped my number in that hot guy's back pocket like six months ago?"

"The hapa?" said Tessa, who had grown up in Hawaii and was herself half Chinese-Korean.

"Yes! Well, I'm going out with him Friday, and it's a beach date."

"What's his name?"

"Dylan. He's a surfer, and he's going to teach me how to surf next week. I just got a wetsuit today."

"Stel! This is exciting. Now this you'll have to tell us about."

And at last they sang.

***

After work, Stella found a pile of her mail on the kitchen table. Most of it was junk, but there were two official-looking window envelopes from the City of Santa Monica that sucked away her oxygen. She opened them and bit her nails as she scanned the bold black writing. "STELLA ROBERTSON"... "FINAL NOTICE"... "if you fail to pay" ... "$130" ... "checks payable" ... "RED PRIUS."

No! No, no, no, no, no. But of course it was so. Of course Wil was running all over town, racking up parking tickets in her name. And of course he wasn't paying them, and they had increased from $65 to $130. A door slammed shut inside her, and any tenderness toward Wil was locked out.

She texted him a picture of the notices.

Are you going to take care of these?

Wil:
I have already called them and they are going to give me an extension.

Stella:
What the fuck. This isn't seventh grade math homework. They don't give you extensions.

She called him, but he didn't answer. She left a voicemail. "Wil. I do not have any extra money, and even if I did, I would not be using it to pay your fucking parking tickets. Either you pay these right now, or I am going to come get that car. I have been trying to be nice, giving you all this time to put the car in your name, but you're not doing shit. You pay those tickets this week, or else."

She took a bottomless breath after she hung up. He texted her again:

I called them and told them my situation and they are letting me do a payment plan. Calm down. I haven't let you down before. Why would I start now?

She chucked the phone onto the couch. *Hadn't let her down yet?*

118

But she didn't have time to worry about this now; she had a dinner date. She tucked the notices under a couple books on her dresser, put on a dress and some makeup, and drove to Main Street.

Mike came outside The Galley when he saw her through the window. He hugged her and guided her to his little bar table. He was 34, tall, with dark hair and a rough Bostonian face and demeanor. He wasn't bad looking, dressed in an Oxford shirt and jeans, the way a frat boy dresses for his Sunday meeting. Stella was looking at the sirloin on the menu, but Mike ordered a beer for himself and a wine for her, then said he wasn't that hungry. After the date with Chip a couple weeks ago, she should have known to eat beforehand.

"You're so wholesome and cute. Not what I expected from the pictures," he said.

"Thanks," she said, taking a gulp of wine.

The conversation was steady and Mike was a good listener with a sarcastic quip for almost everything, but he had an off-putting intensity, and he only wanted to hear about the open relationship. It was snakelike, the way he barely blinked, as if he was trying to bore holes into Stella's skull. At the end of the night, he walked her to her car where she hoped he wouldn't try to kiss her, but he did: two closed-mouth kisses on the lips.

"See you soon, sweetheart," he said.

"Bye," she replied, wondering if maybe she should go out with him again, just to double check that there was no chemistry. *No, probably not.*

In the car, all she could think of was her date with Dylan the next day. She silently prepared for the worst, but her gut said otherwise. She texted him as soon as Mike was out of sight:

> So, are we still on for tomorrow evening, even if there may be surf this weekend? And if so, do you still want to beach it? Where do you live, by the way? (Sorry for the Spanish inquisition.)

> Dylan:
> No problemo. I live in NoHo. And yes beach sounds like fun! I'll bring some water bottles and white wine? I got into a bike accident on Tuesday, so I'll see what the road rash looks like in a few days but it should be fine. Stoked!

***

Stella showered as quickly and thoroughly as she could. She'd spent the day at work skittish with excitement, spinning in her rolling chair. She dug through her side of the closet to find something both practical and nice-without-trying-too-hard. She would need shoes comfortable enough for walking. Doc Martens. She would need to balance out her short hair with something feminine. A short blue skirt. But it was cold and windy; plus, the blind man's massage had left a lattice of bruises on the backs of her thighs. Black tights. And, to make sure she didn't look like a teenager, she put on a button-down shirt and topped it with a peacoat.

She was in the kitchen making dinner, which she planned to scarf before leaving, when Dylan texted.

Dylan:
Alright where shall we meet?

Stella:
Pier? Or do ya want to meet on the promenade and walk to the pier?

Dylan:
Let's go pier.

Stella:
Cool. Are you hungry? I just made some delicious whole wheat penne arabiatta with chicken sausage and I have Tupperware!

She couldn't believe she'd just offered to share her dinner with him. He might not even be hungry. And what if he hated her cooking? She suddenly felt exposed.

Dylan:
Wow. Not sure wine in water bottles will suffice!

Stella:
Haha sure it will! I'll see you there.

She answered her phone as she walked past the guitarists and palm readers on the Promenade.

"I can't find a fucking parking space anywhere." There was his voice, masculine but heart-strong, and using the word "fuck" when he didn't even know her yet, which slightly turned her on. Stella walked as fast as she could to the pier so she could stake out and appear collected.

Dylan:
I just parked. Do you see me? I'm standing beside a silver Prius.

She looked down to the parking lot and ran her eyes over all the cars, but couldn't find a silver Prius or a date. Heat rushed to the surface of her skin.

Stella:
I don't see you!

Dylan:
I see you!

She climbed up onto the pylon and looked out over the ocean where the lights from the ferris wheel reflected glimmering reds and blues. She put the Tupperware down and gulped in a mouthful of fresh salt air. Then, there he was, waving from down below, smaller from up here than the huge memory she'd been carrying. Even at this distance in the half-dark she could detect his adorable dimples. His face was not what she remembered: structured with soft features and strong contours.

"How do I get up there?" he yelled.

"Um—" she looked right, then left. "See where that little stand is, with the umbrella? Your name on a grain of rice? There's a staircase on the other side. I'll meet you there!"

She ran down and waited by the stairs, the white water to her left crashing in the dusk.

"You made it!" They shared a friendly hug, the plastic bowl dangling from her left hand.

"Finally!" he said. "Aw, you really brought me dinner? Oh shit, I forgot the wine in my car!"

"We better go get that," she said, and followed him to the parking lot where he pulled out two Arrowhead bottles full of white wine. "I have more, just in case."

"Sounds good," she said. "Want to walk down and sit by the water?"

"Let's do it."

"So, what were you writing today?" she asked.

"My writing partner and I are working on a screenplay."

"Oh! I'm a writer, too," she said. "Is this a good spot to sit?"

"Sure."

They took turns explaining what they were writing. Stella glazed over the content of her stories, taking care not to allude that they were based on reality and that Dylan might later find himself a character. Luckily, he wasn't judging her protagonist; he was busy eating the pasta.

"This is delicious," he said. "You don't want any?"

"I already ate my share before I came, so that's all yours." She took a drink of the wine.

"This was a great idea," he said. "There is nothing more soothing than being near the ocean."

"I know," she said. "I love living here."

"How long have you been here?"

"Four years now. Whoa. It doesn't seem like that long. How about you?"

"Only seven months so far."

"How do you like it?" She looked down at her size-10 clodhoppers, huge next to his canvas sneakers in the sand. She hoped he didn't think she was a monster of a woman.

"I'm still getting used to it. I hate driving. And parking. I like the attitude around here, and obviously the surfing, but after living in New York for so long, I'm used to constant motion. There was just an *energy* there that I don't find here. Maybe I'm looking in the wrong places, but sometimes I feel like nothing is happening here."

"That's because you're in the Valley! Move to Santa Monica," she said. "You don't have to drive. I ride my bike everywhere. And there's always something going on."

He had finished all the pasta. "That was delicious," he said, putting the lid back on.

They kept talking about acting and art and surfing, their childhoods and daily lives, until the wine was gone and the cold breeze started blowing sand into their eyes. There were no what-do-you-do chats about jobs, no painful lulls, and the more they talked, the more Stella was attracted to him. But she couldn't read his intentions the way she could with most guys. He hadn't said one inappropriate thing. He wasn't touching her or overtly flirting. He was just sharing his thoughts and then listening to hers with disarming courtesy. She was elated to realize that she had not once been duped into discussing the shit tsunami of her recent past. The present seemed to be all that mattered, and the future sat calmly on the ocean's horizon under the night sky.

"I can't believe it, but I'm getting kind of cold," he said.

"Me too," she said.

"Do you want to take this elsewhere?"

"I actually have a hot tub at my apartment. It's really nice."

"Hot tub sounds great," he said.

"Cool, want to just follow me back?"

Dylan pulled into the garage behind her and parked.

"Right this way," she said, leading him toward the elevator.

"Damn, I just remembered I have that road rash all over my leg. It's pretty gnarly," he said. "I feel really bad, but I don't think I can get in the hot tub."

"You did this on purpose, didn't you?" she teased.

"I did," he laughed.

"Well, do you want to just come up and watch a movie or something?"

"Sure," he said.

"Or—"

"What?"

"No..."

"What?"

"Well, just this week, I acquired some mara-joo-wana and it's in my car. What do you think about that?"

A mischievous look crept onto his face. "You wanna smoke some weed?"

"Do you?" she asked.

"I'm in."

"Okay. Let's get in my car."

Stella unlocked the doors and he got into the passenger seat. "Sorry it's so gross in here," she said, grazing his arm as she reached across him to retrieve the little purple pipe from the glove compartment.

"That's okay," he said. "The skunk smell will take over soon."

She laughed and offered him the first hit. "Hopefully," she said.

"I can't believe you got a wetsuit already." He exhaled a mouthful of smoke.

"Yeah, I told you I would," she said, inhaling a bowl full. "I'm used to being broke, but I've been working in this office since the first week of March, so I deserve a daggone wetsuit. I've been dying to start surfing since I moved here, so it's time."

"Well, we have definitely got to go out this weekend. Good waves."

Stella coughed, still clueless about where this all was going. She wasn't sure if it was a friends thing or if he was in fact interested in her. It was such a different feeling from last night's date with Mike.

Dylan was suddenly laughing like a ten-year-old, staring at the label of the little green bottle.

"What?" she said, now giggling for no reason, too.

"This is called 'Headband'," he snickered.

Stella erupted. Everything seemed absurd. "What the heck do you think that means?"

"It's like there's a band going on in your head," he chuckled. "Like a band of merry men. And they are all saying different things."

She howled. "What? You're silly!" Then she started coughing. "More like lung band," she said.

"Lung band."

"It bands your lungs."

The nugget was now ash, so they put the paraphernalia back in the glove compartment. "Okay," she said. "I don't know if my roommates are home, so if they are, don't worry about it. We can still watch a movie. But most likely we'll be alone."

"Anybody home?" she called, opening the door to 411. "Guess not."

This is *nice*," he said.

"I know!" she said. "Danny lives in that room, and Jeff lives in that room. Angie and I share *that* room, but she always stays at her boyfriend's place. Want some water or something?"

"Sure."

They nestled into the corner of the sectional and decided to watch *The Endless Summer* in order to "get stoked" for the weekend. Everything was side-splitting, especially the voice of the 1960's narrator and the unintentionally racist things he was saying about African surfers. Stella was very aware of the outside of her right thigh touching the outside of Dylan's left thigh. She wondered if he'd touch her, or if she would touch him, or if they'd just end up being friends.

"I'm taking these tights off. Sorry," she said, standing up and reaching under her skirt. "They are the most uncomfortable garment ever invented. Do you want to see my bruises from the massage? Look." She turned around and showed him the backs of her thighs.

"A masseuse did that?" he said.

"Yeah. A blind one! Like over a week ago."

"I can literally see his thumb prints," said Dylan.

"I know! It was so painful!" she said, and they started laughing again.

"Man, we're both pretty beat up. I can't even get my leg wet," he said. Stella sat back down beside him and propped her bare legs up on the coffee table. The wholesome-sounding narrator droned on in the background and they looked at each other. Suddenly, Dylan leaned in and boldly pressed his lips to hers.

Happiness surged through Stella. Soft and intense and perfect, the kiss evolved. Her arms were around him now and she felt all of the strength of his back. She ran her hands down his shoulders and arms, surprised at all the well-defined muscles he was keeping under there. She felt the overwhelming urge to be underneath him, the way she yearned to dive deep into the ocean on a scorching day. And then she was. Her back was on the couch, his weight blanketing her, their mouths exploring necks and ears and lips.

"Should we take this to your room?" he whispered.

"Sure," she said. She picked up her tights and shoes and led him to her room, locking the door and hoping Angie wouldn't return

They continued kissing, standing beside the closet. He was the perfect height for looking her directly in the eyes. As she pulled him close, running her hands down the length of his back and over his tight butt, she felt his erection press into her. She heard herself say, "I really want to fuck you." *Oh no.*

"I really want to fuck you too," he said. She was shocked to think back to three hours ago, talking to him on the beach, wondering what he thought of her. "Do you have a condom?" he asked.

"Yes," she said, unbuttoning her shirt and throwing it to the ground, fishing the condom out of a little tin box on her dresser and tossing it on the bed. She remembered a time when she wouldn't have been so confident, but now she knew and trusted her strong body. She had grown to appreciate the steep curves of her hips, her round little breasts, the muscles of her thighs.

Dylan pulled off his shirt, leaving Stella speechless. She touched the bare skin of his torso in disbelief. He felt like the sculptures of warrior gods she had slyly caressed in Rome during her study abroad when the museum guards had turned their heads. She felt like she was getting away with something.

He continued to kiss her, insistent and tender, unhooking her bra and unzipping her skirt, her creamy body yielding to his peanut butter hands. Reaching for his pants, she tried not to tremble, or to be haunted by all those past disappointments when she'd really liked a guy, only to reach this crucial apex and find a penis that was tiny, unkempt, or strangely shaped. But there was no turning back now.

She undid the button and pulled the zipper, her lips on his neck. He helped push the pants to the floor, and she gleefully grazed her palm over the substantial bulge beneath the thin layer of cotton. She slid her fingers beneath the waistband of his boxer-briefs and slipped them off, stepping back to get a look at the craftsmanship of this whole package, naked before her. His dick was beautiful. She wrapped her hand around its thickness, noting how perfectly it complemented his body.

He walked her backwards, laying her on the bed like he owned her. She was shocked at his authority—how quickly he dropped his politeness, climbed on top of her like a Harlequin hero. He left a trail of soft kisses down her neck, taking time with her nipples until she was nearly begging him to come inside. Without hesitation he began to lick her—he needed no coaching.

Although the marijuana might've been a contributing factor to getting them here, Stella now wished she was sober. It was taking forever for her to orgasm, and there was no way she was going to fake anything with this man. Instead, she grabbed his hair. It was coarse and thick and dark. She yanked it until she could see his eyes which were green-brown, pure, intoxicated and devious. She pulled him toward her and kissed his perfect lips again, pushed him onto his back and slid down his gorgeous body, taking his cock into her mouth. He smelled so good. She explored it all with kisses, finding the perfect angle to take every last inch down her throat, until finally he put on the condom and took back control, flipping her over, looking her in the eyes, and pressing the girth of himself into her so she squealed with satisfaction. Something about the shape and size of him produced the finest feeling Stella had ever experienced from penetration.

Time did not exist. Only pleasure and the sound of Stella's panting, like hurricane waves crashing against the shore.

She touched herself—"Do you mind?" "No"—and came after Dylan, who was still kissing her, still touching her where it mattered.

His skin glistened with sweat. She didn't want him to leave yet. She texted Angie to see if she was coming home tonight. She wasn't.

"Your body feels so good," Dylan said.

"So does yours," Stella said, pressing against him. He took her hand and closed his eyes.

"Maybe you should just stay," she said.

"Probably so," he said. He brought her hand up to his chest, put it over his heart, and fell asleep.

***

They were still entangled when his alarm went off at six a.m.

"Do you want me to make you some coffee?" she asked, taking care not to aim her morning breath near his face.

"No, stay here. You are so thoughtful. I'm playing tennis with a friend in a few hours, so I need to get back to the Valley and get my stuff together."

"Okay. Let me remind you how to get out of this building." She slipped on a robe and showed him out. "I'm glad you came over," she said with a hug.

"Me too," he said.

She watched him walk away, wondering if this rendezvous would prove to be a one night stand. If so, it had been the best she'd ever had. Dylan had ravished her like a professional and then held her all night like a boyfriend. She wouldn't soon forget him.

She fell easily back to sleep, beaming from within.

It was a calm Saturday and she had no desire to change out of her sweatpants. She and her roommates ignored all their invites and spent the afternoon like sitcom characters, sprawled on the couch, piling empty beer bottles on the coffee table. Danny was in the middle of telling a story about almost getting killed by a Canadian axe murderer when Stella got a text from Wil:

> Hey, do you know of a good restaurant in Santa Monica to take someone cool?

Mellow from the beer, she responded without thinking.

> Stella:
> Father's Office is pretty good if the person likes beer.

> Wil:
> Oh. She doesn't drink. What else?

He was obviously talking about Tyler the trust fund ho. Stella felt the alcohol turn sharp and she replied:

> I don't know. I'm actually getting on with my life, so I don't have time to plan your dates.

Thoughts percolated in the back of her mind as she finished her IPA. This leech had some kind of audacity. Not only was he blackening her name and ruining her credit with a stack of parking tickets he obviously didn't intend to pay; not only had he baited-and-switched her so she'd leave everything behind for him; not only was he using a car that was legally hers to take her former enemy on a date: he also had the nerve to ask her for a dinner recommendation?

When fury replaced her filter, she dialed the number now listed as "Piece of Shit," with a photo of some dog poo she'd almost stepped in. She wanted her money. She wanted the car transferred to his name. She wanted to wrestle her life back from the grip of his lies. She had a brief fantasy of Wil behind bars, sans his expensive hair gels and Tom Ford cologne, isolated in the corner of a cell.

Thank God he didn't pick up. Stella exercised a muscle she had only recently begun to develop—self control—and left a businesslike message demanding the car be transferred in the next month or else she would call the police to report it stolen.

＊＊

"You're all probably wondering what an Abundance Swap is," India was saying. She was surrounded by twelve people: some businessmen, some artistic-looking women with flowy skirts. Stella hadn't wanted to come, but the sky was desolate gray and her roommates were all gone. She'd come to escape the stillness. "I asked all of you to RSVP by letting me know which of these things you're abundant in: money or love."

Stella had replied with "love," but that was just by process of elimination. She was certainly not abundant in finances. She was the only one in this group who hadn't even ordered a drink: she didn't have an extra ten bucks.

While India was talking, Stella got a text from Tessa:

Hey Stel, I saw Andrew last night. He was at the same restaurant as me, eating with an older lady and her family. I waved, but he pretended not to see me. It was really awkward.

Stella knew it had been Janice and the family that she used to consider her own. She was glad Andrew still had their love, but now she was sure that Janice had picked a side. Stella was the enemy.

"Now, you guys are going to pair off," India said. "Those who are abundant in love, pair with someone who is abundant in the money realm. Tell each other what you're grateful for and how you feel that you arrived at this place. We will reconvene in fifteen minutes to talk about what we've learned."

Stella was paired with an older Indian man named Ravi. He scooted close to her, smiling, imploring her to tell the story of how she became abundant in love. "I need to find a partner to share in my wealth. What is your secret?" he asked.

Stella opened her mouth to tell him. "I guess I'm just honest," she began to say. "I really don't hold back who I am." But then her words got strangled in her throat. "And that's always worked," she managed to choke out. But she was drowning. She put her fingers under her eyes to stop the tears before they fell. What a sham she was. "Honestly, right now I am not abundant in love. Five months ago, I had two men in my life who would do anything for me. Now I'm not even friends with them online. Love is at a low. I have my family back home, and I have friends. But I'm alone right now." She looked in Ravi's eyes and felt guilty for unloading on him.

Ravi assured her she was on the right track. She listened to the financially abundant of the group tell her to keep struggling and follow her dreams until she eventually got paid for it, then she hugged India goodbye and left early.

She drove home knowing she was the only one who could pull herself out of the doldrums. This week, she would focus on her writing. She would not speak to Wil unless it was to collect the money he owed her. She would—*kthunk kthunk.*

The Corolla was slowing, wobbling. Flat tire.

Stella pulled over a few blocks shy of her apartment, aloneness wrapped around her like a fur coat. No one had taught her to change a tire, but she'd seen it done. She opened the trunk and found the spare and the jack kit. Just to make sure, she watched a video on her phone called "How to Change a Flat," then jacked up the car.

As she was tightening the lugnuts, some of her neighbors, a glamorously laid-back movie-producing couple, drove by. Stella waved, hands black with oil.

"Are you changing a tire, Stella?" the lady asked, laughing from the passenger window.

"Yep," she said.

"Hot." The lady took a photo.

***

At 7:30 in the morning, she was waiting for the mechanics to replace her donut with a new tire before work. She'd dreamed she had been following Wil around, saying, "How could you have been so in love with me before and suddenly you just stopped?" But when he started to answer, she looked at him and saw that he was sloppy obese. Suddenly she didn't care what he felt about her. She felt liberated, if a little disappointed at how shallow this might make her.

The car still wasn't ready at 8:35, so she called Chet.

"You need to get here as soon as possible. We have work to do," Chet said.

"They're still not finished. I'll get there as soon as I can."

She made it to work by 9, pretended to be sorry, and feigned being very busy until lunch time, when she walked to Rainbow Acres and got a salad. Wil texted.

I miss you.

Stella took a bite of salad.

Wil:
I miss your friendship. I wish we would have taken it really slow.

She took a gulp of iced coffee.

Wil:
I'm sorry for everything I did to hurt our relationship. I hope you find someone who loves you as much as I do, but better than I did.

She thought of obese Wil from her dream and felt nothing.

***

All day at work, Stella had anticipated her surf date with Dylan. On her way out the door, the phone rang. It was Paul.

129

"Stella! How's it going?"

"Great! How are you? Are you back in town?"

"I am. I got back last night."

"How was Texas?"

"It was good," he said. "I mean, part of it was sad."

"Yeah."

"But I got to spend time with family, so—"

"That's good."

"Anyway, I'm sorry I'm such a flake," he said.

"You are definitely not a flake. You were at a funeral."

"Okay, but I want to make it up to you. I don't know my schedule yet for next week, but can I call you on Monday and we can finally make some plans?"

"Sure. Sounds good!"

Dylan had told her to meet him on a side street in Venice. She saw his silver Prius pulling up just as she was parking. She walked toward him, wetsuit in hand, trying to keep her feet on the ground. Two surfboards split the center of his front seats, obscuring him from view until she walked around to the driver's side.

"Hey!" she said when she saw his friendly face.

"Hey! Did you just get here?"

"Yep."

"Hop in," he said. "Sorry these boards are in the way."

"That's okay," she said. "It adds to the mystery."

Bobbing along on crests of conversation, they barely noticed when Dylan got a little lost driving south toward the spot.

"Okay," he said, finally pulling into the parking lot at El Porto. "Are you ready?"

"Ready!" she said.

She watched him wrap a towel around his waist and take off his shorts. Knowing he was technically naked five feet away was exciting, though last week's escapade seemed like a fairy tale. *Had it really happened?* Stella followed his lead, stripping to her bikini and grappling with the leg-holes of her wetsuit.

"Do the booties go over or under?"

"Under," he said. "That way it keeps the water out. Do you want to wax your board?"

"Sure," she said.

He unearthed the seven-foot board from his car's hatchback and placed it on the ground before her, kneeling to show her what to do. "You just rub it in circles like this," he said, handing Stella the square of pineapple-smelling wax.

She scoured the surface of the surfboard with the little wax-cake. "Like this?"

"Just like that. So you don't slip off," Dylan said.

"I know this is dumb, but would you take a picture of me?" she asked. "I think this is going to be the beginning of something that's going to last." She arranged her neoprene-slicked body in a photogenic fashion by the board.

"Sure," he said, grabbing his phone from the car.

"I think we should just take the one board out this time," he said. "That way I can really pay attention to you and show you what to do."

They walked down the beach path together, through the sand toward the water, where they were the only two people. He showed Stella how to paddle with her fingers stuck together for maximum speed and how to turtle under waves. He swam beside her until they were next to the end of a rocky breakwater and showed her how to sit on the board and eggbeater it around when she saw a good wave coming.

Since it was her first time, Dylan had her face the shore belly-down while he looked out for the oncoming waves. "Okay, now paddle! Paddle hard!" he would yell, but Stella felt like she was just thrashing and getting nowhere.

"How do you know when the wave is coming?" she asked.

"You just learn what to look for after a while," he said. "Want me to push you a couple times, just so you can feel the stoke?" he asked.

She felt stupid, but said, "sure."

"Okay," he said, "Here comes one. Are you ready?"

"Yep."

"Paddle!" He gave the board a push just as the wave came, and off she sailed, flying in Superman position as if propelled by a motor. She smiled into the spray of salty water, then, when the ride was over, maneuvered around toward the horizon and laboriously made her way back to Dylan.

"Did you feel it?" he asked excitedly.

"Yes!"

"Are you stoked?"

"Yes! But I'm going to need a lot more practice!"

"Learning to catch the wave is probably one of the hardest things," he said. "But it's worth it."

Stella said, "Do you want to take the board for a little? I feel bad that you're not getting to surf!"

"I don't have to. I'm here for you," he said.

"After all that paddling, I might need a little rest," she said.

"Okay. I'll take it once."

She pulled the Velcro strap off her ankle and he transferred it to his. He had no sooner mounted the board than he was on his feet, swerving off toward the Southbay atop the rolling whitewater.

As he paddled back toward Stella, she swelled with gratitude. Evening had arrived, the water was glassy, and the sky was turning pink. The sun was sinking over the rocks and into Dylan's eyes, making them glow amber against his wet, tan face. She found him so beautiful at that moment; she had the urge to kiss him but wasn't sure where she stood. What if last week's date had been an inebriated fluke, and he only took her surfing because he felt bad that she'd already bought a wetsuit? She kept her distance just in case he only wanted to be friends.

"Did you see that?" he said.

"Yeah, that was awesome!"

"If you keep coming out with me, you'll be catching them yourself in no time," he said, giving her back the board. So he *wanted* to keep surfing with her? "You want to take one more in and call it a day? If we stay much longer, we'll be shark food."

"Sounds good," she said, and accepted another push from Dylan, which sent her sliding blithely back toward land.

"Are you hungry?" he asked as they walked back to his car.

"Pretty much starving."

"You know what would be really good after that?" he said. "Some pasta."

"Mmm," she said. "Do you want to go somewhere?"

"Why don't we go to the grocery store and then make something back at your place?"

"Okay!" Stella had never known anyone to suggest grocery shopping and cooking together on a second date. She loved the boldness of the gesture, not to mention how he had just assumed that coming to her place was okay.

"How is that road rash?"

"It's actually healed," Dylan said as Stella opened the door to her apartment.

"Danny, you're alive!" she said. "Danny is always working. This is Dylan. We just got back from surfing."

"Nice to meet you, man." Dylan shook his hand.

"You too. Surfing! You guys getting in the hot tub?" Danny asked.

"Do you want to?" she asked Dylan.

"I could go for some hot tub action," he said. He talked with Danny a while about surfing and composing music before Danny returned to his room to get back to work.

"We can't take glass down to the hot tub," she said, opening the wine they'd just bought, "but we can take these paper coffee cups." They took grocery-store baked Alaska down too, and ate dessert first. As they eased into the hot water, Dylan sidled up next to Stella and put his arm around her. Her desire to kiss him grew strong again, but for some reason, she felt she had to leave it up to him, which was new for her. They relaxed. Dylan took her feet in his hands and massaged them. His perfection seemed too good to be true.

"Let's go make dinner," he said, and they went back upstairs where they cooked together. Dylan found her keyboard and spent fifteen minutes relearning Chopin's Nocturne, which he played while Stella put the food on the table.

After dinner he said, "We really need to take a shower and get rid of this chlorine."

"Okay." She showed him to her bathroom. While she was explaining the water pressure, Dylan kissed her at last. They stripped each other and got into the shower, where he pressed her against the wall as the water cascaded over their skin.

***

Upon waking and discovering Dylan's body pressed up against her own, Stella's heartbeat gained speed. He had given her a back massage before bed, then kept her close through the night. She gently climbed over him to make breakfast.

The polished crystal world gleamed outside the balcony window as she made coffee, eggs and toast. Angie was still at her boyfriend's house and Jeff was gone on some trip. Danny was holed up in his room, most likely still asleep, so the apartment seemed grand and luxurious.

"Good morning," Dylan said, emerging. "You're making breakfast?"

They sat on the terrace beside the avocado tree, new lovers waking up together on a lazy weekend. He thanked her for breakfast, gave her a little kiss, and soon was on his way back to the Valley. Once the door shut behind him, she cartwheeled around the room in geeky silence. She wondered how long she'd have to wait to see him again.

When he was gone, Stella realized it was national pothead day— 4-20—and for the first time ever, she actually had celebration supplies. She put on a swimsuit and a dress, grabbed a backpack and stashed her little pipe, went downstairs and jumped on her bike, then rode all the way down to Venice, on the bike path past the skaters catching air, past the vendors selling colorful Mexican skulls. She staked out a spot on the beach and took a couple puffs right out in the open, then lay back and stared at the waves. Time stopped and her mind filled with warm atmosphere.

A while later she saw she'd missed a couple calls from Dustin, a successful and handsome doctor she'd gone to college with, who was in town for the weekend and wanted to catch up. She'd said she would meet him later, but figured she'd take her time. After a little more meditative sitting, She got on her bike and her phone rang again. *Man, Dustin was determined.* She pulled over to one of the grassy knolls and extracted her phone from the backpack. *It couldn't be!*

"Hel-looo?" she said.

"Hey Stella. It's Dylan."

"Hey!"

"I just got back from playing tennis, and I know we hadn't made any plans, but I was thinking, you've been doing a lot of cooking for me, and I just feel like I should repay you. I was actually invited to two parties tonight, but I'd rather cook for you. Do you already have plans?"

A hive of bees was trying to make its way out of her stomach. "Yes! I mean, well, I'll have to blow off someone too, but I would love to! I'm just hanging out in Venice, so I'll have to ride my bike home and de-skankify myself...but what time are you thinking?"

"Maybe six?"

"Yes. I'll be there. Can you text me the address?"

"I can. See you soon! Do you have any food allergies or preferences?"

"I'll eat anything."

She called Dustin back when she got home. "Hey you! I am so sorry I didn't get back to you sooner. I was at the beach riding my bike."

"So when are we going to hang out? And are you inviting your lady friends from the hot girl group?"

"Okay. I am a total jerk and you're welcome to hate my guts...but, first of all, I tried getting the girls together and all of them have stuff they're doing already, so that's out. And then there's me. I really wanted to say hi, but the thing is, there's this guy that I am pretty sure I might be falling for, and he offered to cook me dinner tonight."

"Oh."

"If you never want to talk to me again, I totally understand."

"Stella! I absolutely want to see you. Stop by on your way to your new maybe-boyfriend's house. Does this mean we can't hook up while I'm here?"

"Oh, that was your plan?"

"Well, I've been looking at pictures of you on Facebook since we graduated, and..." he laughed so Stella couldn't tell if he was joking.

She laughed. "Well, if you had gotten here about a month ago, it might have been different, but yeah, something happened this weekend that is making me, like, not want to hump anyone else. I think you missed the boat."

"Damn. Well come stop by and say hi anyway."

"Okay."

She stopped long enough to be polite with Dustin, then she sped off, slightly anxious in her little cutout dress.

She parked outside the house on the corner, and Dylan's Spartan silhouette emerged shirtless from the back door. He hugged her and took her inside, to the kitchen where the smell of garlic and onions mingled with the sound of Jack Johnson's acoustic surf guitar. Dylan sang along as he chopped and sautéed vegetables.

He sat her down in a chair with a glass of wine. "I hope you like apple crisp," he said. "Because I'm making it for dessert. My mother's recipe."

Stella felt like she might break open. *Was it real?*

After the apple crisp, they went for a walk. The stars were bright. As Stella pointed out Orion, Dylan pulled her in and kissed her.

She felt her back hit the wooden fence. "I love this dress," Dylan said as he ran his fingertips over the cutouts on her ribs. Stella's stomach was full of nourishing, delicious food, her skin was tingling from the night breeze and Dylan's firm grasp on the small of her back. Her heart rocketed above it all. She felt all his outlines, her body wilting in his grasp. Finally, he took her hand and led her into his room. By the end of it, her entire body was shaking. They lay entwined and, for some reason, started telling ghost stories.

"We're so sweaty," Dylan said after a while. "Do you want to take a shower?"

"Sure," she said, and he gave her a robe to wear through the house. The bathroom was through the living room, by his roommates' bedrooms. Stella felt like an intruder, but that wasn't a concern right now, because right now they were shampooing their hair and then brushing their teeth together, taking out their contacts and putting their glasses on.

They went back to bed scrubbed and fresh, and though they tried to sleep, they couldn't stop talking. Until two in the morning they talked about everything. Everything except Stella's recent past.

***

Stella woke up lighthearted with the sun in her eyes. *It couldn't be, so soon.* But it was. "You stay right here," Dylan said, and then returned with a glass mug of cappuccino for her, the foam garnished with cinnamon.

"Oh my goodness," she said, covering her mouth with the sheet. Just three weeks ago she'd doubted she would ever feel this again. She took a sip. She would keep it to herself, of course. She'd take it slow. She knew she was a gamble, but wasn't everyone?

She got her things together—she wore home his shirt and

shorts so she didn't have to put the dress back on—and kissed him goodbye.

***

On her way to work, Stella put down the sun visor, and there in the vanity mirror she saw it: the first sunburn of the season, a rose glow across the top of her nose and cheeks. She often put too much stock in symbols and signs, but she really felt it: the winter of her discontent was officially over. Many frowned upon sunburns, but Stella was ruled by the sun, and for her there was no better feeling than getting a little too close to the intense, crazy fire, only to sooth herself by wading into the cool understanding of the ocean.

She knew there were still pockets of tears hidden in her deepest tissues, and that she'd eventually leak them all out and feel so much lighter. She knew there would come a day when she would fully forgive herself, when she'd look at the darkness, say "thank you" for what it gave her, and then release it. But for now it was nice to look into a mirror and see someone who she knew was doing her best. She was proud of all the work she'd done, and now it was starting to show on the outside.

Around lunchtime, Paul called as promised.

"So I'm kinda booked until next Thursday. Are you available?"

"Sure," Stella said, wondering if she should have said no, as she had not yet defined her relationship *(was it a relationship?)* with Dylan.

"Okay. We'll get some awesome food. Have you been to the Misfit?"

"That's one of my favorites!" Surely she could keep it casual with Paul. They could just get drunk and talk, like friends do.

"Really? I haven't tried it yet, but I want to."

"Let's do. You'll love it."

"Okay. I'll pick you up at 7?"

"Sure. Or if you want I could just ride my bike down and meet you there." Stella liked to have an escape route.

"Aw, no. I wouldn't be a gentleman if I allowed that."

"Okay. Pick me up at 7 on Thursday."

"Excellent. I can't wait," he said.

That was when Dylan texted:

I went surfing with my cousin yesterday after you left, and I got stung by a stingray and had to go to Urgent Care.

Stella:
Oh my gosh! Do you need anything?

Dylan:
I think I'll be okay. But some company might help ease the pain.

Stella:
That I can do! Do you want me to bring a movie and we can just be lazy?

Dylan:
That sounds great!

Stella spent the last of her time at work drawing a cartoon stingray with a halo around its head and a speech bubble that said "I'm sorry, Dylan! I didn't mean to hurt you!" to send to him.

***

Dylan was wreaking havoc on Stella's sleep schedule. She was exhausted after another night of ecstasy in his bed, but she had promised her friend Serena she'd go to a concert with her at the Fonda, and she already had the tickets.

She rallied after work and dragged herself to Hollywood. On the way she got a text. The *bloop bloop* of her phone echoed in her ear like a screaming child when she saw it was from Wil.

I can't believe you're threatening me with reporting the car stolen and you won't even answer my emails. I can't get the license until I fill out all these papers to get medical clearance. Obviously I would if I could.

Bloop bloop.

Wil:
You need to get off my back about this. You're the one who broke my heart here.

Bloop bloop.

Wil:
Anyway, you can't take the car back. I've been paying for it and I have proof of that. I can easily get a lawyer and sue you for leaving me stuck with the rent, since you broke the lease when you moved out.

Bloop bloop.
Bloop bloop.
Bloop bloop.

Bloopbloopbloopbloopbloopbloopbloop. 18 texts later, Stella's rage was building. Without reading them, she parked, called Wil, and walked down Hollywood Boulevard.

"What the fuck are you doing, texting me an encyclopedia? It's simple, okay? I want you completely out of my life. I don't even want to know you exist. I want this car situation taken care of immediately, so I can delete your number from my phone once and for all and you can go take your misery elsewhere."

"Oh yeah?" Wil said, pretending to be calm. "Are you sure you're not just jealous because I'm dating Tyler?"

"I don't give a fuck who you date; I just want every last tie I have with you to be cut."

"You don't give a fuck, huh? Well that makes sense since you're the one who cheated on me!"

"You are utterly delusional! This is exactly why I couldn't take another day of being around you!"

"Hold on a minute. Just hold on. I'll be right back."

She held.

"Okay, sorry. So what were you saying?"

"What I'm *saying* is, if you're not going to cooperate with me, I'm going to have to use force to extricate myself from you. I don't want anything else to do with you. So your time is running out. If I have to take the car from you and sell it, I will."

"You obviously don't know how things work. I have lawyers who can take you for everything you're worth," he said.

"What the fuck are you talking about, you dipshit? *You're* the one who has *my* car and owes me hundreds of dollars for parking tickets you've incurred! I left you because you are the most irresponsible, lying sack of shit I've ever met and you were making my life hell!"

Wil broke into slow laughter which soon turned maniacal. "Ha! Did you hear that, Mom? Did you hear how she talks to me?!"

"Well, I think you're both being ugly right now." It was Judy's voice. Stella stopped outside the front stoop of the Roosevelt where she and Serena were supposed to have a burger before the show.

"You have got to be kidding me," Stella said.

"Mom, you will never believe what Stella is doing to me. She is trying to blackmail me. And Stella, I have it recorded, too, so you can't deny anything you said."

"I can't believe this. I have to go, and I don't want to hear from you again unless it's to give me the money you owe me or to transfer the car's title to your name. And don't even bother texting me. I'm not reading any of that shit." She hung up, took a breath, and walked inside with a smile on her face, sitting down at a booth with Serena.

"What the hell is that nut's problem?" Serena said, once Stella had debriefed her. As Serena continued to express her befuddlement, Stella pictured Wil back in the hospital. She saw his black, heroin-addled heart finally give up. She imagined him falling into the darkness of death, never to take advantage of another person.

***

It was raining in L.A. and Stella was sick all the way around. Her throat was a swollen red mess, her nose was somehow both runny and stopped up. Her head felt like a blow-up doll that had just gotten fucked. Fatigue conquered her, and her problems were still around, only harder to trudge through.

Chet actually said a couple sensitive things like "I know you're sick, so just do the best you can on this one," but he also said insensitive things like, "Are you sick, or are you high? Did you not see this third line?" and he still expected Stella to stay at work for the whole day.

By 5:30 she plodded home, focusing on the bed that awaited. Just as she reached her resting place, Dylan messaged her.

How you doin' today, Darlin' from Harlan? (I made that up.)

It was the first time she had smiled all day.

Stella:
Hi!!! Sadly, I feel like a turd on a fork. I'm in bed. So sick.

Dylan:
Who is going to bring you chicken soup?

Stella:
Nobody, I guess.

Dylan:
That won't do! I'll be there as soon as I can.

Was he serious? He was going to come from the Valley during rush hour just to bring her chicken soup?

An hour-and-a-half later, he woke Stella up, carrying two grocery bags.

"Don't catch this nasty bug," she whispered when he hugged her, though his embrace already made her feel stronger. She didn't question her good fortune by asking why he was wearing board-shorts and no shirt. "Whatcha got there?" It took everything in her to eke out the speech.

"All the ingredients for some homemade chicken noodle soup."

"You're going to make it from scratch? I thought you were just going to heat me up some Campbell's."

"No way. You need something made with love," he said. "That's where the healing comes from."

"Thank you so much. You have just given me a reason to live." She went soggy-sentimental. She felt weak at the moment, but she knew otherwise. Her trust in herself, her openness, her inner voice had led her here. If she could manifest a kind, attractive man cooking in her kitchen, she wondered what other surprises life had in store.

"You get back in bed and I'll bring it to you when it's done."

She awoke again when he came to her bedside and whispered, "It's ready," tenderly touching her arm. The soup was warm and nourishing. "I'm sorry I'm not good company," she sighed.

"That's okay." He tucked her in and then lay down beside her. He stayed, with his arm around her, until she fell asleep.

***

The hit-by-a-bus ache still throbbed throughout Stella's body through another day at work. Come evening she was welcomed home by an envelope from Toyota Financial, stamped PAST DUE. She ripped it open, hoping impossibly that it might be a mix-up.

Dear Ms. Robertson,
As of today, your account is past due by $1,202.03. If you have already sent your payment

Her forehead, already hot with fever, became an ignited firecracker. What an idiot she'd been to think the parking tickets were all that Wil owed. Of course he hadn't paid the car payment for the last three months. She collapsed into a fetal position. Even if she had someone to talk to, her voice box was wrapped in barbed wire. Everything was too much.

She sent a Wil an email with the subject "WHAT THE FUCK? YOU'RE NOT PAYING THE CAR PAYMENTS." She put the envelope along with the parking ticket notices under the stack of books on her dresser. She slipped on a bikini and padded down to the hot tub, sat pressed against stinging jets until she felt like a chewed piece of gum that had melted on a hot sidewalk, and then she went to bed without dinner as darkness descended.

***

Wil replied to Stella's email, saying he had a payment plan with Toyota, and that his mom was going to co-sign for the car in a couple months once she finished paying off *her* car. Stella, on her period, still getting over her sickness, and saddled with two overdrawn bank accounts, didn't have the energy to argue. Judy seemed to be a decently respectable woman; maybe she would help him figure this out before it had to get more complicated.

Online, she read about a woman whose ex was ruining her credit, but the woman couldn't report her car as stolen since she had willingly allowed him to borrow it when they were together. The police had shrugged it off as "a civil matter" and the woman was stuck with no car, paying all her ex's bills.

Stella felt like someone had handcuffed her to the bottom of a pool. She regretted searching for worst case scenarios. Was she going to be living in half a room forever, slaving away for Chet, to pay for a car whose location she didn't even know? Or would she have to file bankruptcy, move back to her parents' house, and give up on every dream she had?

She retreated to her usual stall in the cryroom (a more apt name than *bathroom*, she figured), hoping the tears might solidify and become a shield from the endless crossfire of problems. When she returned to her desk, a Motown crooner on the radio was singing, "I love you," over and over. She went numb to think that just months ago, she had given all her power away just to feel tingles in her limbs when she heard a song like this.

It was Friday evening, but Stella headed straight to bed.
Bloop bloop. What now?

Dylan:
Are you feeling better, darlin'?

Stella:
A little. I think tonight is the last of it. I'm hoping I'll be fine by tomorrow.

Dylan:
If you do feel better, would you want to come surfing tomorrow with my cousin and his girlfriend?

She didn't even have to think.

Stella:
Definitely.

***

Gasping, Stella emerged from the spin cycle when she finally figured out which direction was up. She thrashed back onto the board and paddled out again, the ocean smacking her in the face.

"You're actually catching waves today!" Dylan said, floating on his stomach so she could ogle his slick little wetsuited butt.

"Yeah, I'm surprised," said his cousin James.

"I guess you guys aren't able to see what's happening *after* I catch the waves." Her hoarse throat stung from the saltwater, but otherwise, a stuffy nose was all that remained of her flu.

It was a breezy, bright Saturday morning in Hermosa Beach. "This is the perfect way to spend a morning," Dylan said with a contented sigh.

"Yeah. I haven't felt this good...since the last time I saw you, I guess."

He made his way over to Stella, pulled her board next to his, and kissed her, producing a rush greater than getting thrown off a wave. But their first date was only two weeks ago. Stella thought of Paul and the date they'd scheduled on Thursday. She wondered again if she should cancel.

"Too bad you have to babysit," Dylan said as they walked to her car. "Otherwise we could go to lunch. Do you want to keep the board so you can use it when you want to this week?"

"Really? Sure."

He helped her fit it into her car.

"Thank you so much," she said, kissing him goodbye.

At the Duchamps' house, Kara and Evan wanted to watch *Bridesmaids* and eat brownie batter, which Stella thought was a fine idea. Her phone kept *bloop*ing with messages to remind her of her overdrafted bank accounts. The 80 bucks of babysitting money would have to hold her over until Tuesday. She still owed Danny the remainder of the move-in deposit. And now there was the car situation: thousands of dollars she owed because of Wil. Their parents got home at midnight. Before Stella headed home, Dylan texted to ask if she wanted to sleep over.

Before long, she was underneath him in his bed, her body pulsing with electric current. She felt like she'd just seen God.

In the afterglow they touched and played their favorite sad songs for each other. Stella's current favorite was "February Seven" by the Avett Brothers. She must have looked torn up, because Dylan asked, "Does this have special significance for you?" That's when she knew it was time to tell him.

"The story of this song reminds me of what happened right before I met you," she said.

"What was that?"

"Well, I left something good in pursuit of something more, and everything exploded. My whole life fell through. I stomped all over the heart of someone I really love. And I still feel guilty about it."

He listened with understanding as Stella told him the whole story. "But the thing is, Andrew wasn't just a boyfriend."

"Were you *married*?"

She was afraid, but she just said it. "We still are, technically."

"Oh," Dylan said. But he didn't look afraid. He just pulled her in closer.

***

"Would you wanna go to brunch with my friends from high school?"

"Of course," Stella said, too freshly awake to worry about how she would pay for it or if they would like her.

It was hot and Giana and Jacob were as bubbly as the bottomless mimosas they drank. They laughed approvingly at everything Stella said. Dylan sat beside Stella and smiled like he was proud to be with her. She felt like half of a *we* for the first time in a while.

They left in a fizzy dream, and Dylan held her hand as they looked for a park. Up and down hilly neighborhoods they walked in perfect stride. He smelled like coconuts, though by now she knew he tasted like ocean. The park they found was filled with Mexican families grilling, boys playing basketball, little sisters in hammocks and on swings. They found a perfect California Sycamore and lay down under it. The sun shone through its leaves, painting them with glowing amber. His eyes would have been that color, too, Stella thought; but they both had sunglasses on.

She loved the smell of the grass and the feel of his skin, like a ribbon tied around her arm. They were still, and must have looked to the birds like they were cut out of limestone. He usually laughed when Stella took pictures of half-eaten brunch, in hot tubs, and of scenery. She had spent her life trying to capture moments in mason jars, but she didn't have that impulse here, under this tree.

She closed her eyes and let the sounds wash over her: inflated rubber bouncing on concrete, people laughing, and the most terrible club pop bomping out of a nearby stereo. That awful music was a welcome and appropriate sound; Stella couldn't stop smiling as it clicked everything else into place with its cheesy echo.

This was one of those rare instances of perfection that most people wait to notice until after it has passed. But Stella noticed it as it happened this time and was rewarded with the simplest satisfaction. She felt endless.

I am happy, she realized under that tree. And then she was so happy to find herself so happy and not whimpering in the cryroom stall, that two tears leaked toward the grass from behind her cat-eye sunglasses.

"This is the kind of feeling you can't capture with Instagram," Dylan said, as if he had found something, too. He wiped away Stella's two tears with his finger. It was one of those easy-Sunday, simultaneous-orgasm, love-is-all-around, full-belly, wish-granted moments that she would never dare ask for, nor attempt to define.

They held on to it until it passed—and then they left the park.

***

Stella sat at TV partners daydreaming about Dylan and what fun they would have this weekend at Tessa's beach bonfire birthday party. She'd invited him a soon as she had found out, and he'd promised to be her date. All the Ladidahs were excited to meet him.

That's when she realized something: Tessa was friends with Paul. Paul would be at Tessa's party. And Stella still had a date planned this Thursday with Paul. She really liked him, but she was getting so close with Dylan, and to have the two suitors at the same party could be a disaster. Stella sent Tessa a Facebook message to ask her advice on the situation. Tessa replied:

> Wow. Okay, what you have going on with Dylan seems exceptional. Your dates sound amazing. HE sounds amazing. I think it's wonderful to hear that you are feeling something again—and that feeling is admiration, awe, love, even. I also really like hearing how he's treating you. It's like you said—he has the tenderness and care of someone like Andrew and is passionate and romantic as Wil, but he's void of their downfalls. You will eventually learn that Dylan, too, has downfalls—everyone does—but they are quite possibly not as extreme as Andrew's or Wil's, or maybe it will simply be that you won't see his downfalls as anything he's lacking, but beautiful flaws that somehow puzzle piece into your life so they ironically fill out all the spaces they were meant to fill. Regardless, this is exactly where it should be right now, a few weeks in...exhilarating, passionate, wildly romantic.

> Here are my thoughts in regards to Paul. I'm assuming that you're pretty sure Dylan isn't dating anyone else. Going off of that, I totally understand your hesitation to go out with Paul. Does it basically come down to you feeling guilty about dating someone else in addition to Dylan because he is showing you loyalty and exclusivity (even though that hasn't been discussed)?

> I think it's completely fair game to date as many people as you want to until someone tells you they want to be exclusive and

you agree to that. However, I think that naturally relationships build to a point of romance and intimacy where it simply feels weird to date others OR you feel yourself WANTING to only see one person (which is how you felt with Wil). You're not doing anything wrong by dating multiple people, it's just a matter of what you FEEL you want to do.

As for Paul, he's a super cool guy—one that really doesn't hold grudges, and I can honestly say that in either case, he'd handle the situation well. If you decide to cancel on him and you show up with Dylan at my birthday party, Paul will still be super nice, cool, and not offended and will probably be happy to hang out with you AND Dylan. You really can't go wrong with Paul—he's such a cool, mellow guy. So don't worry about the birthday party situation.

Basically, it comes down to this: Who would you rather see on Thursday...regardless of the reason...?

***

Stella's paycheck was late again and she was still overdrawn. She was beginning to look back fondly on those days of scrambling for gigs; she had been just as broke, but at least there had been some variety in life.

She fortified herself and peeked in Chet's office. He was wearing a perfectly pressed fuchsia shirt. She tiptoed in with a knock. "Hey Chet," she mustered. "Correct me if I'm wrong, but wasn't today supposed to be payday?"

He looked at her like she'd just made a joke whose punch line he was trying to understand. "It's supposed to be the first and the fifteenth, so that's tomorrow."

"Hmm. You had told me every two weeks. The first is when my rent is due, so I would need to deposit the money today in order to pay it. My account has been overdrawn since last week, so it's kind of pressing."

He hastily clicked his ergonomic PC mouse as if Stella was wasting his valuable time, then said, "Alright. I'll see what I can do."

"Thanks," she said.

"Do you think it's hot in here?" he said.

She was wearing a sweater and a peacoat. "Nope," she said, returning to her desk. "I'm okay."

MAY

The quarterly advertising calendar took the place of a window above Stella's desk. Beneath "MAY" in bold letters, an infinity of boxes were lined up: four-cornered days exactly like this one, adding up to meaningless rows of rectangular weeks—forty hours at a time, thrown in the office shredder. The "quarters" of her year no longer meant anything, the way they did when they were called semesters, cut with vacations. She scanned the numbered boxes for the next holiday. Mother's day was coming up. *What if...*but no; she couldn't.

She envisioned the faraway comfort of Kentucky: the quiet wilderness of the backyard, the smell of cinnamon bun candles and casseroles baking, the sound of the two dogs' claws tapping around on the hardwood, the soft reprieve of a hug from her mother. Struggling to swim amid the wreckage of her life, she hadn't seen her family in over a year.

Just for dreams' sake, she searched online for a direct flight. Four-hundred-and-fifty bucks round trip.

She called Everly. "What if I came home and surprised Mom for mother's day?"

"What? You would come home? Like in a week? Yes!"

"I'm thinking about it."

"I would help you pay for the ticket," she said.

"Naw," Stella said, thinking about the thousands of dollars Wil had cost her. What was another couple hundred?

"Yes! How much is it?" said Everly.

"Four-fifty."

"I'll pay for half of it. I don't mind." Everly was a teacher. She didn't take many risks.

"I don't know if I could get off work, but to tell you the truth, I really don't care if I get fired. Maybe I'll just *tell* Chet instead of ask. It might actually make him respect me more. You would have to help me with the surprise part, though."

"Okay. I think it might cheer Dad up, too. He's pretty sad about Terry." Their dad's cousin, who they hadn't known very well, had died of cancer this week.

"Okay. I'm going to order it," Stella said.

"Let me know the details," said Everly.

Instead of going home after work, Stella parked by the beach. She wiggled into her wetsuit and pulled Dylan's surfboard out of her car, walking toward the break to brave the water alone. She paddled quickly past the choppy waves. Her shoulders were getting stronger. She sailed in on a few, not really minding that she couldn't yet stand up. As she walked back to her car, hair dripping in the sunshine, she felt free and cool, like the dust of the day had been rinsed away.

Her head was on the pillow when Dylan texted.

I miss you already.

***

Paul was spiffed up in a suit. "Well, you look lovely," he said, opening the passenger door for Stella and commencing to picking out the tunes. They spoke spiritedly, adjectives flowing. Paul blasted some tasteful underground rap and drew attention to the finer points of the songs. "Listen to this lyric coming up," he'd say, then sing along.

They parked and walked. They laughed and talked. But they didn't hold hands and stride harmoniously together. They stood by the bar, drinking cocktails while Stella got jostled by the shoulders of polished hipsters on their way to and from the bathroom. Paul regaled Stella with his whiskey knowledge. They sat down and discussed their love of writing and authors that moved them. They ordered chorizo mussels and maple brussels sprouts and buttermilk-fried chicken. Restaurant noise clanged about them and they moved with it, never stopping to look for the quiet of a moment. They didn't gaze longingly or delve deep. They drank until they blended warmly with their surroundings.

"I hate to be a loser, but I'm falling asleep here," Stella said as he drove her home. She was drunk.

"I don't think I've gotten more than four hours of sleep in the past year," he said.

"Man. I can't do that," she said. An image of Dylan came unbidden into her head.

"Well, I don't know if you still want to hop in the hot tub for a little while—"

"I did tell you about it, like, three weeks ago," she said, and looked at the time. "It is only nine. I guess I could stay up for another hour if you want."

"I brought my trunks," he said.

"Well, let's go then," she said.

Luckily, all the roomies were home when they got upstairs. They looked puzzled, meeting Stella's eyes with looks that said, "What about Dylan?" though Danny gamely shook Paul's hand and chatted.

"We're just going to hop in the hot tub for a bit," Stella said, hoping they didn't think she was a careless slut like the roommate they kicked out before her.

She sat next to Paul in the hot tub, feeling a bit traitorous. This was *Dylan's* spot next to her. She remembered the foot massage, the unfettered affection afterward in her room.

The conversation with Paul bubbled on. He had so many interests, he was never at a loss. Stella's blood was still thinned with whiskey, her brain clouded with questions. She leaned into the hot jets and let them soothe her muscles.

But Paul's stories were getting shorter and quieter, and Paul's body was getting closer. Soon, Paul and Stella were making out, their hands were searching for skin beneath the steaming water, over thighs and across laps.

But something caused Stella to stop. She brought her hand above water and her lips away from his damp face. No matter what discussion or lack-of-discussion had taken place between her and Dylan, she felt beholden to him. Three weeks ago, she might have invited Paul upstairs, but tonight she smiled and said, "So sorry to end the fun, but I better go to sleep. Long day tomorrow."

He kissed her one last time by his car, and said, "I think I could get addicted to you." It was the perfect line to end a first date; or it would have been, if Stella were really single. At once she felt guilty for the kisses she'd let him taste, and for letting him buy her dinner, and for even going on the date at all. But it had taken until now to realize the truth.

"I hope you don't end up in rehab," she stuttered. *What did that even mean?*

***

"Have you met all my roommates?" Dylan asked as they pulled in at his North Hollywood house after dark.

"Nope," Stella said.

"Well, you're about to meet them," he said. "All their cars are here."

He led her into the living room, where a fashionably scruffy guy sat on the couch with his legs propped up over the lap of a skinny, rainbow-haired girl whose style evoked an eighties David Bowie. Beside them was a pale, voluptuous girl with crinkly auburn hair.

"Hey guys," Dylan said. "This is Stella. Stella, this is Trenton, Emily and Cybil."

"Nice to meet you!" Stella said with a wave.

"Hi, Stella!" said Trenton.

The two girls took their eyes off the television for only a second, during which they looked Stella over and proffered a perfunctory hello, smile sold separately, then went back to watching whatever-it-was.

"What are you guys up to?" Trenton said.

"We just got back from the movies," Dylan said. "And this one cooked me dinner. Pretty fun. Where's Ren?"

"In her room," Trenton said. "I think she's getting ready for a party."

"Well, I think we're gonna have a drink and then turn in," said Dylan. "You guys don't want a gin and tonic, do you?"

The girls continued staring blankly, until Emily reacted to something on the screen and grabbed Cybil. "Oh my god! I can't believe she did it!"

Trenton said, half-apologetically, "It's okay, man. You guys have fun."

"How did you meet them again?" Stella asked once they were back in the safety of his room with drinks.

"I went to acting school with Emily and Cybil in New York. We all did a play together that Cybil directed."

"Oh," she said, hoping that their rudeness was a one-off caused by a deep love for whatever-it-was they were watching.

But it ceased to matter once Dylan's hands were wandering toward the zipper of her dress. While the gin and tonics sat sweating on the shelf, she slaked her thirst for him, trying to keep the noise to a minimum for the roommates' sake. Afterward, she knew it was true: she didn't need anyone else at the moment. She would tell Paul tomorrow where she stood—and she should do it before evening, since he and Dylan would both be at Tessa's party.

***

"Do you like omelets?"

"I do," Stella said. It was Saturday morning, and she followed Dylan into the kitchen, where he put the coffee on and began cooking.

Emily, in pajamas, wandered in.

"Good morning, Emily," Dylan said. "Do you want an omelet?"

"No," she said crankily. "Where's the coffee maker?"

"I just put the water in. Coffee should be done in a second."

"Whatever. I'll just have tea," she said.

"There's enough coffee for everybody," Dylan said.

Emily didn't reply; she just started clunking around with her Nutri-Bullet, making herself a smoothie.

Stella felt increasingly uncomfortable, like she was wrong just for being there, so she slipped back into Dylan's room, changed out of her pajamas, and put on a little makeup.

"It's ready!" Dylan called in ten minutes.

Stella walked with trepidation back toward the kitchen, hoping Emily would be gone, but instead, she was sitting at the table, slurping her smoothie wordlessly, ignoring Stella as if she were a bum asking for change. Dylan cheerfully brought the omelets to the table and served Stella. She ate quickly so she could make a quick escape from Emily's vortex of negative energy.

"Thank you so much," she said. "That was delicious. I guess I better get out of here, but I'm going to be seeing you later, right?"

"Yep, at the bonfire party," he said, following her back into his room as she collected her things and approached the door.

She hugged him. "So, people are going to start getting there around five. It ends at ten because you're not allowed to have fire on the beach after that. Did you want to come to my place and go over with me?"

"No, I actually have a party in Hollywood to stop by first, so I'll just meet you there."

"Okay. Tessa and my girlfriends can't *wait* to meet you. I am so excited to show you off." She kissed him. "Thanks for everything," she said, and left.

That afternoon, she reinforced her nerves with a deep suck of poolside air and wrote Paul a message.

Dear Paul,

I feel like a twat, but I have to tell you something that I just figured out. I had such an awesome time with you the other day. But during those three weeks you left to deal with your family matters, I went out with this other guy. No big deal. But this time something was different. You and I had our date planned, though, and I was still looking forward to it. After all, I had only been seeing the other guy for a couple weeks. But I realized after our date that this guy really has a hold on me. I guess I actually started falling in love with him, though I wouldn't admit it to myself until it felt wrong to be with another guy (you) who under normal circumstances I would be thrilled to be with. I guess we can chalk it up to terrible timing. I'm so sorry...but would you be willing to downgrade to just being friends for now?

She hated it. But at least it was honest. She averted her eyes and clicked "send." Gross.

Hey Stella,
Of course we can still be friends. I actually had a feeling this kind of thing might happen. It's just been such a weird couple months for me. No hard feelings. I'll see you at the party tonight?

She bought some s'mores ingredients with her credit card, which was at its limit again. She arrived at Dockweiler and parked on the street, tottering down the hill over the rocks to the beach where at least twenty different gatherings were organizing themselves around oceanside fire pits. Stella found Tessa and the gang, introduced herself to the people she didn't know, and sat down on the blanket with them, cracking open a beer as they waited for dusk and the arrival of the rest of the party.

Paul arrived just as she was getting buzzed. "Monsieur, would you like a glass of bourbon?" Stella said.

"But of course!" he said, giving her a hello hug as if their tongues had never touched.

Stella ate a hot dog and talked to some people about nineties movies, looking up at the hill every ten minutes, anticipating the moment when she would see Dylan walking toward her with a smile.

By eight, they were toasting the marshmallows she'd brought and putting the s'mores together. Stella hadn't wanted to badger Dylan, but there were only two hours left of the party, so she ducked away from the crowd and called him.

"Hey! Are you nearby yet?" Stella asked. "Everybody keeps asking about you. There's s'mores! And the Ladidahs are about to do an impromptu performance!"

"I just left the other party," he said.

Stella was squashed. It was a Saturday night. No matter where Dylan was, it would take at least 45 minutes to get to the South Bay. "Where's the party?" she asked.

"Hollywood," he said.

She felt Dylan fall from grace. What was he thinking? He had RSVPed two weeks ago. He had told her he would come and meet her friends. "Are you serious?" she asked. "You might as well not even come. The party will be over by the time you get here."

"I'm so sorry," he said.

"It's okay," she said, even though it wasn't. "I've gotta go."

She returned to the party and drank some hooch and sang a sad love song in four-part harmony with the girls.

"Stel, I thought we were going to meet Dylan tonight," Jo said.

"I did too," she said, trying not to betray how he had let her down. "But he got held up in Hollywood."

"Aw. Well, we'll meet him soon," said Erin.

"Yeah. I'm sure you will."

She had planned on sleeping over at Dylan's, but instead, she went home and sank into the bathtub. Her phone rang.

"Hello."

"Stella, I am so sorry. I feel like such an asshole. Would you mind if I came over to your house?"

"I don't know if Angie is coming back tonight or not."

"I don't care. I want to see you. Even if it's just for an hour or two."

The thought of seeing him excited her despite his behavior. And if he was willing to go out of his way—"Okay," she said.

"I'll be there as soon as I can," he said.

Dylan walked in the door an hour later and stood facing her solemnly. He pulled her in for a hug. She hugged back limply. He backed up, looked her in the eyes. "I talked to my dad about what I did and he said, 'Buddy, you really fucked up.' I completely agreed with him. I told you I would be there, and then I wasn't. That is not the way I want to treat you." His eyes were full of regret, his voice discouraged.

"I was really disappointed," Stella said. "This has been planned for weeks, and I even chose you as my date instead of this other guy, Paul, who really liked me."

"If you'll give me another chance, I will do my best to keep my promises from now on."

She was silent.

"Will you give me another chance?" he asked.

She waited a while, then said, "Okay."

He embraced her. She put her head on his shoulder.

"Do you think Angie is coming back tonight?" he asked.

"It's midnight, so I'd say not."

"Would it be alright if I stay with you?"

"I guess so," she said.

***

Stella awoke with a heart-thud at six in the morning when the door opened loudly, but she shut her eyes and feigned sleep while Angie came into the room, dropped a bag full of stuff, and then went into the bathroom to take a shower.

"Aw man," she whispered to Dylan. "I'm sorry." She felt like she was in college again, alienating her bunkmate and forcing Dylan to do the Walk of Shame. She found a to-go mug in the cabinet and sent him off with some coffee.

He paused and concentrated on her for a few beats. "You're really great, you know?"

"Thanks," she said, hugging him goodbye. "You're not so bad yourself." Dylan was no longer a flawless mythical creature, but his gaffe last night hadn't changed Stella's heart; it had only reminded her of her intention to be cautious.

Angie came out of the shower looking miffed. "I'm so sorry," Stella said, looking up from her coffee. "I didn't even consider that you might be back this early."

"That's okay," Angie said. "But if he's going to stay over, do you think you could give me a little warning in the future so I won't be startled when I get home?"

"Sure. Sorry."

She left to conquer her embarrassment with a yoga class, and when it was over, she walked to the edge of the bluffs facing the ocean. The breeze chilled the damp skin under her sweat-drenched tank top, and the pier called out to her. People milled all over its squeaky planks, waves smacked it and still it stood, the end of Route 66, always reinventing itself through her eyes: the first place she had set foot the day she moved to L.A., where she'd conquered her fear of heights on the trapeze, and where she'd remembered what hope felt like on her first date with Dylan, not even a month ago.

***

Stella still hadn't told Chet about her plans to take off work the following week. Every time he spoke to her, she shrank to the size of a flea, even at her best. But why? What could she lose but this soul-chafing job anyway? She poked her head into his office. "Hey Chet, are you busy? I have a little issue I need to talk to you about."

"Well, of course I'm busy. When am I not? But come on in. Have a seat. What's shakin'?"

"Last week, my cousin back in Kentucky died." It wasn't the *main* reason she was going home, but it couldn't hurt to lead with it, in case Chet did have the capacity to empathize.

He did look genuinely concerned. "I'm sorry," he said.

"Yeah. He was in his forties and had two young daughters."

"What happened?" Chet asked.

"Cancer."

"Oh."

"So, anyway, my family is pretty torn up about it. My sister has actually bought me a ticket to come home next week." This way, it seemed like she had no choice in the matter. "I feel really bad leaving you guys here alone"—*complete lie*—"and I'll totally understand if—"

"No. You go back and be with your family," he said. Stella couldn't believe it.

"Seriously, if there is anything you guys need me to do remotely, I will have my computer."

"I think Jonas can take care of it. You'll have to give him a little training this week on what you do."

"I can do it," she said.

***

"Dad knows you're coming, right?" asked Everly on the phone.

"Yeah, I told him. I just wanted to give him something to look forward to so he'd get out of the doldrums about Terry."

"Did it work?"

"I think so. He seemed excited. But do you think he can keep the secret?"

"I think so," Everly said. "It's not like he talks much anyway."

That evening, Stella actively loved everything. She loved the sherbet colors of the L.A. sunset, the quiet of the empty apartment. She loved that Chet was going to be gone tomorrow. She loved that she would see her family next week, that she wasn't sad right now, that she was active and fit. She loved that she could write, and had things to write about, like going surfing and Dylan cooking her dinner. She loved the way he felt, the way he looked, the way he treated her. She loved his brain and talents and curiosity and honor and...oh shit.

She loved Dylan.

She loved Dylan!

Oh dear God, she was in love again, and it was with Dylan Campbell, a half-Japanese Michigan sweetheart who was two years younger and had never gone through a rebellious phase or gotten an ill-advised tattoo or attended a university or had anal sex or eaten pickled bologna. A gorgeous, kind, surfing, hockey playing, fiscally responsible, Chopin-picking-out man who had gone skydiving and loved to recycle and spent eight years in New York, alternately starving and acting.

She loved him. And she loved being alone right now, yet having the option not to be.

***

She was in bed reading *Codependent No More* when the phone rang.

"Hey." It was Wil.

"Hey."

"Were you asleep?"

"Uh...kinda but it's okay," she said. "Have you figured out any news on the car situation?"

"No, I was actually calling to see if you knew about any job openings. I know you're all full-time and doing well now, but ever since that asshole Jeff fired me for getting *sick*, I can't find anything. I was only looking for good DP and camera operator jobs, but at this point, I just need cash. Do you know of anything?"

"I don't," she said. "I will let you know if I hear anything, but..."

"Can you put out an email blast to your well-connected friends? I mean, don't tell them it's for me, because they probably hate me now, but I know that Tessa and some of the Ladidahs work in offices and such."

"Um..."

"Or actually, are there any openings where you work?"

She almost spontaneously combusted at the thought of adding Wil's presence to the layers of hatred she had for TV Partners. "You don't want to work here; trust me. I don't think Chet needs anybody right now. If he does, it would be an account executive or something."

"I could do that. Can you put in a good word for me?"

"Sure," she lied. "But hey. Can you please just do something about this car crap? I can't take much more of this mail harassment. I am *not* paying your bills. I will seriously take that car back if you don't do something soon."

"Hey, there's no need to make threats. Literally, by the end of this upcoming month, the car, the gas, any bills at all will be 100% solved. I am in a transitionary period right now with life, but I assure you that everything will be taken care of and everything is already set up with the people so that nothing will affect you negatively. You have my and my family's word, so just ignore the mail unless it's something out of the ordinary and not a bill."

What could she say? It was so much easier to let it go for now.

"Stella. Are you there?" Wil asked.

"Yeah."

"I'm telling you. I am doing everything in my power so you won't have to deal with this anymore. I have all the necessary documents and paperwork filled out and soon I'll be living in a place that costs only eight-hundred a month with utilities included. You have nothing to worry about."

"Hmm," she said.

"Chill, woman! Okay I'm gonna let you go now. Be good. I miss you."

"Bye," she said.

***

Stella and Dylan were making stir-fry at her apartment. "Do we need some music?" she asked.

"Please," Dylan said. She took a break from chopping onions to search for something acoustic. "Want some water?" he asked.

"Yes, please."

He was at the sink, filling up one of the glasses when—"Ow! Dammit!"

She turned to see red streaming down his hand, which was still holding the bottom of the broken glass.

"Oh! Oh no! That's gruesome. Let me get you some Band-Aids. I have Ninja Turtle ones." She ran out and returned quickly, helping Dylan rinse off his hand. "How did this even happen?"

"I have no idea!" he said. "I was just holding it."

"Whoa buddy. You brute!" She laughed, taking the remainder of the jagged glass from his hand, wrapping it up in a paper towel, and tossing it in the trash.

"Don't step on any glass," he said.

"You dingus. The bike wreck, the stingray, and now this? You're a walking disaster!" she said.

"I know. It's only been since I met *you*, though," he said.

"Which Ninja Turtle are you?" she asked, shuffling through the box of Band-Aids.

"Donatello," he said.

"Really? Yeah. I could see that. Do you know which one I am?"

"Which one? The red one?"

"Michelangelo! Duh." She applied the Donatello bandage to his cut.

"Duh!" He laughed. "I love you!" he said.

She tried not to let him see her shock. She just said, "I love you too," laughing it off in case it was only a friendly, appreciative reflex to the laughter and caretaking.

***

At a wrap party for a short film he was in, Dylan introduced Stella to one of the other actors as they'd bellied up to the bar. "This is Stella, my girlfriend," he said.

Back at his place, their heads sharing a pillow, he asked, "Is it alright that I introduced you as my girlfriend?"

She tried to conceal her giddiness. "Well, I'm not interested in seeing anyone else if *that's* what you're asking."

"I'm not either," he said.

"Does this mean I can make it Facebook official?" she half-joked.

"If you want." He laughed. He turned off the reading light and kissed her. "You know, I think it's really important in relationships, though, to keep a little space between partners. Have you ever read Khalil Gibran?"

"I have."

"Well, there's a part that compares the man and woman to the strings of a lute. They can't make music if they're touching."

"That sounds reasonable," she said, hoping he wasn't implying that she was too clingy. "Does this mean you need me to scoot over?"

He rolled on top of her, pinning her under his weight. "Not right now," he said, laying his lips on hers.

***

"See you guys in a week-and-a-half!" she said to Chet and Jonas, more cheerfully than she had ever been within the confines of the frigid advertising office. She ran out the door before they had a chance to respond, hopping down the stairs two-at-a-time, singing the chorus of "Free Fallin'" until she ran into a lady who worked on the second floor.

***

Stella's sister still lived in Richmond, Kentucky, a couple of hours from where they grew up. Stella had gone to grad school there while Everly was in undergrad. They had lived together in a two-bedroom apartment that seemed perpetually decorated for Halloween. Everly still lived there. Stella remembered getting drenched with rain as she biked home from the university where she'd been teaching composition, spending buffalo-wing-and-beer evenings at Hooters with Andrew.

"Going to bed," said Everly's husband Aaron.

"I'm not gonna last much longer myself," Stella told her sister.

"Well, sorry. Your room is completely covered with Aaron's crap."

"That's okay."

"I don't bother him about moving it, since we're just waiting for the house to be done and won't be here much longer...but I swear. You're gonna have to go through a maze of fish tanks and guns to get to your bed."

"Sounds like a typical evening to me," Stella said.

"So, Dylan took you to the airport?"

"Yep. I think he was actually kind of sad to see me leave. We've been spending almost every night together."

"You seem happy."

"I am. I mean, I still have money worries, but things are looking up. I feel like—man, this is corny—but I feel like I've been given a new beginning."

"Corny."

"I know."

"Just kiddin'."

"But really though. He's not like anybody I've ever gone for before. He's like, *thoughtful* and gives things his full attention, and tries not to say anything unless it's completely necessary and true. And even if this doesn't work out, at least it's giving me hope. For a while there I thought I would never love or be loved again."

"I know the feeling."

"Mmm," Stella lowered her volume. "Are things still not going well? He seemed more friendly than usual."

"Things are actually much better than they were. I just wonder if I would have even gotten married if he hadn't been going to Afghanistan."

"I know."

"I guess I'll figure it out."

"You will. It gets better. I had to go through some nasty stuff to get here, and I still miss Andrew sometimes, and I still even think about Wil sometimes. Even though he's making my life hell with this car situation. It's absurd. Obviously I'm not 'there' yet. And I'm trying not to get too deep with Dylan before I know what I'm getting into...I'm just saying that it is possible to bounce back."

"But you're the type of person who can bounce back. You've always been like that."

"You can too! You just have to forget that you have fears."

"Good luck with that. Mom's pretty much made me scared of everything."

"Speaking of. What time are we leaving tomorrow?"

"I figure about nine."

"Okay. I better get in bed, then. Do you think she has any idea?"

"No. I talked to her today and she doesn't even know that *I'm* coming home this weekend."

"Awesome."

"Good night," Everly said.

"Good night."

***

After a two hour drive, they were in Harlan at the Church of Christ where their family had raised them. From the parking lot, tender and heavy, Stella could hear eighty voices singing, "I've got a mansion just over the hilltop," eagerly, in imperfect harmony. When Everly motioned her sister in, leathery men with crew cuts and pantsuited ladies with short, coiffed curls turned to look as Stella scooted into the pew next to her mother.

Linda took her in with childlike eyes, covered her open mouth, and stared for a couple seconds before she burst into laughter, reaching her arms out to embrace her daughter. She hugged Stella close, patted her back, squeezed her and patted it again. Stella bathed in the warmth of her mother's incredible, unconditional love.

"This is the best Mother's Day ever," Linda said, holding Stella at an arm's length to study her face. Through her mother's tears, Stella could almost see her memory of the day 28 years ago when she had gotten the call from the social worker. *Come pick up your baby.* Stella's dad hugged her, then Everly sat down with them. Linda was still holding Stella's hand.

"Mom, were you surprised?" Everly asked.

"Yes! How did y'all hide that from me?"

"I stayed in Richmond last night," Stella said.

Nothing was expected of Stella at her parents' house except to eat and keep eating, which is what she did for three days.

Surrounded by family in grassy humidity of Harlan, she filled up on Aunt Dory's cornbread, chicken n' dumplings, green beans and corn from the garden. She jumped on the trampoline with the little cousins, played with the dogs, caught lightning bugs, talked to Linda on the couch in the air conditioned house, and slept content and swaddled by the plush mattress she had bought herself after college when she'd lived in Louisville for half a year.

Under the bed she found programs from old plays, short stories and poems, and posters of her old bands. Her senior yearbook was filled with notes:

Don't forget me when you get famous!

Everyone thought Stella had moved to L.A. strictly to become an actress. The truth was, Stella had moved to L.A. to feel free, to be at the edge of the land, the last frontier, in a place that changes all the time, with rotating faces and choices and possibilities. But she understood why so many people dreamed of acting for a living. All that was required of an actor was to access a feeling, and then just to *be*. There was no struggle, and there was unlimited praise for the simple act of holding up a mirror to remind people how they had felt at some point in their lives.

Though Stella would have articulated it by saying something like, "It's one of the only jobs that doesn't make me want to kill myself," her love for acting came from the knowledge that whatever despair or joy she was portraying, like the events of her life, did not define her in the end. Underneath, she was always Stella, doing a job to the best of her ability. When she played it well, she could fully immerse herself into anything without fear, knowing that underneath each of the roles she'd have to play was a stable, capable being, doing the best she could.

She went running through gravels and mud puddles, past the Coal Monument, across the bridge over the tunnels, up the pine-studded mountain with its winding road and familiar houses of former teachers and high school friends, breathing in the humid, leafy air. Circumnavigating her past along her old running route felt like hugging the town that had shaped her.

She felt safe beneath the shelter of the mountains. She knew every road sign, every trail, every secret. Nothing had changed. Nothing ever did, besides people dying or having babies. *It would be so easy*, she thought, *to disappear here.*

She slept over at Claudia's one evening, promising Linda she'd be home in the morning.

***

"I can't believe you own a house. Are we grown-ups?" Stella asked as she sat on Claudia's couch sipping wine. She still remembered being in Claudia's room in third grade, pretending to French kiss Joey Lawrence and Jonathan Taylor Thomas.

"I don't know," Claudia said. "I don't really feel like I'm good at it." Her Pomeranian hopped onto her lap.

"Well, you seem to be closer to it than I am. You're the freaking assistant commonwealth attorney! I'm still drifting, and every place I've lived since college could fit into your living room."

"I'll be selling this place soon. It has too many memories." Carter had gone to live with a friend when they decided on the divorce. "And what you're doing is worth more than owning a house. You're living your life. Sometimes I worry that I'm letting all the adventures pass me by. The only real reason I'm staying so close to home is because of my mom."

"I know the feeling. What is it with Appalachian mothers?"

"They love us almost *too* much," she said. "They give up their lives for us. And then we feel guilty, like we owe them our lives."

"Yeah. There's a melancholy that lurks in them there hills," Stella said, drinking her wine. "I think a lot of it has to do with religion."

"It does. Remember how religious I was in high school?"

"Yep. I was, a little bit. But you were really into it for a while, huh?"

"Yeah. When I was hanging out with Rachel Smith all the time. I went to church with her on Saturday nights. It lasted for three hours. Back then I thought it was all or nothing."

"Wow. Well, no wonder. They said we had to 'turn our backs on the world' or else we'd burn in hell."

"It took me a long time to get over that. But finally I looked around and realized that I didn't have to believe exactly the same way as a group of people. What sense does that make? We're all individuals. I wonder what Rachel Smith would think about me getting a divorce."

"Sinner!"

"Finally I realized I could create my own belief system. Because why would I think that listening to some man tell me how to live my life is better than listening to myself? I'm probably smarter than him."

"I know. But when people base their whole life on fear of going to hell, or fear of persecution because they're not living exactly like the rest of the people in town, they tune out their inner voice and don't ever grow. And happiness isn't even a consideration."

"Yeah, because who needs happiness when you're just waiting for the next life," Claudia said. "You're just supposed to live the live they already have planned for you. Even when I moved to New York for those few months, I felt guilty every time I talked to my mom, and she eventually convinced me to come back. And here I am, single again, with the 'perfect' house and job. I'm afraid I'm not going to meet anybody new, because nobody here thinks the way I do. And I want to have kids someday. I think sometimes about just moving to L.A. or somewhere."

"You'll find somebody no matter where you are, but guys in L.A. would go crazy for you!"

"Speaking of...are things still going well with Dylan?"

Stella felt a surge of warmth. The wine was all gone. "I don't want to jinx myself, but yes."

***

In the bread aisle at Don's Super Saver, Mr. Coxton, Stella's sixth grade social studies teacher, approached her with a hug. "You look great, Stella. How's life out in the big city?"

"Really good," she said.

"I saw your wedding announcement in the paper a while back," he said, making a grab for her left hand and seeing her naked ring finger. "Where's your partner in crime?"

"He's not here," she said vaguely, smiling to deflect the pain and possible judgment.

"Well, it's great to see you," he said with a note of apology in his voice.

"You too," she said.

"I'll be looking for you on the big screen."

At the check-out, Stella lay her head on her mom's shoulder.

"Hey Mom," said Stella, eating sesame chicken with her parents that evening while they watched *Dancing with the Stars*.

"What, honey?"

"If I send you some new pictures of just me, do you think you could replace my old wedding photos in the hall?"

"Does it hurt you to see those?" she asked.

"Yeah. It feels like you're still waiting around, hoping we'll get back together."

"Well, I just had those up because you looked so pretty in them," Mom said. "But I'll take them down."

"Thanks," Stella said. "Love you."

"I love you, too, sweetie."

***

That night in bed, Dylan talked to Stella for over an hour. "I'm pretty ready to get back to L.A.," she told him. "I love my family, but the longer I'm away, the harder it is to be myself when I come back here. My mom was on me today to get a corporate job."

"That doesn't sound like you."

"It's not me. I don't care if I end up being known as an actor or an author or a singer or none of the above. I just want to spend more time doing what I love than not. But they don't do it that way in Harlan. They think you have to struggle to survive. Mom won't ever let me be."

"It seems like that's more about her own regrets than about you."

"I think she does have a lot of regrets," she said. "She always says 'I wanted to go there or do that,' but she was afraid to try. And living in this part of the country where nobody has much money, it becomes the most important thing. It's so backward. But this time I just walked away."

"That's good. It's not constructive to express your opinion in that sort of situation. Your mama loves you and she thinks she's doing what's best."

"She makes me feel like a little kid who can't take care of herself."

"Well, from what I've seen so far, you're a powerful woman."

"Thanks."

"You definitely have the power to break this boy's heart," he said.

She hadn't been aware that she held much power over Dylan or his heart, and she felt at once exhilarated and terrified, as if she was looking down from the doorway of the plane, about to stake her life on the reliability of an untested rip cord. She had broken many hearts over the years. "I don't want to break your heart," she whispered.

"Don't worry about it. I'm in it now. I'm willing to risk it."

"Really?"

"Sure. I have no choice now anyway."

"Yeah," she said. "I've just been realizing that no matter what happens, we're going to get our hearts broken again anyway."

"What do you mean?"

"It's kind of depressing. Are you sure you want me to go on?"

"Now you have to," he said.

"Well, I can promise not to break your heart. But I obviously don't know the future of my desire or yours. And even if I don't break your heart, you might break mine. And let's say neither of us breaks the other's heart. Well, even then—even if we stay together forever—one of us is going to die first. Which means the other one's heart is going to be broken."

"Wow. That *is* depressing. But kind of beautiful."

"Yes. So, basically, unless you decide to live your life without love, or unless you die first, you are guaranteed to get your heart broken again."

"It's worth it."

"I think so, too. I feel naïve sometimes, like how could I dare to look for love again after all that's happened? But I think the only way is to ignore that and just be willing."

"I completely agree. What's the use of living if you're going to lock your heart away behind bulletproof glass?"

"Exactly," she said. "You might lose over and over again, but at least you had it while you had it."

"So our hearts are never safe."

"No. Unless—"

"What?" he ventured.

"Well, unless we both die in a plane crash together."

"No heartbreak then!"

"Nope!"

***

Stella's dad, Ron, was sitting in the shade, chewing tobacco and watching cars swoosh by. It was a perfect eighty-degree day with a muggy breeze. A family of bluebirds was flying back and forth to a birdhouse her father had nailed to a telephone pole in the yard. The blue of their feathers dazzled against the greens surrounding them on all sides. She sat beside him, not saying a word, staring out at the mountains, listening to wind chimes and the rustling of leaves. She remembered those years when she rarely saw him, except when he'd come late from the coal mines, black except for the whites of his eyes. She and Everly would rush to the door and hug him, not minding the smell of oil and sweat. If it was payday, he'd bring them some candy from the store and a tiny figurine of an animal to put beside the lamp on their desk. Now he didn't work hard anymore. The black lung had made it hard for him to breathe. But Ron didn't need to constantly beguile himself with activities in order to stay in the present moment. Stella wished she could be a master at meditation like her father. He sat in the midst of the lulls, wanting nothing.

She, at this point in her life, could stay in the present for only a few minutes before traveling to the future, dreading her return to work, getting excited about seeing Dylan and the ocean, worrying about all the things she needed to do. Then she'd look around this house with all its smiling relics of bygone relationships and achievements and fall into the past. Even the sweet country lilt of her family's voices filled the air with bittersweet nostalgia for a time, a place, a version of herself that once was and would never be again.

But today she would be leaving, so for half an hour this morning, she joined her dad and the whispering breeze, finding stillness before she had to move again.

She took one last walk out to Aunt Dory's to hug her and Uncle Hershel goodbye. She hiked once more up the backyard mountain and back down, examining the bear tracks, inhaling the pines and dirt. She rode the four-wheeler as fast as she dared up into the hollers, under the kudzu-choked trees, she cuddled the dogs, made her bed, gave Dad a long hug, and got into the car.

Her mom was driving. They were halfway to Everly's apartment, where they were going to stay a night before Stella had to go to the airport. Outside at fifty miles per hour, mountains became hills, which gave way to fast food restaurants and K-Marts and car dealerships. The Beach Boys played on the stereo.

"Stella Honey?" Linda said as they got on I-75 in Corbin.

Stella bristled. "Stella Honey" was her mother's opener for a "talk," and she still had another half-hour before she could escape this car.

"Hmm?"

"Can I talk to you about something without you getting mad?"

"If you think it's something that will make me mad, I'd rather not," Stella said.

"Well I'm just wondering what your goal is. You still don't have health insurance, you know, and I worry about you. How are you gonna deal with this car situation when you get back?"

"I'll figure it out, Mom. Can we please talk about something else?"

"Well, honey, I'm your mother! All mothers do this!"

"No, Mom, they don't. *You* do this. I haven't lived at home for most of the last decade. I'll ask your advice when I need it, but I don't need it right now."

"Well honey, it's time to grow up. Don't you want to be able to buy things you need? I want to make sure you're settled before I die. I feel like I've finally got your sister settled—she's got a good teaching job and they're about to buy a house—and I *thought* you were settled because you were married and we all loved Andrew."

The oxygen was thinning in the SUV. "Mom. I'm so tired of this conversation. There isn't just one right way to do things. I'm not going to move to Lexington and be a nurse or a teacher and have a white picket fence and a boring husband and 2.5 kids! I do not need you to impose your opinions on me."

Linda went quiet and sad. "I can't believe you talk that way to me. I've never had anybody talk so mean to me."

"Well I've never heard you go up to somebody and offer your unsolicited opinion on how they're living their life." Guilt overtook Stella, but she kept talking. "I bet if you did that, you'd get a different reaction! Thank you very much. Now, not only do I feel inadequate in the way I choose to live my life, I also feel like I'm a cruel person who is 'mean' to my own mother. But I'm not a cruel person. I am a person who is entitled to make her own mistakes. So hopefully someday you'll see that and get off my back."

"That's just the way I am, Stella. I want what's best for you."

Stella thought of catching a wave, and how far-fetched the idea seemed from here. The thought that Los Angeles could even exist seemed impossible. What did she want out of life? She just wanted to live it. She didn't want to obey unquestioningly some "right" way of living, and she didn't want to thrash about, terrified, either. She wanted to find the balance and pop up smoothly, with strength, coasting, at once in control and in a state of surrender to something greater than herself.

Stella's phone started ringing. It was Dylan. She exhaled and answered it. "Hey you," she said.

"Hey surfer girl. What's shakin'?"

"I'm in the car with my mom. We're on our way back to Richmond. Everly's going to take me to her Krav Maga class. What about you?"

"I was just doing a little homework, and I got sidetracked thinking about you. And I realized something that I wanted to tell you. Can you talk?"

"Mm-hmm."

"Well, I've been thinking about you a lot. It must be true what they say about absence making the heart grow fonder, because I've really been missing you."

"I miss you too!" She was suddenly filled with such a love-glow that she forgot all about the fight with her mom.

"I realized...you are the first real woman I've ever dated."

"Really."

"Yes. You may not have all the details sorted out yet, but it seems to me that you have the important things in life figured out."

"Wow."

"And what I was thinking was, my mind has been all over the place. I don't have everything figured out myself. I don't know much right now, but one thing I do know is that I love you."

Her heart stopped. "I love you, too," she said, leaning all the way toward the passenger window as if she could find any privacy in the enclosed space.

"I just wanted to tell you," Dylan said.

"Thank you for telling me." All the colors around her intensified.

"Well, I guess I will see you on Saturday," he said.

"I can't wait," she said, in a daze.

"Me neither," he said.

After she hung up, all the tension in the car was gone. "That was Dylan," she told Linda.

"What did he want?" Linda asked.

"He wanted to tell me he loved me," Stella said, smiling.

Her mom said, "well." And then: "Do you think he might be the one?"

"It's a little too soon to say, but he might be."

"Your mommy loves you too, you know," Linda said.

"I know. I love you, too, Mama."

***

Stella's pulse pounded as she waited on the curb at LAX, ready to see the man she now knew loved her. His silver Prius pulled up. There was his smiling, stubbly face, the dimples, the arms that were soon wrapped around her. She threw her carry-on in the back and jumped in excitedly.

"Are you hungry?" he asked.

"Hungry for you," she joked.

***

On the way to the beach after toast and coffee, Stella unhappily studied her reflection in the visor mirror. She felt bloated from the week of unhealthy eating in Kentucky, and her skin looked worse to her than that of a 14-year-old academic team member. She looked over at Dylan with his nutty skin and wondered if he ever felt unattractive. She wished she had some concealer. Or less self-consciousness.

They joined about ten others in the Venice waves. By the time Stella was walking through the sand again beside Dylan, boards tucked under their arms, heart swollen from immersion in the deep, arms limp from overwork, Stella had forgotten all about the tortured state of her face. Until he stopped her.

"Put down your board for a minute," he said. She did, and he held her at arms' length and gazed into her like she was a magical creature he was seeing for the first time. She averted her eyes at first, putting a hand up to her cheek so he wouldn't look at the havoc of her vagabond skin. "Look at me," he said. She did. "You are so beautiful," he said, his white teeth sparkling as he smiled, the ocean roaring behind him. "Look at those freckles."

She blushed and hugged him. "Thank you."

***

"There she is!"

Chet, in pointy-toe shoes and embroidered jeans, seemed genuinely happy to see Stella. The feeling was not mutual. "Sunshine, it was pathetic here without you. I'll tell ya, Jonas is lousy at what you do."

Jonas shrugged, as if to say, "I did my best."

Soon she was back in her winter coat in front of that computer screen, doing basic math and copying and pasting things. When she needed a boost, she reread a love letter Dylan had sent her, so thoughtfully composed that she knew he had mastered her love language. "You renew me," it said. "You illuminate every aspect of my life." She thought of his sweet face: the prickly plains of his cheeks stretched over chiseled cheekbones, the almond eyes and almond skin and delicate yin and yang of his features. He was incomparable to any man she'd ever known. And she did not need to compare him.

"You got that traffic done?" Chet's voice thundered from his office.

"Yep."

"Sent out, too?"

"No, I was waiting to get it approved."

"What? That was supposed to go out before ten!" It would have been nice if Chet had told her. She was starting to feel like *Alice in Wonderland* after Alice grows so large that her legs and arms are sticking out the windows of the little house.

The small escape of daydreaming about Dylan only filled a little of the dead time at TV Partners. She tried to occupy the rest with writing, running, making plans with friends, and smoking weed or having a beer at lunch so she could coast through the last four hours of the day without the edge. But mainly she spent her time looking for jobs online: jobs where she could move, where the sun would shine, where she could be creative or talk to people.

***

The envelopes under the book on Stella's dresser were stacking their way to the ceiling like bricks, soon to overtake and imprison her. She faced today's mail as quickly as possible—a credit card bill, some junk about consolidating her student loans, two more reminders, now in red, about Wil's parking tickets in her name, and another notice from Toyota claiming that if she didn't pay the amount overdue, the Prius would be repossessed.

If there was an exit sign somewhere in this dark hallway, it was too dim to see. Stella could hardly imagine a world in which she wasn't destitute, avoiding outings lest she had to pay a parking meter. She worried all morning at work, then did the only thing she could think of: she sent a Facebook message to Wil's mom.

Hi Judy,

I have been trying to get my life back in order, but as it stands, there are $245 worth of parking tickets Wil has now rung up on my tab (see attached photo). Not to mention he has been missing the car's payments.

I am trying not to be petty, angry, or cruel, but I am desperate to be untied from this whole situation. Every time I tell Wil this, he says I am "threatening" him. I am not trying to take away his only means of transportation, but I have already been bled dry of everything I once had, and all I want is to start over at zero and be free of this burden.

If you don't want to get involved I understand, but you've helped me in the past, so I thought I'd at least try. I am wondering if you have any advice, help, whatnot.

She saw Judy's reply when she was on her way to Dylan's.

Stella,

I just talked to William. He told me that he is aware of the tickets and he has already taken steps to pay them (in installments).

I'm sorry that you guys are in this situation. I know neither of you expected to be in it...it saddens me that you lost each other. I hear the upset in William's voice and know he understands how difficult it is for you. His priority has been to make the payments for the car and insurance so to not affect your credit negatively at all...and I am helping him do that while he looks for work. He wants the best for you and I read that you do for him. I hope you guys can try to be tolerant of this uncomfortable situation until he gets to a better place. If you feel that your credit is threatened, please contact me again and let me try to help. I am not taking responsibility for William...he wants to do it himself, and I really believe that now. But, despite it being a hardship for me, I will try to help and your credit is top of the list.

Hopefully sometime soon there will be a way to get this monkey off your back.

Mistakes make for wisdom. Please call me if you want to talk or are upset or are happy or pissed or anything. I want only the best for both of you...and know you will both get there!

Hugs...

***

At least three different tourists took their picture as she and Dylan walked past the crowds with their surfboards, holding hands.

"You guys are the perfect surfer couple! You should be in a commercial!" one lady said.

It was windy. Stella was taking the waves despite their size, and then getting taken by them. The ocean was a bully holding her head in the toilet and repeatedly flushing.

The ocean had its moods, but it never held grudges or meant anything personal. It was a teacher, even when Stella wasn't looking to learn. It taught her to leave her expectations behind and to value intuition as much as strength. It taught her the effort required to make it past the breakers, and the surrender required to catch a wave. It trampled her, shook her up, left her gasping. Some days it was grey and it smacked her in the face. She gave up on it; she'd say, "fuck this!" Then a week later she'd come back and it would be a rich aquamarine color and sound like a lover breathing in her ear, telling her she could walk on water.

There weren't many others surfing at the pier. Dylan took a wave and disappeared beyond the white water. Then Stella took one. When she reached the shallows and turned toward the horizon again to paddle back out, she didn't see him anywhere. He was probably already out there, sitting atop his board. She kept paddling, her breath heavy, until she made it to a resting place where she straddled her board, spinning around for a panoramic view. He was nowhere.

"Dylan!" she yelled. "Dylan!" She surveyed the whole scene. There were a couple swimmers in the water a ways down. There was a family building a sandcastle with their toddlers. "Where are you?"

She looked for his board in the water. Nothing.

She took the next wave in and started walking toward the pier, scanning left and right, speeding up to a jog, then a run. The pier was further than she thought. She must have gotten blown nearly a mile south.

Ahead was a speck with a surfboard coming toward her.

"Baby!"

"What happened?" he yelled, running toward her. "I was scared

169

shitless."

"I don't know. I was worried about *you*."

"You were pretty far down there." He put down his board and enfolded her in his arms. He was breathing hard. She'd never seen him in such a panic. "I don't ever want to feel that feeling again," he said.

"Me neither. Let's go."

He stayed silent as they walked back toward the cars. Stella wished she could ease his mind, but she could see he was somewhere else now. He was like the ocean when it went very dark and still, his melancholy a fathomless expanse.

Back at his place they took a shower. Stella went back to Dylan's room to wait for him where she wouldn't disturb the roommates. Her phone was on the bed and it vibrated.

> Wil:
> Still riding the orient express?

Not even funny.

> Stella:
> I'm still with Dylan, if that's what you're asking.

She shouldn't have replied at all.

> Wil:
> But I know you miss this cock. I know he can't compare to what we had. Nobody ever will. What made me cum today, after literally like 25 minutes straight, was thinking of you, me holding onto both of your legs with my shoulders, holding your hands down with one hand, and my other hand around your throat, going as deep as I can inside of your amazing little cunt, you wincing but also moaning and begging me not to stop.

Stella deleted the whole conversation and put her phone on Dylan's shelf without responding.

Dylan came back, slick and refreshed with a towel around his waist. "What are you doing in here?" he asked.

"Just waiting for you."

SUMMER

JUNE

They were climbing up the dusty hillside at Runyon Canyon on their last night together for a while. Tomorrow he'd be flying to Michigan as a surprise for his dad's birthday. Stella stepped high over the wood ties that kept the earth in place while Dylan ran on ahead, fuzzy on the concept of hiking *with* someone. She kept up, and once they had looped down the shady path back to their starting place, endorphins had turned up her vibration.

They stopped to look at the bulletin board where people advertised classes and posted rewards for lost dogs.

"Look at this key!" Dylan said. Tucked into the frame of the board was a silver key no larger than a pinky fingernail. "It's the tiniest key I've ever seen."

"Aw, it's so cute!" Stella said.

"I kind of want it for my necklace," he said. He always wore a tiny ball chain around his neck strung with little artifacts—a Japanese coin, a piece of Jade—which dangled always upon the statuesque center of his chest.

"You should take it," Stella said.

He thought for a second and then said, "No...it might belong to somebody."

"What could it possibly open?"

"I don't know, but I'll leave it for now. If it's still here next time we come to hike, I'll consider it mine," he said.

"Okay," she said, taken aback by his conscientiousness.

***

Over Dylan's shoulder at the Delta terminal at seven in the morning, Stella saw an old lady smile wistfully at her.

"I'll be back before you know it," he said, and kissed her.

With Dylan gone, Stella became a machine. She went to work, got an oil change, ran, bought groceries, and wrote her daily story—this time about their first date by the pier.

In the evening, as she was drilling brackets onto some new shelves she'd bought, a text came.

Wil:
Do you have that extra parking pass? It's not fair that you still have it. You don't even live here.

Stella:
I bought these parking passes with my money, and I gave you one.

Wil:
I need the extra one for my guests. I have a lovely lady over right now and she had to park two streets away. By the way, I'll see you tomorrow. You're coming to get that check, right?

She turned her phone off and went to bed.

**

"Stella, why don't we have your three-month review tomorrow," Chet said from the next office. Stella was busy curating a series of mix CDs for Dylan's birthday, in hopes of sending love and hopefully broadening his musical tastes to include something besides Jack Johnson.

"Sounds good."

"Let's make it ten."

"Okay," she said, and then turned back to the computer to search online for Dylan's parents' address.

She had no choice but to see Wil after work to get the insurance check. The Prius was parked in front of the old apartment, so she peeked inside. Trash completely covered the floorboards. Even though Stella had texted him a half-hour before, Wil kept her waiting at the door for ten minutes.

"Coming!" he finally said, opening the door, smelling fresh, holding a white, expensive-looking, flat-faced kitten. "Hey." He smiled as if he hadn't texted her an unwelcome erotic message, as if nothing unsavory had passed between them. "This is Nora."

"Aw. So cute," Stella said, handing him the fucking parking pass.

"Come in," he said, putting the cat in her arms. "She's a Himalayan. Thanks for bringing this."

"You got a couch," Stella said.

"A sectional," he said. "Yeah. Things are so different from when you were here." He led her to the refrigerator and opened it to show off his organic fruits and vegetables. "See I've changed my habits completely. I'm healthy now! Can I make you a juice?"

"Okay," she said. She looked around and saw no evidence of the lizard, Hemingway. She assumed Wil had let it die, like he probably would with this kitten.

Wil put beets, ginger, carrots, and apples into a fancy juicer. Stella noted the dirty plates piled in the sink—the plates she had bought.

"Here you go," he said, presenting her with a crisp glass of rich red juice. She thought of last week before Dylan had left, when she had had hopped in the shower and poured neon beet blood over her naked body while Dylan took pictures just for fun.

"Thanks."

"It's so good to see you," he said, like he was performing in a play. "Can you sit down for a minute?"

"Sure," she said.

"Look at this book I got," he said, opening a high-priced coffee table book on Allan Ginsberg.

"Cool," she said.

"And I just got these new jeans," he said. "They're Balmain."

"Wow," she said, without saying, You still don't have a job, *right?*

"So what's new with you? You're still dating that guy, right?"

"Yep."

"Is he making you happy?"

"Yes. I'm really happy," she said, without saying, *and the slow burn is so much better than the TNT blast.*

"But is it like what we had?"

Nothing with Dylan is fantasy or forced. Every good feeling is backed up by something real, she didn't say. But she actually felt sorry for Wil, with his pathetic attempts to fill his gaping life-holes with cats and jeans he couldn't afford, so she answered, "Nothing could be like that." *Thank God.*

"I knew it," he said.

"So, you do have that check for me, right?" she said.

***

It took an hour to get to Hollywood. She parked at the bottom of Runyon Canyon and ran through the gate, up the dusty hill just as the evening was turning to night. She approached the bulletin board where they had seen that tiny key, and she shined the light from her phone over it, searching.

There it was, tucked into the corner where they'd left it. She zipped the key into her jacket pocket, running back to her car.

Back in her room that night, she perfected the artwork for the

CDs, attached the little key inside her hand-drawn birthday card, and packaged it all up using the Michigan address she'd found online for Joe and Ayame Campbell.

***

Stella was reading an email from the manager of a potential job. It was an outdoor gig selling cold pressed juice at farmer's markets around L.A., and they wanted to interview her. "Stella, are you ready for your review?" Oh. It was ten o' clock. Stella edged into Chet's office and sat in one of the chairs in front of his big desk.

"So, you've been here three months now," Chet said.

"Yep," she grimaced.

"How do you feel about things?" he asked.

"Well," she started, "I don't know. I feel like I've caught on to most everything, but there are still a lot of times when I have no idea what's going on."

"You know you can always ask," he said. "There are no stupid questions; only stupid people."

"I know," she said. "But you're really busy and I hate to bother you."

"Better to ask than get it wrong," he said. "How are you doing with the full-time aspect?"

"I can handle it," she said, "but to be honest, if there were a part-time option, I'd probably get the same amount of work done. Britt told me that she was down to three days a week at the end of her time here."

"She was. And she ended up leaving right before her six-month raise."

"Would that be a possibility for me? Going down to a few days, I mean."

"I think we could do that. If that would make you happier, I can have Jonas cover the phones two days a week and you could just come in Monday through Wednesday."

She exhaled, feeling lighter all at once. "I would love that," she said, smiling.

"The work here can be pretty repetitive. I know that. But you have a great voice. You're an actor and I know you're not going to be here forever," he said. "But I'd like to keep you as long as you'll stay."

"I'd love to have some days free to go to auditions and such," she said.

"Okay. So let's keep you full time for the next two weeks, but after that, we can start your new schedule."

"Sounds great," she said.

"Another thing is, I'd love to have you do some voiceovers for the radio commercials. I'll pay you per spot, of course. Would you be

176

interested?"

"Sure."

"Okay. Is there anything else you'd like to talk about?" he asked.

"Not that I can think of," she said.

"Why don't you go ahead and take your lunch," Chet said.

"Oh, it's only 11:30. I can wait a couple hours," Stella said. She hated taking lunch so early. It was the after-lunch period that seemed endless, so she preferred to make it as short as possible.

"Well I'm going to have some things for you to get done later, so I need you to take lunch now," he said.

"Okay."

That evening, stuck in a storm of brake lights at LAX, she scanned the faces on the sidewalk. Her pulse raced when she saw him. She parked, got out, and felt a surge of liquid gold energy as she accepted Dylan's strong embrace.

"Did you have a good time?" she said.

"I did. Look," he said, pulling the ball chain out from beneath his shirt to show that he was wearing the little key around his neck.

"You're wearing it!"

"I still can't believe you went all the way back there and got it," he said. "Now this isn't just a key. It has meaning."

"It's the key to my heart," she said goofily.

"And it's right on top of my heart," he said, mimicking her voice.

***

What began as joy for skipping work on a Tuesday ended as one of the most traumatic experiences of Stella's life. She wanted to get an IUD so she could stop pumping her body full of hormones. Dylan drove. When they got there, there was a paper gown and a cold table with stirrups, an octogenarian man with patchy curls of yellow-grey hair and a long metal rod, and a scream when a bear trap had opened inside her. Everything went black and she shook violently. "That's a lot of blood," the old man said. Red everywhere. The nurse looked on frightfully. Stella tried to speak, but nothing came out. She still couldn't see. The old man was gone. The nurse helped her mop up the blood and brought her water. Stella thought she was dead. But then Dylan was there. He took her to the car, drove her to get a giant burrito, then took her to his bed and tucked her in.

"Cybil says she's had an IUD for years and you really got screwed," Dylan said when she woke up. "She wants to talk to you."

Stella gathered courage and peeked out into the living room. No sign of Emily. Just fluorescent-haired Cybil typing on her computer.

"So tell me what happened." She seemed concerned. Maybe without Emily's black aura stinking up the place, Cybil had license to be nice. Stella told her the awful story.

"They didn't give you any medicine to take before?" Cybil asked, dumbfounded.

"No! Nobody gave me anything or told me anything!"

"Honey. I am so sorry that happened to you. They usually give you a muscle relaxer to take the night before, and they tell you to take a lot of ibuprofen. Sometimes they dilate you. If you ever decide to try it again, talk to me and I'll make sure you are prepared."

"Thanks, " Stella said. "If I do try it again, it won't be for a long time. I am scarred."

"I totally understand. That would be terrifying. But if it's done right, it shouldn't hurt too much, and it's worth it to be hormone-free and not have to worry about birth control."

"Cybil was really helpful," Stella told Dylan under the covers at bedtime.

"She's really not so bad. She's just a really strong personality, and she's used to being surrounded by less dominant personalities. So I think she's kind of repelled by how...big...you are."

"Hmm," she said.

Then he told her that in July, he was going away for three weeks. He was working at a theater camp, and then visiting some friends in New York.

"That's so soon," she said.

"It's still a month away. You'll probably be sick of me by then," Dylan said.

Looking at his face she felt a peculiar sensation of certainty. "You really think I'm going to get sick of you?" she asked.

He went quiet and dark the way he had when he thought he'd lost her in the ocean.

"No," she said. "I want to sit on the porch with you when you're 75." She buried her face in a pillow and said, "I don't think you understand. I want to have your babies." She couldn't say where it came from, but it was a place of truth. She raised her head.

Dylan looked at her placidly; his fog had lifted. "I can be a real asshole sometimes," he said.

She wondered what he meant. "You don't scare me."

***

"I just lost a friend in a car accident," said the yoga teacher. "In her honor, I'd like to encourage you to think of a mantra for yourself. Maybe try this mantra: *life is now*. Every time you bring your hands to your heart, whisper it. My friend never realized how short her life would be. What are you doing that is not serving you? What do you wish you were doing that you're not doing? Think about it. Vinyasa."

Stella didn't even have to think. She knew it was time to exhale the stagnation and set herself free. The light was up ahead; She just had to run toward it. She swept her arms high on an inhale, then brought her palms together at her heart, and whispered, "life is now."

It was Wednesday: the new end of her work week. No more Thursdays and Fridays trapped in this office! Dylan was texting to tell her he was "so stoked" about the weekday surf plans they'd made for tomorrow, when Chet squawked, "Hey Stella. I know you're off tomorrow but will you be around?"

"Well, I have some plans..."

"I was thinking I'd like to use you to be the new voice of Fit Universe. Of course I'd pay you separately for that job. You'd have to do the voiceover tomorrow, but it would take an hour tops."

"Oh. That sounds good," she said with trepidation. "I'll check with my...people, and—can I let you know later?"

"Sure. Text me." He left shortly after.

She passed time alone, sitting in Chet's office since it was the only place with a window, thinking about the prospect of coming in tomorrow. Doing voiceover would be more interesting. Maybe she could parlay this into a new way of working for Chet that wasn't so awful. She texted Dylan.

> Would you mind if we moved our surf plans to 10? My boss wants me to come in for what he assures me is only an hour to record a voiceover.

> Dylan:
> Sure. I'll come pick you up and we can go together.

So she sent Chet a text:

> I can do tomorrow, as long as I'm done before 10.

> Chet:
> You'll be gone by 9:30.

But as soon as Stella hit *send*, she got the sensation that her body was being compressed by a medieval torture device. The elation she'd felt in anticipation of a three-day workweek had been squashed. She had allowed herself to be suckered into another day of slavery. Chet would

179

probably convince her to answer phones or do mundane tasks, and then he would concoct some plan to get her here on Friday, too.

During her lunchtime run, self-loathing pumped into her temples and through her veins. Why hadn't she just gone ahead and quit? Fear of confrontation, fear of being broke. How could she have ignored her discontent for so long, numbing her mind with booze and weed? And why was this run so difficult? Her usually athletic frame felt heavy: a result of too many stress-eating binges. *Life is now*, she whispered as she returned to her desk chair and stared at the screen.

***

She arrived at eight on Thursday and Chet, as predicted, gave her a spreadsheet to occupy her while he "got the production stuff ready." 9:30 came and went. She spun her chair around backward, chewing her cuticles.

Ten o'clock came with a message from Dylan.

Are you ready, surfer girl? I'm outside.

Stella hadn't even begun recording the voiceover. Chet was on the phone. While she seethed, Chet negotiated dayparts and budgets. "I'm gonna go ahead and, uh..." he rattled on, as his keyboard clacked and the air conditioner hummed.

10:30 came and Chet was still on the phone. Stella got on the computer, making sure to log these excruciating hours on her timesheet.

Finally, Chet said, "Alrighty, I think we're ready to get off and running!"

She tried to remind herself that even though her personal plans were getting shat on, she was at least making a little money she hadn't counted on.

She stood beside Chet reading from an amateur script about "No start-up fees!" and "26 Cent Tuesday! Only at Fit Universe!"

Dylan texted at 11.

Are you finished yet?

Stella:
No. Still here.

Chet was in the process of making Stella rerecord every line 10-15 times, instructing her to leave behind her naturally appealing coffee-warm elocution in favor of a horrible, speed-freak cheerleader chipmunk voice.

180

Dylan:
I'm across the street. What kind of salad do you want?

The restlessness was creeping up her legs, festering into a palpable rage. Every time she recorded a line, Chet, thief of her time, would stop her to criticize her for "losing enthusiasm."

Stella:
Don't care. In hell.

She was starting to shake and sway back and forth with mounting wrath.

"Smile when you say it! Listen," said Chet. "Do you hear how *this* reading is so much better than *this* one?" He played two snippets of her manic voiceover back. They sounded exactly the same.

"Okay," she said, feeling terrible for Dylan, who was now waiting at Rainbow Acres for her.

She must have been breathing visible fire by noon, because at last, Chet said, "Well, this isn't perfect, but we can work with it; I think I can edit something together."

She bolted toward the door, determined never to enter it again except to return the keys and pick up her final check. She didn't care at this point if he offered her sixty bucks an hour; She couldn't work anymore for someone who had no respect for her or her time.

She ran across the street and sat down at the table with Dylan, wishing she had a punching bag to release her rage. "I can't believe I agreed to come in today! I knew it! I knew he'd do this! And now look— our plans our ruined! I only made a hundred bucks for spending another entire day in that shit hole. I am getting the fuck out of here as soon as I can." She gobbled down the barbecued chicken salad Dylan had bought her, then went into the store and bought a pint of chocolate ice cream, which she ate furiously while Dylan looked on.

At the beach before they surfed, she put on headphones and blasted angry rock, sprinting for ten minutes to jostle loose the vise grip of her anger.

They got into the water.

"I think I need to puke," she said.

"Then puke," Dylan said.

She swam south a few feet and stuck a finger down her throat. The waves beat her gently as chunks of chicken, tortilla strips, and lettuce sailed ashore in a sea of chocolate goo. Then, slowly, the water began to cool her fire.

***

It was the summer solstice and the moon was full all weekend.

Stella always felt wild beneath the pull of such luminescence. On Friday, after her interview with the farmer's market people, she and Dylan acted together in a Hollywood horror movie trailer, hired by Tessa's producer friends. Saturday, the Ladidahs had a sleepover and spent the evening divulging secrets and drinking in the pool. Sunday, Stella joined Tessa, Erin, and Paul (as a friend) for an L.A. taco festival. While she was loaded on margaritas, she got an email from the boss at the farmer's market job. He gave no details—said he'd contact her next week—but they wanted to hire her! She spent the rest of Sunday over at Dylan's, lounging and snacking. She had kept herself so busy with fun over the weekend that she forgot all about the bad dream of TV Partners and her vomit-inducing anger.

"Fuck."

"What is it?" Dylan said. They were squished on the couch on Sunday night watching *Lost in Translation.*

"It's 11:42. That means if I'm going to work tomorrow, I have to wake up in six hours."

"If?" he said.

"I viscerally cannot enter that office anymore."

"You can do it. You can give your two weeks notice this week."

"If I have to spend even ten more minutes in that fucking frozen tundra, I am going to burst into flames," she said.

"It seems to me that you have a penchant for running from anything you find uncomfortable," he said. "Not everything is easy or enjoyable."

"This has nothing to do with running," she said. "This is me choosing not to be miserable. Fuck it. I'm emailing Chet."

Stella <stellawrites84@gmail.com>
to CGoldstein

Dear Chet,

I regret to be doing this at 11:45 pm the night before, but I am having an existential crisis of epic proportions, and I am going to have to be honest about it. I will not be coming in tomorrow for a few reasons, the main one being that I have been growing increasingly attuned to the fact that the majority of my time on this earth lately has ceased to belong to me, and has become something I dread due to stress, boredom, and lack of creativity, activity, sunshine, human contact and fulfillment.

I am, I have discovered, simply not cut out for an office job, full-time or otherwise, and thus I will have to resign my position effective immediately. I don't want to leave you in a pickle because I think you are a nice person and I have learned a lot from you in this short time, but I may have a shaved-head-Britney-Spears breakdown if I don't get my life back ASAP.

This weekend I received a job offer, which, though not fulfilling, will offer me sunshine, human contact, stimulation, and virtually no stress. They asked if I could start Monday, which means I will not be available starting tomorrow. I wish I had known sooner so that I wouldn't have had to make things difficult, but this is one of those desperate times that calls for desperate measures. I have been neglecting my own needs for the past few months, and starting now, I am going to start taking care of myself again.

As soon as I am given my new schedule, I will know when I can come and return the keys and pick up my last paycheck. Or I can always drop the keys in the mailbox and you guys could just mail me the check. Again, I'm sorry, and I'd like to say thank you for all the guidance you've given me this year. I honestly wish you all the best, and I know you'll find it.

Sincerely,
Stella

Stella squinted hard, held her breath, and clicked "send."
***
Chet emailed, called and left messages, but to keep the guilt at bay, Stella didn't read or listen to them: Dylan fielded them and relayed her the vital information. He said Chet seemed like a boyfriend who got dumped for being an asshole, and then was crawling back: "Baby, baby, I promise I'll be better."

But Stella had already gone in to fill out the paperwork for her new job. She was going to help run the summer farmer's markets, selling trendy, expensive juice. Cory, who hired her, was only a year older than her, and chortled at everything that escaped her mouth. The job would have its own trials, but it would not stomp on her living green soul.

Stella hardly knew what to do with a free weekday. She went to the gym in her building and watched *American Psycho* alone with Angie's dog Mary Ann, suddenly understanding more about Wil than she cared to. She chatted with Danny about the psychological perils of being someone's assistant and the particular scrumptiousness of Movie

Theatre Butter popcorn. She went to the juicery store and used her gift card for a three-day juice cleanse. She rehearsed with the Ladidahs. Dylan came over after hockey to sleep beside her. She stirred at 4 a.m. and found that his dick was hard. She couldn't restrain herself. He woke up to find himself inside her. As a thank-you, she let him sleep in and cooked him breakfast. Energy was moving all around her.

***

Andrew <afoss3090@gmail.com>
to me

Dear Stella.

I've had to think a lot these last months.

I don't hate you.

I don't even really blame you anymore.

I just don't see how we can be together again right now.

I just think you and I have to move on.

I haven't proceeded with the divorce thing cause I don't know how.

I'm not happy. I haven't been happy all year.

Every day is horrible.

I know you'll be fine. You always found a way to do great.

I really didn't want this.

Andrew

***

Stella <stellawrites84@gmail.com>
to Andrew

Andrew,

You are a wonderful, honest, kind, human being. And I'm sorry. I hate that there is nothing I can do or say to make life better for you. But I know that you will be happy again when you decide you are ready. That's what I decided finally, after months of crying and wishing trucks would hit me as I walked across the street. It took me a very long time to forgive myself, and even now, there is an underlying guilt every time I smile which tells me I should be paying penance instead. But overall, I am much more cautious now, much more kind to myself, and much more sensitive to my surroundings. It took a while, and it was dark, but I eventually realized that the darkness wasn't going to become light on its own. I know you'll find the light, too. Forgiveness helps. After months of wishing he would die, I am even on good terms again with fuckin' Wil, who basically ruined my whole life, and sometimes I see him and chuckle about the absurdity of it all.

I can't help but think: We are all going to die. This moment is all we have. That is the thinking that got me into this mess, but it is also the thinking that has brought such beauty into my life. I sat right in the middle of my pain, and when I was done grieving, instead of closing my heart off to the world, I left it open, wounds and all. I took responsibility for the chaos I created. I'm still lost when it comes to many things, but I think that now I have a better sense than anyone of the things that truly matter in life. You were one of those things and I lost you. But now I know. At least I know.

You deserve to be living the life of your dreams. Do you know what you want? Did you know really when you were with me? I don't care if you like to hear it or not; I love you and I always will. You are one of the most special people I have ever known, and I will always be waiting for the day we can talk again. I am so grateful for you, and I think the world is a much better place with you in it.

I did what I did. I regretted it for a long time. I begged you to take me back and you made the decision not to. So that is a happy thing—you made a decision! And we are young. Nothing is written in stone. I wish I could make you love yourself, but this is your hero's journey and you will get there. I understand your need to move on. If divorcing would make you feel better, please talk to me and we will figure out how to do it cheaply. There are so many possibilities in this world! You were always very good at putting things in perspective. You've spent a long time thinking. So what is holding you back from happiness?

I love you.

S

JULY

There was bound to be a fight sooner or later.

Stella and Dylan had decided to ride their bikes fifteen miles south to visit Dylan's cousin James in Hermosa Beach. Stella had envisioned a leisurely, sunny ride, singing and chatting like she and Andrew used to do on the bike path, stopping to have beers at the three other parties her friends were throwing along the way. But they were ten miles in and it seemed that Dylan didn't even realize she was there. While she sweated up hills on her rusty cruiser, struggling to keep up, Dylan whizzed past the beauty of the day on his racing bike as if he was trying to win the Tour de France.

"Can you please chill?" she said.

"It's four o'clock. I told James we'd be there already."

"Well we're not. So can we just enjoy the ride instead of racing there? I don't even have gears on this bike! I thought you were going to actually talk to me. If I knew this was what it was going to be like, I would have brought my headphones."

"I thought we were riding bikes. What do you want to talk about?"

"The people over there? The waves? I don't know, but I thought we were together."

"We are together. What do you want me to do, stop every five minutes and ask if you're okay?"

"No. I just want to spend my holiday enjoying myself with someone who is also enjoying himself."

"I am enjoying myself. I guess you're used to someone fawning over you." He affected a gentle flower-child voice. "Is *this* what you want, sweetie? How can I *serve* you?"

"No, that's not what I want."

"What the hell do you want, then?"

"I don't want to feel like some bitch who's just tagging along on *your* bike ride."

"Oh, I'm sorry," he mocked. "I'll just let you go in front so you can feel like you're in charge, since that's what all the rest of your boyfriends have done."

"God. I'm going to kill someone if I don't get a beer."

"What the hell is wrong with you?"

She kept pumping. Her legs burned.

"Oh, let's see. I'm keeping up with a racing bike on this cruiser, I'm starving, and I'm flaking on my friends. My boyfriend has had a frown on his face all day and is acting like I'm not even here. Why are you not talking to me?"

"Because it seems like everything I say is the wrong thing!"

She remembered when he told her he could be a real asshole. Now she understood. "I'm just going to turn around," she said. "Maybe I'll stop at one of my friends' parties, since they actually want to see me."

"Okay. Because this is no fun for me either," Dylan said.

Just then, they were passing a ton of revelers under tents on Manhattan Beach. She felt the day slipping out of her hands, but something told her she could turn it around.

"Can we just stop and rest for a minute?" she said.

Dylan considered. "Okay," he said, huffing toward the sand.

They dropped their bikes and settled in before the ocean. She pushed up his sunglasses so she could see his eyes. He looked hard, but maybe he was feeling inadequate somehow. She didn't know what was going on in there. It occurred to her that her expectations for the day were the entire reason she felt nasty. Stella had thought she was a carefree person who lived in the moment, and didn't need control over everything the way Dylan seemed to, but she was obviously wrong.

"I'm sorry," she said.

"I just don't know what you want me to do in this kind of situation."

"Nothing," she said. "I'm just not used to—"

"Not getting your way?"

"Well," she said, "yeah. There's more than that, but I guess that's one thing."

"I'm not going to cater to you. That's not me."

"Yeah. And I don't need that. I just want you to be exactly how you are. So I will be more direct in the future if I want anything."

They sat and looked at each other. His serious face looked so self-righteous. Stella still kind of wanted to smack it off him.

"Okay," he finally said. "When I don't know how to respond, I just freeze up. And, seriously, you just said—" He launched into an unflattering impression of her.

She cut him off, trying not to laugh. "Fuck off," she said, pushing him.

"I'm going to tell you next time you're being unbearable."

"Good!" she said. "I can't take that passive-aggressive nonsense. Now, before we get on those stupid bikes again, can we please get a beer from these people?"

"I'll go ask."

She watched him traipse down the sandy hill, returning with two bottles of beer. The last five miles, he rode beside her.

***

Blueberries, yogurt, whole wheat tortillas. Ninety-nine cents, ninety-nine cents, ninety-nine cents. Like most broke people, Stella got most everything at the 99 Cent Store. The checkout girl Maribel, a pudgy Latina with a red birthmark across her eye, scanned a Shasta cola, ninety-nine cents. Stella opened it and took an unabashed swig, which effervesced cold and sweet down her throat.

"I've been looking at those all day, thinking about getting one," said Maribel, gesturing to the cooler. "But I was thinking either the Squirt or the Fruit Punch. They're a dollar, but it might be worth it." Her voice was small and exhausted. Stella imagined she had a two-year-old at home, and that she had been at work for seven hours already and would probably change her mind about wasting a dollar on the soda for herself. She looked like the type who never drank or partied or splurged, who prayed nightly and cried alone bi-weekly.

"Which one?" Stella said.

She wouldn't say.

"I'm getting you one," Stella said.

"Oh, no, that's okay. I'm going on my break soon," said Maribel.

"Well when you go on your break, you are going to have this Fruit Punch, on me."

"Oh, I feel bad!" Maribel said.

Stella's mind wandered briefly to this morning when Dylan had lent her eighty bucks. She'd hated to accept it, but the checks for her most recent catering and acting gigs hadn't yet arrived, and she hadn't officially worked her first farmer's market yet. So this morning she'd panicked when she realized it was the first of the month and she was sixty-five dollars short to pay rent. This had, in turn, made her worry prematurely about next month's rent, and she'd begun to sweat so heavily she thought she had a fever. "I promise I'll pay you back in, like, two days," she'd told Dylan as he slipped the money in the waistband of her yoga pants.

Now she handed the checkout girl the red drink and said, "Scan it!"

"I feel bad! I shouldn't have told you I wanted one!" Maribel said.

"You are drinking this Fruit Punch," Stella said. "You've been working all day and you deserve it." Her own Shasta Cola was her reward for having worked as a server at a Malibu funeral in the hot sun earlier.

Maribel tentatively scanned the soda. "Thank you," she said shyly. "I guess I'll take it because my birthday is coming up."

"Oh really? When?"

"July seventh."

"Happy birthday! So you're a...Cancer?"

"Yes," she said, putting her drink aside for later and grabbing carrots to scan.

"Mine's coming up in August."

"How old are you going to be?" asked Maribel.

"Twenty-nine." Stella contorted her face.

"That's not old," said Maribel. "I'm in my twenties, too. How old do you think I'm going to be?"

Stella studied her—young voice, old eyes, slightly frizzy hair, a certain innocence in her words—then ventured, "Twenty-three."

"Close!"

"...Twenty-two."

"Yes!"

"Well I hope you have an awesome birthday!" She swiped her card and pushed the requisite buttons.

"I hope you do too," she said, handing Stella her receipt. "Thank you! And God bless."

"You too." She smiled, grabbed her bags and walked out to her car.

When she got home, there were two checks on the table with her name on them.

***

Stella was on the Duchamp's sectional. She was a lazy babysitter, feeling lethargic after a long, sweltering day she'd spent in the Valley, acting in a film directed by a blockbuster cinematographer. It had been a small role and Stella had spent about eight hours sitting, talking to hairdressers, snacking on hummus, and reading a book, while she waited to deliver her two lines: shot, reverse shot, that's a wrap.

The kids, immune to their proximity to the ocean, were entertaining themselves indoors. Evan was watching a loud baseball game while shaking a gallon Ziploc bag of icy ingredients, hoping it would turn to ice cream. Kara had gotten tired of yelling at her brother and retreated upstairs to finish a movie.

Stella sat looking at this week's calendar, noting with dread that Thursday was approaching, when Dylan would be leaving until August. She knew from experience that for her, three weeks could change everything. Stella moved more quickly than most people. She could fall in or out of love in three weeks. She could decide to go back to college or move to Europe. She could change jobs three times. She could lose or gain ten pounds. She could become a riotous success. She could get a new tattoo or change her name. She could rediscover a lost dream or friend or passion. What she could never do for three weeks was stagnate.

She drove to his house when her babysitting was done. He wasn't back from his referee gig, so she let herself into his private entrance with the key he'd just had made for her. It was red and shiny like a kid's balloon, and it meant that she no longer had to sit outside in the car waiting for him if she got there first. She slipped inside and posted up on his bed with her laptop.

She could hear someone in the house and hoped their paths didn't cross without Dylan as a buffer. He would be home from work soon.

At midnight, after an hour of writing, Stella couldn't hold back her urge to pee. She thought of going outside, maybe finding a cup in her car so she didn't have to go near Emily's room, which was right next to the bathroom. But that would be silly. She wasn't hurting anyone. She tiptoed as softly as she could through the house, though the old wooden floor creaked.

She emptied her bladder, and was further relieved to find Emily's door still closed when she opened the door. She quickly tiptoed back to Dylan's room as if a lion was sleeping two feet away. She passed the kitchen.

An angry voice: "How did you get in here?"

Stella jumped.

Emily was in the kitchen making a cup of tea.

"I just used a key Dylan gave me to his room. He's going to be back any minute now."

"He *gave* you a *key?*" she sneered.

"Just for nights when he's not going to be back until late." Stella scuttled through the curtain to the safety of his room.

Soon, Dylan arrived. He brought her a beer and chocolate chips.

"I have to drink less beer," she said, taking a frothy swig of hefeweizen. "I'll do it while you're gone."

"Are you scared of what could happen?" Dylan asked.

"I'm not *scared*. Are you?"

"Kinda," he said. "That somebody will snatch you up."

Three weeks had been the exact amount of time Andrew had been gone on his work trip when Stella had fallen in love with Wil, which changed her life's trajectory and led her to this very moment.

"I choose you," she told Dylan. "I just hope you'll like the person I am in three weeks."

***

Dylan was gone, and Stella was busy with her new job at the farmer's market, which was such a relief. Instead of wasting away trying to look busy, she got to fill coolers with fresh juices from the factory, heave the coolers into a giant van, and drive it to a market where she hung out in the sunshine, talking to people as she sold and sampled cold colorful nectars.

At each market she had a partner, and today at Beverly Hills, her partner was Zeke, an actor and self-described total mess who vibrated with the same frenetic energy Stella had a few years back: a new-to-the-planet quality that made the current her feel world-wise and full of gravitas. Sometimes he sat like a statue; other times he paced and said things like, "See? I wish I could be more open like you are. I mean, I *can* be open. But usually I'm so compressed and I just bottle everything up inside and it is dying to get out. *You*, you just put it out there, you know? Like you don't even care if anybody is listening or cares, you just say what comes to you. You're so relaxed about it. That's what I need to make me a better actor. I'm working on it. Have you had any auditions lately?"

"They keep sending me out for commercials where I have to play moms," Stella said, laughing. "Can you see me as a *mom*?"

"Now that you mention it, I kind of can," he said.

The heat was cooking their brains so that toward the end of the day, they kept forgetting things. Zeke drove three miles in the wrong direction and Stella didn't notice. They forgot the cash box in the van when they went into the office to count the money. Then, when they went outside to retrieve the cash box, Zeke locked them out of the office.

"I'm going straight to the pool when we're done," Stella said.

Zeke said, "Oh my gosh, I was just telling John yesterday that I am on a mission to swim this week. I've been talking about it for days!"

"You can come," she said reflexively.

"What, really? Well, I have a class. But I could come after my class. Would that work?"

"Okay."

By evening when Zeke arrived, a fog had rolled in.

"It seems too cold for the pool now," he said.

"It does. We have the hot tub I guess," she said.

"Sounds good to me," Zeke said.

"Want to just bring some wine down, too?"

"Great idea," he said.

Stella poured 2-buck-Chuck into some coffee mugs and they headed down four floors.

Heat bubbled up past her thighs, the steam releasing her exhausted muscles. Zeke squirreled his way underwater, one step at a time, and sat across from her. They talked about the people they worked with, acting, relationships, and goals. Stella found out she was nearly five years older than him. They finished the wine. Her fingers were getting wrinkly. They stopped talking for a minute.

She recognized the look flitting across Zeke's eyes, turning them from childlike to resolute. And that's when she realized: it had been a while since she'd been in a situation with the opposite sex that required boundaries. Pre-Dylan, there was the string of one-daters. Prior to that, there was the Wil affair, and before that, the open relationship with Andrew. Hence, for the past four years, she'd been free to pursue anything she desired, whether it was making out with guys at bars, fostering tawdry conversation, or giving out her phone number out like candy.

But what now? Was she allowed to be friends with guys she'd have likely seen naked if she were single? Was it kosher to sip wine in a hot tub with a likable guy when the man she loved was out of town? She was not good at rules. She was only good at following her own internal compass.

But now, she thought—and she said it out loud to Zeke since he so was so fond of her openness—she had begun a new chapter which marked a new romantic style. She would still keep an open heart and mind to all that surrounded her, but maybe when it came to one-on-one interactions with men, she could draw a line and decide not to cross it.

"You know when a miracle happens, and you suddenly have something that's so perfect, it's exactly what you've been looking for?" she said.

"Yeah," he said, "and you are always thinking of how you might screw it up?"

"Yes. Well, I am just *deciding* this time that I am not going to screw it up."

***

The next few days Stella sold juice and had adventures. One afternoon driving the unwieldy juice van, she dinged the bumper of an anxiety-ridden man's car, which was parked in an illegal spot at the gas station. The old Stella would have stressed over this, but she kept her composure and was even able to comfort the man before they parted ways.

Another afternoon as she left the Beverly Hills market, an older lady with fried blonde hair and a European accent asked if Stella could take her to a job interview. She had missed the bus. Stella decided the risk was low, unless the lady had a gun, which wasn't likely. So she drove the lady to her interview. She worried that the lady might ask for money, but instead they had an encouraging conversation.

After a yoga class on a day off, Stella walked down the Promenade, talking to Dylan on the phone. "I was really impressed with the rough cut of your movie," he was saying, about one of the short films she'd worked on earlier that year. "There were things I would have directed differently, but I couldn't stop watching you."

"Well, in 16 days, you can watch me in person," Stella said.

As she hung up, she noticed she was passing the Apple store where Andrew worked. She looked through the glass, and there he was. He was wearing new shoes and skinny trousers. He looked handsome, though his beard was overgrown and he had a large new tattoo on his forearm.

Stella felt chilled, as if she had left a window open somewhere in an otherwise comfortable room. It was a distracting draft she felt every now and then, and the window was stuck. She wouldn't have walked in, but something told her that Andrew controlled that open window, and she might persuade him to close it if she could just talk with him face to face.

She tread softly through the lions' den of his coworkers, loosely holding onto the peace from yoga class. Some people she recognized ignored her, others sneered, and one, she swore, muttered "bitch" as she walked by, now conscious of her damp clothes and bare face. She wanted so badly to hug Andrew and tell him everything would be okay, but when she got within a foot of him, she saw his pretty eyes were dead crystal marbles. His body seethed with hatred as if for seven months he had been using his memories of their last days together to brick-and-mortar himself into a little box of misery.

His words were as poisonous as the air he exhaled. "You can't love," he said quietly. "You're just an addict. And you're not even addicted to real love. Just that stupid butterfly feeling. And when that goes away, you don't care about the person anymore. You're just going to keep doing that until the day you die. Falling in love over and over again and then throwing it away for the next guy."

Stella felt like she was choking on saltwater, gasping for air. What if it was true? What if she was no better than Wil? No wonder everyone in this store hated her, and no wonder Janice and Jen and Rob and others had cut her out of their lives. The sadness in her recognized what it must be like to be Wil, to do the best you can and find that reality is always on the other side of a dirty window. Everything then became frustration. *Fuck you*, she suddenly wished she could say to all the people who thought they knew the inside of her heart. *Have you never had a relationship go awry? Would you rather I had lived a lie, locked in a stagnant marriage? Would you rather I had made both myself and Andrew miserable by keeping up a charade that made a mockery of the relationship we once had?* She knew truth was the only savior in any situation, and whether or not it looked good now, her strength, her leaving—had saved them both.

"This is not fair. I can't leave," Andrew spat. Stella breathed into the brief, intense pain of his final rejection.

"It's okay. I'll go," she said.

It was somewhat freeing, knowing there was no chance of ever laughing again with the Andrew she had fallen in love with seven years ago. The baby-faced artist who empathized and protested others' injustice, the good listener who was open to damn near anything, her sweet, mild-mannered lover was dead. And officially, their marriage would now follow.

***

The morning was smooth: just Stella riding waves as they came to her, answering to no one. She let the cool water slide through her fingers and toes, sensing the movement of the ocean, feeling out the delicate balance between the external and internal, reading as best she could the torrents that came, and judging how much control she could have. Now that she was aware of this balance, she knew that everything from here on would hinge on her ability to glide from the crest of certainty to the trough of uncertainty and back again. How had it taken her this long to see the beauty in this game?

She returned to her car after an hour and tugged off her wetsuit, finding the little key pocket to unlock her—

No. There was no car key in the pocket. She retraced her steps over the sand, but it was futile. The key was probably at the bottom of the sea. She ran back to her car and looked inside. There on the passenger seat was everything she needed: her phone, apartment keys, and clothes. But she couldn't get to them. The meter had 24 minutes left on it. She'd get a $64 Santa Monica ticket if that expired. Not to mention she had to work in an hour.

"Shit," she said to herself. "Shit." She slid the surfboard and wetsuit under the straps on top of her car and ran into Cha Cha Chicken in her bikini. Only the cooks were there: all Mexican men.

"Puedo usar tu telefono, por favor?" she said.

One of the guys lent her his phone, whose commands were all in Spanish. She was about to dial someone when she realized: she had nobody's number. Except her mom. Stella called Linda.

"Hey Mom. It's me. Remember how you made me give you my roommates' phone numbers? Do you have them?"

Linda's slow, sweet voice drawled patiently, "Let me see if I can find 'em." She shuffled around for a few minutes. "I think they're at work. I can get 'em for you."

"I'll have to call you back from someone else's phone."

"Okay."

"Don't worry; I'll be fine. Call you soon. K, bye." She hung up, handed the phone back into the kitchen, and ran out the door. "Thank you!"

What else could she do? The meter would expire in fifteen minutes. There was only one person Stella knew who lived close by and was likely home. She took off running for Wil's place.

Her bare feet hit the sidewalk, boom, boom, boom, as her eyes scanned the concrete for glass. "Damn, girl!" someone cat-called from a car window, reminding her to be self-conscious of her ass bouncing past all the cars at the Pico stoplights. The sidewalk was hot. Her breath was choppy. She had four shoeless uphill blocks to go. She finally reached 7th Street and ran up the stairs. Strangely and wonderfully, she felt no association with the apartment or the door she now pounded on.

"Wil! It's me! Are you home? Wil!"

A minute later Wil cracked the door with heavy-lidded eyes. "What's wrong?"

She told him the story of the lost key and, with profuse apology, laid out her requests for parking meter money, two rides—one to the parking meter and one to her apartment—and a phone to borrow. "Seriously, if you can't, I'll figure it out."

He exhaled a stream of cigarette smoke. "No, I'd love to drive you. It's okay."

"Really?"

"Yeah. It's no problem."

"Thank you so much."

Wil put his shoes on.

What a strange event being human was. Stella got into the passenger seat of the Prius that was technically hers, sweeping away the empty water bottles, candy wrappers, and receipts.

"There's some quarters here in the cup holder," Wil said, folding his long arms and legs into the driver's seat, "but they're covered in gunk."

"I don't care," she said, picking out four gunk-covered quarters. "Thank you. Really. Like this Spanish woman said to me the other day when I gave her a ride because she missed the bus"—Stella did a Spanish accent—"You are my angel today, my dear. You have saved me."

Wil laughed sweetly, a laugh filtered through melancholy. Then he was silent. Stella wondered if he was thinking about that moment in time when there were not enough hours in the day for them to pour out their words. What a verbose six months they'd shared.

She thought about what Dylan had said when she'd first told him about her weakness for men who were dexterous with words. "I understand the appeal there," Dylan had said. "Words can be beautiful. But words are like boxes, and if you don't fill them up with actions, then they're just empty."

Now as Wil drove her east on Olympic, she drank some water from one of the bottles on the floor. They chatted a little about music, and how poor they were, and how everything they thought was theirs getting stolen away might not be such a bad thing. Then a song came on. Stella recognized it from the mixtape he had made her back in September.

Heaven knows there's not one thing left to say, went the refrain.

Wil parked at her apartment and stayed until she returned with her extra car key.

***

All Stella had known about missing someone, really, was the reaction her brain had produced after she left Andrew. Not having him there for those first few months had been disorienting and dark, like falling into a well.

Missing Dylan was a completely different and new experience. Her days were filled with a sweet discomfort, like surfing in a winter ocean until she couldn't feel her fingers. The contrast of her living body atop the moving water showed her the purpose of the numbness. One could not exist without the other. Dylan's absence, she knew, would likewise show her the beauty of his love, and vice-versa.

Nonetheless, Stella found herself filling every hour with activities—working on her fictionalized life stories, going out with friends from Ladidahs, enforcing arbitrary workout goals, making playlists, browsing Goodwill, going to yoga, reading voraciously, selling juice at the farmer's market, even modeling designer clothes for a photo shoot Rebecca had organized—but she missed Dylan's calm, his conversation, his cuddling, his cooking, his care. Love was her source of greatest joy. When she woke up, he had sent her a picture of him holding a coffee. She texted back:

Gaaah I miss you. Misery, pure misery!

Dylan:
Oh I hope that's not the case. That's a lot of pressure to be in

charge of your happiness. :) I miss the shit outta you too.

A record scratch killed the fluffy romantic music in her head. She reread his text. "That's a lot of pressure to be in charge of your happiness?" In what world did a lighthearted remark about missing one's boyfriend after two weeks away equal "a lot of pressure?" Up until now, Dylan's fears had come from Stella's sordid relationship history: fears that she was a fair-weather lover who would dispose of him like last month's magazines. That made sense. But was he now afraid that the opposite was true? That she was so weak she needed him to fill gaps in her empty soul?

Stella:
Don't fucking worry, I'm in charge of my own happiness. I'm just a human who hasn't had sex in two weeks, or intimacy or love, and I don't know why everything I say has to scare you to death. I'd like to be able to share my feelings with you, whether good or bad. So tell me now if you're looking for something else.

Why couldn't he just let her love him, free and easy? Based on empirical evidence, she knew he loved her. Whose feelings was he afraid of, Stella's or his own? Was he afraid of losing Stella, or was he afraid of losing himself to her? And, moreover, why was it impossible for Stella to ever stop herself from saying exactly what came to her mind?

Stella:
But I assure you...I have made it almost three decades living a mostly magical life, which is my own doing. I am very happy, and what I want in a partner is someone to share it with who is kind, creative, funny, responsible, open, adventurous, sexually adept, ambitious, and loving. In my estimation, you are all that and then some. So it only makes sense that after two weeks without you, I'd miss you. Duh.

Dylan:
I appreciate your honesty and straightforwardness. I also have a hard time sugar coating the truth. I do want to go balls-to-the-wall with you and I love you. But I'd be lying if I didn't at least respond to the way you seem to feel about time apart. It alarms me a bit and because it's our first time away from each other for this long, I just want to communicate how I feel towards you in an open way. That's all. If my responses scare you, I'm sorry, but I need the freedom to say what I need to say. In this case I

just wanted to see if this text about being miserable was a sweet way of saying I miss you, or literally, I am fucked without someone to love me and hold me. Because if it's the latter, then we need to talk. I've always seen you as a strong and independent woman, so I'm pretty sure it's not the latter but I need to make sure.

She felt like she was wearing an apron and rollers in her hair, like she had just baked her man a pie and he had thrown it on the ground at her feet, yelling, "You know I don't like rhubarb!" It was incomprehensible that a comment, meant only to make him smile, could be taken so seriously.

Stella:
Frankly, I'm insulted and hurt. What do you need, proof? If ya want, we can stay apart for another two months if that would convince you. I'll stay single and just get on with my life, be happy alone...then you can come back when you think I've "proven" myself. I mean...come on! Would you rather I not miss you?

What had he wanted? Clinical terminology? ("Dylan, I want you to know that I am, at the moment, perfectly content without you; however, I cannot help but think that my life would be much improved if you were currently in Los Angeles rather than in New York.")? Stella thought of her mom's voice saying, "Stella, you never know when to quit," as she typed more.

Stella:
FYI, I don't NEED you and I'll never say I do. I just WANT you, but if that's too much trouble, I can stop doing that easily.

That's when Dylan called. He told her he'd been hanging out with his old friend Ryan and Ryan's new, clingy girlfriend. "It was disgusting," he said. "I guess that influenced me a little." Then he went silent. Stella didn't feel better. Why the hell would he compare her to this codependent girl she'd never met, as if he didn't know her at all?

"I'm still getting to know you," he said. "We've only known each other for a little over three months, technically." And she remembered; Dylan was more cautious than anyone she'd ever been with. This, she guessed, was his way of getting to know her. She'd have to really work on this Mars-Venus communication breakdown. At this point, Stella saw herself as Los Angeles: warm, hazy, in-the-moment, given to fits of road rage, but mostly rife with pleasantries and dreams and neighborhoods so eclectic they felt like different cities. And Dylan was still New York: self-sustaining and brash, too cold or hot at times, but always genuine and full of bustling energy and underground tunnels that went to amazing places.

"Yes, I've only known you for a short time," she said in his silence. "But there is such a thing as a true connection. You can just trust. I know we're coming from different places, but I have absolutely nothing to lose. We both know what's the worst that could happen in this relationship. It could end and we'd both be heartbroken. That's it. We've discussed it. We can live through that. But there is no end to what the *best* can be if we stop with the fear and the analyzing and just *love*. We have everything to gain."

Later she was deleting music from her computer that she'd probably never want to listen to again: music that reminded her of past lives. She came across a recording called "Andrew High." She pressed play and smiled, even through the cement-boots feeling of nostalgia.

"People are the same as this," he was saying in a pot-brownie voice.

"As that little duck on the TV?" came Stella's voice.

"Yes," said Andrew.

"Tell me about it," said the Stella-on-the-recording.

"Because," said Andrew, "that's what I like about people, where you have...*you*! Like you! You are a beautiful picture." He spoke slowly. "You are a beautiful goddess woman. Of a woman. Like, the ideal of all fuckin' women."

"Hmm," said Stella-four-years-ago.

"The thing that all real fuckin' dudes want some of," High-Andrew continued. "But you're also so quirky and crazy, and totally bat—drivin' me batshit."

The sound of a silent room took over.

"Driving you?" said Stella's voice.

"Driving me and all of us batshit. Like, you don't make any sense!" Andrew was saying.

"Mmm-hmm!" She could hear herself munching on chips.

"No, little duck in a TV, you don't make no sense. That's why we're so fuckin' similar," he said. "And so interesting for each other. I find you—do you find me really interesting?"

"Yes," her voice said. "Except for when you're boring." Here there were sounds of fabric shuffling over the microphone. Then her voice said, "Well. I'm merely saying—"

"Well, *I'm* merely saying," said the version of Andrew who no longer existed and would never again exist, "you're no good when you're performing."

She couldn't bring herself to delete it.

**

The market was slow; it was so hot in the Valley. People must have been at home under fans, eating takeout by the light of the evening news. Stella spent her day in a tent next to John eating bartered food, drinking the juice from their coolers, and quoting lines from *The Philadelphia Story*.

When things went quiet, she stared into the stale air of the parking lot and thought of how her skin had been grazed by no foreign hand for three weeks. Her nerves ticked in time with the seconds that passed. But none of her fears had come to pass during these 21 days; she was generally the same person. And tonight, Dylan was coming home.

AUGUST

"I love you." Stella opened her eyes in North Hollywood to Dylan kissing her forehead and putting a slice of nectarine in her mouth. There hadn't been more than a foot of space between them since the airport. They ate breakfast outside in the morning quiet, daydreaming about owning a house someday on a shady street with wind chimes.

***

It was the weekend of Stella's 29th birthday. She had 48 hours to make a film for a competition with a team of people she'd just met. They had drawn "musical" as their category, so they'd stayed up all Friday night writing lyrics, then heading to a recording studio to produce four songs. Stella had napped on a couch, and then consumed at least eight cups of coffee Saturday while they spent twelve hours filming.

Sunday, while the editors worked all day to make the 7:00 deadline, Stella treated herself to a birthday dinner, a movie, and a hike to the Hollywood sign. She sat for a half-hour on the dusty mountaintop looking over Los Angeles, and received an unexpected text from Andrew.

I wish things could have been different, too. I am sorry for a lot of things, but not for taking care of myself.

Half-dead with exhaustion, she drove to Dylan's house. She could tell he was excited as he led her to the garage. "I've been working all weekend on this, so I really hope you like it," he said. She had an idea what it was, but pushed it out of her mind to make room for surprise.

Dylan opened the garage door and there was a surfboard,

covered in polka dots and a neon sun, and Stella's name in careful lettering. "I spent all weekend shaping it and painting it," he said. "I barely got it done in time." He looked so proud.

Love overwhelmed her and she felt almost embarrassed, like a spotlight was shining on her. "Thank you. I love it." She hugged him tightly.

"You'll have all week to try it out on the family trip!" he said.

"I'm so excited."

They were both worn out, but they drank a bottle of champagne and crashed together. And so began the final year of Stella's twenties.

***

Dylan drove them through a guarded gate at the beach rental near San Diego. Stella had been thrilled that he'd invited her to his annual family reunion, but though she got a little wobbly thinking of her past experiences with boyfriend's families.

A sunburnt man in tennis shorts and a baseball cap came walking toward the car, smiling. "Son! You made it!" He waved and approached Stella's passenger window.

She introduced herself and he hugged her through the window.

"Stella. I'm Joe. Good to meet you. Welcome, welcome."

They parked and took their bags inside. A tiny, lovely Japanese woman was cooking. "Mama," Dylan said, hugging her.

"Hello!" Stella said.

"Stella, this is my mama, Ayame," Dylan said.

"We're glad you could come, Stella," she said.

***

The Campbells took Stella in. There were aunts, uncles and cousins, family friends stopping by, everyone holding hands and giving thanks before sharing their meals. Dylan's brother couldn't make it, but his sister Ava, an elegant dancer, asked Stella to teach a yoga class to her and Ayame, and she did, out on the balcony. Ava was so different from Andrew's sister, who had once accused Stella of stealing her yoga mat. There were cousins playing monopoly and others watching TV, eating, and talking.

Stella's own loving family was quite small and had rarely gone on vacations. She had never known how rich it could feel to be included in such a clan. The seed of a dream planted itself in her: a future sprinkled with days like this, waking up when she felt like it to the sound of family laughing, drinking rich coffee out on the deck, playing around on the guitar for hours until she learned a few new songs, singing in harmony with her beloved, sneaking away to the bedroom in the afternoon, surfing for hours, eating burgers for dinner and drinking gin and tonics until the sun went down.

"What if this was what our lives were like every day?" Stella said.

"I'm not sure if I'd want that. I love this relaxing lifestyle, but I think it's important to have something you're working on. If you had the choice to eat dessert for every meal, would you?"

"No way," she said. "But there could be a balance. Here's an idea," she joked. "I'll turn this writing project into a best-selling novel, and then a series we can act in, then we'll have the money to have this leisure whenever we want. But we'll have projects to keep us busy so we're not having dessert for every meal."

"That sounds good. If you can do it, do it!"

She laughed. "Okay." But that dream would have to wait until she got her life in order. It was a long way off.

"Do I get to be a character?" he said.

"Yeah. I already write about you."

"Bad things?"

"Just the truth. Do you want me to read you something?"

"I don't know. What if I get mad about it?"

"You won't! How about the one where we first met?"

"Okay," he said. "I wonder if we remember that the same way."

"Let's see," she said, and found the story on her computer. "Are you ready?"

He nodded.

"Okay," she said. "If it sucks, please pretend otherwise." And she started to read.

"Back at the end of 2012 when I was still living on 9th Street in an open marriage, and also suffocating on infatuation with Bad Idea Boy, there was a day when I worked two catering events back-to-back. The first was some corporate buffet near Culver City. The second was a warehouse party in Downtown for a bunch of graphic designers.

"By the time I made it to the stark metallic Warehouse District with my coworker Jesslyn, much had gone wrong. The company had given us the wrong address, so we were late. Half the food was missing, not to mention my feet were killing me. I was sure that I smelled of sweat and tacos and looked about the same, with my dyke-chic haircut and black tie. To counter the severe butchness, I smoothed on some bright lipstick, went inside and tried to make the best of it."

Dylan laughed. "Butch? I thought you looked hot!"

"Thanks, baby!"

She continued with the story. "'I hope they get drunk enough not to care that all we have is a cheese plate and some meatballs,' I told Jesslyn, arranging the cheese.

"My wish was granted, because, in addition to the full bar, there was a little wine station set up across the way. I couldn't help but notice a very attractive, vaguely Asian guy that came with that territory. I hadn't, in the past, felt much of a pull toward that direction (East), but I loaded up a plate of meatballs and took it over to the handsome wine pusher.

"'Are you hungry?' I asked him with an eye-twinkle.

"'I could eat,' said the hot guy. He had a nice smile, decorated with perfectly placed dimples.

"'Well, for the price of one glass of wine, these meatballs could be yours,' I said.

"'I think I could do that,' said the increasingly handsome guy. 'Do you like red or white?'

"His eyes were the color of sunshine on swamp water. I looked into them and said, 'Always red.'

"He poured, and handed it to me, saying, 'Has anyone ever told you that you look like—'

"'Emma Stone, I know.' I heard it once a day. It was not true, and was starting to get annoying.

"'I was going to say Olivia Wilde.'

"'Oh!' I said. 'Thank you!' I took a sip of the wine."

"Then there was that whole thing about me telling you that my name means 'ocean,'" Dylan said.

"Oh yeah. I'll have to add that. I'll find a good name for you. Okay, here's the rest. I saw the hostess coming by and decided I should return to my bleak food station. 'I'll be back later,' I said, chugging the last of the wine.

"'Alright,' he said. 'I'll be right here.'

"I made quite a few trips to that corner of the room. Every time, we'd talk, our conversations moving with the ease of Malibu waves, and it would feel like we had known each other forever. I circulated, slightly giddy and evermore buzzed.

"When there was no more food and the job was done, I removed my tie, undid the top buttons, untucked my shirt, and reapplied my lipstick. As I was nearing the exit, though, I stopped myself. Or a feeling stopped me. I couldn't leave without at least having a way to contact him again. Maybe it was the wine. I tore off a piece of paper and wrote down my phone number.

"He was occupied, helping to move a table. I brushed past him like a lynx and slipped my number into his back pocket. I walked out the door without looking back."

Dylan was laughing. "Wait a minute," he said. "I seem to remember you scampering away like this." He got up and tiptoed like a sneaky meercat.

"Not true at all!" Stella said. "I was totally slick!"

"You tell your story and I'll tell mine," he said.

"Well, whatever I did, it worked," she said. "Now, let me finish."

"Go on," he said.

"When I got home, he'd sent a text, asking to hang out soon. I was about to reply, when I realized that I was not, so to speak, ripe for the pickin'. I was in two doomed relationships at the same time: one that was dead on the table with nobody willing to work the defibrillators, and another that was The World's Largest Stick of Dynamite whose fuse had been recently lit.

"I knew I was not going to entrap someone so seemingly wonderful in this toxic lovetangle. So instead of responding, I simply saved his number in my phone, where it lay dormant for six months." Stella closed the computer.

"Have you written the story about our first date?" Dylan asked.

"Yes."

"I can't believe you went six months without contacting me," he said.

"I can't either," Stella said. "I have never in my life exercised such restraint. But it just wouldn't have worked otherwise. You're different from the rest of them."

***

Stella had been taught that God was a force outside herself and that life was something that happened to her. Love was "meant to be" or not, and she had no control. But this year had changed that. For the first time, she saw that the happenings in her life were in fact *because* of her.

Writing herself as a character helped. Taking a step back from herself, seeing her persona as exactly what it was—an identity she had created—she could study the details without investing in them. She could surrender for the moment to the endlessness beneath this silly 98.6 degree body, beneath "Stella" and all her adornments and attachments, and feel the joy of that stability.

But this new power was scary at times, finding that she was more than just a pawn of fate. Living with intention was difficult when the answers didn't come readily, and as she navigated these new waters, she often overthought. She felt the need to ask herself multiple times a day, *Are you happy? Are you sure you want to be here? Because you can leave if it's not working.*

She loved Dylan more than ever, and now that worried her. She found herself employing a mental points system to figure out whether she should risk wholeheartedly committing to their relationship. He cooked her dinner, +1 point. He ignored her when she said something, -1 point. He told his cousin he was crazy about her, +1 point. He refused to kiss her with toothpaste on her mouth, -1 point.

By Day Four of the beach vacation with his entire paternal line, the points had been adding up in Dylan's favor. After dinner, they were all hanging around one of the cousins' vacation houses, when Joe piped up. "Are we ready for poker?"

"I'm in," said cousin James, pulling two dollars in quarters out of his pocket.

"You know I am," said Dylan.

"Do you play poker, Stella?" Ayame asked. "They love to play when we come down here, just for quarters."

Stella thought of all the experiences she'd had with playing cards over the years, none of them enjoyable. But in the spirit of the moment, doing her best to participate in the family traditions, she said, "Okay, I'll play. But I don't have any quarters."

"I have a few," Dylan said, sitting down at the table. Stella sat down beside him. "Do you know how to play?" he asked her.

"I've played poker before. I'm probably a little rusty, but I'll learn as I go."

A few more family members joined in and sat down at the table. James started dealing the cards. "Everybody put in a quarter to start," he said.

"So, can I use one of your quarters, babe?" she asked.

"You don't even know how to play," he snarled, placing his own bet and accepting the hand he was being dealt.

Stella looked around at everyone else, picking up their cards. She felt the same way she had in pre-school when she had wanted to play at the sandbox and the kids started calling her a "sand witch."

"Are you seriously not going to let me borrow twenty-five cents?"

"I'll let you borrow it, Stella," said Ayame.

"That's okay," she said. "Thanks, though." Her stomach dropped as she watched Dylan looking at his hand, drinking a beer, as if she didn't exist. "I'm gonna go." She got up and walked out the door. She heard Joe say, "you screwed up, son."

-20 points. *Fuck Dylan.* Stella walked down to the beach in the dark and sat in the sand. Nobody she'd been with had ever treated her so coldly for no reason. She felt so vulnerable, doing her best to be accepted by these people she'd just met, and getting rejected by the one bridge she had to them. *Was she forcing this relationship? Was he already bored with her, or annoyed for some reason? Was Dylan actually an insensitive person, or was he trying to test her somehow? Should she end it before he broke her heart?*

He never came to look for her. She sat and cried for a while and then took a shower and went to bed alone.

***

The next day was gloomy and Dylan was stonewalling Stella. She wrote all day and kept away from him. Dylan's Aunt Neen and Uncle Don were celebrating their 45th anniversary. Neen glowed from the inside. Don looked at her like she was the most stunning woman alive.

"What's the secret to a long lasting relationship?" Stella asked Aunt Neen at the tennis court.

"Commitment," she said. Light went through the prism of the word and came out the other side as a rainbow. Stella could finally see the full spectrum. Commitment.

Stella went surfing alone. For the first time ever, she stood up and became one with multiple waves. She took rights and lefts and felt sure and steady, sliding down slopes of water until the whitewash stopped her, smiling ceaselessly with no witness but herself.

***

The sun lit the ocean on their last day, and the clouds surrounding Dylan burned off. He was kind again, laughing, and even apologized in his way (gravel-kicking shame under a thick mask of strength and justification). They surfed together and as Stella sat on her board looking at the endless horizon, she could see the waves coming. They were easy to catch.

If there was no such thing as a perfect match, at least Stella knew what she didn't want. She didn't want a lake like Andrew—still water where she knew every inch of the perimeter that contained her. And she didn't want to be dragged over rocks in the current of a rushing river like Wil, paddling against the stream to avoid waterfalls.

She wanted something that was dynamic with or without her splashing in it. She wanted something she could explore for a lifetime and never get to the bottom of. She wanted something that would lay her flat under a torrential wave, spin her around roughly, and then heal her with its salt and cool her with its tickly foam.

***

The week was over. No more sports challenges, children's laughter, bottles of beer, kitchen full of cooks. The moon was a waxing crescent. Dylan kissed Stella goodbye and the kiss became a universe all its own. She took hold of his arms, the mass of them rigid around her waist, his jaw stubble scraping her chin, lips soft and meaty. She undid his belt buckle, grabbed his hips, and pulled him to her, under the hem of her dress, against the broken spoiler on her Corolla. Later, Dylan insisted on Aquasealing the spoiler back onto the car.

Back in her empty apartment, Stella stepped in a steaming pile of truth as she checked her email. "Credit Alert: Your Rating is Now Poor."

She forwarded the email to Wil.

Now you have officially ruined my credit. This has got to stop.

He responded by telling her that next month, he was moving into a much cheaper apartment with his friend Spence, and then he

207

would have extra money to put toward the car payments. The damage was done, but on the bright side, if he was moving out, Stella no longer had to worry about the lease she had abandoned.

***

"Look at this shit!" Dylan said in his North Hollywood kitchen. "I just cleaned this entire kitchen this morning and it's already disgusting. Who leaves a knife covered in peanut butter on the counter? Look at those ants!"

"Man," Stella said.

"This has been getting on my nerves since I moved in here, but since we got back from the family reunion it's gotten worse by comparison. If you want to live in filth, do it in your bedroom. But when you do it in a common area, it's just disrespectful."

"Have you talked to your roommates about it?"

"Yeah, but they lived here before me, so I don't really have any jurisdiction. If it wasn't for me doing these dishes, they'd just stay in the sink until they grow mold on them. So I have to do it every time."

"You don't *have* to do it."

"But I can't stand to have the place where I prepare food to be unsanitary. Maybe they can live like this, but I can't. It sucks, because back in Brooklyn, I was the one in charge, so if things got out of control, I could call a house meeting. But not here."

"Let's get out of here," she said. "I'll buy you lunch at that sushi place around the corner, how 'bout?"

"Okay," he said, taking a last indignant look around the kitchen.

***

This month's existential crisis came on schedule. It amazed Stella how large-scale disasters were something she could put off, but when a string of small things went wrong, her mind withered. On top of plans that went awry, checks that didn't arrive, and miscommunications, she had spent three days in a doctor's waiting room to get rid of a urinary tract infection which was undoubtedly the result of too much sex, coffee, and alcohol during last week's vacation. "What if" scenarios crowded Stella's head. All the problems she'd been avoiding would conquer her; she would soon be hospitalized, homeless, dumped, and perpetually unsuccessful.

She called her mom and complained through a mouthful of cookie dough. "Honey, you don't need to worry," Linda said. "There's something you said when you were a teenager that I've never forgotten. You said, 'I see my life as a work of art, and a work of art is never finished.' You said you didn't ever want it to be."

"Hmm," Stella said. "I guess I don't. But I feel like I can't even control the brush right now."

"You will."

208

Stella imagined the cluster of colors that her life had become. It was abstract. But she wanted to find the forms and make them clearer. What would it all look like? How could she paint health, abundance, creativity, freedom and, above all else, love, without the muddling strokes of self-doubt?

***

An unrelenting wind buoyed the sails and chopped the salty water as Stella sprawled on the prow of the yacht, sipping her champagne. Behind the chilly breeze, the sun was warm and she looked over at this dark, sexy man who smiled at her with perfect teeth.

It wasn't a perfume ad; it was Stella's life. In this moment, she was rich.

The boat's gentle rocking quelled her mind. Dylan pressed his nose up to her face and she turned to kiss his wind-chapped lips. It wasn't their boat—it was a friend's—but it was their moment, and in that moment Stella became sharply aware of her ability to find the abundance that was all around for the taking. The more she recognized it, the more her riches seemed to grow.

On their way home, singing along to the radio, she took out her phone to attempt to capture the black palm tree cutouts against the rosy Huntington Beach sunset.

She had a voicemail from her farmer's market manager. Weird. She listened in case something had changed for work tomorrow.

"Hey Stella, it's Cody. I'm calling everyone to let you guys know before you hear it from someone else. As of September, Farmers Markets are going to be dissolved, and we have two options. We have been guaranteed positions at the stores, although that job pays three dollars less per hour than you guys make, or if you would like to cut ties with the company, you can file for unemployment. I'm sorry. I'll send a follow-up email to let you know the details. Thanks, Stella."

She hung up. "Nothing gold can stay," she said.

"What?"

"The juicery is going to stop selling at farmer's markets. But fuck it. I was feeling abundant today, and I'm gonna ride that out."

"What are you going to do?"

"I don't know," she said. It had been a sweaty, healthy, happy summer of work, but she'd had a feeling the job wouldn't last long. She threw the phone in her bag and turned up the radio. Maybe she was tens of thousands of dollars in debt and had just lost her main source of income. But today she knew one thing that nobody else in the world knew yet, and maybe nobody ever would: She was rich.

***

"Well," she said, squatting to boost a heavy juice cooler into the back of the dented van, "we're about to lose our jobs, huh?"

209

"Yeah. I'm kinda freaking out," said Zeke. "I think I'm going to go work at the store."

"I don't think I will," she said. She hated the fishbowl feeling of being trapped inside. "That would take away everything I like about working at a farmer's market, plus they're cutting our pay by a lot."

"I know," he said.

Stella wasn't worried. It was all part of the game. She'd had "stability" with Chet, and she'd had volatility from nearly every other job. She knew now that true strength was being steady through instability, since that's really all life was. Just the way she trusted the elements and her feet on a surfboard, she'd trust in her own ability to survive.

Later that day, four other farmer's market vendors approached her, saying they'd heard Stella was available. They asked if she wanted to work for them, and she said yes to two of them.

***

Claudia had finalized her divorce and gotten her old name back.

"Congratulations!" Stella said.

"Thanks. But I don't want to celebrate too early. Not until I find out for sure that I'm free of everything."

"I know how you feel. That's how I feel about Dylan."

"What do you mean?"

"The heart is such a fickle master. I don't want to jinx myself."

"That makes sense."

"But I do have him on lease until Christmas," she said. "We bought our plane tickets."

"You're coming to see me, right?"

"Of course."

"And he's meeting the fam for the first time?"

"Yeah. I'm kind of nervous. Do you think everyone will get along?"

"Your family is wonderful. Are you kidding me?" she said.

"You're right."

"This is a big deal," said Claudia.

"Is it?"

"You're basically proclaiming that you're going to be together four months from now. It's like you got married for four months."

"I guess you're right." Stella laughed. "But I'm not going to get too far ahead of myself."

***

Stella had been writing for about half a year, hundreds of pages. She knew she could have idealized her heroine, cleaning her of flaws and naïveté. She could have written her to always make the "right" decisions in an always-thrilling life with lessons that came in neat little boxes. But that wouldn't have been true.

"Hey. Do you have a minute?" Angie interrupted in a way that made her nervous. Stella turned from the computer, mentally scanning the past few weeks to reflect on anything thoughtless or offensive she might have done. Nothing came to mind.

"I've been thinking. I just turned 30 and I'm starting to feel kind of awkward about sharing a room. I've been working all the time on this nanny gig and I know I'm not here a lot of the time—"

"Oh," Stella sighed.

"But I am making enough money now that I think I can afford my own space."

"Dylan had recently said that he was starting to dislike his living situation, so it might be perfect for him to move in and split rent with me. Danny *loves* Dylan. And I know Dylan would enjoy having roommates who are actually nice, without the pressure of signing a year lease."

Angie looked confused. Then she said, "Yeah, well, Danny had actually told me that if there are any more roommate changes, that he wants to go down to just one person living in this bedroom, because there's been so much turnover and it's a lot of trouble."

Oh. Stella had thought Angie was going to move out. But was she asking *Stella* to move out?

"Huh," Stella said.

"Well you don't have to figure anything out immediately, but I just thought I'd talk to you about it."

"Okay," she said. "Well, I've got to go down to the farmer's market. My juice job is over soon, but now I'm selling pasta and Korean food. Better get ready."

***

Stella lay with Dylan on his bed, studying the symmetry of his eyes to see if they might be the same shape upside down. They might. "What would you change about your life to make you happier?" he asked.

It came pouring out. "I'd have a room of my own, and I'd live closer to you because all this driving really cuts down on productivity. And I'd be getting paid for writing and acting. I just want to feel a little secure. I used to not care about that, but now I do. I want to feel like I have a home." Stella was vexed, remembering the conversation she'd had with Angie yesterday. She'd only lived with these roommates for five months. She hadn't planned on moving a fifth time this year.

"Didn't you have all that with Andrew?" Dylan asked

"No. I guess I could have, but the thing is, I didn't make the choice to. Neither of us made any choices really; we didn't ever even talk about the future."

"I didn't talk about the future with my ex either," he said, "and I think that's because I didn't really see a future with her."

"I just wasn't conscious. We never talked about having a family, or made plans. I guess that's why we got open-married. Everyone thought we were making a commitment to be only with each other forever, but secretly, we were making a commitment to being noncommittal together."

The vagrant life had always called to Stella, but only if it was by choice. She liked owning little and needing only her sturdy self and the sunshine. What didn't appeal to her was becoming a vagabond accidentally: realizing that she'd gone years without making any real choices, and finding that she had no true home, no place or family or niche to call her own. She thought of what moving had stolen this year: money, objects, sanity, hope. "I'm already starting to feel like my apartment isn't my home. But I really don't want to have to go through that again so soon," she said.

"That doesn't sound like you," he said.

"What do you mean?"

"You're spontaneous."

"Yeah, I'm spontaneous like, 'Let's go eat at Roscoe's Chicken and Waffles.' I'm not spontaneous like 'Let's change my entire life right now.' Not anymore. I am over that portion of my life. Chapter closed."

Dylan kissed her a ton of silly little kisses like a pecking chicken on the lips.

"You'll figure it out," he said.

212

FALL

SEPTEMBER

"I'm in a rut," she told Everly while driving to her apartment from a surf where she'd caught no waves. "Nothing is moving. I don't know what the heck I'm doing. I need a real job. I need a real home. I need a purpose. I don't feel positive about anything except Dylan at the moment, and I don't want to put that kind of pressure on him to be the only good thing in my life. I'm broke. I don't know what to do next."

"I'm in a rut, too," her sister said. "Aaron hasn't been himself for a while, and it's really affecting me. I'm on Zoloft right now. It's making me numb and tired all the time."

"Ugh; I'm sorry."

"But it will get better. And then, you know, it will get worse again. That's how it goes."

"True." Stella pulled into the parking garage at her apartment and turned to get her—"Oh no. Oh no." *The surfboard.* Her guts all sloshed together as she realized that *her* polka-dot surfboard—the one Dylan made her with his own hands—was not in the car.

"What?" said Everly.

"My surfboard. Oh no, no, no, no, no." Her voice rose in trembling timbre. "I left it on the street in Venice. Oh my God; I am freaking out. It'll take me thirty minutes to get back there. It's not going to be there. I have to turn around. Will you stay on the phone with me?"

"Yes. What happened?" Everly asked.

"I was parallel parked on a side street, and I had to pull out of the spot so I could pop the back hatch. So I propped the board against a fence to move my car. But after I moved from the parking spot, you called, and I forgot to get back out and put the board in. I just drove off!"

"Don't freak out. It might still be there."

It was dark outside when she made it back to the parking spot.

"Is it there?" Everly asked.

She put her flashers on and got out of the car, barefoot. "No," she shrieked. "It's not there." She sobbed, not because she'd lost a surfboard, but because she'd lost the greatest tangible gift anyone had ever given her. Dylan was so proud of that board; he had put so much love into it. She had hoped to keep it until it broke down and then hang it on the wall when she was old. "I'm sorry, I'm gonna go and call Dylan."

She left a sloppy message on his voicemail, then walked frantically around the block, the concrete warm on her bare feet. "Excuse me, have you seen a surfboard?" she asked a man. He hadn't.

How reckless and stupid she was. She wondered why Dylan bothered loving her.

He met her at her place, holding her as her snot poured all over his shoulder. "It's just a surfboard," he said.

"But you made it for me," she cried.

"You lost the board; you didn't lose me," he said.

She felt helpless. Dylan stayed, but she woke up throughout the night, afraid this was a metaphor for where she was in her life, doomed to fail at everything. "I'm sorry," she repeated.

"No need to apologize to me," Dylan said, squeezing her steadily.

***

Stella stayed busy for a week at farmer's markets and catering gigs. Labor Day was her first day off. Dylan's, too.

On the "Lost Items" section of Craigslist they put up some photos of the surfboard.

She went to yoga. It occurred to her as it sometimes did that she, a mess of hopes and medium-rare schemes who owned nothing, was not one of the people out there who had real problems. She got stoned and ate watermelon with Dylan, then they watched documentaries in bed.

"Cybil sat me down and talked to me yesterday. I've been meaning to tell you."

"Okay..."

"I see her point, so don't get mad. Basically she said that she was glad I have a great sex life, but because I have a curtain instead of a door, I've been sharing it with the whole house."

"She was telling you that we need to have quieter sex?"

"Yeah, or just try to do it when they're not around."

"There are four of them," Stella said. "When are they not around? And we can't freely do it at my place because Angie could walk in anytime. I have to get my own place. I just want to live!"

"You can live, but you have to understand that when you're in someone else's house, you have to respect them."

"I'll just be celibate from now on."

***

Stella was soaked through with sweat from selling Korean food in the Valley. The end-of-summer heat wave signaled finality; fall was upon her. In L.A. there weren't too many leaves that fell away, but other things always did. This time it had been her juice job and her surfboard. She'd probably lose more. Maybe her apartment. But then she'd gain some things, too.

As she drove away on the 101, she wondered what it would be like if she moved to the Valley. It would be a lot cheaper, and she'd be a lot less exhausted since she'd be closer to Dylan. She was always living out of a bunch of bags, driving back and forth. She needed a place to settle down. A place with privacy and peace.

When she got back to the apartment where her roommates were watching Netflix, her phone buzzed.

> Hi. I saw your photos on Craigslist. And I also saw a post called FOUND SURFBOARD IN VENICE. Here is the link to their ad!

"No freaking way. Oh my gosh; someone found my surfboard!"

"Terrific!" Danny said.

She called Dylan.

"Aw, I was going to surprise you!" he said. "I just left Calculus class and I'm on my way to get it right now. This guy named Doty found it and kept it for you. He seems like such a nice guy. I offered to pay him, or at least buy him some beer, and he refused."

"Wow. I can't believe it. There are some good people out there."

"You're one of them," Dylan said. "That's why you're getting good vibes back."

"Thank you so much for getting it for me, baby. You wanna come sleep over at my house? Angie is going to be gone."

"Okay," he said.

"I'm going to be more careful," she said once her surfboard was safely stowed in the corner of her room. She hoped she could keep her word.

***

The heat wave was unrelenting, and after hours of sweaty rehearsing with the Ladidahs for their upcoming gig at the Roxy, Stella crashed in Dylan's bed. It had been three days, she noticed, since she'd been back to her shared room on the Westside. Since the conversation with Angie, she felt strange and unwelcome at her apartment. She never felt that way around Dylan, who didn't mind if she wore the same dress for days on end.

"How can I show you how much I appreciate you?" she said, peering over the book she was reading.

"You can lie there and accept my massages and eat the food I cook for you," he said.

"You're everything I've been looking for."

He looked serious. "You won't always feel that way."

"Why do you always say things like that?" she said, pressing her nose into his cheek. "If I say it in twenty years, will you accept it? When will I be allowed to say it?"

"When I feel like you really know me," he said. "You know a lot of me now—" but he seemed to feel the ever-present need for a disclaimer when things felt too perfect. He was bracing himself for disappointment, just in case.

***

Stella couldn't really move on until she extricated herself from her past completely: Andrew, Wil, and the debt. After the farmer's market, she returned to her apartment and excavated the stack of bills, parking tickets, and overdue car payments she'd been ignoring for months. After hours on the phone, quaking back and forth like a wind-up toy with various officious people who offered advice, she had not come up with a solution, but she had acknowledged one truth: Wil was never going to take legal ownership of the Prius. It was legitimately hers, and she had to get it back.

When she hung up the last phone call, anger and impatience had her fully wound. She drove to the edge of Santa Monica and parked, walking down the bluffs and inhaling the greens and blues around her until she felt safe and relaxed.

"How are *you* doing?" a bootcamp instructor flirted as she passed.

"Good," Stella said.

On this same grass for years she'd meditated, walked many dogs, done handstands, taken professional photos, ridden her bike, and spent hours looking out over the edge, casting wishes into the saltwater. Here she had cried when a homeless man serenaded her with "A Change is Gonna Come." Here she had sat laughing with Trev as they listened to the sermon of a manic street preacher on a bad acid trip. Here she and Wil had come with a laptop and a blanket and watched a movie after dark. In this tree she'd seen an owl one night. She wished she could call Andrew and ask him if he remembered.

This was the first city she'd ever chosen to be home, but she knew she couldn't keep clinging to it. She had already begun searching for places in the Valley.

The sunset was painting a strip of the ocean orange. A man in eyeliner walked by with a parrot on his shoulder. An old couple held hands on a bench.

How can I get this back? She asked silently. The answer came when she turned away from the water, stepped toward the curb and pressed the button for the crosswalk.

"Wait," came a mechanical voice, tailored for those who couldn't see what was in front of them. "Wait," it said. "Wait."

***

September 11th. Exactly one year ago, Stella had met Wil, and had chosen not to heed the symbolic red flag of the date, or any of the red flags that followed. And now she was standing on a chair in the closet, pulling down the box she'd been afraid to open for months. Claudia had given her the idea. She had kept Stella on the phone yesterday while she threw out every single artifact associated with her ex-husband. "Stel, I kind of already regret doing that," she said once everything was in the trash.

"I know," Stella had said, "and you probably will for a while. But eventually you won't think about it anymore, and then the only memories left will be the good ones that your brain actually wants to remember."

Thus she sat on the carpet exhuming the letters, knick-knacks, concert tickets and cards. Sadness took her when she found a garland of flowers from her wedding, and again when she found a note from Andrew that read, "Stella Robertson, you are the best thing that ever happened to me and I am going to love you forever!" She reluctantly threw out the lot of these memories, but she kept the flowers.

She was less resistant to discarding Wil's mementos. She took a whole pile—a notebook full of emotional outpourings, a few cards she now felt had been designed to manipulate her, and a little caviar box from that late Valentine's dinner—straight to the trash chute and sent it to rot along with the moldy banana peels and soiled tissues. For a bit of celebratory flair, she took his Joy Division T-shirt, set it on fire in the bathtub, and watched it burn.

***

Stella had to get to the Valley in an hour to see the first of three apartments, but a delicate green hummingbird was dead on her doorstep. Or no—its chest was rising and falling in a panic. She crouched down. "Are you okay, little bird?" Its eyes were closed.

She went inside and Googled "help injured hummingbird." Back outside, she lay on her belly. At the touch of her index finger down its back, it opened its eyes and looked at her. It seemed to be saying, "I made a miscalculation. I have hit a wall. I am stunned. I can't go on right now."

220

Stella tried to pick it up, but it clung to the indoor-outdoor carpet, letting out a loud "cheap!" Stella examined its wings. Perfect feathers glistening with oily rainbows of blue and lime. "Oh, little bird!" she said.

She ran inside and got a bowl, filled it with water and a scoop of sugar crystals, and stirred it up with a finger. When she knelt down and put the sugar water up to its mouth, tilting the bowl, the water leaked all over the carpet and the bird sat staring at her. But then, it opened its needle-like beak and took a few drinks. Its shiny breast dipped as it took in three gulps, each no larger than a tear.

Again Stella tried to pick it up. This time, it flapped its wings fast, but lost confidence and gave up quickly. The bird needed time to rest and receive the nourishment of the sugar water, so Stella went inside to get her things. "Please be gone when I come back out," she said.

A few minutes later, she opened the door again. The hummingbird was still there. It had closed its eyes again, but was no longer gasping for air. Stella pet it on the back and it opened its eyes as if to say, "What do you want from me?"

"You are going to fly again."

She gently cupped the bird in both hands and lifted it up. It flapped its wings so quickly that they became a green streak in the air, and it flew. It flew in the wrong direction, further into the hallway, stopping at a wall. Stella caught the bird.

"Wrong direction, but you can do this, Birdie! Up and out!"

She gave it a little push out over the balcony and the bird flapped with all its might, up, up, up, until it was far from the building, and out of sight.

***

"Guys, we're in the headliners dressing room," Erin said. "The other guys are in the *openers* dressing room. Just sayin'."

They laughed beneath kohl eyes and black lace. Stella had ghetto-rigged some big gold chains with a dangling dime-store crown-bling, and put a couple cornrows in her hair, which was growing out. It was Friday the 13th, and if bad luck was to find her, she was going down in fun.

Before they went onstage, they huddled amidst the walls of posters and Sharpie scrawls. "We've worked so hard for this," said Tessa. "When I was a little girl and dreamed of coming to LA, I never thought I would be performing onstage at the Roxy. Do you guys know how many great acts have been here? We've grown so much as a group this year, and this is the strongest we've ever been. So let's prove it."

They marched out behind the red curtain into a semi-circle of twelve mics. The band got their instruments and settled in. The sound guy came out and said, "You have two minutes. Do you want to wait or start early?"

"Start early," they said unanimously.

The curtains slowly opened as the announcer introduced them, and what they saw was a pleasant shock, as if they'd just opened the door to a house full of friends yelling "Surprise!" with streamers and balloons. The entire house was packed; people were inches from the stage.

"One, two, three, four," Victoria counted in. The band struck the first chord, and as they moved into harmony, Stella couldn't see the darkness because the light was shining right into her eyes.

***

"I haven't seen much of you lately," Danny said through a mouthful of popcorn.

"Yeah. Ever since Angie hinted that she'd like me to move out, I feel kind of awkward around here."

"She told you to move out?" he asked.

"Well, not in specific terms, but she said she wants a place of her own, and that she talked to you, and that you said you only wanted to have one person in our room."

"Really?" he said. "I definitely have *not* talked to her, but what about Dylan? You two could live in that room."

"Interesting," she said. "Well, I looked at three places in the Valley this weekend to see if I could live closer to Dylan."

"I wish I would have known this." But Danny was smiling, as always.

"Yeah, but it might be for the best. I have so many things in my life to clean up right now."

"Yeah. Your life is like a video game right now."

"It is. And I'm the hero. Dude, I'm done with this rut. No more 'letting things happen' to me. I'm going to conquer these levels."

"Is there a certain order to them?" Danny asked.

She thought about it. "There is," she said. "Okay. Level 1: I have to get the Prius back in my possession and figure out how to pay for it or sell it."

"Good. Good."

"Level 2: I have to get Wil out of my life for good. Which means, legally remove my name from any bills or money-related situations I'm in with him, and then delete him from my phone and my life."

"I like it so far," he said.

"Level 3: I have to sell one of the two cars. That's going to be a pain."

"Okay."

"Level 4: I'd like to find a place to live, cheap and closer to Dylan."

"Aw. We'll be sad to see you go, but okay."

"Level 5 is where I have to blow up the mountain range of debt I've acquired, partially thanks to Wil. So that probably means getting a good paying job. Level 6 is where I have to take care of all the paperwork and actually talk to Andrew to get officially divorced."

"Whoa. Anything else?"

"That sounds like enough for now. If I conquer Level 6, I'll have a permanent place to live, I won't be driving all the time, I'll have a good job that pays my debt, I'll be legally single, and it will be like Wil doesn't even exist."

"Well, you better get past Level 1," Danny said.

"Level 1: The Car Fiasco."

***

Stella had only driven the Prius once, to Vegas with her friends. She didn't even know its current location, since Wil had allegedly moved in with a friend this month. She did know, according to her threatening letter from Toyota, that it would be repossessed if she didn't pay $1260 by Monday.

She called the Toyota Financial people one last time for advice. A helpful guy named Jamal predicted that selling the Prius would be near impossible since there was twenty grand left and nobody would want to take over the payments. If she sold it, he said, she'd end up paying the difference for years, with or without the car.

"What would happen if I just let you guys repossess it?" Stella asked.

"If I were you, that would be my last option," he said. "What happens is, we take the car and sell it at auction, and if we don't get the full amount, you're still going to owe us the difference."

"Okay. So, I guess I could sell my old Corolla, somehow get the car back from this ex of mine, and then just keep the Prius?" She would have to get a job that would cover the payments.

"That's probably gonna be your best option," said Jamal.

She went for a run to burn off stress, and checked the mail on her way back upstairs. A severe looking letter from the State of California was addressed to her. She opened it and couldn't believe what she saw.

It was a late tax rebate. Hundreds of dollars to help her pay this bill so the car wouldn't be repossessed. *Thank you, Karma.*

***

Stella had four bags of loot from the farmer's market: two giant loaves of bread, two scones, two enormous pretzels, ten different gourmet pestos and tapenades, two boxes of fresh pasta, some hummus and feta cheese, peaches and grapes, and a tiny plastic container that housed a rock of pure opium. The flower lady, an old Chinese woman who raised her own poppies, had made it at home with her husband and given Stella some. After she laughingly showed it to Dylan, her roommates, and some other friends who had come for a barbecue ("I guess I could smoke it…but isn't opium just proto-heroin? And I could sell it…but then I'd be a drug dealer,") she settled on flushing it.

"My plan is to move out by October first," she told them through a mouthful of Lay's.

"Do you have a place?" Angie asked.

"Not yet," she said, "but it seems like the right time. I've found a few decent places so far. Mostly shares in the Valley, if they pick me."

"Well, you know you can come back and sleep on the couch anytime you want or need to," Danny said.

"Thanks. I might have to take you up on that."

Stella was so grateful for the six months she'd spent here. She'd regained her strength and relearned how to laugh. Now, whatever happened outside, she felt bulletproof on the inside.

When everyone left, she called Wil. He didn't answer, so she left him a voicemail. "Just so you know, not only have you caused my credit to drop 62 points, not only do I now have four-hundred dollar's worth of parking tickets in my name thanks to you, but also, Toyota is going to repossess the Prius if I don't pay them twelve-hundred dollars by Monday. Black and white. You pay this shit by Monday or I am taking the car."

She left Wil's mom the same voicemail, in case Judy wanted to jump in and pay for it.

Before bed, she had heard nothing from Wil, but she got a text from Judy that read

I got your message. I'll call you tomorrow.

***

The weekend was over. Judy never called. So Stella turned off her empathy, patience, and communication, and engaged Level 1.

She paid the outstanding Prius balance, with help from Dylan. The threat of car repossession was over, but after he lent her the money, which she hadn't asked for, Dylan's stress seemed to mount, along with his perception of what a "mess" Stella was. He picked little fights with her, implied that she was not where she should be, and briefly convinced himself that she was using him. Even after she paid him back (with money she borrowed from Linda), he withheld his affection and said she was needy for even wanting a hug. It was hard for Stella to believe in herself when the image he reflected back to her was so ugly and distorted, but tears couldn't deter her mission.

She stayed focused when she got a text from Wil's dad during her dinner of leftover farmer's market noodles.

> Stella, this is Pat Mallory. I understand you are trying to take Wil's car from him. FYI, I am good friends with a high-powered attorney, and he has informed me that legally, Wil has rights to the Prius since he paid the down payment and has been making payments on it. If you decide to proceed with taking his transportation, we can sue you for breaking the lease on the apartment, among other things. I don't think you will want to pay the court fees.

She didn't know what came over her, but she didn't blink before responding:

> Interesting, because I am also friends with a high-powered attorney, and my friend says that since my name is on the title and registration, the Prius is my car, and I can report it stolen if it is not returned to me promptly.

She finished her food and headed to bed to read a book. Angie was gone for the night.

> Pat Mallory:
> She called my bluff. Best to lay low. If anything bad happens, I'll do what I can for you.

Ha! Stella felt almost a little embarrassed for Pat. He texted her again in a few minutes.

> Pat Mallory:
> Sorry Stella. That was meant for Wil. I love him so much and I just want to protect him, you know.

> Stella:
> I know.

***

Dylan and Stella had made up. She had heeded Aunt Neen's "commitment" advice and decided to stick it out through Dylan's disillusionment. She had learned by now that he had many personalities, and the sweet one would rotate back around if she had patience. Maybe his Gemini manner was the universe's way of ensuring she didn't get bored.

They were at Wahoo's eating fish tacos after surfing. The waves had been so perfect that Stella had briefly forgotten about all the money she was going to have to come up with to pay back her mom. The company was so nice that she was able to ignore her struggle to get the Prius back. The chips and salsa were so delicious that she wasn't thinking of her move-out that was supposed to happen in two weeks, despite the fact that she still hadn't found a place.

And then Dylan said, "Certain things about my living situation are really getting on my nerves. I'm starting to think I need to change it up."

"Well, I'm looking for a roommate," she said casually.

He looked at her across the table, serious. "Would you really want to live with me?"

"Of course I would," she said. "We stay together at least five nights a week anyway." If they lived together, she figured, there would be no more driving, no more worrying about roommates, no more not being able to find her dental floss because it's in a pocket somewhere in the bottom of a bag. Not to mention, they could split the rent, and maybe she could begin to afford her life. "I told my roommates I'd be out by October, though, and that's coming up."

"I'll tell you what," he said. "I'm going to first talk to my roommates about you staying with me for a little while, and maybe we can find a place by November 1st."

She was shocked. She hadn't even mentioned living together because she assumed it was too early. Stella thought of crabby, hate-filled Emily. The thought of living with his roommates for any amount of time seemed unfathomable.

He came to her apartment and she showed him the rental site with all the rooms she had looked at for herself. He said, "let's create a new search. I'd love to live in a guest house. I just want some yard so I can have a garden."

She altered her search to fit his tastes, doubling the budget and looking for a one-bedroom guest house with a kitchen and a yard. They wrote down a couple phone numbers. Dylan called and left some messages to see if they could take a look that weekend. It all seemed too easy.

***

Stella worked catering at an office party. Vince was bartending. They ate coconut shrimp in the back room and talked about how happy they were that they weren't 9-to-5 slaves. The office workers' expressions were so resigned, their clothes so uncomfortable.

When she returned to Dylan that evening, he seemed to have something on his mind.

"I talked to my best friend today," he said as they walked hand in hand in the dark.

"Cool," Stella said. "What did she say?"

"I told her about the living together idea."

"Oh," she said.

"Yeah," said Dylan. "And I've been thinking. I think I made that decision too hastily."

It was as if Stella had been kicked in the stomach with a steel-toe boot. "What?"

He was measured and detached, the way he always was when he discussed matters that had the potential to make her emotional. "Don't you think it's too soon?"

She had stepped off a cliff and the ground was rising toward her quickly.

"Well, yeah, I thought it was soon, but that's why I never asked you to move in with me. You're the one who brought it up," she said.

"I know," he said, "but I've had time to think about it, and I'm not ready."

A barrage of thoughts and emotions infiltrated her mind. *Does this flaky behavior mean he is a selfish, untrustworthy coward? Have I just spent the past six months trying to build something with someone who is just going to end up breaking my heart? Should I go back to Kentucky and stay with Everly to save some money? Does he not understand that only an asshole would put such a life-changing offer on the table, then just take it away and expect me not to feel anything?*

They misunderstood each other for hours. Stella felt sick. She had reached her threshold of being taken advantage of and walked on, and she wouldn't take it from Dylan. Sleep dragged her to bed, but nothing was solved. She knew one thing: she had to put herself first, because nobody else was going to do it. But with her new understanding of commitment, she didn't let this mean anything dire. She pulled the fuzzy blanket over her shoulders and turned toward the wall. Love was the most important thing, she knew. She had only to love and everything else would figure itself out.

***

The police had told her to be at the station at seven in the morning to see the auto detectives. Dylan came with her, upstairs to a room so cold Stella's teeth chattered.

"I'm Detective Miller," a man finally said. "What can I do for you?"

"I have a situation in which a car that I own is being driven by someone who should not be driving it. I want the car back, but I don't know where he lives now."

"Did you initially give him permission to drive it?"

"Yes. In January, I said that this would be his car as long as he paid the bills on time and didn't get tickets in my name. The idea was that he was supposed to transfer the car to his name as soon as he was able. But he has defaulted on the payments and ruined my credit. I had to pay $1,200 last week so that it didn't get repossessed, and I'm going to have to keep making payments if I don't want my credit to keep going down."

"Well if he agreed to make the payments and he's not making the payments, he broke your verbal contract. You want your car back, so if he doesn't return it, this is a stolen car situation."

Confetti cannons went off inside Stella. Thank God she wouldn't have to hire lawyers and chase justice to the ends of the earth.

"So what you're going to have to do," said Detective Miller as he printed out a report and began to make notes on it, "is write a certified letter of demand and send it to his last known address. If that was your old address, you just send it there. It doesn't matter if he gets it or not; all you have to do is mail that letter and if he doesn't return the car in 30 days, you come right back here and we will report it as stolen."

Stella felt hope once again.

"Thank you for your help, Detective Miller," Dylan said as they left.

"No problem," said Miller. "It's just a cut and dried case."

***

She wrote a letter, got it notarized, made copies, and sent it to the 7th Street address where she lived with Wil for two weeks. She didn't call to tell him. She wondered if she should just wait in the shadows for 30 days so she could report the car stolen. How satisfying it would be to see Wil go to jail.

And then another piece of red-inked mail came. The parking tickets Wil hadn't paid had been sent to a collection agency, which meant another hit to Stella's already destroyed credit. She returned to the police station alone to find out if there was anything she could do about it.

"You can sue him later if the car gets reported as stolen," Miller said. "But if you want my opinion, you should just let me call him now. You never know: He might just bring the car back."

Stella thought about it. Was her thirst for revenge so great that she needed to wait three more weeks for them to throw Wil in jail? No. The sooner she conquered Level 1, the sooner she could get on with her life Wil-free. It wasn't her job to punish him; the universe would do that without her. "I'm just afraid if he knows I'm coming for it, he'll damage it or drive off to the east coast with it."

"Look at it this way," said Miller, "if he doesn't bring it back, he'll be responsible for a stolen car. And if he does something else to it, he'll be charged with that."

"Okay." She gave Detective Miller his phone number.

"Hello, is this William Mallory?" asked Miller. Stella paced back and forth one floor tile at a time. "This is Detective Miller from the Los Angeles Police Department," he said. "It has come to our attention that you are driving a car that is owned by Stella Robertson. Is this true?" Miller paused, listening. Three minutes of silence passed while Wil no doubt spun a story that only a professional liar could spin. Stella got nervous and took her mala beads off her wrist, running a finger over each one as she measured her paces back and forth.

"Well, have you been making the payments?" asked Miller. Another pregnant silence. Then: "Mister Mallory? It sounds like you're cutting out. Mister Mallory?" She kept walking and taking in slow sips of air, exhaling them all the way out. "I understand what you're saying, but the fact is, you two are in a very precarious situation. Your relationship has changed since January and if you're not paying, Stella wants her car back." Again he stopped talking. Stella stopped pacing and stared at her shoes. Blue flats with an ankle strap. "Okay. I'll leave that up to you two. Thank you, Mister Mallory."

Miller looked at her. "He's gonna bring it back. You two will have to work out the time and place. You can do it here if you want."

"Oh my gosh."

"I'd do it in a public place, you know. But if you need us, we're here."

"Thank you so much," she said. "I'm going to call him right now."

"No problem," said Miller, and he retreated back into the office.

She stepped outside the police station to call, and Wil actually answered.

"Hello," she said.

He immediately launched into dramatics. "You could have just asked for the car, you know. You didn't have to get Detective Miller involved. I can't believe what a big deal you're making. I would have brought it to you."

"Your word is not something that gives me confidence," she said, "and I want the car back. I'm at the police station right now, so you can bring it here."

"Well, uh, actually, Spence has to go to work so he can't bring me today and I still need to get all my stuff out of it and everything, so would there be any way possible that I could bring it to you tomorrow?"

For some reason, she agreed. "Okay. I work until 3 tomorrow, so I'll see you after that."

"Okay," he said. "We'll get in touch tomorrow to see what time after 3."

***

Stella spent the morning at the farmer's market lost in neurotic what-if scenarios. During slow times, she made a list with a red marker in her journal, and crossed off the first item to give herself encouragement.

~~Level 1: Get Prius back~~
Level 2: Get rid of Wil
Level 3: Sell car
Level 4: Home
Level 5: Get Job
Level 6: Divorce

She texted Wil to give him the address.

I will see you at 3:30 at the police station.

Two hours later, he hadn't replied.

Stella:
I don't think I need to tell you what happens if you don't show up with the car. It's called an arrest warrant in your name. See ya there! Or else Detective Miller will see you later.

Wil:
I'll be there.

But then, an hour later, he texted again.

Wil:
Actually, Spence has to bring me and my sister is coming and it's out of their way to come to the police station, so why don't we meet somewhere public like Miller said, like the Whole Food parking lot in Venice. Will you meet me there instead?

He called. Stella didn't answer. In what world did this joker think he had leverage to negotiate? No way in hell would Stella ever again adjust her plans for him.

Stella:
Dig your own grave if you want. It's the police station or jail.
***
Dylan walked to the station with her at 3:30.
They waited on the curb until nearly five o'clock.

She finally went inside the station to call Wil from the police phone, but as soon as it was ringing, Dylan knocked on the glass door and motioned for Stella to come outside.

There was Wil in the passenger seat, two hours late, sunglasses on, hunkered down and fumbling with stuff for at least five minutes before he got out of the car. His sister, who had driven him, gave Stella a death stare and then walked to the waiting getaway car with this Spence character. Dylan stood behind Stella like a bodyguard. Wil looked like a wreck when he got out. He had gotten skinny-fat and reminded her of the smog monster from *Ferngully*. He gave her the key and explained how to use it, and then Dylan, for some reason, got into the driver's seat of the car, so she took the passenger seat. Wil was still standing outside her open window, muttering about how she owed him for rent from all those months ago when she'd moved out and broken the lease.

"Just don't respond, baby," said Dylan. Stella didn't. They pulled out. "God, this car stinks."

It smelled like a year's worth of chain smoking and decay. There was—puke?—ground into the floor of the back seat. Stella shuddered when they parked and she found a syringe in the pocket on the driver's seat door.

But then she smiled, an authentic smile, because Level 1 was complete.

***

Her muscles twitched. Her body was baptized in sweat. Her yoga teacher was reading a passage about forgiveness.

Stella left the studio full of compassion. Her problems felt within her control. Now that she was finally free from Wil, she wanted to release him with kindness. As she walked to her bike, she composed a final message to him in her head. *As I remove your number from my phone for good, I forgive you for everything and I wish you the best.*

She turned on her phone to write him, but there was already a message waiting for her.

Wil:
You believe in karma, right? Well, at least I do, and you may not be able to realize this through your delusions, but when your disgusting behavior and treatment of me catches up to you, I just hope that you remember why your life will become a living hell (and why you'll burn in Hell for all of the wreckage you've caused with all of your victims that you tricked into thinking you had a conscience or a heart, and then crushed with your utter selfishness and complete lack of empathy.) See how far playing the victim card will get you in life, and see how many people eventually see through your facade and acting skills of

pretending like you are actually capable of caring about anyone or anything that isn't you. Good riddance, you fucking psychopathic monster...

Stella shook her head and deleted him from her phone. She had a brief thought that said *He knows where you live.* She wondered if she should worry, but decided to feel light instead as she deleted the very last trace of him from her life (besides the soul-stank she was still trying to erase from the Prius).

***

She shared the text with Serena while they stood at the Getty Museum looking out over the stirring city.

"Are you kidding me?" Serena guffawed. "Yeah. You're psychopathic because you let him drive a car in your name for nine months, and you are so selfish and heartless because you wouldn't let him continue ruining your credit. You monster!"

"I know," Stella said. "I'm so *delusional.*"

"Did his mom ever get back to you like she said she would?"

"Yes. She texted me and said, 'And now I really understand what William has been talking about all along.' He forwarded me an email that she had sent to him that said, 'I'm so proud of you for handling the situation with dignity and grace.'"

Serena's face registered shock. Then she said, "You know why she's mad at you, right? Because now she knows *she's* going to be the one to have to deal with his antics."

"Thank God."

"Imagine how awful it would be to have a kid who is such a loser! That's one of the things that scares me about having kids. But I'd hopefully not raise my kid to think he can do whatever he wants and step on everybody along the way."

"The most unbelievable part to me is that after all of this adversity, Wil has obviously not changed or learned anything," Stella said. "He squanders every opportunity he gets. He's just going to continue manipulating people, bleeding them dry, lying, relapsing into drugs, and taking no responsibility for his own actions until he kills himself. It's always somebody else who wronged him. But forget him. Level 1 is done. I got the car back. And as of today, I beat Level 2. I paid all the bills connecting me to him. Wil is out of my life for good! I have to cross it off my list."

"He's totally out of your life?"

"I blocked him and all our mutual friends on Facebook. I put his phone number and all his family's numbers on the block list for my phone. I went online and paid for all his parking tickets, which took my entire bank account. The fee had gone up to six-hundred bucks. So yeah. I should never get another piece of mail telling me I owed something that isn't mine. I took his name off the car insurance. So hopefully I'll never have to see or hear from him again. I mean, unless he tries to kill me or something."

"Seriously, Stella. Do you think that could happen? He is so unstable."

"I honestly don't know. But my building has good security and I'll hopefully be moving soon anyway. So, onto Level 3."

"That's cause for celebration. What is Level 3, anyway?"

"It's either selling one of the cars, getting a steady job, getting a place of my own, or getting a divorce. I guess I'll try all of the above and see which happens first."

That evening, Stella researched no-fault divorce in California. She found all the documents for a "summary dissolution," when both parties want out of the marriage, and she printed them out. She filled out her copies and put Andrew's in an envelope.

Stella:
I'm sending you the divorce papers. I'll pay for it. What's your address?

She was surprised when he replied with a Mid-Wilshire address. It was uncanny to picture Andrew anywhere but Santa Monica. If he had found a new home in a place they had never visited together, he must have been a new person. Stella addressed and stamped the envelopes, intent on mailing them tomorrow.

***

September had two days left. Stella told Angie how unlikely it was that she would make her move-out deadline of October 1st. Angie was fine with it, but the tension was building; Stella needed a space of her own where she could go inside and lock the door.

The one place she was still considering was a five-minute bike ride from Dylan in the Valley. The roommates, two lesbians and their dog, seemed nice enough. The place was about eight rungs down the ladder of luxury Stella was used to, but she would bloom where planted, she knew.

It was a beachy Saturday. She biked down to Venice and went surfing alone. She made new friends in the water and ran into an old friend on the street. She did yoga with one of her favorite teachers, got lunch at a food truck, and sat on the bluffs, content. That's when the women from Dylan's street texted her:

We've made our decision and we would love for you to live with us. You could move in on Tuesday, but please let us know by tomorrow so we can tell the others.

***

The Valley girls said it was okay if Dylan came with Stella to see the place before she gave them her final decision. They biked over and the house was as Stella remembered: dark but livable, with a slobbery, friendly dog that jumped on everyone and shed all over the couch. Her potential room needed a paint job and had a strange sloping ceiling, but it was private and decently-sized.

"It's ghetto, but I would at least have a place of my own," she told Dylan after they left.

"I think you could do well there," he said. "There's a nice little park nearby, and the library, too. Wanna ride over and see?"

"Sure," Stella said.

They rode off, and though the wind sailed past her face, her heart felt leaden.

At the park, Dylan led her through the grass to a Eucalyptus tree. He took a leaf between his fingers, rubbed it, and inhaled. "Doesn't the oil smell good? It reminds me of my childhood."

"It is nice," she said, and gave the tree a hug. Then they lay down.

"What a perfect day. Look at that bum," said Dylan. "He is never going to get as close to peace as he is right now." The breeze blew. It felt a little like the Westside. Except the beach wasn't within walking or biking distance; it was an hour away in some nasty traffic.

Stella offered a smile while she asked her soul why it felt torn up.

Her soul told her it didn't want to move to the Valley.

Her soul said Santa Monica was home. She loved not having to drive when she went places. She loved the weather that stayed between 65 and 70, the *om*-chanting, lavender-smelling, goodwill-spreading, farmer's-market-going people, the pier and the Promenade and Montana Avenue and Main Street and Abbott Kinney and the PCH. She loved Swingers and Cha Cha Chicken and all the movie theaters and the trapeze school and the gazillion yoga studios. *So why are you thinking of moving to the Valley?*

Her self answered with the only reason it had: *I'm moving to the Valley for Dylan.*

And she replied, *No you're not.*

"Nickel for your thoughts?" Dylan pried. "Inflation, you know."

Stella hadn't rescued herself from the dregs of rock bottom just to bend her wishes to fit another man's. Besides, Dylan wouldn't want her to.

"I was just thinking," she said at last. "I'm going to text those girls. I've decided I'm not moving to the Valley."

His face dimmed. He had, for the duration of this bike ride, been envisioning a new world where Stella lived two miles down the street. But she knew that when he wanted her close badly enough, he'd come to her. Until then, she would choose to live where her soul felt at home.

The stone was rolled away from Stella's heart. "I'm staying on the Westside," she said, "because I'm a fuckin' Westsider."

OCTOBER

Stella left the farmer's market with two bags of loot and a bouquet of autumnal flowers, and drove straight to El Porto to surf with Dylan where they'd first gone six months ago. "We have come so far," she said when they were done, walking hand-in-hand into the setting sun, carrying their boards toward the parking lot.

"You mean surfing, or our relationship?"

"Both, I guess." They still argued, but it felt different now. Their understanding grew every day as they got better at allowing each other to be themselves. Stella felt the beauty around her and licked the salt off her lips.

"Yeah. I've learned so much from you already," he said.

"Ditto."

As they put their boards into the red Prius that was now hers, a van drove up and parked facing the sea. "Should I go give this person my parking pass so they don't have to buy one?" Stella asked. She'd seen Dylan do it before; this lot was expensive.

"Sure," he said.

She ran toward the van in her wetsuit, hair dangling damp in her eyes. "Hey, do you want my parking pass?" she called, and then she saw the driver, a fit thirty-something woman, sobbing.

"Yes," said the woman. "Thank you. I just need to cry it out."

Stella didn't know what to say. She wondered what it was: a death, a divorce, a revelation about someone she loved. But the woman was tan and virile, and obviously knew the healing power of the ocean. Stella touched her arm as she gave her the pass, "You are going to be just fine."

She realized in that touch that the woman was her. Even after she settled all her current dilemmas, there would be more sadness,

236

more heartbreak, more pain to come. But there would also be more love, more happiness, more first-time experiences, more small triumphs.

"I'm sorry," the woman said.

"Don't be sorry," Stella said, walking away to give her space.

The woman gave her the shaka, the universal "surf's up" sign, and by the time Stella made it back to Dylan at the car, she had wandered out onto the sand.

The flowers were still in the Prius from the market that morning. Stella found a piece of paper and wrote,

A. You are beautiful
B. You are loved
C. You <u>GOT</u> this!

She left it on the woman's windshield along with the bouquet.

***

Wil's soul-stench was fading from the upholstery of the Prius. Dylan had advised Stella to try to sell it and keep her old Corolla. ("Think about it. Were you planning on getting a new car *before* this all happened? No. You can barely afford your lifestyle. This is not a sensible time in your life to get a new car.") But that seemed wrong to her. If she sold her old car, she could use the money to pay off one of her credit cards, and sans that monthly payment and the hundreds of dollars she'd been spending on gas, it would all even out.

When she got back from a day of errands, she parked the Prius outside her apartment and opened a little drop-down door in the ceiling that she'd never noticed before. Inside were some sunglasses: three-hundred-dollar Persols that Wil had bought when she was with him a year ago. She laughed out loud, then, upstairs, listed them for sale online, along with the old Corolla.

***

Stella's purpose in life had become conquering Levels 3 through 6. She woke before the sun most days, driving pentagram shapes all over Los Angeles for gigs: farmer's markets, babysitting, personal-assisting, bartending, babysitting. For the money she was saving on gas, she was glad she'd listened to her own advice about keeping the Prius.

She still didn't know what Level 3 would be: getting one good job, selling the old car, finding a new home, or finalizing the divorce. Angie was making great money as a nanny for these rich people, so Stella went online and signed up on some nanny-finder websites. She was also applying for education jobs and administrative jobs. She even spent a Saturday morning taking a four-hour test to qualify as a substitute teacher in California.

A few people had responded to her Craigslist post, inquiring about the Corolla. She told them she wouldn't take anything lower than six grand and most of them balked, but there was one guy who wanted to see it next weekend for his son.

She had started looking for rooms of her own on the Westside, having told the roomies her new move-out goal was November 1st. Home was still something Stella couldn't quite define. She'd felt it before, on 9th Street with Andrew, and before that, growing up in Kentucky with her family. But now it was elusive. Did it come with a specific latitude and longitude, or was it proximity to certain people? Was it the place where she grew up as a child, or the place where she grew up as an adult? Was it a room of her own, or room in her heart for her own identity? She yearned to know.

She went to see a place near El Porto: a nice room in a house with a yard and her own bathroom. The roommates were two dudes who were "420-friendly" and made good use of the adjective "mellow" in casual conversation. It could have worked, but the move-in cost was a thousand dollars plus first and last month's rent, which Stella was nowhere close to having, so the boys had to find someone else to take the room.

Every place she checked out seemed to have at least one thing stopping her. There was a place in her price range in her favorite Santa Monica neighborhood, but it required a credit check, and thanks to Wil, that was out. There was a room in a Manhattan Beach house with good people, but the room was barely big enough for a bed. She saw a few ads for beachside rooms with their own bathrooms, but each ad had specific requirements for roommates: raw vegans or devout Christians only. A couple more were ideal if Stella was willing to live amongst twelve cats or take care of someone's paraplegic uncle in the mornings. There had to be a better option near the water.

***

She was singing a song as they biked back to Dylan's house from his community college campus. While he had been in calculus class, she'd hung out in the library, spilling coffee and reading. It was autumn in the Valley and the air was crisp.

"You went flat," Dylan said.

Stella was tired of getting stifled by his perfectionism. "I wasn't singing it to impress you," she said. "I was singing because I felt like singing. I have a question for you."

"What's that?"

"Do you love me for who I am right now, or do you love me for some imagined perfect future version of me with a perfect body who doesn't ever sing flat? You don't have to answer me, but I would advise you to ask yourself that question."

Dylan turned and said from under his bicycle helmet, "I was just thinking of that the other day, and I love you for who you are." Stella paused and considered this character flaw—his nitpicking—and the paradox of her wanting him to be more perfect than he actually was by getting rid of it. That's when she realized she'd have to love him for who he was, too.

They rode on a few blocks. Then she said, from under no helmet, "That cute house is for rent."

"I like it," he said.

***

The gigs came when they came. It was normal now to work 48 hours straight with only a couple 6-hour sleeping breaks. But Stella didn't complain the way she once would have. All the working, applying for jobs and apartments, and planning was creating some major momentum. The inertia made her forget her basic human needs and long to do more. She spent a Friday evening training to be a volunteer to help students write. Being this busy left no time for worrying about money, and the lack of worrying was working in her favor: she had four different emails in her inbox from people who wanted to interview her for jobs.

One was to edit textbooks for a major publisher. One was to be the office manager at an acting school. One was to be a nanny to a baby girl. One was to be the assistant to the teenage daughter of a CEO. It was as if the universe had been waiting for her, not just to *say* what she needed, but to *prove* it through hard work and to trust that it would come.

She waited to respond to the acting school and the mom with the baby girl. She called the textbook people and they wanted to interview her in three weeks. She also responded to the CEO. He wanted to meet her tomorrow.

She felt like a skier poised at the top of a snowy slope, full of potential energy ready to turn kinetic.

***

She was sitting at Dylan's desk looking for more Westside rooms online. He said, "I feel shitty. I feel like there's still something wrong between us."

It was true; they'd never really gotten closure after the fight about Dylan pulling the plug on living together. And last night a stupid conversation about celebrity gossip had escalated into an assault on each other's ideologies. Dylan had insulted a starlet for behaving in ways he deemed bawdy and out-of-control. When Stella defended her, he compared Stella to the tabloid darling, insisting that her life was pure chaos and she was "just spinning." Stella had introduced him to her

239

video game analogy and explained that she had very quickly conquered Levels 1 and 2, and had just scheduled two interviews for good jobs. She asked him what more he wanted.

"I just want to be in a relationship with someone who is my equal," he had said, and then had become impenetrably silent, leaving her to sleep with acid in her veins and fog in her head. She was tired of believing she'd never live up to his standards.

"Something *is* wrong," she said. Stella liked to resolve issues quickly and lovingly. Dylan, however, was all business until an argument was over; he could not love in the midst of conflict, and last night, as he was unleashing the anger he had been apparently hoarding for weeks, he had told her she was "bat shit crazy" when she'd tried to touch his arm softly to express her understanding.

This difference seemed insurmountable and grave. Stella's mind always went automatically to Andrew in these circumstances. *Andrew and I never fought*, said the voice in her head. *And if we did, it was so easy to resolve.*

But she came back to the present moment and remembered commitment. She and Dylan loved each other. She had walked out on Andrew for a reason. She brought her computer to the bed to lay with Dylan, her head toward the foot of the bed, and continued her Westside apartment search. He put his hand on her ankle and some of the ugly particles stopped swirling and settled inside her.

He came down to the bottom of the bed, cradled her in his arms, and said, "I've been taking you for granted, and I'm sorry. I've been feeling like you might just get up and leave me at any time."

"I've been feeling that way, too," she said. She propped herself up to a cross-legged position. His face was blank and handsome like a G.I. Joe. "You can be very cruel."

"How?"

"Sometimes you say really hurtful things, and sometimes you're just not very thoughtful."

"Give me an example," he said.

"Like when you said I was *so far* from your perfect prototype of a woman, was that necessary?"

"Well, do you want me to be dishonest?"

"No, but there are times when you should ask yourself if the thing you're about to say is something I need to know, and if it's not, and if it is going to hurt me, maybe you should just...not say it."

"Well it's actually a good thing that you're not my prototype, because I told you, I'm in love with you anyway."

"Then maybe it's time to let go of your idea of your perfect woman and just make me it," she said. "Otherwise, you're wasting your time with me."

Words sailed back and forth until some hit and penetrated the soft places. They found compromise, face to face, arms wrapped around each other. Then they went for a hike.

"I wonder how many more breathtaking views we'll see in our lifetimes," Stella said, her hand in his at the overlook.

"A lot, I hope," he said. He turned toward her and softly studied her face. "Wait," he said, "I thought your eyes were green."

"No—"

"They're blue," he said.

"Wow," she said.

"I can't believe I thought they were green this whole time."

A past version of Stella would have been offended, would have read too much into this. Other loves had written her poems about her blue eyes, and this one took six months of gazing in to even know their color. But the current version of Stella knew that it didn't matter. Dylan had a problem half the time with seeing her for who she was, but he was opening more and more to let her in. As long as Stella knew who she was most of the time, she could wait for him to catch up.

"It's like that Elton John song," she sang: "You see I've forgotten if they're greeeeen or they're bluuuue!"

"There are flecks of green, though," he said, looking deeper, holding her around the waist. "Do you know what color my eyes are?" he asked.

"Hazel."

He seemed surprised, as if knowing your lover's eye color was an achievement. He pressed his forehead up against hers and said, "I think this is one of those relationships that's going to keep getting better with time."

***

Stella met Chadwick at the tables outside the health food store where she used to go when she worked for Chet. He was tan, 40-ish, laid-back, and impeccably dressed in a button-down lavender shirt. She had researched him before she arrived and found that he had been a heroin addict as a teenager and now, after more than a decade of being clean, ran one of the fanciest rehab centers in Malibu. He bought her a kombucha and told her about the job.

"So it's really easy. My daughter Sam is 14. She's pretty self-sufficient; she just needs someone to pick her up and take her to school in the mornings, bring her home after school, and then help her with her homework if she needs it."

"I could definitely help with that," Stella said. "I've been a teacher before."

"Great. You seem like someone she would like. She's not typical. She's really into horror and she likes to draw a lot."

"She sounds like someone I'd get along with," Stella said.

"It would pay twenty an hour, and I'd pay you while she's at school, too. Since it's so far away, you'll have to wait around to pick her up. Does that sound okay?"

She tried not to gasp. If this worked out, she could quit all her gigs and still have time for auditions and writing. "That sounds great. I could just work in a café while I wait."

"I used to go to the gym near her school while I waited for her. I just wasn't able to get any of my work done because of all the driving. It's an all-day thing."

"I see."

"Also, do you have a car that you don't mind driving a lot? I could get one for you to drive, but I thought if you'd like to use yours, I could just pay you a stipend every month—maybe three-hundred dollars?"

The payment Stella had been worried about was four-hundred a month, and this would nearly cover it. "I actually have a Prius, so I could just use that," she said.

"Perfect. That's what I would have gotten anyway."

They chatted a while longer about Stella's interests, where she lived, surfing. Then he said, "I have one other person I'm interviewing tomorrow, but I'll let you know as soon as I can."

"Sounds good," she said.

When she left, she briefly considered that she wouldn't need to look for another job for years if Chadwick hired her. It would change everything financially without crushing her spirit. She got excited for a minute, then she assumed the same attitude she took on after an audition: She consciously forgot about the interview. She'd done her best and had been herself, so there was no need for further concern. If the job was hers, she would get a call.

***

Days blurred by. One night Stella slept at her apartment on the Westside, the next at Dylan's in the Valley. She worked the farmer's market way up north in Calabasas, and the one in the winding Palisades hills. She drove to the Southbay to feed cats, Silverlake to hang with friends. She looked at two apartments in Venice. She took the Corolla down to Long Beach where her friend Cameron from the Ladidahs wanted her husband to take a look at it.

She tried not to get annoyed by the phone calls she didn't have time to answer from friends inviting her to events she couldn't attend. Outside of Level 3, life still insisted that she get an oil change and do her laundry, sleep, eat, and make it on time to all her appointments. Life made no concessions excusing her from showers and paying bills and needing exercise and love and the occasional overindulgence in red wine.

Dylan's living situation was beginning to sandpaper the edges of his nerves. At first Stella figuratively plugged her ears to his daily griping to stop herself from saying what she wanted to say ("If you hadn't backpedaled on your idea to live with me, you wouldn't *have* these complaints!"). But she could tell he was reaching a serious breaking point. He was unsatisfied with a few things in his life, and none of those things was her.

"You know that house that you pointed out when we were riding bikes the other day?" he said over the phone.

"Yeah."

"I called the realtor. If we did it together, we could rent out the extra rooms and it might work."

She kept mum, not knowing exactly how she felt about it.

***

It was only nine o'clock at the farmer's market, and the mustachioed Mexican fruit vendor had already whistled Jingle Bells five times.

"I am betting he'll do it twenty-two times today. What do you bet?" Stella asked Andres, the Bundt cake salesman in the next tent over.

"I'll bet twenty-three."

"The winner gets...what does the winner get?" she asked.

Andres pointed to the ground behind Stella's tent where a beat-up plastic hair comb was lying. They had been tracking its whereabouts for a month. Every Tuesday, the comb was there, in the exact same square foot of the parking lot.

"At this point I think we should name it," Stella said. "I think it looks like a Herbert."

He laughed. "I don't know. I was thinking more like Momo."

She crashed back onto her cooler, cracking up. "You are so right. Momo it is."

The man whistled Jingle Bells again. "That's six," Stella said, opening her journal to the last page and adding another tally mark. Her phone rang and she saw that it was Chadwick. She ducked out of her stall and answered it.

"Stella?"

"Yes?"

"I'm calling to find out if you'd like the job. I think you're the best choice for Sam."

She jumped up and down and accidentally kicked Momo.

"I'd love to," she said calmly. Or what she thought was calmly.

"Great. You can come by tomorrow and meet Sam. I live on a boat so I'll text you the address."

He lived on a boat? "Perfect. See you then."

And like that, she knew what Level 3 would be: getting a job that would be her ticket out of financial slavery. Today would be her last day selling Korean food. She rearranged her list.

Level 1: Get Prius back
Level 2: Get rid of Wil
Level 3: Get a Job
Level 4: Get a Home
Level 5: Sell Car
Level 6: Get a Divorce

At the end of the day, she counted her money, turned in the fee, did the inventory, and stacked up the coolers. She called her boss Frank with dread, to report the sales and tell him she was leaving, but he didn't answer and his voice mailbox was full. Stella was so grateful not to have the confrontation—she whispered *thank you* to the sky.

She took her pay out of today's sales and stuck it in her pocket. She wrote a note to Frank on the inventory sheet, briefly explaining why today would be her last day. She walked to her car, waving at Andres, who had won Momo when the fruit vendor had whistled Jingle Bells 24 times total.

***

Chadwick's boat was a yacht with four bedrooms, an upstairs and a downstairs, and a TV that rose up out of the floor at the push of a button.

"Sam! Come meet Stella," he called as Stella stood awkwardly behind him.

"Coming!" said a little voice, and soon she was sitting on the leather sectional: a skinny, pale, sweet-faced girl with long brown hair parted in the middle. She was wearing jeans with rips and a distressed flannel shirt, looking much like Stella had in eighth grade.

"Hey! I'm Stella!"

"Hi," Sam said. A little white dog jumped up next to her and Stella sat down to pet him. "Is this your dog? He's so cute!"

"Yeah," she said. "Killer."

"Hi, Killer."

"Sam. Stella is going to start taking you to school during the week."

"Cool," she said.

"So your dad said you like to draw?"

"Yeah," she said.

"Show Stella some of your drawings, Sam."

"They're in my room." She got up and Stella followed her to a small bedroom. There were at least twelve drawings on notebook paper hanging on her wall: half-naked girls, zombies, teenage cartoons making out, lots of blood and knives.

Stella was impressed. "Wow. These are really good." They chatted a little more and then Chadwick escorted Stella out, thanking her and telling her to come back next Monday at seven in the morning.

***

Stella knocked on Dylan's door. He opened it, surprised, and said brightly, "What are you doing here?" He was on his way out, leaving for the weekend for hockey referee business.

"I just thought I'd say 'bye in person and bring you some things for your trip." She handed him a mix CD, and some snacks for the road.

"Thank you, baby! Did you make this?" she nodded. She had fashioned a case out of cardboard and pressed autumn leaves, and earnestly titled it, *Fall in Deep*. "It's like a piece of art," he said. "I'm scared to take it in my car!"

"It'll be something to listen to on your way."

"Oh, by the way, babe, I meant to tell you. That house I called about? It fell through."

"The one we saw in the Valley?"

"Yeah. It would have been so nice if we could have rented out rooms, but I guess they went with someone who had more income."

"It's ok. I'm actually going tomorrow to look at another room in a house near the beach. I think this could be the one."

A look of vague distress fleeted across his face as he said, "where?"

"Venice," she said.

***

Stella was in Malibu, hiking Solstice Canyon after she'd turned in some paperwork to Chadwick at his office.

Claudia called to say she'd met a guy on a dating website just a month before, and was already in love. "People are going to think I'm crazy. I just got divorced. But I can't help it."

"I'm the last one who would say you're crazy," Stella said. "I'm in the same boat over here. 'Hey everybody! I'm in love again! I know that you all came to my wedding a couple years ago and that went to shit, and then I know I said I was in love with the second guy who I left my husband for, but *for real* now, y'all! This time I've found the *one.*' Really. Why even bother worrying about other people's opinions. For a long time, I just felt like turning my back on the world."

"Yeah. Who cares. I'm just somebody who believes in love. So I've found this, and I'm going for it. If it doesn't work out, it's still worth it."

"Good," Stella said.

When she hung up, she turned off her phone. She wanted to

hear only the sounds of now.

Somewhere up the mountain, amidst the smell of sweat and wild rosemary and sunshine, the past took hold of her for a minute. A few tears dropped down her cheeks as she remembered Andrew getting lost with her, sitting here looking out over the ocean, eating a can of peanuts. But now she was as alone as possible; a solitary human at nature's mercy. Los Angeles was far away.

She kept ascending as the path grew narrow, the grasses tall on either side. Cactuses stood and lizards scurried. Beneath her, her feet jumped over rocks, her strong thighs carrying her as far as she dared. She heard nothing but her rubber soles crunching in the dirt, creatures rustling in the underbrush, crickets chirping, wind rushing through leaves. She felt only the sun on her shoulders, sweat dripping off her elbows, her heart beating powerfully in her chest, the gentle breeze on her bare skin.

She passed an old bathtub. In it, there was a furry black tarantula as big as her hand. It had to be a Halloween prank. Stella threw a small stick at it. Its hairy legs moved it fluidly through the tub. She sprinted away yelling "aaaah!" until she reached the peak of the mountain where she could see the ocean for miles. She spun around and took in the craggy mountains and sky.

There was no way she could really turn her back on the world, she noticed, because everywhere she turned, the world was right there in front of her.

***

Dylan called as Stella was eating falafel alone in her apartment. "I think I just jumped onto a new train," he said.

"What train is that?"

"The Stella train."

"I thought you were already on that train," she laughed, stepping out onto the balcony and taking in the view of the West LA buildings lit up in the breezy evening air.

"I was. I mean, I haven't considered myself single for the past six months, but I think I still had one foot back at the station."

"And now?"

"Now I'm on it, and it's moving. I've been thinking about how good it would be to fall asleep next to you every night."

"Where did this come from?"

"I don't know. I was just listening to the CD you made me. It really tells a story."

"I hoped you'd get that."

"And then my dad called. I told him I wasn't looking forward to getting back to my house, and he asked what happened to the plan to live with you. I realized after we talked a while: I want to live with you. I know it's not as big a deal for you, but this is a big step for me."

"Hmm." She had just gone to see the latest room in Venice: a two-bedroom to share with a lady named Karma.

"Would you still want to live with me?"

Dylan thought it wasn't a big deal for Stella, but it was. Not only would she be entwining her life with this person she loved, she would also have a chance to find home again in the physical realm.

"Yes. I would."

***

Everything was pending, as if Stella had been jumping over a great gulf and someone had paused the footage mid-leap. Levels 4-6 orbited just outside her reach.

First, finding a home. She was back to searching with Dylan, but he was away for another day, so she was on her own, working to get as close as she could to his criteria. Her requirements were simple: "residence where I can put all my stuff and be naked when I want to. Kitchen preferred." She had a feeling that Dylan's fastidious tastes would postpone her prospective move-out date once again.

As for selling her old car, after personally sanding its scratches and touching them up, posting the ad, hustling all over Los Angeles to let people test drive it, and staying resolute after being low-balled by cheapskates offering her less than half its Blue Book value, Stella finally had a buyer: her band mate, Cameron. She and her husband were, she admitted, in no financial place to buy a car right now, but they needed one absolutely, so they applied for a car loan. Now Stella had to wait with them to find out if they'd get approved.

Then there was the divorce. Stella had been avoiding contacting Andrew, but she texted him.

Did you get the papers I sent you?

Andrew:
Yes. I sent them in.

Stella:
Oh okay. Thank you.

Life was one big audition, and Stella knew that the only way to keep sane was to do the work, listen to her intuition, and not depend on any certain result. Even when it was uncomfortable, she already had everything she needed.

***

She made it to the boat just in time (7:15) to retrieve Sam and take her deep into the Valley for school by 8:30. Stella let Sam pick the music and was nostalgically surprised when Sam selected the same Blink-182 albums she used to love at 14. Sam went to a private school where there were only a few students and teachers. She clearly hated it, but dragged herself through the front doors, leaving Stella to write at the coffee shop next door.

Sam was back in the passenger seat in four hours and wanted to go to some Halloween stores. The best one was practically a haunted house inside, with rooms full of smoke, strobe lights, and gory, life-sized dolls that moved. Sam approached Stella with a blood-covered teddy bear. "He's so cute," she said. "He's just a display, but they told me they'd sell him to me for twenty bucks."

"Awesome," Stella said, and followed Sam to the checkout counter.

"So, twenty dollars," the guy said, putting the teddy in a bag.

Sam looked back at Stella.

Oh.

For some reason, she hadn't anticipated this. She was in charge. She got out her card to pay for the bloody bear. Chadwick would surely reimburse.

"What did you name him?" Stella asked.

"Sweeney Todd," Sam said, hugging him tightly. "Did you see the checkout guy? He was hot."

Stella laughed. Sam was a little like her at fourteen, except richer and more morose. And then Sam wanted to get spaghetti.

She ate a total of three bites, and Stella offered up her credit card again. As they left the restaurant, Stella hadn't noticed that Sam had placed her box of leftover spaghetti on the ground in the parking lot.

"Hey Stella," Sam said as they closed their car doors.

"Yes?"

"Look." She pointed to the abandoned box in the parking lot.

"What did you do?"

"Will you run over it with your car?" Sam asked.

Stella pursed her lips. "Okay," she said. "Just for an experiment."

"Sweet!" Sam searched through her phone's music library for the perfect pop-punk song for squishing a spaghetti box with a car.

Stella made a donut in the parking lot, crushing the box with the left wheel.

"Yes!" Sam said. They got out to look at the defeated doggie-bag, whose entrails were spilling out the busted white sides of the box in a most satisfying way.

"Okay but now we have to pick it up because we don't want to ruin Mother Earth," Stella said.

"Yeah, I don't want bad karma." Sam said.

They parked and walked through the yacht-studded marina to start Sam's biology homework. As the sea lions barked and a sailor waved, Stella felt that the curtain had been pulled back on a world she'd only glimpsed before. She was no longer an outsider, an impostor from the coal fields held back by her stories of struggle. She could never have known that this would be the answer to Level 3, but now that she had access to the world of riches and ease, she understood that life was far more unlimited than she'd imagined.

***

While Sam was at school, Stella's writing churned forth like a Pipeline wave. She didn't know the exact obstacles that awaited her at each level, but she, the creator beneath this character, was capable and free in the not-knowing. The intense focus in beating this life game created exhilaration, which sparked momentum and became clarity. The pages stacked up and read almost like a novel, showing her how far she'd come and how much further she wanted to go.

When she had begun this writing task, she'd thought chronicling her journey could help her become stable by forcing her to face details she might have otherwise glazed over. But she'd only half-beaten the six levels of this life journey and surprisingly, she already felt steady. She knew she could finish what she started, and now that she knew of the limitlessness that existed outside her tiny experience, she wanted a trophy at the end of the game.

She always loved to have something concrete to be proud of, and of her long-term creative goals, she'd thought writing a novel was far-flung. But nothing was unattainable if she created it. It seemed like the perfect reward, so for herself, she dared to add a new level to the list.

Level 1: ~~Get Prius back~~
Level 2: ~~Get rid of Wil~~
Level 3: ~~Get Job~~
Level 4: Get a Home
Level 5: Sell Car
Level 6: Get a Divorce
Level 7: Write Novel

***

Dylan returned and joined Stella in the search for apartments during the evenings. They looked at one in the Valley, but after seeing two in Venice and one in Santa Monica and finding them only a fraction smaller and a couple hundred dollars more expensive, Dylan was as determined as Stella to live on the Westside.

Stella's weekdays began to follow a pattern. She took Sam to school and then spent the day writing. Her character quit her dismal job, returned to her rural roots to face her past, argued with her lover for the first time. The more understanding Stella gained from detailing the through-line of her past, the better she got at creating the story of her present.

She closed her computer and picked Sam up. She did what Sam wanted, and then what Sam had to do, running around town, eating lunch, buying Sam things, doing Sam's homework, thinking of all the things she'd do differently if Sam were her own.

Thursday morning, Chadwick called and said Sam was sick and staying in bed. That same morning Stella received a text message from Cameron:

> The loan came through and I have the check. When do you want to do it?

> Stella:
> I can bring the car down to Long Beach now if you want!

She started up the Corolla for the last time. It was an all-day affair with the smog check and the title transfer, but she and Cameron sat on the metal bench at the gray DMV, talking about their moms, their men, the Ladidahs, their money issues, the city. At last Cameron handed Stella the check. "Now I have so many options! I can go to the grocery store while he's at work!" she said as she dropped Stella back at her place.

She took a last look at the car as Cameron drove it away. She had defeated Level 4.

> Level 1: Get Prius back
> Level 2: Get rid of Wil
> Level 3: Get Job
> Level 4: Sell Car
> Level 5: Get a Home
> Level 6: Get a Divorce
> Level 7: Write Novel

***

The air was chilly and they were in their thicker wetsuits. There had been reports of a great white in the waters nearby, but most wonderful things were worth their risk.

Dylan was beginning to realize this. "How do you think our relationship will change when we move in together?" he asked.

"I don't know."

"I know it will change. I hope it's for the better. I think there will be a whole lot of little things at first. Like, 'Woman, you didn't put my knife back where it belongs!' But we'll get used to it."

"It'll be easy, I think. We'll gain three hours a day just because we don't have to drive to see each other."

"I know." She could sense his excitement lately. He propped up his chin with the heels of his hands like he was on a daybed. Stella crossed her cold, wrinkly fingers that they'd find the right place by the ocean. "But we aren't going to find anything unless we set a goal. We can't just keep leisurely browsing; we need intention. I need to move soon."

"I know it's more urgent for you than it is for me, but I understand. I'm starting to feel it."

"I'm going nuts in this limbo," she said. "If we don't set a definite date, I'm going to go back to finding a place just for me and I'm gonna move by November."

"Okay. Let's say December 1st."

"Really?"

"Yeah. I'll tell my roommates today."

She exhaled. They floated next to each other and shared a salty kiss, then bobbed along for a while, waiting for waves that never came.

Stella thought back to that final text Wil had sent before she eradicated him from her phone and her life—

when your disgusting behavior and treatment of me catches up to you, I just hope that you remember why your life will become a living hell

—and closed her eyes to see how long she could blindly balance on her board. She laughed.

"What are you laughing at, weirdo?" said Dylan.

"Man. You get what you put out in this world," she said. She didn't even have to wonder how Wil was doing right now.

***

Slugging down pumpkin-spiced coffee, Stella haphazardly pulled into the Marina to pick up Sam. The sun was just rising in the distance, the water was rippling, and the ducks were swimming. It felt like fall: slate silhouettes of the boats' masts in the foreground of the pink and orange sky, the majestic forms of the cotton candy clouds, and the water reflecting it all back.

Chadwick was shirtless, drinking green juice, when Stella stepped onto the boat. "Hey Stella."

"Hey! Happy Halloween!" she said.

"You too."

"Do you have any plans?"

"No, just working," he said.

"Yeah, I think I'm going to go to bed early." Stella was mystified when she remembered her excitement last year, when each of the Ladidahs dressed as a different Mario Kart character. Wil had tagged along for party after party while Andrew stayed home.

"Sam is almost ready." Chadwick was so nice, but he always seemed distracted, like he was programmed with static responses that didn't quite follow the conversation at hand.

Killer jumped up onto her lap.

Just then Sam appeared, wearing her little black angel costume that they'd bought at one of the Halloween stores. Her long hair was crowned with a fuzzy black halo, and she had black lacy gloves and black feathered wings.

"You look great!" Stella said.

"Thanks," she said. "I have the perfect soundtrack for the car ride."

"Oh man."

"Dun-dun-dun-dun-dun-dun-duh-duh!" She sang the Halloween theme as they stepped off the boat. Stella joined in. "Dun-dun-dun-dun-dun-dun-duh-duh!"

Maybe that's what kids are good for, she thought. *The second you give up on something, they show it to you with new eyes.*

"Wow. Great parking job," said Sam, surveying the Prius, sitting lopsidedly, half in the road.

"Yeah. Well, it's early."

While Sam was at school, Stella took the money Cameron had given her for the Corolla and paid off her most ghastly credit card, then wrote for hours in a café. Before picking Sam up, she worked out at Equinox.

She stripped in the locker room after a kickboxing class, catching her own gaze in the mirror and noting how much sturdier she'd become—glittering eyes, dewy skin, arms shadowed with lean muscles—since she used to work at the gym for peanuts. Of course she had no urge to dress up for Halloween. She felt like she'd finally taken off a costume she'd been wearing for years.

NOVEMBER

"I am gonna want an In-N-Out burger after this!" Surfing made Stella hungry. She looked at Dylan. "I love you! You hungry?"

Dylan frowned at her. "Do you want a pointer to help you surf better?"

"Um—"

He had ignored every joke she'd attempted since they'd arrived, and now he unsmilingly offered his unsolicited advice. "You're paddling like this. You have to scoot up on the board. See that? If you don't, you're going to be struggling for years." She swallowed her response and looked to the blue horizon. "Yeah, I know. 'Fuck you, Dylan,'" he said.

She paddled south to where a bunch of surfers were waiting for waves, finding it difficult to enjoy herself because she could feel Dylan watching her with his critical eye. Her brain jumped into an imagined future in which Dylan was a father whose children had an insecurity complex because nothing was ever good enough for Dad.

"You know, I'm not feeling this," Stella said after a while. "I think I'm gonna go." She took a wave in and walked onto the beach. He followed her.

"What's wrong?"

"Last week, you were texting to tell me you were overflowing with love for me, writing me notes, and cooking for me. This week, you've been making fun of me, mocking and criticizing me, and not appreciating anything I do for you. It seems like you need to pull away right now, so I am just going to let you do it. Call me when you feel like seeing me." She gave him a hug, and she left the beach.

Learning Dylan was a lot like learning the waves. Nobody could tell her how to do it; she'd have to figure it out herself. She was willing.

But for now she headed to In-N-Out and got a burger alone.

When she arrived full-bellied at her apartment, she had a piece of mail from the Santa Monica City Clerk that made her feel lonely and triumphant at once. All she had to do, it said, was go to the courthouse and pay the fee, and the divorce would be officially underway.

***

This time, she didn't contact Dylan.

Days passed. She spent time with Sam, wrote, and worked out at her fancy gym. She kept looking for apartments for the two of them. December was less than a month away, and she had to vanquish Level 5.

One day, online reports said the swell up north was four-to-five feet plus. Stella packed her gear and drove up to Malibu, where a line of cars were parked bumper-to-bumper along the dusty shoulder of the road. She yanked on her wetsuit, secured her car key inside with a safety pin, took her board under her arm, and walked barefoot down the dirt road past the lagoon, to Third Point.

At the edge of the sand, Stella looked toward the horizon and saw the waves churning relentlessly. The horde of surfers teemed like ants on an anthill. Every wave had a surfer ripping down its face, or sometimes tumbling over the falls. Every so often, an overhead wave left the whole Point deserted. The day was dreary with no sign of sun, and the water looked dark grey and uninviting. Stella's knees felt a little shaky and she considered turning around. Even if she didn't have trouble paddling past the big breakers, she'd have to fight the veterans for waves. It would be pointless. She looked behind her at the rocky dirt path. She was sweating inside the neoprene.

Maybe she should just paddle out. It would be good to get wet. And anyway, how could she ever improve unless she got comfortable with something bigger? She walked into the chilly water, over the rocks, up to her knees, then her thighs, before she could change her mind. She waited for a wave to pass and then placed her board, mounted it belly-down, and started paddling.

She felt like she was on a treadmill. At least a huge set hadn't come through. She found she could scale the tall crests if she clicked her heels together near the top. She was getting close enough to see the rest of the surfers, who were dropping in on each other left and right. Her arms were shaking, but she couldn't turn back now. *Please don't run over me.* She paddled as fast as she could, but the wind was picking up. Her board repeatedly slapped against the choppy water.

"Outside!" someone shouted.

A set was coming. *Oh God, no.* She was still 20 yards away from being able to sit on her board safely. She was stuck in the path of anyone who was going to take a wave, and if they weren't good enough to steer around her, she'd be roadkill.

The first wave came. Five feet, probably. Stella turtled, praying a huge rock wasn't underneath the water waiting to hit her head. It was rough underwater, and she tried not to struggle, even when the second wave came and the ocean kept her down longer than she could comfortably hold her breath. When she finally made it to the surface and sucked in a gasp to fill her lungs, she saw it: a seven-footer, about to crash right onto her head, with a surfer poised on top, ready to slice down her face. She panicked and let go of her board, diving as deep as she could as the wave cracked down.

She was glad for her flexibility as the wave tossed her in circles, hollowing out her back so she became a human wheel. She no longer knew which way was up, but she used all the strength of her arms and legs to find air. *Conk.*

"Fuck!"

She had finally made it above water, but something—her surfboard—had hit her hard on the head. "Ow! Fuck!"

The waves had calmed and a few surfers were heading back toward the drab horizon. "Are you okay?" a man asked.

"I got hit. Does anything look wrong?"

He paddled closer and sucked in through his teeth. "Your ear. You should get out," he said.

She propelled herself toward shore, terrified that another set would crash on her.

She climbed out over the rocks on trembling legs, unzipped her wetsuit, and pulled off the sleeves so it fell down around her waist. "Can you take a look at my ear?" she asked the silver-haired lifeguard.

"Let me see," he said. She pulled her hair back. "Yeah. You're gonna need stitches."

"No, it's not that bad," she said. "I'll be okay. I'll just wait a few hours and see how it goes."

"I think you should drive right over to Urgent Care," he said.

"Really?"

"Yeah."

She walked down the path, past surfers heading toward the beach. "Ooh. What happened to you?" a young guy asked.

That's when she caught, from the corner of her eye, a pool of blood dripping down her bare shoulder.

At Urgent Care, the nurses told her they didn't have anyone qualified to fix her. The fin from her board had come down precisely to slice the back of her ear into a gaping gill. She'd have to drive an hour over the mountain to a hospital that had a plastic surgeon who could repair cartilage.

She played cheerful music and sang along on the way. Part of her wished Dylan was here, but another part was glad he wasn't. It stung terribly when her salty hair dripped into the wound. She tried not to look in the mirror because the entire right side of her neck looked like a scene from a horror movie.

"You're lucky it didn't go any further," said the surgeon after she'd put Stella through the cold tube of a CT scan. "It could have damaged your ear drum."

"Yeah, and I'm lucky it was the back of my ear instead of my face or my neck."

The surgeon anesthetized her with a dangerous looking needle, then threaded another needle to sew her up. Stella closed her eyes, but could hear the slow *shrrrip* of thread drawing slowly through her skin and cartilage. She sang "I Will Survive" quietly to herself until it was over.

"No more surfing for a month," said the doctor. "Try not to get this wet."

***

It had been four days when Dylan finally called and asked her to come over. She talked to her mom on the way, unloading all her fears and not mentioning the ear incident. What if she always fell short of Dylan's expectations? What if every time she was upset and needed support, he left her hanging to deal with it all alone? Would she learn to cope, or eventually seek comfort elsewhere, or would he learn what she needed in a relationship and finally provide it?

"I feel bad for you young people," Linda said. "You worry so much about everything being perfect. When you get older you see that nothing is that big of a deal. You're still in the beginning stages of your relationship. I think it takes a few years to really understand each other."

She was right. Stella didn't need to worry about what was down the line. The truest thing was that she wanted to see him now.

Soon, there he was through the window, sitting at his desk with the light on, concentrating hard on something. Stella was overwhelmed with love for this strange creature.

"Hey mister," she said.

"Hey."

He pulled her onto his lap. "I was talking to Cybil earlier about Love Languages. Do you know about those?"

"Yeah," Stella said.

He spoke slowly and thoughtfully. "There are five of them, and you usually give in the same way you like to receive. Mine is Acts of Service. And Words were way down at the bottom for me. Because I've always believed that words don't mean anything unless the actions match them. But I think for you, Words is probably at the top."

"It is."

"Well, that's not my style. So, I was really confused the other day, because I felt like I had done all these things for you, and just because I wouldn't say 'I love you,' it erased everything I did."

"Yeah. Instead of giving me loving words, you were criticizing me. You do that a lot, and it stacks up. Just like anyone, I need to know I am loved. Every day. If you're going to go into your cave for a few days, or if you're mad at me, I need to know beforehand that you are going to love me on the other side of it."

"I just don't really see the point of all this verbal reassurance. I mean, I love my mom and she knows it. She doesn't expect me to tell her every day." Stella had never met anyone more frustratingly stubborn than Dylan. Over the course of seven months, she had influenced him in many ways, but he always, always resisted at first. She had to plant the seed and then wait for him to come around to the decision on his own.

"I bet she feels differently when it comes to your dad. I am telling you, Dylan: You will not find any woman on this planet worth loving who does not need to feel loved every day in her way. Why in the world would anyone get into a relationship otherwise?"

"Well, when I offer you advice, you don't have to take it, but it's good to at least listen before you throw it away."

"I do listen, but if it's not something urgent, I'd rather you just wait until I ask for your advice. Otherwise I feel like you're always trying to change me."

"What? You're the one who is trying to change me right now."

"I am not trying to change you. I am telling you what I need to be happy in a relationship, because I trust that you can give that to me if you are willing to do so. I really appreciate everything you do for me, but you don't have to do anything. I'm not asking for any grand gestures. I'm not asking you to spend any money or put me on a pedestal or cook for me or leave me sweet notes. Although sometimes those things are nice. All I want is for you to let me know verbally that you love me, however you want."

His eyes registered some recognition. He didn't say anything immediately, but she felt some space open up.

When they finally went to bed, he stroked her hair.

"Oh. Don't touch that ear," she said.

"Why not?"

She showed him the back of it. Every time she closed her eyes, she still saw the wave that had trampled her.

"Baby! What happened? It looks like an ear vagina!"

She told him the story, bracing herself for a lesson on what she did wrong and how she should be more careful. But he didn't scold her. He just pulled her closer and said, "I'm glad you're okay." Then: "I looked at an apartment in Santa Monica two days ago. It was only twelve hundred."

"What? No way!" she said.

"I put in an application."

"Thank you!"

Then, with perfect diction, he said, "I love you. You know that?"

***

"Sam still has a ton of homework she couldn't finish over the weekend, so she's gonna stay home today and knock that out," said Chadwick when Stella arrived. "So you guys just hang out on the boat today. And if you feel like it, maybe you can go out to lunch or something," he said.

"Sounds good. I'll help with any homework Sam needs me to."

But Sam said she didn't need homework help. So Stella lay reading a book, sunning herself on the deck for the first half of the morning, grateful and astonished at life.

"Are you finished with your biology?" Stella finally asked.

"Almost."

"I can help," Stella said, and sat beside her. Sam was easily distracted. She was listening to music and playing with some singing monster app on her phone between biology questions.

"Can I see your ear again?"

Stella showed her.

"That is so cool! I bet I could do horror makeup that looks like that. Can Dylan come hang out with us? I can do it on him." While Sam hated school work, she was a professional-caliber special effects makeup artist with an arsenal of gear to turn people into zombies or burn victims.

"I think he's doing a film project today, but maybe tomorrow."

"Boo. He needs to show me his abs," Sam said.

"Want to get some food?"

"Sure. Let's go to Café Crepe!"

People always tried to figure out their relationship.

"Are you her mom?" asked the waiter.

Stella was momentarily aware, the way she was at commercial auditions for "mom types," that she may have officially exited her youth. "I don't look old enough to be her mom, do I?" But she couldn't be a nanny; Sam wasn't exactly a kid. Chauffeur certainly didn't cover it. Stella decided she was more like Sam's surrogate big sister.

She still vividly remembered being 14, brilliant, opinionated, and not at all innocent. So when Sam asked questions, she answered them.

"Do condoms really come in sizes?"

"Well, really only two sizes. Regular and Magnum," Stella told her. "But usually the guys who buy the Magnums don't need them and it's just a good way to tell who's a douchebag."

She didn't know the story about why Sam's mom wasn't in the picture, but she figured it would come out eventually. Sam had told her a few things in the past two weeks, though: She missed her old school where all her friends were. She was afraid they were going to forget her. She was desperately in love with a boy, Zach, who was her friend. She had never been kissed.

Sam jumped on Stella's back when they were walking to the car and Stella laughed and ejected her into the passenger seat.

Chadwick texted when they were back at the boat.

If Sam doesn't need any more homework help and you guys have eaten, you're free to go if you want.

"Do you need anything else?" Stella asked. The sun was setting.

"Nope. You can go if you want. Go hang out with your Dylan." She petted her little dog. "Or you can stay and hang out with your Sam."

"Well, Dylan is going to be busy, so I can't see him," she said.

"We could watch a movie!"

Stella could have used a long evening alone...but for what? She wondered if it was wrong to stay and get paid for watching a movie. Sam clearly didn't want to be alone. Stella wanted to do the right things so that Chadwick would keep her around—not just for her own gain, but to protect Sam from the inevitable pitfalls of being a teenage girl desperate for love.

"I could watch a movie," she said.

***

It was Veteran's Day and Stella and Dylan were eating fruit leather and watching *South Park* in her apartment after having spent most the day in bed. The four-day weekend had snuck by. Other than recording some tracks for Ladidahs' first album and going to a premiere for one of Dylan's short films, Stella had nothing to show for it.

"You still taking your birth control every day?" asked Dylan.

"Yep," Stella said. "Why? Do you want me to stop so I can pop one out for you?"

"Nope."

About a year ago, even the joke would have been too much for her. The thought of being a mom grossed her out, and every time she used to talk to her mother on the phone, Linda would subtly suggest that she and Andrew have a baby, using reverse psychology. "Now, I'm telling you, I don't want you to have a baby and you livin' out there in California."

"Well, trust me," Stella had said, getting more miffed each time the topic arose, "you don't have to worry. I have absolutely no plans to have one of those parasitic creatures until I've lived enough of my own life to want to give away my energy."

"I can barely support myself now," Dylan said. "I'm thinking maybe in about seven years."

"Hmm. Okay. I'll be 36." Stella didn't let him know there was a voice in her head that was saying, *How about three or four years?*

"Do you think when we live together that we'll miss the whole buildup of missing each other that makes us so passionate?" he said.

"No way."

"Really?"

"I'll still be gone for, like, six-to-twelve hours a day most days, so don't worry; we'll still get to miss each other."

"I've got to go to work soon," he said. Then his phone rang.

He was sounding professional and saying things like, "Great. I'll let you know as soon as possible." He hung up and said, "We've been approved for the apartment in Santa Monica."

Stella was stunned for a second, but then she sprung into the air saying "Yes! Yes! Yes!" with a little dance.

"So you want it?" he asked. "It's really nice, with a bedroom, a nice kitchen, and wood floors."

"Yes! Aaaahhh! I'm so happy!" She hadn't even seen it yet, but she wanted it. Santa Monica was finally going to let her back in. And this time she understood its importance.

"Then I'll take the deposit on Tuesday," he said. "They said we can move in the week of Thanksgiving."

When he had to leave, she walked him to his car. He reached up and pulled a grapefruit down from a tree and handed it to Stella. "We've spent a lot of time together these past four days," he said, a slight smile bringing out the dimples. "Are you sure you're not sick of me?"

She had to tell him the truth.

"All I want is more."

***

"Wow, you're eatin' fancy over there," Kerry said. While the band waited to record their album, Stella sat on the arm of the couch eating stuffed grape leaves and drinking a single-serve glass of red wine.

"I know," Stella said. "I had to grab dinner from the grocery store before I got here. I haven't had a chance to eat."

"Were you with your kid?"

"Yes. I woke up at six at Dylan's house, drove to Marina del Rey to pick her up, drove her back to the Valley for school, drove her back home after school, and drove back here again after helping her with her homework. I've been in the car at least six hours today. I could have driven to San Francisco."

"Ugh. Well, drink up."

"So you guys, the Tinder guy and I finally had morning sex," Kerry said.

"Awesome—it worked!" Stella said.

"Well, it was three in the morning..."

"That doesn't count!" Jo said.

"Stella, what's been going on with you? Tell us a story," said Erin.

She told them of the surfing accident story, which horrified them. Then they wanted more. "What about the girl you're taking care of? Sam?"

"She's great. I'm just so glad I'm not fourteen."

"Me too," said Rebecca.

"I can't save her from the shit she's about to go through. Like, she's in love with this total idiot who treats her like crap, and she just lets him. We all went through that. I made the same mistake over and over, of course. And when you feel that way, nobody can tell you anything."

"She really needs you right now," said Rebecca. "You came at a good time."

"Yeah, I totally did," Stella said. "I showed her how to use tampons the other day."

"Really? How?"

"I just took it out of the package and showed her. Not *on* anyone."

"I wish I would have had you around when I was 14," said Jo.

"Yeah, she came back later and was like, 'I'm never using pads again!'"

"Yeah, they're gross," said Kerry.

"I still have this friend who wears them!" said Cameron.

There was a collective groan, then Tessa came in and said, "It's your turn to record."

"Finally!"

***

Since Dylan had missed Tessa's last party, Stella was glad he could make it to her dinner party, where they dressed up and ate shortribs and gelato. Her friends expressed their approval when Dylan was out of earshot.

Stella had seen Paul a couple times since she'd sent him the "friends-only" text. And now when she looked over, she saw Dylan standing with him. She wondered if it would be awkward, but walked up anyway, joining in on one of Paul's pop culture discussions—something about the Beastie Boys that Dylan had no opinion on.

Dylan said later, "That guy Paul is cool."

"Yeah, he's awesome," Stella said. "Kind of funny. Do you remember how I had gone out with a guy right after we had our first date? Because it had been planned for weeks?"

"It's him?"

She nodded. "I wonder what would have happened if I hadn't met you when I did. I feel like I might have kept dating him. But after you, I knew I couldn't keep going out with other guys."

"I can see why you liked him," said Dylan.

"I did! We got along really well."

"Cool."

"And we didn't bone."

"Thank God," he said.

***

Dylan texted Stella around noon when she and Sam were exploring a thrift store.

> For some reason I started thinking about stir fry, which reminded me how utterly blissful it will be to cook for you and eat with you, just me and you in our new home. Put a smile on my face in the middle of the hockey game. I lied to you when I said I'd FALLEN in love with you. I'm STILL falling. I know it's gonna be hard for me in the beginning adjusting to the different way of living but if you can bear with me and my need for independence, we'll do just fine. I can't wait to experience this new chapter with you. WOW!!!

That night before she went to sleep in his bed, he reached over and squished her cheeks with his palms, then he wrinkled the flesh of her forehead. Through her half-open eyes, she saw him smiling.

"What are you doing?"

"I'm just trying to imagine what you're going to look like when you're old."

***

Stella's right calf was ceasing up from eleven hours of pedal pushing. She reached the recording studio at 7:30. She, Kerry, Cameron, Diana passed two hours talking and eating while they waited to sing.

She tried not to get cranky when she thought of her five a.m. wakeup call tomorrow so she could make it to the Marina from the Valley. She was so tired of the song they were recording, but she closed her eyes and tried to conjure memories of singing it to full audiences when she meant it. On the second and third full renditions of the song, she gained enthusiasm, coloring in all the empty words with real memories.

Then through the speakers came the Brad, the producer's

262

voice—"Okay. Now it's time to go piece by piece and punch in the parts that need work." This hadn't taken long in previous sessions.

They sang the same phrases over and over. "I can see no way, I can see no way." And again. "I can see no way." And again. And again. Ten times. Twenty times. After every take they did, they heard muffled talking from the other room and then some criticism through the speaker from Tessa, Brad, or Val, the visiting member of the Ladidahs who had been absent for the past year because she was singing professional backup with a famous act. Was it Val's presence that was making everyone so nitpicky? What happened to "raw" and "real" and "interesting"?

It was too loud. It was too quiet. Too much vibrato. "Can you just hit that last word harder?" "No, you hit it too hard." "Can you just crescendo?" It was too airy. It was too dark. The vowels were not matching. Thirty times. Forty times. Stella was so tired and had needed to pee for the past hour. She was getting flashbacks of her last day with Chet, before she puked in the ocean. Each take sounded exactly like the one before it. Cameron and Kerry were still laughing amenably. *Did they not have to wake up early?* She was now deducting each minute that passed from her night's sleep. As of now, she'd only get five hours max after driving home and getting ready for bed, and tomorrow would be another 12 hour workday.

11:13. "I can see no way, I can see no way."

"One more."

11:17. "I can see no way, I can see no way."

"One more."

"One more."

"One more."

Stella's hot blood was heading down through her fingers and toes, up to the top of her head. Little comments began to come out of her mouth each time they would insist on another take. "You can't be serious." At first it was under her breath. "Are you fucking kidding me?" Then she was sighing out loud and withdrawing. "Let's just *do* it." Soon—"I'm about to snap this microphone in half"—she reached her breaking point.

"This is my last one," came out at last around 11:30, "I have a fucking life!"

"Yeah, 'cause none of us have lives," said Cameron.

Good point, she thought, feeling bad for accidentally insulting her friends, but not so bad that she didn't want to get the hell out of there.

"You can go, Stella," said Tessa, clearly rattled by the unbridled bitchiness. Everyone else in the studio looked at her like she was the kid who was about to blow up the school.

"Thanks. Bye." She walked out the door as fast as she could, her mind hell-bent on a glass of bourbon and her four hours of sleep.

Dylan embraced her when she arrived at midnight, listening to her curse the interminable hell of a recording session. She felt like a brat, but in sixteen hours, she hadn't even had a half-hour of personal respite. She looked into the face she'd been missing and the boiling rage began to cool.

"I got the Costa Rica tickets!" he said, pouring water on the embers.

They'd had a brief conversation about his family planning a trip to Costa Rica in the spring. Stella had said yes when he'd asked her, since she could technically afford it with her new job—but it hadn't seemed real. Now it was. Life had opened in a way she could only have dreamed of six months ago. "I'm so excited! I'll give you a check tomorrow for my part. Do you want to jump up and down?"

"Sure. I've been sitting here working on math for hours, so I probably need to jump up and down," he said. Stella threw in a few air punches and kicks for the finale.

"So if you were planning on breaking up with me," he said, "you're going to have to wait until after March, because those tickets are non-refundable."

She knew this was real love because Dylan had been wearing a ridiculous mustache for a week now and even so, he still melted her with a glance.

"Well," she said, "this relationship is non-refundable. So."

***

Stella unlocked Sam bit by bit through hours together in the car, singing along to silly music, stopping at shops to look at knick-knacks, eating at restaurants and making friends with the waiters. Sam loved to go to the same places over and over. It bored Stella, but she figured it was a search for stability in a place to feel welcome, so Stella indulged her.

Today while Sam was in her one-on-one math class, Stella went shopping for a few things for the new apartment. She still hadn't seen it—she was simply trusting in the location and the pictures Dylan had showed her—but this evening they were going to pack up their cars and drop off all the small items. Stella counted down the hours as she bought a shower curtain rod and a couple trash cans, then picked up Sam from school.

She returned Sam to the boat, ready to make a getaway. Then Sam asked, "Hey Stella...could you help me with this essay?"

Of course today was the one day Sam wanted homework help. "Sure," Stella said. She sighed a little on the inside as she helped Sam write: a task akin to pushing a dead truck up a hill. Sam got distracted every three words. When Stella was finally finished, she drove through

Santa Monica and beheld her new apartment. The sun was setting as she bounded up the stairs and through the door. Dylan was standing on the wood floor, surrounded by boxes.

He hugged her as she took in her surroundings: granite countertops, space enough for the two of them. She thought of all the memories they'd make. "Isn't this romantic?" Dylan said.

"It is," she said, feeling like she'd just gotten off a long, cramped plane ride. "I can't wait to spend the night here tomorrow."

***

Stella waited in line at the courthouse and paid for her divorce, and then took Sam to the dentist's office. The receptionist and hygienists called Stella "Mom" and consulted her as if she had a long-term stake in Sam's teeth. Stella didn't have the heart to correct them with Sam standing there; maybe Sam needed someone to care about her teeth. So Stella nodded as she listened to their schpeel on how Sam needed to floss.

As she sat in the waiting room getting antsy for moving this evening, a text arrived.

Hey Stella. It's been a long time.

It was Jeff Barnard, Stella's last remaining connection to Wil, who had given Wil the porn editing job all those months ago. While Stella had blocked all of Wil's acquaintances, she hadn't blocked Jeff, since she knew he was no longer in contact with Wil. After Wil had abused his kindness, drinking on the job and showing up late every day, Jeff had fired Wil and cut him out of his life.

Jeff:
Is it true about Wil?

Stella knew. Even as she texted back,

What?

Jeff:
I heard he was dead.

Stella waited for that sinking, stomach-drop feeling. But all she felt was mild relief beneath the caffeinated twitch from her overindulgence in the dentist's office Keurig machine. Whether or not her feeble fears had been unfounded, she would never again have to worry about Wil coming to destroy her or anyone she loved.

Sam came out and they took the elevator down. Wil had

probably done it to himself, but Stella wondered how.

"Remember Wil?" she said to Sam.

"Oh yeah, the hot one who was crazy?"

"Yep. He died."

"What?"

"Yeah. I don't know what happened."

"Are you sad?"

"Oddly, I'm not right now," Stella said. She had other, forward-moving things on her mind.

***

Andrew <afoss3090@gmail.com>
to me

Stella.

First I apologize for not being able to speak to you in person. I do not trust my tongue or my mind to be clear.

I wish that so many things had been different.

I didn't take you back when you asked because I believe that you are still the person who is addicted to love and could not be satisfied with me.

I thought that you could be. That's why I married you.

I know that you have grown through this and so have I, but someone who wants me doesn't need other people as a backup.

I want you to be happy.

I hope that you have a good holiday season.

Thank you for paying for the divorce.

I hope someday we both can feel better.

ANDREW

Stella got Andrew's email after she dropped Sam at the boat, on the way to Santa Monica to move into her new apartment. She pulled over and cried after reading it, the way she should have cried when she heard Wil was dead. But she wasn't entirely sad; she sensed a hope in Andrew's letter—a chance that he was starting to move on. The holidays rumbled toward Stella like a train fast approaching. She knew her world would be brighter this year, and she hoped Andrew's would.

She got to 16th Street and helped Dylan carry bookcases and a mattress. Ten trips up and down the stairs and it was done. They sat on the floor drinking champagne.

She felt newly vulnerable now that she had things to lose. "I have failed so many times," she said. "I so don't want to fail again."

"Well, there will be times when we think we've made a mistake," he said.

"Yeah. So what do we do then?"

"We stick it out."

"I'm willing to stick it out," she said.

"I am, too. Do you want to shake on it?" he said.

"Yes." Stella proffered her hand. "We will stick it out."

"We will stick it out," he said. "I think it will be worth it."

At last they made their bed. She was happy to lie in it.

***

Giana and Jacob were orphaned in L.A. this Thanksgiving, so Dylan invited them along to northern California to spend it with his Japanese grandparents. The prospect of being around family comforted Stella, even if it wasn't her family. Dylan was already in the Valley with their friends and Stella was on her way to pick them all up for the trip. Her phone *bloopblooped* with a text.

Jeff Barnard:
It was a suicide. I just talked to his sister on the phone. She said he did it in the worst way. He texted her the address of where he was and wrote 'I love you sis.' Then 20 minutes later it happened.

Stella didn't write back to ask for more details. She assumed Wil had overdosed. But she did realize that, with all the hubbub of moving and working and holidays, she'd had no time to process all the huge changes that were happening. She still hadn't bothered to shed a tear for Wil, which she found curious and slightly repulsive. She thought of Judy and Pat Mallory, in their respective homes, probably weeping, partially from sadness, partially from guilt for their small sense of relief. *Should I write them?* But she couldn't; she was an outlaw to them.

As she waited in traffic, she tried to squeeze out a tear. She thought back to the things she had loved about Wil before it all went pear-shaped. His hair and lips and dick, his boldness and words and wit, his mixtapes, his thoughtful creativity. But the tear wouldn't come; all Stella felt was anger. It felt to her like he had chosen to die in the same way he had lived: destroying himself and then expecting others to clean up the mess.

Giana, Jacob, Dylan and Stella packed into the car. They played question games that revealed deep personal sensibilities: "Would you rather your partner go deaf or become a paraplegic?" They talked for hours as the sun disappeared. Eventually, Stella told them about Wil's death.

"That's severe," Jacob said. "How did it happen?"

"An overdose, I assume," she said. "It was suicide."

"Wil Mallory?" Giana said.

"Yes?" Stella said, wondering how Giana knew his last name.

"He was on the front page of Reddit this morning," she said.

"What the hell?" Stella said.

"Yeah." Giana found it on her phone and showed Stella: a selfie he'd taken in the hospital when Stella was in the room. He was shirtless, with heart monitors stuck to his chest and an IV in his arm, smiling a huge Joker smile, all his scribbly stick-n-poke tattoos visible. "You dated him?"

"Oh my God," Stella said. "Yes. This is him." Giana handed Stella the phone and she scrolled down. Instead of mentioning suicide, the post amplified his good qualities and said "His heart was weak and it finally gave out." That was true in a way. Thousands of people had responded with comments that either mentioned his looks or turned him into a martyr. Stella read them aloud.

"Ugh. This chick says, 'I'd go necrophilia for him!' And here's somebody saying, 'What a pity. He was two years sober.' Not true. He started drinking in January right after one year of sobriety, and even that year is suspect. Oh geez, this person says, 'He looks like such an amazing person! I wish I could have known him.' Is it wrong that I have the impulse to post the truth on here?"

Dylan started, "I wouldn't—"

"I'm not *going* to. I just can't believe that after all the people he dicked over, the world is acting like they lost a great humanitarian or something." She handed the phone back to Giana.

"My mind is blown," Giana said. "Wait. But here's one from an ex-girlfriend. It says, 'None of you people really knew him. He hurt me worse than anyone ever has. He was a complicated person, but he was part of my life for a while.'"

"Wow." Stella was grateful. She remembered stories about this girl—Jackie. She and Wil had been together for a couple years back east. And Jackie was right. These internet morons didn't know him. Neither did Stella. But she knew some things. She had cleaned up his vomit. She had helped the nurse put a catheter in him. She had waited up for hours amidst beeping machines while he slept catatonically under a heavy morphine drip. She had ruined her own marriage for him, lived with him and cooked for him. She had paid his bills and was still paying some of them.

"Are you okay?" Jacob asked.

"Yeah. I know everyone expects me to be sad, but I'm just not." Maybe she had no tears to spare because she had already mourned his loss back in February when she'd found out who he really was. That's when the Wil she loved had died.

"I'm just glad you left him when you did," Dylan said. "Just think if you had stayed with him."

"I shudder to think. I might have been the dead one."

"That's what I was thinking."

"Really? He was that bad?" asked Giana.

"Really. Life got so dark when I was with him. I sometimes wished I'd die. He was so obsessed with psychopaths and so convinced of the lies he told himself; I actually wondered if he'd try to kill me."

"Stella, I am so glad you're here right now," Jacob said.

"Me too," said Dylan, reaching for her hand.

"Thanks, guys. Okay, new subject," Stella said.

They pulled into the driveway at midnight, finally silenced by the brightness of the stars. Dylan's grandfather greeted them with hugs at the door, a glass of red wine in hand.

"You didn't have to wait up, Jiji," said Dylan. "But I see you've been enjoying yourself."

"Oh, this is nothing. Aiko and I usually don't *start* our wine time until eleven. Are you guys thirsty?"

"We're pretty tired, but we could have a glass with you."

They sat on sofas talking for hours. Dylan's grandmother didn't speak English, but she brought them little wasabi crackers and shrimp puffs and sat beside Jiji. They listened to stories about the Korean War and how Baba and Jiji had met. He talked about K-pop, Facebook, and the virtues of boxed wine. Every time they would finish a glass, Jiji would gesture to Dylan and say, "Waiter! There are empty glasses on the table!"

By 3 a.m. the young folks had to insist on going to bed.

Dylan was already asleep beside Stella in the guest bedroom, but she was lit and her brain wouldn't shut off. Songs from that original mix Wil had made kept playing in her head. She was stuck on this line from "Mother of Pearl" by Roxy Music: "I've been searching for something that I've always wanted that was never mine." She remembered Wil telling her that she was that something for him: the holy grail. Even after they broke up, he still said she had done him the greatest favor: she'd taught him that he could love and be loved. Wil had the ability to bring such intense joy. Everything he did was full of either panache or drama. Stella still didn't know if he really ever felt any of the extreme emotions he put on, or if he had just been trying desperately to understand what it was like to feel. Either way, everything with Wil had always begun with big dreams and had ended with despair.

She put in her headphones and found his mix buried deep in her music. Her heart began to soften as she closed her eyes and let the songs take her to a place she hadn't visited in a year. A sad acoustic song called "One Two Three" unspooled a reel of good memories. There was the white dove on the roof that let Wil and Stella hold it in their bare hands. There was Wil sitting behind her on the couch in the east Hollywood sublet, four hands around one guitar neck, playing the bass and the lead at the same time. There was the scarf he knit her, the necklace he hired a friend to make her. There they were, dreaming through the staged kitchen windows at IKEA.

The song ended, repeating "I love you," and Stella felt her cheek get a little wet. The tear didn't represent sadness; just the beginning of understanding. Wil was an innocent baby. Under his spontaneity and his cruelty was an endless tunnel of fear that said *None of what I'm doing will ever fill the void in my soul.* Even Wil wanted to be a good person. He just sucked at it a lot of the time. Maybe he knew that.

Simple as that, she could see here in the dark. Life and death: It really wasn't a big deal. You were alive one second, and the next second you weren't.

Stella took off the headphones and scooted close to Dylan. She could thank Wil now. He had guided her to the darkest place so that she could find the strength in herself to walk toward the light. Wil was the inciting incident that led her here. Dylan put his arm around her, and she fell asleep.

***

It seemed early. Stella could hear Dylan in the kitchen, adorably speaking Japanese with his grandmother who, from the smell of it, was cooking something delicious. "Daijoubou, Baba! I do." It was Thanksgiving day and Stella was comfortable aside from the Jiji-encouraged wine headache. After breakfast, Jiji and Baba began cooking the afternoon feast. They wouldn't allow help, so Stella, Dylan, Giana and Jacob split off to sing and play guitar in the extra bedroom. They felt like kids.

"We always put up our Christmas tree after Thanksgiving dinner at our house," Stella said.

"Us too!" said Jacob.

"Later we should watch a Christmas movie."

"Guys. I brought some special chocolates. Do you think we

should eat them?" Dylan asked.

"At ten a.m.?"

Dylan fished the cannabis chocolates out of his bag. "We can take a hike, and by the time dinner is ready, we'll be back to normal."

"I'm down," Stella said.

Giana and Dylan split a chocolate. Jacob looked nervous, but Stella broke a chocolate in half and he ate his share.

"I'm strapped in," Jacob said.

They took a crisp walk around the neighborhood, watching deer and wild turkeys crunch through autumn leaves, skipping over bridges, to a park where they swang and seesawed by a lake.

"Are you guys high?" Giana said.

"I am in a different dimension," Jacob said. They were lying in the grass.

Dylan was telling jokes that made no sense, and occasionally pulling Stella aside and saying "We *live* together now!"

"I am gone," Stella said, watching the clouds dance. "How long is it 'til dinner?"

"It's at four," said Dylan.

"It's three right now," said Jacob.

"Oh no! We are going to be total ignoramuses! They're going to know!" Stella said.

"We should probably head back," said Giana.

The table was set and Baba and Jiji were putting the food out.

"Do you want me to help with the turkey, Jiji?" Dylan asked.

"Sure, Dylan. Why don't you get it out of the oven and start cutting it?"

Giana and Stella were sunk into the couch watching everyone else in the kitchen. Stella felt paralyzed. "Look at Jacob," she whispered.

"Oh my god," Giana laughed. Jacob was lurking uncomfortably behind the table as if he was trying to help, but he wasn't moving. Jiji and Baba put out the stuffing and the potatoes. Jacob looked terrified.

"Oh I'm sorry!" Dylan said. He had just spilled a quantity of turkey juice all over the floor. Baba chided him in Japanese. Giana and Stella giggled.

The dinner was interminable. Jiji kept trying to converse, but everyone was silent except Giana, who kept saying the wrong thing.

"Mmm, this is a good turkey," someone would say once in a while.

"Are you guys going to drink wine with me again tonight?" Jiji asked.

Stella looked at Dylan for help.

"I think we might just be really tired from staying up so late last night, Jiji," he said.

"Party poopers!"

After dinner Stella found Giana and Jacob in the hallway. She whispered, "What the hell is wrong with us?"

"I couldn't even cut the pumpkin pie! Thank you so much for taking over, Stella!" said Giana.

"When will this end?" said Jacob.

"Dylan put poison into our bodies!" Stella said, before they all went to bed around eight o'clock.

***

The long drive back was hot and congested.

"Do you realize that yesterday we spent at least an hour inventing a televised public service announcement to promote efficient Cheeto eating?" Stella said.

"Yes, and I still think it would be a very helpful message for the Cheeto eaters of the world," said Dylan.

But when they ran out of games and conversation, Dylan became grumpy and expressionless. Stella thought again about Wil. She was curious to see if his obituary had made it to the internet. When she searched his name, she found a headline in the *Santa Monica Mirror*: "Coroner's Office Identifies Santa Monica Man Who Died After Walking Off Roof."

The Los Angeles County Coroner has identified the man who walked off the room of the Medical Center as William Mallory, a Los Angeles resident.

"What the hell," Stella said.

"What?" said Giana.

"Wil didn't overdose. He jumped off a fucking building."

The building was the office of the incredulous pain doctor. Stella remembered standing with him on top of the parking garage, looking toward the horizon from ten stories up. Maybe he'd been thinking about jumping even then. Maybe he'd researched it for months, Googling "minimum stories for death jump" and "do you die before you hit the ground?" He'd probably created a suicide playlist and listened to it on the way. Stella pictured him filling a prescription and then walking up to the roof, taking in the view of all the squat rectangular buildings and deciding now was the time. She pictured him texting his sister, putting in some headphones and playing the perfect song, stepping toward the edge, his weak heart thumping beside the defibrillator in his chest, and then diving off headfirst. She pictured his thick bones shattering, some of them poking out of his pale skin; his skull caving in and guts splattering on the pavement outside the IHOP.

She pictured the people walking by, the clerks on the other side of the pharmacy window, horrified by the gruesome image they hadn't chosen to see, and the cleanup crew coming to scrape the carnage off the concrete.

"This story just gets crazier and crazier," Jacob said.

Stella and Dylan dropped off their friends around 8. Dylan held Stella's hand as he drove to their new home. November was over.

They got into bed—their bed—early. Stella fell into sleep, safe in Dylan's arms, but a few times throughout the night, she woke up with a tightening around her throat that felt just like Wil's big clammy fingers.

DECEMBER

Despite her tormented sleep, Stella woke up at 6:30. She could feel a bright new day breaking. Winter had come to southern California. The sun was shining, but Stella could see her breath. She crawled over Dylan, who was wrapped up like a sushi roll, and put her feet on the floor, grabbing a sweatshirt and tiptoeing through the boxes in the living room—no couch yet, no TV, no gas heat—but this home didn't feel temporary. She scooted her fuzzy-socked feet over the tiles in the kitchen to make coffee. It smelled so rich and promising. Stella hadn't gotten here by chance. She had built this life around her, and she was giddy at the ownership she felt.

That afternoon, the mail man brought an envelope from the Santa Monica City Clerk. Inside were the divorce documents, stamped and signed by the city. Now all she had to do was wait six months, and she would officially be a single woman. She texted Andrew.

> I just got the notice that our divorce will be official six months from today.

> Andrew:
> I got the same notice. I guess that's the end of it.

Though the era had long since ended, they were now formally single, as if there had been no colorful celebration with all their family and friends, no vows they'd written to each other to mark a time in their lives when they believed their love was immune to the pitfalls of promiscuity. The photographs lived on, as if they were a couple from a magazine, perfect and impersonal. She wondered if she should apologize one last time, but figured it wouldn't help.

I guess so. Goodbye, Andrew.

She opened her journal and found her list. She crossed off Level 5 and Level 6.

~~Level 1: Get Prius back~~
~~Level 2: Get rid of Wii~~
~~Level 3: Get Job~~
~~Level 4: Sell Car~~
~~Level 5: Get a Home~~
~~Level 6: Get a Divorce~~
Level 7: Write Novel

***

The routine was similar every day, but it felt dependable and not stuffy. Some days Stella drove to an audition after she dropped Sam at school; other days she wrote for hours. Sam's company was welcome, though her repetitive pop-punk was starting to rattle Stella's eardrums. She thought of her own mother and the words *poetic justice.*

"This is Zach's favorite song!" Sam said. She called Zach her friend, but everything she said about him revealed him as a manipulative little delinquent, using Sam for money and trying to move in for physical gratification. Stella cringed dozens of times each day when she heard his name, knowing she couldn't do anything to change Sam's feelings. Stella did tell her stories about bad decisions she herself had followed to the bitter end, and of people she wished she'd let go of earlier. But Sam likely didn't hear anything Stella said, since she punctuated her day with various flickering videos, messages, songs, photos, and other such noise that overloaded Stella's circuitry to the point that she feared for Sam's generation.

Sam was wearing the Alkaline Trio t-shirt Stella had handed down to her, featuring bloody cartoon children flying kites. When her three-hour school day was over, they drove to Stella and Dylan's apartment for lunch. Sam seemed pleased to be in their little apartment, a far cry from the yacht she lived on. They still didn't have a table, so Dylan laid a towel down and they sat amid the boxes on the floor to eat the quesadillas he made. It was a rough sketch of what a family might feel like in a couple of decades: a teenager eating two bites of food and then abandoning it without a thank-you, Dylan and Stella following her into their bedroom where she declared, "I'm taking a nap!" and lying on either side of her. Sam watched videos on her phone and the three of them ran their legs up the wall, comparing to see whose were the longest. After a while, Stella said, "We probably need to let Dylan study his calculus, and you've got homework."

They got in the car and drove a couple of blocks, passing some high hedges.

"Is that a cemetery?" Sam asked.

"Yep."

"I've never been to one. Can we stop?"

"Sure," Stella said. They walked through peacefully, reading the 19th century dates on headstones in the grassy graveyard, not saying much at all.

***

Stella hadn't seen Dylan all week because they'd been working on opposite schedules, but after a hard, sweaty day, they had finally made it home with a couch and a table. They got rid of the boxes and Stella found a place for everything. She painted geometric blue waves across one wall, underneath the surfboard rack Dylan had built and hung up high, stacked with yellow, white, and orange boards. Together they hung the Santa Monica sign brightly in the kitchen.

"Where'd you find this again?" Dylan asked.

She made a silly, devilish face. "I stole it."

"I thought you *found* it," he said.

"Well, yeah. It was on the ground on 13th street."

He laughed at her. "You know, there's a big difference between something being stolen and something being found."

"I don't know, man. Sometimes they're one in the same."

Dylan insisted on cooking. They still didn't have kitchen chairs, so he sat on an overturned bucket and Stella sat in the desk chair to eat fresh salmon and pesto linguini that smelled like heaven. A strange feeling of déjà vu came over Stella as she tasted the intense flavors: tart grape and oak wine, nutty basil and olive oil, the warm pink fish falling out of its skin.

"This reminds me Janice," Stella said, sinking.

"The lady you lived with when you came out here?" he asked.

"Yeah. Every time Andrew and I would go over to her place for dinner, we'd have this exact same thing. Pesto pasta and salmon, with tons of red wine. She loved wine. We'd get buzzed and talk about everything. It was so much fun. I told you about that first California earthquake we had when I was over there, watching the wine swish back and forth in the glasses! But I haven't heard from her since the shit went down, and I guess I'm scared to try again."

"What shit went down?"

"You know, when I left Andrew. Not many people took sides, but I know that Janice still sees Andrew, and she obviously doesn't talk to me. I definitely approve of her being there for him, but she and her family were the only family I had out here. Now I don't have any."

"You have me," he said. "You know, I think that we expect people who are much older than us to be beyond that kind of behavior. We think it's about us, but the truth is, it says a lot more about what's going on inside of them. Maybe at this point in Janice's life, you remind her of something that's too painful for her. The same thing actually happened to me once."

"Really?"

"Yeah. I had this teacher in New York named Max who sort of took me under his wing. I had dinner with him every couple weeks and he'd give me advice and foot the bill. I thought we were close. But once we got to talking about this one teacher at my school who everybody hated. I told him I respected the guy for giving it to us straight and really preparing us for the harsh world of acting. Nobody else was doing that. He disagreed and we argued for a while. I thought it was just a friendly argument, but every time I tried to contact him after that, he ignored me. I never saw him again. I was really hurt for about a year and I kept trying. But then I realized that he must have some deeper issues that he needed to address, and that doesn't mean that the time we spent together wasn't valuable."

"You're right. No matter what, Janice was very important in my life and nothing can change that. She helped me and Andrew out of so many pickles, and I never even considered that she was having hard times of her own. I mean, she got divorced last year, and right around the time that her husband moved out, Andrew and I had to come stay with her again because that was when the bed bugs ran us out of our apartment."

"So, she was going through some stuff."

"Yeah, and I never really talked to her about her personal stuff. I tried to, but she sort of seemed uncomfortable once we went deeper than surface level, you know?"

"Yeah."

"But I was probably wrong. If one of my friends who was my age was having relationship trouble, I would have asked about it and tried to help. But since Janice was in her sixties, I didn't feel like I had anything to offer her. It's my perception of people older than me. Where I'm from, it was considered disrespectful to question adults, so I never interacted with them person-to-person. I was beneath them, and in Appalachia, nothing was going on in adults' lives anyway. We kids *were* their lives."

"It was totally different for me growing up," Dylan said. "I got along better with the old people than the young ones."

"I believe that," Stella said.

"So do you think it's a lost cause, or should I try one more time, like send her another card or something?"

"I think it would be fine to send a card, but if you do, just don't expect anything. Don't apologize for anything or try to make plans. Just tell her what you told me: that you think of her often and you appreciate her for being in your life during that time."

"Yeah."

"And if she replies, great. But if she doesn't, you've at least let her know what she means to you."

"You know, I bet that's how Sam feels about me."

"What is?"

"The same way I felt about Janice. She probably sees me as an adult and thinks she has nothing to offer me. She does tell me things. I guess all I can do is listen and treat her like a person, and give her love."

"I think you have the right idea."

"It's definitely hard at times, but I can't believe how perfect this is for me. It's like the universe knew all along what I could never have foreseen. I knew I needed a job that paid enough for me to live, and wouldn't exhaust me, would keep me interested, and give me the freedom to write and act and sing, but who knew *I'd* become a mentor?"

"Do you feel unprepared?"

"No, in fact. I feel perfectly prepared," she said.

***

Stella drove Sam past Malibu mansions overlooking the ocean. She peered toward the waves at Sunset, jealous of the longboarder she spotted on a perfect wave. She still had another week before she was allowed to get back in the water.

"I realized something this weekend," Sam said. "I can't say 'I love you' out loud. I can do it over text or something, but in real life I can't. I've never even said it to my Dad."

Stella felt an overwhelming responsibility toward Sam. She wished she could make Sam's life easier by "fixing" her: the obsession with boys who didn't deserve it, the hesitancy to try anything new, the resistance of hard work in favor of instant gratification. But Stella couldn't expect instant gratification, either. Like finishing a novel, being there for Sam would be a daily choice, and the beauty would not hinge on the end product, but in the daily challenges and small moments. Sam, like everyone else, would have to fail in order to learn, and Stella would have the often painful job of watching.

But Sam was strong. She knew from an early age something that Stella had only learned this year: how to be there for herself. Even though Stella had been adopted—something that made Sam feel closer to her—she had grown up with two parents who had smothered her with love. No wonder *I love you* rolled off her tongue so easily.

"It's really hard, but you know what you have to do at first?" Stella said. "You just have to blurt it. Like, when you text someone, you know how you can say anything because you just type it and you're sitting there thinking, 'I'm too scared to send this! AAAH!' but then you just force yourself to push 'send'?"

"Yeah. I can say anything through texting."

"Well, just pretend you're texting. Just make up your mind to say it and then just puke it out the first time. It's way easier after you break the ice." She thought about all those nights with Dylan early on, when she had to bite her tongue to keep it from bubbling out as they fell asleep together. "It's definitely worth it," Stella said.

"I'm scared!"

"Just do it!"

They got some lunch and then did homework on the boat, and soon it was time to leave. Christmas was coming.

"You're leaving me!?" Sam said in mock surprise.

"Yep, but I'll be back."

Sam fake-cried.

"Hope you have the best Christmas ever," Stella said.

"You too! And tell Dylan, too."

Stella grabbed Sam for a sloppy hug and said, "I love you!"

Sam blushed and said, "You're messing up my hair!" but Stella knew what she really meant.

***

"I can't believe I'm finally meeting your mom and dad," Dylan said as they walked up to security. "This is the first time we're going on a plane together!"

Stella found him adorable. In this age of irony, who still took note something sentimental as it was happening and dared to say it aloud? Due to the conditioning she had received during the past decade from jaded hipsters, her first impulse was to release a snarky laugh and assume he meant it tongue-in-cheekily.

But when she looked through his glasses to his early-morning eyes, they were completely earnest, so instead she replied, "I know, babe!" just as excitedly.

The best thing about Dylan was that he did not deal in sarcasm or ulterior motives.

"All these milestones," he mused, cataloguing the moment as they rolled their tottering bags behind them.

***

The only thing she was nervous about as they drove to her childhood home was the dinner conversation. Her family never talked: There was nothing to say. They used to eat in front of the TV when she was a kid.

Dylan had never seen the kind of road that slices right through a chunk of mountains, framed to the left and right by walls of black coal reaching to the sky. He was mesmerized by it, and by the green vines that dripped from power lines and climbed trees like a green sheet covering the furniture in an old room.

"What is that plant that's everywhere?" he asked.

"Kudzu. It's a Japanese invasion, not native to these parts."

"Like me," Dylan said, switching the radio to the local country station.

"This is the station I was a DJ for!" she said. "But it was pop back in the day."

Dylan starting singing along to a song about trucks and sweet tea.

"It's right up here at the end of the road." He looked at the three doublewide trailers that sat next to vegetable gardens beside the gravel road. "Past the trailers. My cousins live up this mountain, and they have wild turkeys that eat out of your hand. We'll have to take the four-wheeler up there."

"Your house is nice."

"The cost of living is pretty cheap around here." They walked up and Stella saw her mom through the glass door, approaching with a smile that turned her eyes into slits. She threw open the door and embraced Stella with a warm, doughy hug. "There's my baby!"

"Hi, Mommy." Stella's dad was right behind Linda. Ron's hug was stiffer, but just as heartfelt.

"Glad you're home," he said.

"Me too."

Mom was already hugging Dylan. "Hi, Linda," he said over her shoulder. "Nice to finally meet you."

She squeezed him and said, "I know I just met you, but I feel like I've known you forever!"

Dylan shook Dad's hand. "Nice to meet you, sir."

"Good to meet you, too," Dad said.

Linda made fettuccini, garlic bread and salad, and they sat down at the table. Stella looked at Dylan to see what he was thinking, but he was engaged in conversation with her parents, who were asking him about his childhood. They talked about the way things were when they were growing up "across the mountain," they shared ideas for what Stella and Dylan could do over their visit. Ron even offered them a Bud Light, which would have been contraband in this house a few years ago. Stella's fears faded.

"I can't believe it's not a dry county anymore," she said. "We're meeting Claudia for dinner at that new pizza place this weekend. Have y'all been there yet?"

"No, but I heard it was good," said her mom.

After dinner, Ron put a chaw of tobacco in his mouth and grabbed his spit cup. "You wanna see my guns?" he asked Dylan.

"Sure," Dylan said.

***

No boyfriend had ever been so accepted by even the extended family. Uncle Hershel, who talked even less than Stella's dad, had invited Dylan to come "across the mountain" to look out for elk and shoot guns. Stella stayed home to lie in the recliner reading a book and listening to her mom clang around the kitchen, making a huge dinner for Everly's birthday that night.

As Stella was debating going for a run without waiting for Dylan, Everly came in through the kitchen door, plopping her purse down on the counter.

"Happy birthday to you, happy birthday to you!" Stella sang horribly-on-purpose.

"Where's Aaron?" asked Mom.

"He's not coming," said Everly. "I don't know what's wrong with him. He was laying around all morning and wouldn't move, and eventually I was like, 'If we're going, we better go,' and he got really mad and said, 'Well, I guess I'm not going then.'"

"Why am I not surprised," said Mom.

"On your birthday?" Stella was appalled. "That is ridiculous. It's not about him."

"Well, he said he already celebrated my birthday when he took me ice skating."

"Do you think he just didn't want to be around all our family?" Stella asked.

"I don't even know. I'm just used to this kind of stuff by now," Everly said.

Dad was on his way out the door with his beloved shih tzu, Kiki (originally Everly's dog) on a leash. "Come on, witta girl. Let's go pee-pee."

"Did you see your cake, Everly?" Mom asked.

Stella went to the sun room and retrieved her cake, in the shape of a penguin with a bow on its head. "Isn't that cute?"

Everly smiled, "Yeah."

Dylan returned at last. "Wow, you were out with Hershel for a long time. What in the world did you guys do?"

"We had a good time. Hershel was driving his truck over these steep mountain trails and I was just gripping the door. I was nervous. I was looking over at him with his spit cup of tobacco juice, thinking 'he is definitely going to spill that,' because the truck was just bouncing everywhere, but that cup never moved. He has definitely done that more than once."

"So it wasn't awkward? Like, did Hershel talk?"

"Yeah, he actually talked a lot. I was asking him all about the wildlife and the mountains and everything, and he can talk forever about that stuff."

"I'm shocked," said Everly. "I think I have probably only exchanged 200 words ever with Hershel."

"I think you just have to talk about stuff that he knows about," said Dylan.

Mom said, "Hershel knows more about the mountains than anybody I know. He is just like our dad was."

"Yeah, he does," Dylan said. "We saw this elk that was just lying down. Its antlers were the hugest things I've ever seen. And Hershel just knew it had a brain worm."

Stella took Dylan on a run through the foothills of her hometown. They barely had time to return and take a shower before family was filling the house for Everly's birthday dinner. Hershel's wife, beloved Aunt Dory, came bearing a Ziploc bag of homemade deer jerky.

"Mmm," Stella said, ripping into a piece. "Aunt Dory, this is Dylan."

"Well, nice to meet ya, Dylan." She gave him a hug.

"Nice to meet you. This is the best jerky I've ever had," said Dylan.

"Well, you'uns keep it. Jason killed that deer with a bow and arrow."

"Wow. That is truly impressive," he said.

"Yep. Fifteen years old and he's up in the mountains every morning at five o'clock before school," said Dory. "Now Dylan, are you from China?"

"No, I'm from Michigan," Dylan said good-naturedly, "but my mom is Japanese."

"Oh. Well we are glad to have ya here. Any friend of Stella's is a friend of ours."

Dory's grandson Jason came in followed by his 17-year-old sister Miranda and her one-year-old baby girl. Then came the rest of the aunts, uncles, and cousins, and Hershel, shyly helloing everyone including his new friend Dylan. Though Aaron never came, his mom arrived with Aaron's brother and his wife and baby. Everly seemed okay once everyone was lining up and filling their plates with hunks of honey ham and casseroles, green beans and mashed potatoes—all of Linda's delicious work from the day, plus the penguin cake. The house felt warm and full amid the Christmas decorations. They ate once, then again, before playing boys-against-girls Catch Phrase and watching embarrassing home movies of Everly and Stella playing basketball in turtlenecks.

***

"If y'all want to come up and shoot guns, get you a jacket," Dad said.

They climbed into the soft-sided Jeep Wrangler and Dad drove them up the gravel road of the mountain that was his backyard, past Lynn and Terry's house, then deeper through the pines until they reached a little clearing at the top of a steep dirt path.

"Ya wonna set 'em up?" Dad asked, handing Stella a beer can and a plastic bottle.

"Maybe you should stick it on that tree up there," said Dylan.

Stella ran up the hill about thirty feet and sat the can on a stump, then plonked a plastic bottle onto a bendy branch.

"Is that good?" she asked.

Dylan wasted two bullets before hitting the can. The bottle was harder. "You want to try?" he asked, giving Stella the gun.

"Sure." She hit the can in two shots.

"I can't believe you live here and you've never shot guns," said Dylan.

Stella couldn't believe it either. But living in the middle of this culture didn't always mean being a part of it. While Everly's friends were slightly more country folk, choir and theater were Stella's high school activities. All her friends were wanna-be cosmopolites who just happened to live in a tiny Appalachian town. Sure, Stella rode the occasional four-wheeler or hiked up to Kingdom Come, but, whether it was because she was female or just eccentric, nobody had ever asked her if she wanted to shoot guns.

Ron pulled out the .45 when the .22 ran out of ammo. "Now this one has a lot of kick, so hold it good and tight," he said, placing it in Dylan's hands.

Dylan gave it a shot. It punctured the silent mountains with a cloud-shattering explosion. The sky began to sprinkle a little rain.

"Let's set in the car and we'll come back out when it stops," said Ron.

"So, how long were you a coal miner?" asked Dylan.

"All the way up 'til about ten years ago. I got black lung from all the dust and it took me this long for me to get my money for it."

"Did you have to go in the mines?"

"Naw. I ran a machine called an auger. It has a big drill bit that drills into the side of the mountain and pulls the coal out. But where I was sitting, that's where all the dust would come. And that guy I worked for, he was supposed to pass these inspections, but he would make us put towels over the air monitors, and when the inspector would come around, he'd take 'em off."

"That is horrible," Stella said.

"Yeah. He did all kinds of stuff like that. The worst thing about it was in the winter. It was so cold up there. I'd put on so many layers I could barely move, and I was still freezin' to death."

"What about the people inside the mine? Was it colder in there?" asked Dylan.

"Naw, inside the mines it stays about the same temperature."

"Looks like it stopped raining," she said.

"Wanna shoot some more?" asked Ron.

"Alright."

Outside the Jeep, the air smelled like pine needles and fresh mud. Stella took in a big breath.

***

She woke up to pancakes Dylan had made for everyone. They were tasty, but Stella briefly resented his tireless perfection as her family took him in with love. The more eager and helpful he was, the more she felt like a nuisance for just being herself.

"Are y'all coming to church with me?" Mom asked. A feeling of dread arose in Stella.

"I'll come with you," said Dylan.

Stella said nothing but went into the bathroom to put on her makeup. Dylan came in. "Do you not want to go? You can stay here, and I'll just go."

"No, it doesn't work that way. If you go, then everybody is going to ask who you are, and then when they find out, they'll know I'm in town—never mind the fact that you're not my husband, who they know I just married a couple years ago—and they'll be like 'Is Stella okay?' and when they've found out I'm not sick and just elected not to go, they will all judge me and talk about how I 'don't believe in God' or something."

"Yikes. I'm sorry that I put you in this position, then."

"No, don't worry," she said, smiling so that the blush would hit the apples of her cheeks. "I'm sure I would have ended up going anyway."

"How bad could it be?" he asked.

Back home after the church service, Stella sat under a blanket watching *Home Alone*, hating herself for eating another slice of penguin cake. "I liked the music," Dylan said. "I've only been to church a couple times. Everybody was singing. Even the people who couldn't sing. But there *were* actually some good voices in that group."

"I know. The only thing is, isn't the subject matter kind of depressing? I mean, it's all like, 'I can't feel at home in this world anymore.' Like, 'Just live miserably according to this specific prescription. Don't worry! You'll die soon!' I counted at least four times when the preacher mentioned some kind of 'us versus them' thing. Like you can't be part of this world and a Christian, too. It's all based on fear. I know I sound bitter and I just need to get over it. But I resent it. I feel like that's why it's taken me so long just to be independent. The God I believe in actually wants me to be happy and enjoy living in this world."

Stella loved her family, but she was starting to miss that freedom that let her open the door in Santa Monica and feel the sunshine, then run fifteen blocks to watch the sun set over the ocean. She couldn't fully be herself if she couldn't "sin" and see miles of ocean and sky where the land drops off at the edge.

***

Linda always piled packages under the tree; she even had four or five for Dylan. Dylan had written funny poems for all Stella's family members. Stella sat in the corner of the sofa, feeling like a little kid. Only grown-ups had presents for everyone. Only grown-ups had it all together and didn't doubt every move they made. This year was almost gone and she was closer, but she wondered if she would ever make it to "real adult" status. Here in the confines of her parent's house, she felt so far off. She thought of Sam back in L.A., and wondered if this was how Sam felt most of the time, being a forced participant in someone else's plan and never living up to expectations.

Stella opened a box and pulled out a robe. "Thank you, Mama," she said.

"I don't know if that's the one you were talking about," Mom said. "Is it?"

"It's not the exact one I had seen. But that's okay."

Stella immediately regretted her words when she saw her mother's face fall. "Oh. I hate that," Mom said. "I made a special trip to Knoxville just looking for that robe you were talking about."

Why hadn't Stella just answered, "Yes. It's perfect"? Her heart plummeted. Gifts meant nothing to her. She always told her mom not to get them. But they meant everything to Mom, who was chasing the lost joy of watching Stella and her sister rip into presents when they were kids.

But now she had done it. She'd made her sweet mother feel inadequate, when her love was the only gift Stella cared about. Stella tried to explain this, but she could tell Mom didn't understand. Linda wouldn't accept that Stella was fine, even when they dispersed and started winding down for the night.

That evening, Stella called Sam through video chat. Sam appeared on the screen, messy-haired, on her bed in bad lighting, holding her white puppy.

"What did you do for Christmas?" Stella asked.

"Nothing really," she said. "I got a new PlayStation and I've been playing this zombie game."

"Oh. Did you guys get a tree?"

"Yeah. We went today but we couldn't get a big one, because it wouldn't fit on the boat."

"Aw."

"I don't really like Christmas," said Sam. "Nobody's around to hang out with and I never see my friends."

Stella looked out the window and saw nothing but jagged limbs of poplar trees. "Well I'll be back in a few days," she said, "and after that, I'm not going anywhere for a long time."

"Okay."

"What do you want to do when I see you again?"

"We could go to the art store and get a bunch of supplies and make something."

"That sounds great," Stella said. "I'll see you before you know it."

***

"Where'd Mom go?" Stella asked her dad through a mouthful of cereal. She and Dylan would be leaving in a few hours.

"Ah, she went to the store for something."

By the time Stella finished her bowl, Linda had returned with a Goody's bag in her hand. She handed it to Stella.

Stella opened it to find a big fluffy, flowery robe.

"Mom," Stella said, hugging her, feeling as low and unworthy as she possibly could.

"I saw this the other day and I thought it was the softest thing I'd ever felt. I know it's still not the one you wanted, but—"

"Mom," Stella tried to hold back tears. How could anyone love her this much? Stella felt the dishonor of being an ungrateful, terrible person. "You didn't have to do this. I seriously didn't care at all. But I love it. Thank you." She put on the robe and knew that every time she wore it, she would feel like she was getting a hug from the person who loved her most in the world.

Later they packed up the rental car. Her dad never used to cry, but his sixties had softened him. He hugged Stella multiple times as she and Dylan walked back and forth to the car with bags and presents, and in a never-before-seen act of tenderness toward a daughter's boyfriend, he even hugged Dylan. Linda hugged them both too, again and again, making silly threats to keep them prisoners as she tried to hold herself together.

"The house is always so sad and quiet after Stella leaves," she said.

"I love you, Mommy," Stella said.

"I love you, too, baby," she said, squeezing Stella as if to capture her essence. "I love you, too, Dylan," she said, hugging him tightly.

"And I love you, Mama," Dylan said, making his way toward the car.

"Be careful," Ron said as he always did, pronouncing it *cure-ful.*

"We will. I love you."

"Love you too."

The doors were shut and the ignition was started up, and here was that goodbye moment that always brought tears. Stella waved, her parents getting smaller and smaller as they watched their daughter disappear. Dylan drove them over the familiar crunching gravel. Having him by her side eased the hurt of leaving a little.

"Goodbye, little mountain cocoon," Stella said with love.

Instead of losing herself in the passing majesty of the mountains outside, she sat stuck to the passenger seat, loathing herself. She hated that she had hurt Mom. She hated that her mom had gone out of her way to make her happy when she didn't deserve it. She hated how she'd felt disconnected from her own family, sub-par and unthoughtful in Dylan's perfect shadow. She knew the problem was her own, but she couldn't loosen the tightness in her throat. Outside the mountains, the highway was a dismal straight grey line stretching to infinity. Dylan was silent. Something was amiss.

"Is something wrong?" she asked.

"I'm just thinking about the way you were acting, and I really don't like it. It seems like because you were at your parents' house, you regressed to a bratty teenager."

"Well I guess I should have been as perfect as you, and maybe they wouldn't think I was a complete degenerate."

"Oh. You're going to blame me for your behavior?"

"I'm not blaming you for anything. I'm just saying that it's really hard to feel like I even belong when you're writing them poems and cooking them breakfast and they're inviting you to go riding around the mountains. The fact that I've never even been invited to come shooting until *you* were here. And my mom looks at you like you're the freaking second coming."

"Your family loves you. Maybe there's something deeper that makes you feel like you don't belong—"

"Like the fact that I *don't!*"

"If you think I was doing so much to violate your territory, maybe *you* should have grown up and done some nice things for your family instead of acting like a child. You could have helped me make breakfast. You didn't even try."

"Yeah, that sounds great," she said sarcastically. "If I had thought of it, I would have changed the entire dynamic of my relationship with my family before I went home. Thanks for that. You always act like you know exactly what I should do. I'm so fucking tired of it. You don't know anything about what it was like to grow up there. I didn't get to move to the big city when I was fucking eighteen, because my parents guilted me to stay nearby! I didn't get to make my own decisions until I was halfway through my twenties because I was paralyzed with fear! I didn't even know that listening to myself was an option! You're the spoiled one who had every opportunity. I'm tired of your fucking judgment when you know nothing."

He didn't respond; he just kept driving. She waited. A stormy ocean raged between them. She hated how she felt but she didn't know how to change it.

"Well?" she said.

He wouldn't talk.

Fuck you, she said under her breath, to him, to herself, to everything that ever held her back.

They didn't speak as they waited at the airport, or as they crammed into the tiny plane seats. Stella tried to keep her tears contained as she fought her demons. Hours passed and she wondered what she could do to fix herself. She was never enough. Never.

The plane jerked. The intercom crackled. "Folks, this is your captain speaking. It looks like we've hit some unexpected turbulence." The plane jostled and shook. "I'm going to turn on the seatbelt sign. Flight attendants, please return to your seats." The plane dipped and quivered. Babies screamed. The old lady across the aisle crossed herself. The plane dropped altitude and kept dropping.

Stella wasn't afraid of turbulence, but when she looked down at the desert below, she pictured what it would be like to plummet to her death. She imagined her parents sobbing as they saw her photo next to Dylan's on the news. She touched Dylan's leg, and he put his arm around her. She leaned in. Soon, the plane leveled out and steadied.

"I'm sorry for what I said in the car," she said. "I just didn't need you to scold me at that moment. I was already feeling bad about myself. Nothing I can ever do can repay my mom for what she's done for me. If it weren't for her, who knows where I'd be. I could have been an orphan, or I don't know, a cult member. But I always just make her feel bad," Stella said.

"That's the thing about Moms. We can never repay them. And we're not supposed to," he said.

"What am I supposed to do then?"

"Love yourself and your family as unconditionally as she loves you," he said. He grasped her hand and held it for the rest of the flight.

***

Soon they were back in the alternate universe of Santa Monica, putting their winter clothes back into their shared closet, along with Stella's new robe. She was unleashed.

Dylan fashioned surfboard racks for their bikes out of PVC pipe and finally, Stella's month was up: She could surf again. They strapped the boards in and pedaled toward the beach break at Bay Street.

"I can't believe we live here!" Dylan said. Along the way, people on the street pointed and asked about Dylan's homemade bike racks.

They made it to the coast in ten minutes, parked their bikes, and ran toward the water. Stella was timid as she paddled out, even though the waves were tame. It felt good to be back, but she couldn't fully trust the ocean or herself. While Dylan took wave after wave, she let them roll right past her. She'd find the balance in due time.

At home they made stir fry together and sat at their little kitchen table, which finally had chairs. The food was colorful as confetti and smelled delicious. Before they ate he took her hand, closed his eyes, and breathed in deeply. She waited. He opened his eyes and looked at her with appreciation.

***

Stella barely noticed New Year's Eve when it came.

She woke up manic beside Dylan in their bed, delirious in holy-shit, what-the-fuck love. This happened sometimes, and when it did, she wished she could multiply their every second together into an infinite time warp.

He was asleep. She devoured his caramel skin with her gaze, she traced the sharp cut of his jaw with her fingers, feeling the prickle of the black stubble on his cheek, she listened to his soft breathing and watched his unmoving eyelids—the straight line of lashes. She softly rested her hand on his bicep, moved it over the muscle and then across the firm landscape of his chest and abs. He stirred. She grazed her lips over his neck and let its potential energy rile her until she couldn't wait for him to wake up. She wanted to watch him transform from this soft peace into something rough, something with an agenda and the skill to carry it out.

He blinked awake and she fell into the deep green wells around the burnt amber of his irises. Goosebumps rushed up her bare arms. She had a sudden inclination to prostrate herself before him and offer him everything she had from now until forever. *I belong to you*, the urge begged her to say. But she didn't say it.

And then in the aftermath of what happened in their tangle of sheets she could not silence the cold truth that whispered, *these feelings are fleeting; you've felt them before.* She chose this time not to give herself away. She, too, was someone to fall in love with—someone with a bright face, a gleaming smile, wild hair and dazzling deep-sea eyes that took in all the world's contrast. Her skin was salty and her love was pure, and she was open to receive all that came her way. Her body tingled and dopamine stuck like honey to the sides of her brain.

By night there were echoes of music and hollering, searchlights in the sky, and the buzz of a city forgetting a whole year. Stella and Dylan heard it all, but they only wanted to drink champagne and stay in.

"Do you want to pop this baby?" he asked.

"What do you think?" She took the green bottle and pulled off the foil-and-paper seal. She untwisted the piece of metal that released the little cage around the cork. She sat the bottle on the counter, remembering—"Oh. We can't do this without music." She went to her computer to select a festive playlist for two.

"Did you just leave this on the counter?" Dylan came into the living room, holding the champagne bottle. He twisted the cork and pulled it out. The sound of the pop was unceremonious and no glasses awaited.

"Hey! I was picking some music, so we could do it right!"

"You left this bottle on the counter without the cage on?"

"Yeah?"

"Do you realize how dangerous that is? That's like leaving a loaded gun lying around." Not a hint of a smile crossed his face.

"Are you serious?"

"Yes, I'm serious. You took the cage off and just left this here. I thought you were a bartender. You don't know that you're not supposed to just leave a champagne bottle unattended? Why do you think they have the cage?"

Stella had finally found the perfect song—"Under Pressure" by Queen—and she played it. "Wow. You are hilarious. Now can we please drink that?"

"You don't think this is a big deal?"

"No, Dylan. I don't think it's a big deal. And yes, I have been a bartender and I have also lived on this earth for twenty-nine years, and guess what—I'm still alive! Twenty-eight of those were entirely without your help. So if we could just pour the champagne and have a good evening to celebrate New Year's, that would be awesome." She took the champagne, dancing a bit to Queen and David Bowie, found their two glass flutes, and poured it in. She reached out to hand Dylan his. He stood there, not accepting it. "Seriously? You're going to ruin our New Year's Eve because I left a champagne bottle on the counter with no cage on it? Is that really worth it to you?"

Dylan went to their bedroom and put on some sneakers. "I'm going to go for a run," he said.

"At eleven-thirty?"

"Yeah." He zipped up a jacket and walked out the door. She watched him run down the stairs and into the night.

She let him go. She swallowed his champagne and laughed at the absurdity of trying to communicate with another person. To be understood by someone who inhabited a different body, you had to translate your feelings into language—a made-up gobbledygook of syllables with randomly assigned meaning—and then the other person had to take those syllables and interpret them through their unique faculties, and turn those interpretations into feelings. No matter how superbly entwined you were, you were always alone and at best just approximating what the other person felt.

She started sipping her glass of champagne and sat down to write. Today was the last day of her original challenge. She had stuck it out and written to the end of the year. She guessed she'd spend 2014 editing, if she was ever to beat Level 7. She knew she was alive because she could feel her pulse just beneath the skin of her neck. She knew that this life of hers was going to be much different from the one she had envisioned a year ago. She knew that no relationship was perfect, that people and things could be lost to her forever at any time, but as for Stella, she would never lose herself again.

She closed her eyes and for a second she heard Wil's voice. *Your life is fucking changed. Are you happy?*

She opened them again and looked around to write the universe she had created. Here was the apartment, warm and still smelling of cinnamon pine cones and the chicken they'd cooked earlier. Here were the waves on the walls, Dylan's racing bike on a rack, their snug couch, the sign reflecting "Santa Monica," the city that was hers again. Here were voices floating in on the ocean breeze—*Ten! Nine! Eight! Seven!*—and Stella Robertson at 29, sitting in a chair, safe beneath the champagne bubbles, her fingers on a keyboard typing the last words of the year: *Your life is fucking changed. Are you happy?*

Four! Three! Two! One!

Yes. She was.

ACKNOWLEDGMENTS

The following beautiful souls were indespensible to the creation of this book:

Kai Chapman, Holly Pennington Lewis, and Tiffany Shinn for the words you let me borrow and the love and inspiration that came from your very existence.

Nevada Martinez, Emily Brooks, Tanya Besmehn, and Supra Parthasarathy, for brilliant, selfless editing help.

Bryarly Bishop, Karen Biscopink, Sean Hathaway, Andrea Datzman, Lynn Jose, Wendy Williams-Burton, and Crystal Cantrelle for support, early reading, and/or giving me a lift somewhere along the way.

www.ingramcontent.com/pod-product-compliance
Lightning Source LLC
Chambersburg PA
CBHW020237180626
46810CB00006B/2238